I was particularly impress███████████████████████eak, and
sardonic howl—from the souls of these y███████████writers.
Their willingness to bear witness to the nightmare of racism's
wretchedness is matched by their devotion to the possibilities for
illumination that only serious literature can reveal. Full of astonishment over the woe, and pride, of the contemporary Black condition,
they provide us with an important understanding of the driving
forces behind those youthful participants in the Million Man March,
so misread by the media masters of the Black experience. We must
hear the lucidity behind the rifle fire of their rhetoric pitched from
the foxholes of their version of America's Black condition . . . even
as they offer up these burnished evidences, laments, and yearnings
snatched, culled, and honed from our contemporary American civil
war, with guts, grief, and wonderment.

—Professor Leon Forrest,
African-American Department,
Northwestern University

America has a case of denial so severe that, if it does not diagnose
and treat its disease soon, it is doomed to commit the social equivalent of suicide. Our society desperately needs to be jolted into a
sense of realism. *Soulfires* has the conscious energy to provide such
an awakening. Anyone who wants to understand and transform contemporary America should confront these words.

—Michael Warr, author of *We Are All the Black Boy*

PENGUIN BOOKS

SOULFIRES

Daniel J. Wideman's work has been featured in *The Langston Hughes Review* and *Uwezo* and on television in the PBS documentary "One More Look at You." He is the son of John Edgar Wideman.

Rohan B Preston is the author of the poetry collections *Dreams in Soy Sauce* and the forthcoming *Lovesong to My Father*. His feature arts writing has also appeared in *The Chicago Tribune* and *The New York Times*.

YOUNG BLACK MEN ON LOVE AND VIOLENCE

SOULFIRES

EDITED BY

DANIEL J. WIDEMAN

and ROHAN B PRESTON

PENGUIN BOOKS

PENGUIN BOOKS
Published by the Penguin Group
Penguin Books USA Inc., 375 Hudson Street, New York, New York 10014, U.S.A.
Penguin Books Ltd, 27 Wrights Lane, London W8 5TZ, England
Penguin Books Australia Ltd, Ringwood, Victoria, Australia
Penguin Books Canada Ltd, 10 Alcorn Avenue, Toronto, Ontario, Canada M4V 3B2
Penguin Books (N.Z.) Ltd, 182–190 Wairau Road, Auckland 10, New Zealand

Penguin Books Ltd, Registered Offices: Harmondsworth, Middlesex, England

First published in Penguin Books 1996

1   3   5   7   9   10   8   6   4   2

PUBLISHER'S NOTE
Some of these selections are works of fiction. Names, characters, places, and incidents either are the product of the authors' imaginations or are used fictitiously, and any resemblance to actual persons, living or dead, events, or locales is entirely coincidental.

Page 399 constitutes an extension of this copyright page.

LIBRARY OF CONGRESS CATALOGING IN PUBLICATION DATA
Soulfires : young Black men on love and violence/
edited by Daniel J. Wideman and Rohan B Preston; with an introduction
by Henry Louis Gates, Jr.
p.   cm.
ISBN 0 14 02.4215 5
1. Afro-American men.   2. Afro-American men—Correspondence.
3. Afro-American men—Poetry.   I. Wideman, Daniel J.   II. Preston,
Rohan B
E185.86.D57   1996
305.38'896073—dc20   95–31585

Printed in the United States of America
Set in Trump Medieval
Designed by Jessica Shatan

For Angela
and
Maimuna
for their courage, insight, persistence, and love

and to our literary elders and ancestors,
who have carved the path for us and on whose shoulders
we stand

Editors' Notes

When one proposes a book on love and violence from the perspectives of Black males—issues that define not only how we conduct our lives but our very humanity in America and indeed, every place where Africans live—one is confronted by the limited, even deflated expectations of such a project. Indeed, when one hears the terms love and violence, alongside the code "young Black men," one already has pre-formed notions of their contexts and meanings. Even young Black men (who are everything and manifest the full range of human genius) fall into these reflex mindsets, often believing that love equals sex as it relates to violence equals rape equals gang-bang. The permutations may be numerous but the formula remains— those things have been a part of our dispensation in the Americas.

In America, "young Black men" has served as a catch-all repository of social woe. The Black male body, especially in its youthful vigor, has been and continues to be a site of grafting, of graffiti and branding. It functions as a never-neutral palette where voyeurs, politicians, academics, sociologists, criminalists, morticians, artists, and what-have-yous inscribe their fears, adoration, disdain, dis-ease, and fantasies. But it is ours—though we are not objects, not just our bodies. Whether in prisons, colleges, laboratories, boardrooms, or in the athletic arenas, this reviled and revered physique is the very intersection of sex and violence. Indeed, the overwhelming emphasis on our very physicality reduces the gleaming, glowing bodies of Black men to just that. Our tender and virtuous hearts, our spilling souls and expansive dreaming—all become gratuitous and extraneous to our daily pressures. Yet we possess a very great capacity to love, to learn, to live full-bodied, full-hearted and of full minds in this, our world. We have contributed greatly to human culture, to the arts and sciences, to theology and philosophy, even to politics.

We see such faraway places in the eyes of our brothers on any city street or in any grocery store, church or mosque. And yet, as far away as we are, we are right here, in it all—on the nightly news (being chased and shooed), on stage (being cheered and oohed), everywhere, it seems, but at home, with each other, with our loved ones. Our eyes slant away so as not to cause fear—because we know that they think they know what they don't know, namely us. Sometimes we look just to see them squirm but mostly, we would rather just be. We do not seek invisibility, just to be taken on as individuals, to be given the benefit of the doubt—not pre-read (really un-read), preknown (unknown) or pre-judged (guilty). We could be innocent.

We hurt, even if it's hard for some to "feel our pain." When we see Michael Jordan rising triumphant, his tongue outstretched, over a basketball court, we also see his slain father in him. But our pangs are not always illuminated so well. We know the government catalogs of our brethren killed, raped, wounded. We live with the casualties. Of course, we have hurt too. Each other. Our families, and ones whom we have loved, tried to love or loathed. We rarely have a second opportunity, so our mistakes illuminate the headlines. Everyone knows them. And as teenagers, wayward or not, we are treated as adults. Where a thirty-something Neil Bush, the son of ex-president George Bush, is called "a kid" by commentators after he is implicated in serious shenanigans in the failure of a savings-and-loan institution, young Black men are never afforded a childhood, or innocence, or the benefit of the doubt. But in all of it, we are growing. We seek nothing less than a full humanity.

> *Rohan B Preston*
> *Chicago*
> *October 10, 1995*

━━━━━━━

A moment. A snapshot in a life. The closest I can come to explaining the genesis of this project. Why I embraced it. What its completion means to me.

Two and a half weeks before my twenty-fifth birthday, on November 8, 1993, I became a statistic. Unlike most, however, who find their complex human essence reduced to a number, their life story distilled to digits in a formula, I was not six feet under but approximately 35,000 feet over solid ground.

On a plane somewhere between Chicago and Pittsburgh, like a bolt of lightning, a terrifying number flashed through my mind, cutting through the roiling stew of fury, grief, and depression I had descended into upon hearing that my oldest male cousin, Omar Lateef Wideman, had been shot dead at age twenty-two.

One.

One left.

Me.

In a single, overwhelming instant I realized that I was on my way to bury Omar, and that that act would leave me the sole Black male Wideman of my generation not behind bars or beneath ground. One voice, a single pair of eyes, a solitary set of life-promulgating genitalia. A statistic. To be measured and weighed. The sole surviving evidence of one family's generation of young Black men, a mere sum of flesh, now precariously suspended thousands of feet in the air, at the mercy of wind, rain, and other natural elements whose power and permanence are eternal and unquestioned; elements which are assured survival as long as the earth's axis continues to turn. One. Suddenly the loneliest number in the world.

While in town for the funeral, I held in my lap the newest member of the clan; the youngest of the next generation. Jordan Darryl Walters, my cousin Tameka's second son. Jordan has wildly bright brown eyes and a headful of angel's hair—thin-spun alpaca fluff of such unearthly fineness his mother has not let scissors within earshot of the child since the day he was born. In a family notorious for the devilish cuteness of its babies, I could see with my own eyes Jordan was by far the cutest. And if all reports are true, he is also the most devilish new one to arrive in quite a long time, perhaps as long as a generation.

A generation. A community bonded by the accident of birth and incubated in the crucible of a common era; emerging intact into adulthood and beyond with a shared cultural template, a linked historical repository, a set of experiences that tie its members together, stories fastening them to each other and to the world; myths, music, and memories to be passed around and, most important, passed on.

What happens when a "generation" is not any of this? When "a generation" becomes the pat answer to questions like "how much decimation?" Or "who was destroyed?" What happens when a generation is the yawning, bloody void between a young man and his nearest free, surviving male kin, gurgling innocently on his lap? What do you do when "a generation" is the empty pit in your stomach, the lump that rises in your throat when you are holding a baby in your arms knowing the moment you put him down, if not sooner, you could lose him? What happens when "a generation" is how much the evidence weighs, the evidence you must surmount to begin to craft strategies to insure a baby's safe passage through this world?

This book is part of my attempt to answer these questions. To help introduce a generation of black men to each other and to themselves. To reach out to a circle of survivors and gather their secrets, their shouts and whispers. To try to learn to love each other before it's too late. For, as writers and storytellers and griots and documenters, we bear a unique responsibility. We possess the tools to cobble together and re-unite a family. We must birth a new voice borne aloft by the winds of a reinvented, reconnected spirit. We must tend the hearth, stoke the embers of thousands of soulfires into one eternal flame. One flame. One. Perhaps we can rediscover the truth of that numeral, which holds not just the promise of naked isolation and solitude, but also the key to the language of unity.

Daniel J. Wideman
Evanston
October 10, 1995

Acknowledgments

Much thanks (and love) to our respective spouses, Angela Shannon Preston and Maimuna Mahdi-Wideman, whose unswerving belief in this project literally kept it alive during the most trying periods.

Our deepest thanks to Sarah Chalfant, our tireless agent whose infectious enthusiasm and advocacy helped carry us through the process of turning a simple idea into the book you hold in your hands; to Hal Fessenden, our indefatigable editor at Penguin, and to all those who submitted pieces to the project. Space limitations preclude including everyone, but to all the contributors who made this project what it is—big up and X-amount of respect!

We are also deeply appreciative of our nuclear and extended families.

Rohan B Preston especially thanks Mum (Gladys Elizabeth Holmes), Mama (Gloria Mercedes Holmes Folkes), Papa (James Sylvestre Folks, February 11, 1909–March 6, 1994) Rudolph and Evadné Jones, Karen, Kim (plus Shé-Shé), Lee and Andrea (love you all more than scoveitched fish), Aunty Pauline Folkes Livingston, Maria, Angelee, Aunty Chauncy and Uncle Osmond (Dorothy & Osmond Russell), Joan, Wayne, Nicole, Aunts Juanita, Jascinta, Tatlyn, Pal, Uncles Hubert, Roy, Carl, Peter, Alwyn, cousins Noel, Michelle, John, Andrew, Dwight, Terrell, Sherrell, O'neil, Grand Aunts Celie (Cecele Moncrieffe Butler), Aggy (Agnes Moncrieffe Whitter), Cassetta Moncrieffe Parchment, Theresa Juanita Moncrieffe Schaaffee; all the Folkes, Holmes, Jones, Isaacs, Moncrieffe, Schaaffee, Whitter, Blackwood, Livingston, Campbell, Bennett, and Parchment generations in Jamaica: Preston Hill, St. Mary, St. Ann, Kingston; and a Foreign: New York, Miami, San Francisco, England, Canada, and wherever else we are scattered. Thanks to Drs. John L. and Juel L. Smith, Aunt Erma Coburn, Babette Shannon, Lisa and James Flagg (plus Shannon and Juelisa), and to Gina and Oliver Spicer (plus Angelica), Kenneth Shannon, Chris Coburn, and many, many others whose names have not been called but whose love, spirit and wisdom have sustained us.

Contents

PART TWO: LOVING EACH OTHER

FOR THE LOVE OF YOU

TRIALS TOWARD TRIUMPH

VIOLATIONS: EYE OF THE STORM

PART THREE: BROTHERTALK

Introduction
"Camp Meeting"

I remember when I first kissed my father—not the *very* first time, of course, because I am sure that I kissed him as a child; but the first time I kissed him as a young adult. I had been thinking about this whole matter of male affection since the afternoon that I saw my cousin, Greg, so casually kiss his father, Uncle Joe, on the cheek before we went off to bed.

Shut my mouth wide open!

I was struck dumb when no one even feigned surprise, when no one laughed or giggled nervously, when Uncle Joe—a taciturn and moody man, the son *of* "a white man—some Irishman," and given to drink "like his father's people"—treated the whole thing like it was normal, like he was appreciative, like it was the way it was supposed to be between a daddy and his son.

I envied the casualness of their intimacy, the sharing of affection between a parent and a child; open, natural. I was ashamed at my own astonishment, at my own unease. I managed to close my gaping mouth, averting my eyes from Greg's, ashamed that I had been ashamed, wondering what was wrong with me, and with *my* father, determined to make kissing him on the cheek, goodnight, or good morning, as normal a part of the day at our house as it was down to my cousin Greg's. My father, for his part, seemed only as startled as he was pleased, as he gestured toward his cheek, pretending to rub my lips off his face. He seemed to have been waiting for that for a long, long time.

I thought of this long-buried memory while watching the Million

Man March. Rather, while attending to my mail in between all these speeches, and reading a fax from a colleague at George Washington University, who had scribbled a hasty "P.S." to a typed letter, saying "gotta run . . . I'm taking my son to the March!" The memory returned as I watched all those fathers and all their sons, hand-in-hand, wide-eyed, creating together a day that America would long remember, in awe and terror, black boys gathered together to atone, waiting over two hours only to realize that the Great Atoner himself would not heed his own great and terrible call. Jake Wideman's haiku suddenly came to mind:

Why, I cry, do I
see myself so clearly now
nestled in your midst?

And it *was* a stroke of genius: attempt to trump the Jewish people with a black day of atonement, in the very shadow of Yom Kippur, and assume Dr. King's mantle, on the very space where he enunciated himself as the voice of a truly integrated America. How can we not admire that? Whether the idea came from Louis Farrakhan's *hunger* for center stage among mainstream leaders, or whether it came from God, as he so modestly claimed, that Monday was Louis Farrakhan's moment, the orgiastic apex of his long march from obscurity out of the shadows of Elijah Mohammed, Malcolm X, and even Dr. King himself.

Anyone who says it wasn't didn't see the march that I saw.

Colin Powell realized this. The usually decisive general did not waver idly: he *knew* that Farrakhan's idea had captured the imagination of African-American men like nothing else in a long, long time—even more than the Fuhrman tapes. During his book tour, Powell had, after all, had more face-to-face contact with "normal" people—of whatever hue, sexual orientation, or religious belief—than any other American could possibly have had in the recent past.

The unprecedented book tour, breaking all records for autographs, sales rivaled only, perhaps, by the Pope, brought more voices of the inarticulate to his ears in three weeks than most of us hear in a lifetime. "The march has struck a chord with thousands of young brothers," he told me on the Sunday night before the march. "I had to think about that, no matter who had thought of it." In the end, Powell—at the time considering a run for the presidency—had to protect his one constituency, the great American center, rather than to go one-on-one with the grand master of black camp, Minister Farrakhan, and the greatest black camp meeting of all.

And the march *did* have all the hallmarks of a traditional camp meeting, a traditional religious revival in which rival preachers share a rostrum and, like a sacred jam session, take their turn at blowing each other away with the force of their own greased and practiced oratory. Make no mistake about it: The stakes are high at these rituals. He with the grandest delivery captures the day. And their audience of holy connoisseurs is *most* demanding; lacking sympathy for *poseurs*, they will not be fooled.

In a sense, every black public speaker since 1963 takes the stage with "I have a dream" ringing in his head as a silent second text. If anyone was to supplant King's unrivaled moment, the Monday march was the place for it to happen. That it didn't speaks volumes about the confusion that reigns among black male leadership.

Each speaker was confined to three minutes only, a remarkable restriction given the format and the depth of talent assembled on that stage. Most black preachers take three minutes saying hello, let alone delivering an entire message to a million men. The three-minute handicap was enforced to give Farrakhan his time to show the world whose march this was; and in case anyone still doubted the matter, he thought it wise to tell us at a morning press conference the very next day.

The speech smacked more of one of Fidel Castro's all-day orations than a sermon in the black tradition. And, despite its length, it never really found its text, it never actually reached its oratorical climax. Farrakhan—oddly enough—failed to find his voice, hence the speech's jarring rambles from Allah and Jehovah to Moses and Jesus, from Masonic numerological symbolism to Nixonian black capitalism, from profoundly moving calls for black male accountability to condescendingly patriarchal nods at "black womenfolk" whose rightful place, it seems, remains at home. No, the day did not belong to Farrakhan; it belonged to a million black fathers and their sons.

I was forced to wonder about all this on Monday during the march, as I drove up Cambridge's elegant Brattle Street. There, pulled over to the curb, just outside of Henry Longfellow's mansion, officers from two police cars had pinned a black man against his car, hands held high over his head. Driving while Black, I thought.

The publication of *Soulfires* is, to my knowledge, unprecedented in African-American literary history. Most of our anthologies, certainly until recently, have been dominated by the work of black males, despite the fact that a woman, Phillis Wheatley, launched our tradition, and another woman, Toni Morrison, is arguably our greatest novelist. But a selection of imaginative work by and about young black males—in which black males are the subject and the object, the text and the pretext, the form and the content is, I believe, unprecedented.

What is as unusual about *Soulfires* is the remarkably broad array of voices unfolding in this collection, the hundred ways it shows how to be black and male, gay and straight, left and right, nationalist and not. Far too often, the trope of "the black male," even within black discourse, is as stereotyped, as univocal, as mythic, as totalized as it is in white discourse. The diversity of voice and face as contained here signifies *strength*—the strength to define the whole as *all* of the aspects contained in its parts—and the self-confidence of a tradition to tolerate and promote a cosmopolitan sense of otherness from within. For who, this volume asks, can be other to his own brother? After all, as Jabari Asim writes in "Spitting Image":

your sass is safe with me.

Maybe this is what true community depends upon?

And now I am a father—of two teen-aged young women. They kiss me goodnight, they kiss me hello, and admitting out loud that we love each other is just what we do. When my father, now eighty-two, heads across town after Sunday dinner, he would think it odd if we all didn't kiss him good-bye.

Henry Louis Gates, Jr.
November 10, 1995

PRAISESONG FOR THE ANONYMOUS BROTHERS

PETER J. HARRIS

See ya, I wouldn't wanna be ya!

See you plait daughter hair. See you massage son soul. See you spin their hours into gold. See you join the Y. See you coach boys & girls. See you ballet on blacktop. See you maestro. See you Osagyfo. See you comrade. See you Rev. Doctor. See you teach public school. See you pick private school. See you open Freedom School.

See you. See you. See you.

See you baggy clothes. See you white collar down. See you wear holes in cold. See you & Homies chill. See you wax car. See you slap dominoes. See you mumble to yourself. See you answer back. See you tell the truth.

See you. See you. See you.

See you ride bus. See you drive cab. See you walk mall. See you clear counter. See you clean floor. See you hold baby's hand. See you hold woman's hand. See you hold man's hand. See you show love in public. See you on the J.O.B.

See you. See you. See you.

See you done right. See you do right. See you live right. See you through my own damn eyes. See you fail. See you try. See you like we got the same address. See you bow tie. See you left coast dread. See you Black Caucus starch. See you push cart of cans. See you carry mail. See you guard doors. See you tame motors. See you barber holler next. See you farmer stroll rows of food.

See you. See you. See you.

See you bedroom. See you boardroom. See you laundry room. See you talk shit. See you make me laugh. See you stress. See you call your baby. See you give her a rose. See you cook her favorite meal. See you call your baby. See you give him a rose. See you cook his favorite meal.

See you. See you. See you.

See you 100 Black Men. See you Big Brother. See you Simba mentor. See you choose Allah. See you praise Jesus. See you drum Olorun. See you told what to do. See you run the show. See you punch the clock. See you speak. See you mute. See you cup your ear. See you hope. See you hustle. See you burn the flag. See you sprawl for police. See you up against the wall. See you slouch in court. See you Garvey. See you union. See you Duke Ellington. See you Maroon. See you brave.

See you. See you. See you.

See you stumble. See you graceful. See you dance. See you 9 to 5. See you after hours. See you cradle bean pies. See you statesman. See you dropout. See you restless. See you portrait. See you collage. See you emblem. See you word like a song. See you stutter Rodney King. See you opinion like it's fact. See you old man. See you Black boy. See you link the two.

See you. See you. See you.

See you jailed. See you caged. See you tamed. See you pain. See you fronting. See you lamping. See you want. See you need. See you dissed. See you Blood. See you Crip. See you Brother. See you sober. See you loved. See you peace. See you home. See you listen. See you love. See you on it. See you faithful. See you chumped. See you challenged. See you change.

See you. See you. See you.

See you confide. See you fried. See you still got my back. See you sick. See you used. See you beat. See you offed. See you suicide. See you blues. See you ballad. See you jazz. See you straight. See you gay. See you with sister. See you with blond. See you America. See

you Europe. See you Africa. See you redbone. See you Wesley Snipes.
See you serene. See you home.

See you. See you. See you.

See you city. See you country. See you tired. See you silk. See you
denim. See you dare. See you risk. See you hip. See you get props.
See you surge. See you Turn. See you Tuned. See you Man. See you
Living. See you *Live*.

See you. See you. See you.

I definitely wanna be you.

PART ONE

DEAR BROTHER

LETTERS FROM
REGIONS IN OUR MINDS

———

HAIKU

Why, I cry, do I
see myself so clearly now
nestled in your midst?

—JAKE WIDEMAN

LETTER TO MY BROTHER, EVERETT, IN PRISON

MICHAEL ERIC DYSON

Dear Everett,

How are you? You're probably surprised to hear from me in a letter. I suppose because we have talked almost nonstop on the telephone over the last five years I haven't written too often. Perhaps that's because with writing, you have to confront yourself, stare down truths you would rather avoid altogether. When you're freestyling in conversation, you can acrobatically dance around all those issues that demand deep reflection. After five years, I guess it's time I got down to that kind of, well, hard work, at least emotionally and spiritually.

I've been thinking about you a lot because I've been talking about Black men quite a bit—in my books, in various lectures I give around the country, in sermons I preach, even on "Oprah"! Or is it the other way around, that I've been talking about Black men *because* I've been thinking about you and your hellish confinement behind bars? I don't need to tell you—but maybe I'll repeat it to remind myself—of the miserable plight of Black men in America.

I am not suggesting that Black women have it any better. They are not living in the lap of luxury while their fathers, husbands, brothers, boyfriends, uncles, grandfathers, nephews, and sons perish. Black women have it as bad as, and in some cases even worse than, Black males. That's one of the reasons I hesitate to refer to Black males as an "endangered species," as if Black women are out of the woods of racial and gender agony and into the clearing, free to create and explore their complex identities. I don't believe that for a moment. Or that Black men are separated from the rest of humanity.

I just think Black women have learned, more successfully than Black men, to absorb the pain of their predicament and to keep stepping. They've learned to take the kind of mess that Black men won't take, or feel they can't take, perhaps never will take, and to turn it into something useful, something productive, something toughly beautiful after all. It must be socialization—it certainly isn't genetics or gender, at least in biological terms. I think brothers need to think about this more, to learn from Black women about their politics of survival.

I can already hear some wag or politician using my words to justify another attack on Black men, contending that our plight is our own fault. Or to criticize us for not being as strong as Black women. But we both know that to compare the circumstances of Black men and women, particularly those who are working-class and poor, is to compare our seats on a sinking ship. True, some of us are closer to the hub, temporarily protected from the fierce winds of social ruin. And some of us are directly exposed to the vicious waves of economic misery. But in the final analysis, we're all going down together.

Still, it's undeniable that Black men as a whole are in deplorable shape. The most tragic symbol of that condition, I suppose, is the Black prisoner. There are so many brothers locked away in the "stone hotel," literally hundreds of thousands of them, that it makes me sick to think of the talent they possess going to waste. I constantly get letters from such men, and their intelligence and determination are remarkable, even heartening.

I realize there's an often justifiable fear that millions of Americans harbor toward prisoners whom they believe to be, to a man, unrepentant, hardened criminals. They certainly exist. But every prisoner is not a criminal, just as every criminal is not in prison. That's not to say that I don't believe that men in prison who have committed even violent crimes can't turn around. I believe they can see the harm of their past deeds and embrace a better life, through religious conversion, through redemptive social intervention, or by the sheer will to live right.

But the passion to protect ourselves from criminals, and the social policies that passion gives rise to, often obscures a crucial point: thousands of Black men are wrongfully imprisoned. Too many Black men are jailed for no other reason than they fit the profile of a thug, a vision developed in fear and paranoia. Or sometimes, Black men get caught in the wrong place at the wrong time. Worse yet, some males are literally arrested at a stage of development where, if they had more time, more resources, more critical sympathy, they could learn to resist the temptations that beckon them to a life of self-destruction. Crime is only the most conspicuous sign of their surrender.

I guess some of all of this happened to you. I still remember the phone call that came to me announcing that you had been arrested for murder. The disbelief settled on me heavily. The thought that you might have shot another man to death choked me emotionally. I instantly knew what E. B. White meant when he said that the death of his pig caused him to cry internally. The tears didn't flow down his cheeks. Instead, he cried "deep hemorrhagic intears." So did I.

Even so, a cold instinct to suspend my disbelief arose, an instinct I could hardly suppress. I was willing, *had* to be willing, to entertain the possibility that the news was true. Otherwise I couldn't offer you the kind of support you needed. After all, if you really had killed someone, I didn't want to rush in to express sorrow at your being wrongly accused of a crime you didn't commit. Such a gesture would not only be morally noxious, it would desecrate the memory of the man who had lost his life.

If I wasn't able to face the reality that you might be a murderer, then I would have to surrender important Christian beliefs I preach and try to practice. I believe that all human beings are capable of good and evil. And regarding the latter, wishing it wasn't the case won't make it true. Too often we deny that our loved ones have the capacity or even inclination for wrongdoing, blinding us to the harm they may inflict on themselves and others.

I eventually became convinced that you were innocent. Not simply because you told me so. As one lawyer succinctly summarized it: "To hear them tell it, there are no guilty prisoners." But after discerning the controlled anger in your voice (an anger that often haunts the wrongly accused) and after learning that the police had discovered no weapon, motive, or even circumstantial evidence, I believed you were telling me the truth. Plus, you had been candid with me about your past wrongdoing. And in the wake of your confessions of guilt, you repeatedly bore the sting of my heated reproach. For these reasons, I believed you were not guilty.

But I realized then, as I do now, that these are brothers' reasons. They are the fruit of an intimacy to which the public has no access and in which it places little trust. Many of the reasons that led me to proclaim your innocence are not reasons that convince judges or juries. Still, I felt the bare, brutal facts of the case worked in your favor. A young Black man with whom you were formerly acquainted was tied up in a chair on the second floor of a sparsely furnished house. He had tape tightly wrapped around his eyes. He was beaten on the head. He was shot twice in the chest at extremely close range, producing "contact wounds."

After breaking free of his constraints, he stumbled down the flight of stairs inside the house where he was shot. After making it outside, he collapsed on the front lawn of the house next door. As he gasped for breath while profusely bleeding, he was asked, first by neighbors, then by relatives who arrived on the scene, and later by a policeman, "Who did this to you?" Something sounding close enough to your name was uttered. The badly wounded man was pronounced dead a short time later after being rushed to an area hospital.

In the absence of any evidence of your participation, except the dying man's words, I thought you'd be set free. After all, he could have been mistaken. Given the tragic condition in which he lay dying, he might not have had full control of his faculties. Was his perception affected by the gunshots? Was his mind confused because of the large amount of blood he lost? Unfortunately, there was no way to be certain that he was right. There was no way to ask him if he was sure that you were one of the culprits (he said "they" a couple of times) who had so barbarically assaulted him. Surely, I thought, it took more than this to convict you, or anyone, of murder.

I was wrong. The murdered man's words, technically termed a "dying declaration," were admitted into court testimony and proved, at least for the jury, to be evidence enough. I was stunned. In retrospect, I shouldn't have been. Detroiters, including the ones who peopled the Black jury that convicted you, were fed up with crime. How many times had this apparent scenario been repeated for them: Black men killing other Black men, then seeking pardon from Blacks sitting on a jury in a mostly Black city?

When it came time to sentence you, the judge allowed me to say a few words. I felt more than a little awkward. Although I didn't believe you were guilty, I knew that if I said so the judge would ignore my presentation. In his mind, the jury had settled the issue of your culpability. I didn't know how much I should refer to your past, or to the social forces that shape human action. I figured that the last thing I needed to do was sound like a hotshot intellectual trying to enlighten the masses.

And yet I knew in my heart that I shouldn't avoid mentioning those beliefs I held to be true; for instance, that economic misery can lead to criminal activity. Still, I didn't want to be mistaken for defending the belief that social structures alone determine human behavior. I also wanted to avoid inflicting any more pain on the murdered man's family, most of whom believed that you were guilty as sin. And I didn't want to sound like the brother who was righteous, who had made it good, making excuses for the brother who had gone completely wrong. I wonder if you remember what I said?

Your Honor, I'm a minister of the gospel, and I'm also a scholar and a teacher at a theological seminary. I, of course, want to express first of all my deep sympathy to the family of the man who died. They have endured enormous hurt and pain over this past year. I want to say to you in my brief remarks that I am deeply aware, in an ironic sense, of why we're here. Sentencing is a very difficult decision. I have been deeply committed over the years to justice in American culture and also to examining the workings of the legal system.

On the other hand, I also understand the societal forces—such as poverty and joblessness and structural unemployment and limited social options and opportunities for legitimate employment—that many people of our culture, particularly Black men, face. It is also ironic that I'm here because I write in my professional life about . . . social forces which often leave young Black men feeling they have no other option but to engage in . . . criminal activity in order to sustain their lives. Unfortunately many make that choice. I grew up in the urban poverty of Detroit, as did the other members of my family. Therefore I understand not only from a scholarly viewpoint, but from a personal viewpoint, limited life options and the kind of hopelessness and social despair they can breed in a person. I come here this morning pleading and praying for leniency in my brother's case. As his lawyer has already stated, the mystery that surrounds the events of that day continues to prevail. In any regard, I can attest to my brother's character, that he is not a hardened criminal. He has made unwise choices about the activity of his life in the past. He has made choices which have encouraged him to engage in a life-style that I'm sure at this point he is not proud of. At the same time I think the penalty far exceeds the crime that he has been involved in. Above all, my brother is, I think, ripe for a productive future in our society. Although he has indeed made a noticeable change in jail, a prolonged stay in prison, I feel, will not greatly contribute to any sense of rehabilitation that the Court might think prison offers. Unfortunately the prisons of our land often reproduce the pathology that they seek to eliminate. Because of his own poor beginnings in our city, the death of our father at a crucial time in his life, and because he's been subjected to the forces I've already referred to, my brother has made poor choices. But he's also shown a remarkable strength of faith and renewed spiritual insight. He's shown a remarkable sense of concern . . . about all the people involved in this case and not just himself. . . . In conclusion, Your Honor, I would plead and pray that . . . your deepest discretion and most conscientious leniency prevail in your sentencing of my brother this morning.

I have rarely been more depressed, or more convinced that my words mean absolutely nothing, than when the judge's words, all-powerful words, revealed your future. Life. In prison. An oxymoron if I've ever heard one.

But you have managed to squeeze an ounce of invention, or should I say, self-reinvention, from the pound of cure that prison is said to represent. When I first learned of your new identity, Everett Dyson-*Bey*, I was neither dismayed nor surprised. Frankly, my position is simple: do whatever is necessary to maintain your safety and sanity in prison without bringing undue harm to another person. You're a strong, muscular fellow, and I didn't think you'd have much trouble staying safe. And I took your change of religion—from the Christianity you inherited as a child to the Moorish Temple Muslim belief of your new adulthood—to be an encouraging, even creative defense of your sanity.

I am disappointed, though, by the response of the Black church to your predicament. I suppose since I've been to see you countless times over the last five years, it could be claimed that those visits count for my church's mission to those locked away. But we both know that's bogus. That line of reasoning insults the integrity and slights the example of so many who've followed Jesus in "visit[ing] those who are in prison." You haven't been visited a single time in prison by anyone visiting *as* a Christian minister, or *as* a concerned church member. Thank God our pastor visited you in jail before you went to prison. But the church is larger than he is. Several times I asked the minister in charge of prison visitation to go see you. My requests were futile.

I don't know why so much of Black Christianity avoids the prisons. Of course, I realize that hundreds of Black churches have prison ministries that make a real difference in inmates' lives. But the average pew-sitting member, or for that matter, the regular church minister, rarely gets into the thick of prison life in the same way, say, as members and ministers of the Nation of Islam. Or the Moorish Temple. Perhaps it has something to do with how Black Muslims, with smaller numbers than Black churches, must proselytize when and where they can. Since many of their members have served time, they may be more willing to reach back to help those left behind. Then, too, the application to prisoners' lives of the stringent ethical code taught in Black Muslim settings often brings welcome relief from the moral chaos into which so many inmates have descended.

Another reason for their success may be that Black Muslims take seriously their theological commitments to racial uplift and reconstruction, especially among the poor and imprisoned who are most in need of that message. Perhaps it's a simple class issue. The more legitimacy some Black Christian denominations gain, the higher class-status they acquire, the less they appear inclined to take care of "the least of these." In the end, I'm glad you've discovered in the Moorish Temple what you couldn't find—or perhaps what couldn't be found in you—through Christian belief.

Many people think the sort of religious change you have experienced is a "fox-hole" conversion, a transformation brought on by desperate circumstances that will be rejected as soon as you're set free. That may be the case. If it is true, you certainly won't be the first person it has happened to. But as long as you can, hold on to the hope your religion supplies. There will be other desperate situations after you leave prison. Besides, so-called normal religious people experience a series of crises and conversions over the years in settling down to a deeper faith. And even those folk who don't walk through its doors every time church opens often have meaningful conversations with God.

I think Daddy was one of those people. He was a complex man who worked extraordinarily hard and who believed deeply in God. But he wasn't very religious, at least not in any traditional way. When people discover I'm a Baptist preacher, they often ask if preachers run in my family, if my father was a preacher. I laugh inwardly, sometimes out loud, thinking of what an odd image that is, Daddy as a preacher. It's not that he cussed like a sailor. I know too many preachers who do that as well. And it's not because he had a short fuse. So do most prophets, biblical and current ones too.

I guess it's their righteous rage at evil, their ill-tempered tirades translated as holy damnation. But the line between their baptized fussiness and plain old invective is sometimes quite thin.

I think what causes my bemused response is Daddy's genuine humility. Most preachers I know aren't that humble. I don't think that's all bad. Many can't afford to be. The tribulations of their office are enough to shatter a fragile ego. But the annoying hubris found in so many ministers was completely absent in Daddy. And yet his ferocious anger frightened me. True, it didn't last long when it surfaced. But its concentrated expression had devastating consequences. And often—I think too often—it had its most harmful effects on his children's behinds. And, perhaps, on their minds.

As you know, a debate about corporal punishment is raging in our nation. There used to be a belief that there was a racial divide on these matters, at least when we were growing up: Black folk in favor, white folk opposed. Even though I don't think it's that simple (where one lives, either in the city or the suburbs, and one's class identification are important too), I don't deny that racial differences exist.

Recently, though, I think the gulf between Black and white views on child rearing has probably narrowed. A new generation of Black parents has questioned and often rejected the wisdom of whipping ass. To be sure, you still hear Black folk saying, "The problem with white folk is that they let their kids get away with murder, let them talk and act any way they want to without keeping them in check." But you also hear Black parents and the experts they listen to arguing that corporal punishment encourages aggressive behavior, stymies the development of moral reasoning, hinders self-esteem, and even causes children to be depressed. No such theories prevailed in our household.

I must admit, I tend toward the newfangled school of thought, even though I haven't always put it into practice now that it's my turn to parent. In fact, during your nephew Michael's childhood and early adolescence, I didn't know anything about "time out." As a teen father, I had barely survived the pain of my own rearing and the violence I'd encountered. I knew what I had seen, repeated what was done to me. And I regret it.

One of the most painful moments I experienced involving punishment occurred when I was a teacher and assistant director of a poverty project at Hartford Seminary. Mike, Brenda (then my wife), and I were in our car driving to work to pick up some papers one evening. Down the street from the seminary, Mike had behaved so badly in the car that I pulled over to the side of the road to discipline him—

three licks on his hands. In my view, it was a very light and well-deserved spanking. After administering this punishment, I drove the single block to the seminary.

But before I could park my car, two white policemen drove up in a squad car. One of the policemen approached my door, instructing me to get out of the car. His partner walked up to Brenda's side of our car.

"Can I ask you why you're stopping me, Officer?" I asked politely and professionally. I'd learned to do this, as most Black men in America have learned, to keep the blue wrath from falling on my head.

"Just get out of the car," he insisted.

As I got out of my car, I informed the policeman that I worked at Hartford Seminary.

"I'm a professor here," I said, pointing to the seminary behind me.

"Sure," the policeman shot back. "And I'm John Wayne."

The policeman instructed me to place my hands against the car and to lean forward. I knew the drill. I'd done it too many times before. I could hear the other policeman asking Brenda if everything was all right, if my son was harmed. Mike was in the backseat crying, afraid of what the police were going to do to me.

"I'm fine, I'm fine," Mike cried. "Why are you doing this to my dad?"

From the pieces of conversation I heard between the second cop and Brenda, I gathered that someone—a well-meaning white person no doubt—had spotted me spanking Mike and reported me as a child abuser.

Just as Brenda told the cop how ridiculous that was, two more police cars rolled up with four more white men. "Damn," I thought, "if I had been mugged, I bet I couldn't get a cop to respond within half an hour. And now, within five minutes of spanking my son, I've got six policemen breathing down my neck."

As the other cops surrounded our car, the policeman hovering over me still refused to explain why he stopped me. He forcefully patted me down as we both listened to Brenda and Mike explain again that nothing was wrong, that Mike was fine.

"You sure everything's all right?" the cop talking to Brenda asked once again for degrading emphasis. She angrily replied in the affirmative.

Finally my knight-in-shining-armor spoke to me.

"We got a complaint that someone was hurting a child," he said.

"I can assure you that I love my son, and that I wasn't hurting him," I responded in a controlled tone. "I spanked my child now so that he wouldn't one day end up being arrested by you."

"We have to check on these things," the second cop offered.

"Just don't be doing nothing wrong."

He shoved me against the car to make his point. With that, the six cops got back into their cars, without apology, and drove off.

I don't have to tell you that the situation was utterly humiliating. I resented how I'd been treated. I felt the cops had deliberately intimidated me. They had embarrassed me in front of my family. I think their behavior is fairly typical of how many white men with authority treat Black men. They are unable to be humane in the exercise of power. They run roughshod over Black men in the name of serving a higher good, such as protecting Black women and children from our aggression.

The irony of course is that white men ignore how their violence against Black men has already hurt millions of Black families, including Black women and children. In fact, the intent of much of white male hostility is not to help Black women and children but to harm Black men. Fortunately for me, Brenda and Mike understood that truth. Neither of them trusted the cops' motives for one moment.

Still, the incident forced me to imagine the impact my punishment had had on Mike. I thought about how he might interpret the discipline I gave him. I wondered how spankings made him *feel*, despite the reassurances of love with which I prefaced any punishment I gave him. The irony, too, is that I was reading social and cultural theorists who were writing about discipline and punishment. While I found many of them extremely enlightening about big social forces and how they molded people's habits of life at home and in the world, I sometimes wondered if they had any children. I continued to talk to Mike about these matters, apologizing to him about my past disciplinary practices, promising him, and mostly living up to it, that I would look for alternatives to physical punishment.

Of course Daddy lived in a world where such considerations were impossible. If you don't control your kids, they'll control you. That's the logic that informed his decisions. If you don't beat their asses, they'll beat yours one day. I guess depending on where you stand on such issues, the rash of recent slayings of parents by their children either proves or undermines such a theory. In any case, I eventually grew to hate Daddy for the violence of his punishments. I can still hear him saying "Get me that 'hind pepper," referring to the quarter-inch-thick, twelve-inch-long piece of leather he used to whip us. Occasionally, he'd plant his size-twelve foot right up my posterior.

I know, of course, that no one on our block would have called that child abuse. And neither did I. Given the Black cultural logic of the time during which he was reared, and during which he and Mama reared us, Daddy was simply attempting to keep his brood in line. (What we must not forget is that during an earlier time in our nation, Black folk beat their children at home so they wouldn't give white men lip in public. If a Black child wasn't strictly disciplined, he might say or do something that might cause him untold danger away from the protection of parents. Even though that logic may be long exhausted, some habits die hard.)

My resentment of his whippings got so bad that he once told Mama that he thought I hated him because he wasn't my biological father. When Mama told me that, I was crushed. For despite his discipline, I knew he loved me like I was his very own, like I was your full-blood brother. For that reason, I have never made the distinction between any of us five boys who came up together. In my mind, not only did we have the same mother, but we shared the same father. He was as much of a father as most of my friends had and often much, much more. Since he adopted me when I was two, he is the only father I have ever known. He was Daddy to me, just like he was to you.

No, I was very specific about my beef with him. It wasn't blood, it was those beatings. The same ones he gave to you, Anthony, Gregory, and Brian. And probably to John Everett, Etta James, Robert, and Annie Ruth, our late brothers and sisters from Daddy's previous marriages.

My conflict with Daddy came to a head when I was sixteen, the same age Mike is now. He had ordered me to do something, what I can't remember. But I do remember feeling the familiar threat of physical punishment behind his words if I didn't immediately obey. I had had enough. We were at the house, upstairs on the second floor. He barked his orders, but I wasn't moving fast enough.

"Move, goddammit, when I speak to you," he bellowed.

But the resentment weighed me down, slowed my legs. I knew instantly that we were heading for a showdown. Daddy jumped up from the bed in his room and moved toward me. Even that gesture failed to speed up my pace. This wasn't worker slowdown, a domestic uprising against an unjust guardian. This was sheer frustration, anger, and weariness.

"Move, I said," Daddy repeated. I didn't.

Then he grabbed me by the arm and pushed me against the wall. Something in me exploded. Or did it snap? Either metaphor, or perhaps both of them, captures my state of mind, my state of soul.

"Fuck it, man," I heaved. "You just gonna have to kill me, 'cause I refuse to be scared anymore."

I guess he took me seriously. He literally lifted me off the ground with his left arm, and his massive chocolate hand sunk deep into my yellow neck as he pinned me against a hallway wall. They didn't call him Muscles for nothing. I thought for sure that he might really kill me. But I didn't care anymore. I was tired of running. But Mama saved me.

"Everett," she hollered. It was all she said. But it was enough to bring Daddy to his senses, to make him drop me to the ground before he completely choked me. Never mind my gasping. I felt free, delivered of some awful demon of fear that no longer had power over me. It was my emancipation proclamation and declaration of independence all rolled into one moment. It was a milestone in my relationship to Daddy.

For the next seven years, his last ones on earth, Daddy and I got along much better. After I got Terry pregnant at eighteen and married her, and after Mike was born, Daddy and I grew much closer. In fact, he'd often cook for me and Terry because we were so poor at times that we didn't eat every day. In fact, at times, we didn't eat for two or three days in a row. But then we'd go by the house, and Daddy would always give us a good meal. I even sent Daddy a Father's Day card in 1981 when I was in Knoxville attending college. I told him how much I loved him, and how much I appreciated the fact that we had overcome our differences now that I was a man with major responsibilities. A few weeks later, he was dead from a heart attack at sixty-six. So young when you really think about it.

But I must confess, even now as a thirty-five-year-old man I have dreams of Daddy doing violent deeds to me, whipping me in vicious ways. The lingering effects of the whippings Daddy administered are illustrated by a story I heard about a boy and his father, who sought to rid his son of his habit of lying. The boy's father hammered nails into a piece of wood for each lie his son told. Finally, when the board was nearly full, the boy pledged to stop lying. And his father promised to pull a nail out each time his son told the truth. When the board was completely empty, the boy began to cry.

"What's wrong, son?" the boy's father asked. "You should be happy. You've stopped lying, and the nails are all gone."

"Yes," the boy replied. "The nails *are* gone, but the holes are still there."

Well, the holes are still there for me as well. My psyche bears the marks of spiritual and psychological violence. But I am not bitter toward Daddy. I honestly believe he was a good man trying to do his best in a world that was often difficult for him. The older I get, the more clearly I understand the forces he faced.

I guess I'm sharing all of this with you now because we never enjoyed this kind of intimacy before your imprisonment. A shame, but it's true. And even though we grew up in a household where we knew we were loved, we rarely, if ever, heard the words "I love you." Daddy taught us to be macho men, strong enough to take care of ourselves on the mean streets of Detroit. And though Mama protested, thinking Daddy was trying to make us too rough at times, I'm sure we both appreciate many of his efforts to prepare us for an often cold-hearted, violent world.

I yearned for a home where we could be both strong and vulnerable, tough and loving. But Daddy's reading of the world led him to believe it was either one or the other. He chose to teach us how to survive in a city that was known then, in the seventies, as the murder capital of the world. And because I loved books, and not the cars that you and Daddy and Brian loved to work on, he sometimes thought I was "too soft." But Daddy was really proud of me later when I excelled at school. He wanted me to be better than he was.

I remember once when I was about eight years old, I was mimicking his pronunciation of the number "four." He pronounced it "foe." I followed suit. But he stopped me.

"Don't you go to school, boy?" he asked.

"Yes," I replied.

"Don't you know how to say that right?"

"Yes."

"Then do that from now on. Okay?"

I've never forgotten that exchange. He didn't have a great education, but he sure wanted me to be learned. Indeed, he wanted the best for all his boys. I imagine if he was alive he'd be heartbroken that you're in prison. Daddy was the complete opposite of so much of what prison stands for. He rose every day before dawn, even after he retired from the factory, and worked until evening, cutting grass, laying sod, painting, or working as a maintenance man. I learned my work ethic from him. I can still hear him saying, "Boy, if you gonna do a job, do it right or don't do it at all." I've repeated that to Mike at least a million times. And of course, his other famous saying was "If you start a job, finish it." That is, other than his maxim: "Laziness will kill yo' ass."

And even when he worked those thirty-three years at Kelsey-Hayes Wheelbrake and Drum Factory, he often put in sixty or seventy hours. I swear I once saw a stub where he had worked nearly eighty hours, pulling a double shift for an entire week. It was Daddy's example that led me to work two full-time jobs after Terry got pregnant with Mike. (But he warned me then, "The more money you make, the more you spend." He was right, of course.) I'd go to a maintenance job from one A.M. to seven-thirty the next morning, and then work a menial "construction job" (a misnomer, to be sure) from seven-thirty to four-thirty in the evening. And I still had to get food stamps while Terry was enrolled in W.I.C. (Women, Infants, and Children)! That stuff saved our lives.

I'm glad that you and I have learned to talk. To communicate. To express our love for each other. It hasn't been easy seeing you cooped up like an animal when I visit you. But the one good thing to come out of all of this is that at least we're getting to know each other better. That's why I feel good about telling the world about you.

Even as I talk about you on television and radio, though, I always try to impress on the audiences and interviewers in the short time I have that ours is no "one son makes good and the other makes bad: what a tragedy" scenario. I'm not trying to pimp your pain or commercialize your misery to make a name for myself. That's because I believe in my heart, and I hope you do too, that it could just as easily be me in your cell. I don't want people using our story as a justification for rewarding Black men like me who are able to do well while punishing brothers like you who've fallen on harder times.

No matter how much education I've got, this Ph.D. is no guarantee that I won't be treated cruelly and unjustly, that I won't be seen as a threat because I refuse to point the finger at "dem ghetto niggers" (a statement made by Black and white alike) who aren't like me. I'm not trying to erase class differences, to pretend there's no difference between a Black man with a Ph.D. and a Black man who's a prisoner. I'm simply saying I can't be seduced into believing that because I've got this degree I'm better.

How could I be? I was one of "dem ghetto niggers" myself. Even now I think of myself as a ghetto boy, though I don't live there anymore, and I refuse to romanticize its role in its inhabitants' lives. Not even survivors' guilt should make us that blind. But being from the ghetto certainly leaves its marks on one's identity. Don't get me wrong. I'm all for serious, redemptive criticism of Black life at every level, including the inner city. But there's a difference between criticism that really helps and castigation that only hurts.

I should close this letter for now. I fear I've touched on many sensitive spots, and you may sharply disagree with some of the things I've written. But that's all right. The important thing is that as Black men, as Black brothers, we learn to embrace each other despite the differences that divide us. I hope you write me back. I'd really like to know what you think about what I've said. In the meantime, stay strong, and stay determined to renew your spirit and mind at the altar of devotion to God and our people. In the final analysis, it's the only thing that can save us all.

Peace and Love,
Mike

Magic

Tyehimba Jess

us.
staring
stupid eyed
at your prestidigitation.
we watch you floating, mid air
like peace
and fire
and power
and grace
as we ask
what did that nigga god do to make him so bad?

and with a 360 swish you answered
i'm never comin down
i own this air
and all in it

we believed and we believed

but now heroman, you fly the courts no more
now you be walkin mortalized with mortal steps
crushin naïve dreams we had of livin carefree forevers
and things are a little more solemn now.

no more *that shit don't affect me!*
no more *i clean, i ain't like that*
and *only faggots get that shit!*

and the face of genocide has become just a little clearer since
you brought it home to every basketball court in the hood.

you, smilin giant
you, sleek-footed move master
you, once slidin, pushin, leapin, dribblin, weavin down a court
through forests of flashin arms and legs takin it to the hole
you now serve up in yo face images of   ·

syphilitic tuskegee graves,
smallpox blankets,
disappearing hospital beds in the hood,
needle-spread sickness,
and a horror called doctor bills
all a part of the game played on these asphalt streets.

and now, on all the networks,
the tv smile,
the brave words
as you remind us the magic is still here
we only thinking of the day we last saw you floating, mid air
thinking of peace, grace and power.

how all the rules have been broken at our feet.
magically.

BROTHER LESS

TYEHIMBA JESS

i was not when the lead ripped
   Malcolm to pieces.
   Six months later,
   i came out screaming.

i was three when the bullet
punched through Martin's jaw.
   Now i would know neither.

i was five when Fred slumped
   forward in his blood.
They took him from me too.

Before i could know them our
   voice was ripped
   away calling

   Sometimes I feel
like a brotherless child
A long way from brother's
   arms

Fear-tied, tourniquet-whipped, broken arms.
Trackmarks waiting like dark ghosts.
Look castaway.

Eyes crushed
mirrors for monster reflections.

Lips tremble familiar confusion of
slow, stalking streetcorner sickness
Hands, fists, curled around death,
wrapped on skull of my sister.

> *Some*
> > *timos*
> *I feel like a brotherless child*

Seeking to be whole,
finding you in holes 6 feet deep,
shallow watery tombs of streetcorner blood, liquor, piss,
5 × 7 cell graves
where you wait to die like what you think is a man.

Only graves don't talk, they scream.

And corpses don't reach out to embrace brothers.
They are too busy embracing themselves,
aching hurt away,
coffin-style.
Marble-slab-in-the-coroner's-office-cool-to-the-end.

And dead lips can only tell dead words
or ask me to die too.

To a Lot of People, for Many Reasons . . .

Matthew McGuire

Dear D*,

What up in Illinois, D—? A lot on my mind, don't know where to start. Earlier this evening I spoke to a former student of mine and it got me to thinking, so maybe I'll start there. Back when I was teaching I used to write your Pops after I had finished covering one of his books; I figured it was the least a teacher could do for someone whose ideas he was using to work with young students. A colleague once told me that college professors taught subjects, but that in high school we taught people. Corny as it sounds, it stuck with me and I began to think about what it was that I hoped to teach people. A simple question, and one that is easy to gloss over, but one that can provide an important pillar for the framework in which someone operates.

I tend toward the belief that we all have to ultimately do for self, and that there is no better skill to have out there than the ability to fashion one's own way through the mazes and obstacles that inevitably arise. Maya Angelou once said that "You had better learn to create yourself, because if you don't, someone else will do it for you." More importantly for my understanding, my mother raised me that way. Whether she realized it or not, through her example and her stories, she told me very clearly that Matthew was responsible for Matthew, and that living right was an important matter. Whether *I* realized it or not, I believed her.

* Daniel Wideman

Mom knew what she was doing. The importance of self-creation is a crucial lesson when you are raising biracial kids who look white and are growing up in a middle-class black—yes black and yes middle-class—neighborhood while hanging out on both sides of the tracks. I remember being at the playground one day when I was four, down around 12th and Vermont, near our kindergarten school. It was me, my brother (Eric), Andre, and Gary; and we were playing ball of some sort when a tall brother came to the fence bellowing to the world and to our teacher about the evils of little white kids and little black kids playing together. They should be separated, he said, pointing to me and Eric. The game had stopped, as had most of the motion on the playground, and this cat's words kept things still for the five minutes or so he needed to vomit up whatever it was he had to get out. Thankfully, he eventually finished and Gary released the pause button by saying, "He's crazy and besides, you're not white anyway." (So much for thinking that awareness of racial categories and their "logic" is unclear to children until they begin to date or something like that.) From there, tension gone and group solidarity ensured, we began laughing and demonstrating all of the karate moves that we would have done on the guy if he had entered the playground and tried to mess with us for real.

I take two things from this story. The first is that if you try to think through all the implications of the episode and how it struck me, you will end up in a nasty vortex of confusion and disbelief. The larger point is that via such experiences, I realized early on just how important it is to take the reins for myself. *If you don't create yourself, someone else will do it for you.*

With all of these stories and ideas in mind, I began to construct my syllabi and my philosophy for the courses I was supposed to teach. I wondered how I might translate my experiences and opinions into something that students a few years younger than I could use. I was especially concerned about a course on African-American literature I was going to teach to seniors. Before long I decided that working to understand the context we live in—this place called America (though we mean the United States) during the postmodern era (who knows what that means?)—was as useful as anything else we could do. So we jumped into it, and your father's book (*Brothers and Keepers*) was a great springboard. It raises some of the issues that surge through adolescence: freedom and what it really means once you get away from constitutions and diplomats, responsibility, personal demons, prisons, brothers, love, reckoning with the past, and how such an act is about survival in the present. . . .

(I know, Dan, I know; MTV, *Newsweek*, and Grandma all keep saying that the only things kids think about today are guns, sex, and new ways to self-destruct. But look at my categories again and then look at theirs. Seems to me that if you take "guns, sex, and new ways to self-destruct" and you stretch it out like you might stretch a piece of rubber, you'll come up with something that looks like "freedom . . . personal demons . . . love . . . the past.")

Neither teaching nor *Brothers and Keepers*, however, is the point of why I'm writing or where I am headed. I was headed toward telling you that I remember writing your dad and saying that his words and his vision of this society had served as "valuable currency for my students as they negotiated the tolls that come with being young and black in the United States." And I was only headed there because it is on the way to telling you that right now is a time to suspend sending letters to the fathers of our generation. This is a moment when we need to begin rotating that circle; we need to look toward each other, toward self. You know?

I have a couple streams of thought running through my head, and they're battling. Both seem important. The first has to do with my father, who has been dead for damn near twenty years—and I mean damn when I use it there. I don't know about other people in my family, but I think about him almost every day. Don't ever let anyone tell you that you get over the deaths of those near you, especially if they die when you are young. You move on and continue living, yes (what choice do you have?), but death and the spaces it creates become part of who you are and it's not something that you shuck off like an arm tackle. I'll be worried if the day ever comes when I think my father's death is just something that happened and that I'm over it. To me it will mean that I'm denying the complexity of his absence and the various pains it has caused, and that will be a sign of weakness. Ain't nothing wrong with hurting, you know; it's being afraid of hurting or not trying to come back from a wound that shows trouble in your life. So Papa is one of the things on my mind, and I'll come back to him a little bit later.

The other stream of thought is Dianne, whom I call "Dee." She comes to mind because that's the way Dee is, just flowing in with a smile and a presence you wouldn't believe and then she is "here to stay," as Billie Holiday put it long ago. Dee manages to shake my head whenever she gets into it, swirls around for a nice long time, and I thank her for it always. Yet this time she also comes into things because you said the book is about love and violence. My discussions of the former often incorporate her, so as I weigh these two themes and how they shape my life, Dianne ambles on in and takes her place among the people and the experiences that have landed me where I am.

Now Dee will always be important to me because she was the first person who loved me who didn't have to. Family is under some obligation, I think, and folks who have known you since you were little just care for you because it's a habit. OK, I'm overstating; but Dee was the first person who I remember saying, "I don't know you but I see something there that is live and just being around you makes my day so why don't you let me peep what else is inside your head and then maybe we'll both end up breathing a little easier." Which is what I did and is what happened. The effect Dee had on me was what I imagine it would be like if Novocain was coursing through your heart and then someone came along to turn the nerves back on. Like when you switch the TV from mute back to sound. She did that for me.

Now I don't know if Dee was my proverbial first love or not (it doesn't fit what I think first loves are about—with them I think of blank stares and the luster fading badly after the initial separation, neither of which was the case with us), but I know that the point when we became close is a concrete marker in my memory bank. "Before Dee" was one way; "since Dee" is another. There are a few other such markers, the most important of which is at age six, when Papa died. (It appears this is the "little bit later" when he comes back in.) When Papa died I saw the side of love seldom talked about, the part that should make it more precious and therefore less thought-lessly given. When Papa died the love fled as well, pulling tissues from my heart as it receded. Forever. From Mom's heart, from my brother's; if one was to go by the praise I've heard since, from a long list of hearts. And this is what I weigh heavily.

I take James Baldwin seriously when he asks if we are willing to pay the price of love's ticket, because it is an expensive ticket and not all of us have unlimited checking accounts. Mom sometimes says, "You can't control everything in life, but you *can* cut down on the risks." I don't believe that she is advising anyone to forgo love as they weave through life, but I do believe she is touching on an important point. Simply put, there is enough pain coming into our lives as is, so why not try to regulate some of what we have a say in?

The friction I keep running into is women who only give lip service to the perilous sides of love and commitment. They seem to think that love is something that, once given, must be accepted, as though they are doing you a favor by offering it up. Yet from where I often stand, it is much more complicated. Offering someone love is a magical thing, but it is also an imposition. It demands a lot, and many women assume that every man automatically wants the returns that come from such an offer.

What I question is the motivation behind these declarations of love and eternal bonding. It seems fairly self-serving for someone to offer a gift that binds so thoroughly and then to expect the receiving party to automatically fall in line with the intensity that follows. It seems that such gifts are nothing of the sort; they are a means to acquiring—security? identity? money? . . . Which is cool as long as you are honest about what you are after, and aren't fooling everyone involved by cloaking it in the language of purity. But discussions of love contain such language, and "love" seems to have become such a necessary acquisition that many lose sight of why they want it. As though love is simply one more thing to pick up as you roll through life, like a car or a job.

To put it bluntly, everywhere I turn I see hearts with gaping holes in them consuming other people's energy and affection to no end. And when men don't provide all of their resources to fill those holes (regardless of the expense to themselves), the call of "emotionally inaccessible" goes out, right along with "no good." Well, it may be that he is no good, but what was it again that you wanted him to be good for?

My point is simple. There are many men who don't seem to understand what it takes to sustain a loving relationship, and who don't fulfill the obligations that come with the blessing of such a union. There are at least as many women who think that the gift of love is their due, and who won't acknowledge the flip side of this blessing, which is a curse. One always contains the other. So when someone (myself included) doesn't want to dance, it may be just that nakedly simple.

A related point is this: when all is said and done, I might end up living where Mom lived for a time, having lost her loverbestfriendconfidantsupporterfatheroftwochildrenandsomuchmore. Perhaps worse (?), I could end up on Papa's side of the equation and become the person who embeds himself so deeply in another's heart that his memory always evokes departure. And most likely, I will grow old slowly and predictably with a wife, several kids, and the standard dose of ups and downs. We simply don't know which direction our futures will take, but I *do* know that I can't casually roll the dice and assume that my life's major traumas are behind me. And I don't plan to.

This isn't where I planned to end up when I started writing, but that doesn't really matter now. If this is what came out, then this is what was really on my mind. I think I planned something more "literary," but I'm glad it didn't come to that. You said the book was about love and violence, which means it is about something raw, and that is how this letter feels. Let me know how all of the above strikes you—it is meant as conversation, you know.

Take care, and be sure to love your wife every day. I'll say it again: love her each day. You are lucky to have one another, so keep on. . . .

Be easy,
Matt

LETTER TO MY BROTHER

ROHAN B PRESTON

When they cross the street before they pass you,
do not be offended. It is not you that they are afraid of—
sixteen years old, with a high-top fade and kenté scarf—
they are afraid of their own wills and consciences.
It is not you who deliberately gave smallpox-infected
blankets to frigid and trusting "Indians,"
it is not you who fed a hundred million bodies
to the sharks which define the mercantile trade winds.
No, you did not perform "biological tests" at Auschwitz
or in the ghettoes of Warsaw or Washington.

Lee, you must remain firm, unbowed—you must
walk with neither a hiccup nor a spasm in your step.
For when they hold up a mirror to your face,
place it on presidential campaign ads or in police albums,
it is only Frankenstein seeking his true genius.
And when they flag you down on I-95 or the Turnpike,
and ram a night-stick into your rib-cage, hands
behind your back and Gestapo boots grinding your neck,
you will know the bottomlessness of their power,
and they think that your hatred runs just as deep.
You must walk well, Lee, head high even if maimed.

In the elevator, those women are not really afraid of you—
their first definition of carnal twitching, unctuous savagery—

because they know what their fathers have done to Sister,
not even four hundred or a hundred years ago, but yesterday.
They know that their daddies were on the lacrosse team
when all seven peeled ears of corn and sprayed cum in her face,
then dragging Sister by the hair, face down, from room to room.
So when these ladies cringe and gasp and are about to faint,
bury your smile, swallow, and know that you are not a hyena
or shaggy ogre prowling across their Savannah,
just a teenager whose very skin bares their daddies' little secrets.

DISPATCHES FROM THE FRONT

—

HAIKU

Violent summer nights
sky lit up with orange streaks
red pools dot the streets.

—JAKE WIDEMAN

SECRETS

Red fire rages
Way down below
In our bellies.
Watch us consume
Ourselves with deception.
Our black smoke
Hides our truth.

—CHARLES W. HARVEY

To Black Folks and Bass

Omar McRoberts

Car after car booms by: Bass
like thunder claps and rumbles
at the command of Blackyouthgodzz. Bass
filling my chest inspiring fear
awe and a desire to move from rest.
Robbing my breath, Bass, sometimes
sinister Bass, creeping past like superslow
uzi fire: "Boom, Boom, Boom, Boom, Bass
Jum Jum, Jimbe Bass. . . ."
Black as the space in which it moves
coming from superfat grooves, Bass.
Too much for the rattling car frame to take, Bass
shake aloose concrete shackles, Bass
massaging pain from mental muscles forgetting
daily hustles and bustles, Bass:
The sound Afros would make if they could be
played. Bass
got me swaying, swinging curlin' kinkin' up in
a sea of burgundy brown Black Earthvibes, Bass.

I love Bass.
The kind Ron Carter and Charlie Mingus would be
proud of, Bass.
Thumpin' like Art Blakey, Bass—
hell naw, Bass ain't new

Bass is You, the sound of sisters and brothers, Bass:
Africasoulfoodcornrowsundayservice. Bass
making mind/spirit/body share the same space
tearin' up the place, Bass is you.
The sound of creation and of
nations within nations the sound of rebels
the cosmological precursor of treble, Bass.
Bass is grabbing hold of you, telling you
the News in rumbling blues
mesmerizing paralyzing Bass
which is your voice 1000 times
speaking of the sublime:
"Boom, Boom, Boom, Boom, Bass
Jum Jum, Jimbe Bass. . . ."
So I just sit still, while bopping my nappy head.

Peace, Dog

A ONE-ACT PLAY

Jabari Asim

CHARACTERS
Brandon Joseph ("Boo Jay") Simmons, 16
Terrell, 16
Flex, 16
Gracie Simmons, 63, Boo Jay's grandmother

TIME
The present

PLACE
The Ville, somewhere

SCENE 1:
An alley. Despite the earnest attempts of a few conscientious residents, the alley is in serious need of a bath. A nearby dumpster is overflowing with rubbish. Occasional bits of glass and aluminum glint in the sunlight. In the distance, the rumble of a bass-heavy rap rattles the afternoon air. Other sounds fill the gap: babies crying, horns honking, dogs barking, police sirens blaring, people in the hood laughing and talking. Boo Jay, a slender youth, is busy scrubbing the back of a garage. Armed with a bucket of lather and a stiff brush, he is attempting to rid the garage of the graffiti scrawled on it. Streaking red letters tell the world: Flex is in the house! Lambdin Posse. Throughout the play, the surrounding sounds should rise and

fall in volume, especially the thudding bass of the "jeep beats" and police sirens. Boo Jay is rapping to himself as he scrubs.

BOO JAY: A bop, a swing. Of funk Ah sing. A rat-a-tat scat, a way cool cat. A glow, a buzz. Ah can kick beats like music does. Like dancers doin dips on the crest of a ridge, and Sonny blowin licks on the edge of the bridge. Be at ground zero as a new slick is born, in a poet throwin notes like the bell of a horn.
(Terrell enters.)
TERRELL: Yo, Dog!
BOO JAY: Whassup!
TERRELL: Can you git slick wit the vibe that Ahm bringin?
BOO JAY: All depends on the lingo that you slingin.
TERRELL: Rhythms and rhymes and beats datz phat . . .
BOTH: Ahm fresh, Ahm fly—an' you *know* that!
(They slap high fives and turn them down.)
TERRELL: What's it like?
BOO JAY: You the man.
TERRELL: Naw, *you* the man.
BOO JAY: You the man.
TERRELL: *You* the man.
BOO JAY: Ite den, Ah am. Ain't peeped you much lately. Don't tell me you been hidin out at the library or somethin.
TERRELL: Tryin ta jone, huh? Shoot, if Ah *wuz* at the library, you sho wouldn't know where ta fine me.
BOO JAY: Terrell, Ah know where *everything* is in dis hood.
TERRELL: Yeah, Boo Jay, fourth generation on th' block an' all that.
BOO JAY: Damn skippy. Mah granmotha wuz born in uh house on Enright.
TERRELL: Zat right? Well, gimme a sheet an' call me Klansman! Can we git off dis dusty ol history book stuff?
BOO JAY: You callin mah granma dusty?
TERRELL: Step back, man. That skin you in is way too thin.
BOO JAY: You right, ace. Ahm buggin. Must be cuz Ah ain't had none in oh, six hours uh so.
TERRELL: Uh-oh, here we go.
BOO JAY: Whut choo mean, here we go? Like Ahm lyin uh sumthin. Lemme tell you sumthin. Ahm the mackinest mack daddy this side uh Natchel Bridge. Any woman'll tell ya Ah knows how ta please her.
TERRELL: If she's a skeeza, you ain't got ta please huh!
BOO JAY: Say whut?

TERRELL: Bein Ah am the kind of stud that Ah am, you'd best lend an ear ta the lesson Ahm blessin.

BOO JAY: Now whut if somebody said sumthin like that bout cho sista?

TERRELL: Man, Ah wish some fool would. We'd juss hafta step, dat's all.

BOO JAY: Yo skin's too tight, all right. You bust so much yang, yo nose is growin. On th' real tip, though. Where you been?

TERRELL: Juss chillin in the crib, Boo.

BOO JAY: Straight?

TERRELL: Word. Stayin outta trouble, know whut 'm sayin?

BOO JAY: Trouble, huh.

TERRELL: Yeah, Dog. Stranjuhs in th' hood. Writin's on the wall.

BOO JAY: In livin color an' all that. Got me out here scrubbin own a lovely Sairdee afternoon. Ah could be out, uh, gittin me some.

TERRELL: Damn, Dog. An' Ah thought *Ah* had uh one-track mine.

BOO JAY: Well, if it wuzn't fuh this garage that's whut Ah'd be doin'. . . . Course, when it comes down to it, this is bout th' only thing that's more fun.

TERRELL: More fun nen whut?

BOO JAY: Gittin some . . .

TERRELL: Man, you rilly should be wearin uh hat out here. Th' sun's bakin yo brain.

BOO JAY: That's right. Go own and jone me if it makes ya feel good. You juss jealous cuz Ah git ta do this an' all you git ta do is watch.

TERRELL: Too bad Homa G. ain't open. Ah think you need a checkup.

BOO JAY: Terrell, since we boyz an' all, Ahm willin ta share this oppatunity witcha.

TERRELL: See Dog, Ahm hip ta Tom Sawya. No way Ahm fallin fuh dat scam. You ain't th' only one dats read uh book before.

BOO JAY: Damn. You *have* been hidin out at th' library, haven't you? Oh well, guess Ah'll hafta finish this myself . . .

TERRELL: Betta herry, too, Boo Jay. Be dark before ya know it, an' th' fools'll be shootin. Ahm audi, home. Peace.

BOO JAY: Peace, Dog.

TERRELL: Watch ya back, ace.

BOO JAY: Always, dude.

(*Terrell exits. Boo Jay resumes scrubbing for a brief interval before resuming his rap.*)

BOO JAY: We dress up the word like elegant birds, in lids and vines, in fact the whole nines. Yes, Ah be rockin wit th' fly verse, kid—
(*Suddenly Flex hurtles from the wings and knocks the brush from*

Boo Jay's hand. He tries to pin Boo Jay against the garage. They struggle, leaning into each other.)

BOO JAY: Whut th' hell is wrong witchoo? Git off me!

FLEX: This is whutchoo git when you mess wit me. Lucky Ah don't smoke you on th' spot!

BOO JAY: Dude, Ah don't even *know* you!

FLEX: Like hell you don't! Screwin up mah tag!

BOO JAY: Yo tag? Aw, ya meanniss here?

FLEX: Word, punk. Ah see you can read.

BOO JAY: Git off me, man.

FLEX: F-L-E-X. Flex. Rhymes wit sex. Dat's muh tag.

BOO JAY: Look, man, dat may be yo tag, but this is mah granmotha's garage. She don't want no graffiti own it, an' neitha do Ah. This stuff's hard as hell ta git off. Probly hafta paint it.

FLEX: An' Ah'll juss tag it again.

BOO JAY: Me an' mah granma, we mind our own business. You should mind yours.

FLEX: This hood *is* mah business. Ah live here now. Wherever Ah go, mah set goes wit me. Folks need ta know dat, so Ah spray mah tag. Keeps th' low-lifes away.

BOO JAY: What's that got ta do wit me an' mah granma?

FLEX: Everything an' nothin, chief. When Ah see uh nice, clean wall like this was, Ah think, Hmm, look at this nice clean wall. It looks okay, but it's missin that final touch ta complete the pitcha. Ah supply that final touch. Ah couldn't care less who th' wall belongs to. Whennuh wrong set comes around, they'll see mah tag an' herry they sorry asses straight outta Dodge. Mah tag gives ya protection. You should be grateful. One day Ah might start chargin folks.

(Boo Jay breaks loose from Flex's grip.)

BOO JAY: All Ah know is this tag's comin off.

(Boo Jay grabs his brush and begins to scrub. Flex grabs him and wrestles him to the ground. They begin to fight in earnest. They roll over a couple of times. Flex ends up on top.)

FLEX: Shoulda known betta nen ta waste mah time tryin ta reason wit yo ass. Ain't but one kinda lingo you undastand.

(They roll over again. This time Boo Jay's on top.)

BOO JAY: Ya talk like ya can step to it an' do it, but you cain't back it up.

(They roll again, with Flex on top.)

FLEX: You ain't nuthin but a yellow-bellied alley rat.

(Another roll. Boo Jay's on top.)

BOO JAY: See a rat, kick his ass.

(The rumble continues. Flex begins to get the better of Boo Jay. He beats him up pretty good, gets up, and laughs. Both boys are breathing hard.)

FLEX: You took it, punk. Know sumthin, you stupid. Stupid an' dead. Hope you an' yo granma got a nine, cuz me an muh boyz will all be packin tonight. We comin back ta buss a cap in yo ass. Tryin ta step wit th' Flex, sheeit, you muss be buggin. Stay away from the windows tonight, punk. Wut they say in Wellston? Me an' mah boyz comin ta cancel Christmas!

(Flex picks up the bucket of suds and empties it on Boo Jay. Flex exits. Boo Jay slowly reaches a sitting position. He wipes the suds from his eyes and rubs his jaw.)

BOO JAY: Damn!

(Terrell enters.)

TERRELL: Dig, there goes th' neighbahood an' shit.

BOO JAY: Aw yeah, *now* you show up. You shouda had mah back, man.

TERRELL: Like Ahm spozed ta have ESP uh sumthin. Or Ahm spozed ta hear you all the way in th' confectionery wit all nem pinball machines goin? Who dropped ya?

BOO JAY: Flex. Rhymes wit sex.

TERRELL: That's messed up. Lucky he didn't try ta buss a cap in yo ass. Whut he say?

BOO JAY: Say he comin back tonight wit his set. Say they all gone be packin.

TERRELL: Ah don't undastan it, homes. Yo old girl's a schoolteacher. Ain't like y'all cain't afford to move. If it wuz up ta me Ah'd say bump dis stuff an' git outta Dodge own uh one-way play.

BOO JAY: Well, it ain't up ta you, so save yo air.

TERRELL: Touchy, touchy.

BOO JAY: Yeah, Ah gotcho touchy.

TERRELL: Boo Jay, you den already had yo ass kicked once t'day, know whut 'm sayin?

BOO JAY: Ain't that nuthin. Spozed ta be mah boy an' didn't even git mah back. Probly wuz watchin from behine a tree.

TERRELL: Actually it wuz a telephone pole.

(Boo Jay looks at Terrell for a moment. Realizing the joke, he reluctantly laughs.)

BOO JAY: You bugged, man. Come own, help me up.

SCENE 2:

Inside the Simmonses' living room, which is neat and well furnished, a cozy oasis from the turbulent world outside. Gracie Simmons is grading papers, while Boo Jay studies. Boo Jay rises and peers nervously through the blinds.

GRACIE: Sure you don't want me to put something on that eye?

BOO JAY: No, ma'am. I'm all right.

GRACIE: Brandon Joseph Simmons, you know better than to stand in the window like that. Especially with it almost dark. You expecting somebody? Terrell maybe?

BOO JAY: No, ma'am. . . . Granma, can we move?

GRACIE: Where would we go? We run away from crime and the white folks run away from us. Ahm sixty-three years old and Ah tell you, Ahm not studyin runnin, not for a single minute. This house has been in the family for four generations, including you. If we did sell it, we'd never get back what we put into it. Your great-grandfather bought this house with the sweat of his brow, working in the packinghouse. When Ah married his son, Ah came to live here too. Ah like to say Ah was born on Enright, but Ah grew up right here. If your mom hadn't passed, it would be hers now. Instead it will belong to you. This house is our tree, Boo Jay. Its roots go way down.

BOO JAY: Cain't we at least put some bars on the windows? We're about the only folks around here who don't have any.

GRACIE: Ahm not a criminal, so why should Ah have to live in jail? You know, maybe Ahm getting old because Ah could have sworn we had this conversation before.

BOO JAY: Aw, Granma, you know we have. It's juss that we need some protection, that's all.

GRACIE: Speaking of protection, Ah hope you and that Wanda girl are—

BOO JAY: Granma! Don't try ta change th' subject. You know how it is aroun here. Our good neighbors either die or move away one by one. All kindsa low-lifes take their places. You know it's bad. You won't even let me sit own th' porch at night.

GRACIE: Yes, Ah guess you're right. Times are changing. The old things, old feelings, old people—they all turn to dust. Ah ever tell ya how Ah met your grandpa, God rest his soul?

BOO JAY: Yes, ma'am. It was at the Pine Street Y.

GRACIE *(overlapping):* Pine Street Y. Charles was a lifeguard. And one pretty man. Ain't no accident you're as pretty as you are. And muscles? We're talking muscles on top of muscles, thanks to Pop Beckett's gym class. Ah used to love to swim. My girlfriend Stick and Ah were the only girls at Sumner who weren't afraid to get their hair wet. All the girls used to try to catch Charles's eye, but none of them could. Seems like his mind was always occupied by something faraway, something real important. One day, after Ah figure he's been eyeballing me awhile, Ah ask him, "What would you do if Ah was drowning?" He looks over a minute and says, "Ah guess Ah'd have to give you the kiss of life, now wouldn't Ah?" We started dating after that. He'd walk me home from school—six months before he ever got a kiss. On Saturdays we went to the Comet to see a movie. We'd stop at Billie Burke's for a bite, or we'd grab a tamale from the man on Finney. He made the best tamales this side of Mexico. Ah've never been to Mexico, but you catch my meaning. Sometimes we didn't do anything at all but walk. Cool breezes blew through on summer evenings. The stars twinkled high above, and young people could talk and laugh and dream of a glorious future. You talk about bars on the window. Half the time we went to bed without locking the door. We didn't have to worry about drive-bys or wearing the wrong colors. All we had to worry about was whether Sumner was going to beat Vashon in the big game. It was safe to walk anywhere, as long as we stayed on the Black side of town. Funny, white folks act all scared of us now. Back then, we were scared of them.

BOO JAY: Just walkin around an lookin at th' stars sound kinda whack ta me. Didn't you an' grandpa know how ta party, ya know, dance?

GRACIE: Did Ah hear you say dance? Nobody could cut a rug like your grandma Gracie. Nowadays, folks just get nasty, like they oughta be off in a bed somewhere. In my day, we *danced*, honey. It wasn't about doin' the butt. My sisters and Ah were sophisticated ladies and, for a time, jazz was our religion.

(A lilting jazz ballad softly plays as Boo Jay takes his grandmother's hand and they begin to dance.)

GRACIE: Ella Fitzgerald was queen of the bandstand, and nobody could move me like Billy Eckstine could.

(Gracie is transformed as for a magical moment she becomes young again. Her movements are smooth and graceful as she begins to sing along with the tune. Boo Jay watches, fascinated. The moment soon fades as the soft jazz is gradually overwhelmed by a thumping,

bass-heavy hip-hop riff coming from outside. They stop dancing. Gracie sits on the sofa and rubs her knees. Boo Jay peers nervously out the window, taking care to remain out of range.)

GRACIE: Well, what's past is past, and Ah know my knees are happy to hear that!

BOO JAY: What about your heart? Is your heart happy?

GRACIE: You sure ask grown-up questions to be such a youngster.

BOO JAY: Granma, Ahm sixteen.

GRACIE: Ah know, Ah know. Almost a man. My heart's happy, sure. It's had its hurts, you know that. Losing my Charles, then your mother. . . . But for every hurt, there's been happiness, and most of it right here under this roof. If these walls could talk, son, oh, the stories they'd tell.

BOO JAY: Granma, you can't expect me to stay here forever.

GRACIE: Just sixteen and already itching to spread your wings.

BOO JAY: It's not that. Ahm itchin to stay alive. When Ahm a man, Ah wanta be able ta take mah children to th' park. Ah want them ta be able ta play without worryin about gittin shot. You talk about walkin aroun an' lookin at th' stars. Now, juss spoze me an' Wanda wanted to do that. We'd have ta git own the bus an' ride ta Ladue uh sumplace. Am Ah makin sense, Granma?

GRACIE: You are. But you a Simmons. A fighter.

BOO JAY: Try tellin that ta Flex.

(Suddenly there's a very loud and persistent knock at the door. Boo Jay stops a few feet from the door and yells.)

Who is it?

FLEX: Ahm lookin fuh Boo Jay. You know who Ah am!

GRACIE *(moving toward the door):* He can't come out right now.

BOO JAY *(urgent whisper):* Granma, stay back! Hit the lights!

FLEX: Yo, man! You let cho bitch take up fuh you?

(Gracie strides purposefully toward the door. Boo Jay tries to stop her, but she pushes him aside. She unfastens the door's several locks.)

GRACIE: Sounds like you better learn to watch your mouth!

BOO JAY: Granma, no!

(Gracie opens the door and comes face to face with Flex. After a moment they both speak at the same time.)

GRACIE: Francis!

FLEX: Mrs. Simmons!

BOO JAY: *Francis?!*

FLEX: Mrs. Simmons, Ah swear Ah didn't know it was you.

GRACIE: Are you in the habit of calling women disrespectful names?

FLEX: No, ma'am, Ah juss—

GRACIE: Just what? You used to have manners when you were in my class.

BOO JAY: *Francis?!*

FLEX: Yo, man. Ah didn't know you was related to Mrs. Simmons. See, Ahm new ta this hood an' all that. Mah trip.

BOO JAY: Ite den.

GRACIE: My grandson tells me you're in a "set." Ah take that to mean a gang?

FLEX: No, ma'am. It's juss me an' muh cousin Pierre. We juss wanted th' fellas, ya kow, ta think we hard. We new, so we needs ta git props an' all that. Ya know . . .

GRACIE: No, Ah *don't* know. . . . If you hadn't recognized me, would you have shot me?

FLEX: No, ma'am. Ah juss wanted ta dis, ya know, scare yo grandson, thass all. *(To Boo Jay:)* Hey, man, yo granma, she definitely th' bes' teacha Ah evah had. She down, ya know?

BOO JAY: Yeah, Ah know. What about our garage?

FLEX: Me an' Pierre'll knock it out. We'll take care uh it. Cool?

BOO JAY: Cool, *Francis.*

FLEX: Aw, you jonin, but thass awright. Ah'll be seein' ya, Mrs. Simmons. Nah Ah know where you live, maybe we could talk sumtime.

GRACIE: As long as you watch your mouth.

FLEX: Yes, ma'am. Ah'll do that. *(To Boo Jay:)* Peace nah.

BOO JAY: Peace.

(Flex exits. Boo Jay and Gracie lock the door.)

BOO JAY: Granma, you sumthin else, ya know that?

GRACIE: Ahm a Simmons. Good stock. Like you.

BOO JAY: Like this house.

GRACIE: Word.

(They both laugh.)

BOO JAY: Granma. How bout some music?

GRACIE: Brandon Joseph, if you play that Keith Sweat one more time—

BOO JAY: Aw naw, uh-uh. Ah meant some Ella Fitzgerald.

GRACIE: Don't think Ah have any.

BOO JAY: Then Ah guess we'll hafta sing.

(They join hands and begin to dance. Softly, Ella Fitzgerald begins to sing.)

CURTAIN

AMERICAN HUNGER

TONY MEDINA

there is beauty
in vacant eyes,
wide eternal
dark spaces
where somewhere
somehow hope
lies
there is beauty
in abandoned
spots &
dirty spaces
where dreams
slip through
concrete cracks
& race along
hopscotch chalk
there has to be
some beauty
there where
solitary tears
crease the dirt
on a little brown
girl's face and
little boys
go hungry

playing cops &
robbers in
broken-down lots
with nappy head
of hair and eyes
and eyes laugh out
despair

Soul Survivor

Daniel Edwards

INHALE . . .

The sky was usually shiny and gleaming when Shade cleaned and polished his chrome 9 mm in his backyard. Today he worked feverishly and nervously. Today was not like the other days. The sun was crippled and frail against the great might of the dark thunderclouds. Evil was present in the air. But he felt a bit more relaxed when he thought about the great deal of chaos he was soon to cause. The time was now. He knew there would never be another chance. Those niggas had this shit coming to em. They were the number-one brothers on Shade's shit list. At last he was through with cleaning the assault weapon. He scratched his head. He seemed confused. He thought of the little daughter he once had, whom he could never ever forget. His daughter's life was taken by some crazy-ass loc-ed-out niggas around the corner. These gang-bangers were riding Shade because of his unique gangster-like qualities, which enabled him to run blocks upon blocks of the drug-drenched streets. Two years ago those crazy cluckhead fuckers shot up his Lexus coupe, killing his ho and toddler. He was stripped of his crown, dethroned.

He screamed, cursing and swinging at the air. He walked toward his house, and burst in through the backdoor. He ran straight for the long woola that was left in the ashtray in the kitchen.

Sweat was dripping down his head; he smelled and looked like a punk-ass nigga. He snatched up the woola, put down the shiny 9, and then paused for a minute as he held the shit to his lips. The rock and chronic smoke filled his lungs. He looked around the room

and felt the dark worm twist in his gut. He frowned, trying to expel
the feeling. For it was this feeling that drove him to his wild-ass
tactics, taking drugs and slangin shit. He felt powerless to combat
the feeling. The worm implant he could not control. It made him
squeal like a pig as he looked around at his filthy house.

CUCCCCHHHHH. The match scraped loudly like a bloody knee
on cement and lit.

He lit the shit and took a long pull, then brought it down from
his lips. The room was somewhat dark. He looked like Rudolph the
reindeer, slicing through the dark with the glowing flame from his
woo. He was slowly but surely becoming what he had fought against
for so long. A punk buster, lighting the path for the powerful red-
skinned, white-bearded devil. Shade was like many other black
males who have come to this treacherous path before him. The path
that would help lead the devil to his higher plateau. The red-skinned
devil, who would sit back and control the Black's plight and path,
fulfill his kinds, wants, and needs.

The hit drove the nigga into a frenzy. He thought of how much of
a fool he was for hitting this beautiful but deadly shit, but he could
not resist the temptation. For whenever he was under the guidance
of the good shit, he felt wiser, and also that his decisions and actions
were carried out correctly. Sometimes he wondered why make decisions. His family was slain; he felt there was nothing to make
decisions or actions for.

He was and would always belong to an outlaw subculture. And
the system that was in control of things disliked his kind. The system he knew of as bullshit. He tried to walk the right path, or white
path. The one-way school system, the two-way job, and the multi-
path highway to heaven, religion. He would get as far as he could
walking against the opposite flow of an escalator. So now he was
back to his shit, fuck it. He snatched for the woo he had put still lit
in the tray. He stumbled and knocked the tray on the floor.

The house was already a mess, but for some reason he dropped
down to the ground and picked up about thirty of his woo roaches.
They seemed to call out to him. The drug was part of him. He could
not stand and watch the baby woolas lie helplessly on the ground.
He placed all of them back in the ashtray. He looked upon the tray.
The roaches were piled as a mountain in the tray. Even though they
had risen that high before, he tried to act like he didn't notice it.
See, to Shade this was a bit embarrassing. When his wife was alive,
the nigga swore on his only child that he would quit the crazy habit.
Now look at his bitch ass, thirty woo roaches in a week. The broken

promise is what killed his family. That nigga's crazy. He grew ashamed of himself, and quickly emptied the tray in the trashcan right next to him.

He hoped to suddenly wash his record clean for his deceased loved ones. Still on the floor, he rose up on one knee, frustrated and heated. He stood and said silently with an angry-ass face, "What the fuck am I doin? I pray to no one. I am under no god." He stood there for a minute, trying to boost his ego by looking all hard and tough and shit. Then he began to look around for the lit woo. His search was cut short when the front door suddenly burst open.

"Nigga, come on which yo shit. Nigga, come on." It was that crazy nigga loc-ed-out Bub-G. He ran back out of the house the same way he had come in. Shade snatched the 9 off the counter and dashed out of the front door. He didn't even bother to close it. "Nigga, stop looking all paranoid and shit, ya bitch, and let's get this shit on," Bubs screamed out. Out in the front of the crib sat Lullaby's ride. Bub-G jumped in the passenger side still yelling the punk shit about Shade. Shade jumped in the back and they sped off.

"Shade is you on, nigga, or what?" Lullaby asked.

"Shit, hell ya fool," Shade replied.

"Then all right then, niggas, let's get shit on," Lullaby said, and then began laughing, coughing, and spitting all at the same time and shit. He was somehow still able to maintain the wheel. Lullaby was a crazy-ass nigga, known to break a fool off sumthin. His name signified how swiftly he could put a head to bed. He spent time in the county for seven years because of manslaughter. The fool had killed about five brothers so far and was still going strong while on parole. Lullaby reached down toward the pullout and turned up the sounds. The shit was booming. Lullaby was a tall muthafucka, skinny but swift. He was one of those niggas that had been rushed too many times. So now he settled beefs by peeling caps.

As expected, chronic was then lit by Bub-G and smoke filled the boys' lungs. Bubs took a pull and started choking. Bubs reached back and held the blunt in Shade's face.

"Nigga, this that old lethal smoke. Couple of hits will get yo ass lifted," Bubs said, still holding the blunt. He stared at Shade as though he was checking his soul's pride through the lens of his brown eyes. "Fool, you don't want none of this," Bubs said.

Shade jumped to his defense quickly. "Nigga, hand me that bud." Shade snatched the bud out of Bubs's hand. Bubs was always testing Shade. He would always bother Shade for no reason. But the two were tight, they had known each other since they were children.

Shade was already used to Bubs's pestering. Bubs felt he could lecture Shade on how to survive the woe from his tragedies. He had been through so much himself at a very young age that he knew of Shade's heartbreak.

At ten Bubs had lost all of his family to a bunch of jackers. Bubs had woken one night to screams of horror and cries for dear life. The screams had marked his soul with their own private frequency. He had never heard anything like it. For it was his sweet dear mommy screaming, not a lady on TV being tossed around like an inflatable doll by a mob of death-row convicts. It was his brave strong daddy who he had watched put so many niggas head to bed in his days, now being treated like a bitch, a busta, a mark-ass nigga. Bubs had seen the shit go down, peeking down from the top of the stairs. His dad somehow knew he was there. His daddy had stared him in the eyes while the punks held the steel to his grill, and blasted his brains all over the living room. It was an ill scene. It changed the young boy forever. He was just a helpless young boy when he watched the G's destroy his daddy the pimp, the drug hustler. But he grew to be a man in the short time after he had seen the G's topple his daddy and claim his drugs, which were drenched with his father's own bloody medulla.

He had run to his father's safe spot to grab the Mac 10. If he could not save whoever else was left alive, then fuck it, he would avenge them all.

As he grabbed the gun, the house suddenly became quiet. He knew he had made too much noise opening the safe. All he could hear was his fatally-wounded family, their bodies jumping and twitching on the hardwood floor downstairs. The reflexes of the death-fighters ticked on for a few seconds and then were cut short, slicing complete silence into the air. The G's were onto his little ass. He could hear them creeping through the crib, silently but swiftly. As the G's crept up the stairs, Bubs clicked on the TV, turning it up as loud as possible. Any real nigga knows about or has once possessed the TV tube that would not make a sound or a picture until a couple of minutes after you had turned it on. Once he did that he dashed to his bedroom. He stood in the doorway, peeking out. The hallway was dark, so when the G's reached the top of the stairs they could not see. The light switch was all the way at the other end. The fools never bothered to flip the switch at the bottom of the stairs. He could see their silhouettes moving in the dark. Three bandits began stalking toward his parents' room. The TV suddenly turned on blaring wild rock music. The shit had the brothers buggin. The one farthest from the leader of the three got caught out in the hall and blasted the leader's head clean off.

One ran up the stairs and Bubs ran out of the room blasting. He had one of em already targeted, so this fool didn't stand a chance. He hit the one coming up the stairs, knocking him back down on his ass. The other he blasted in the knees first. This was the sucker who had slain his daddy. Bubs was going to kill him immediately but he thought twice about it. Instead he walked around to face the fool crawling away and knelt down right in front him. "Look at me fool! Look at me," Bubs yelled. "Stare me in the eyes like my daddy did when you took his life. I want you to see death coming for you, just as my father did, bitch, before you killed him. Now fool say your prayers, because death becomes you." BOOOM! Fade to black.

Bubs's life story explains why he is so cruel, provocative, daring, yet protective. That nigga got his medal for the hard rock mufucka of the decade.

The gray skies soon became black and the thunderclouds thickened, rich with the smog from the hot city. Thunder shook through the land, scaring everybody in the ride. "God damn, this shit is crazy," Bubs said, staring up at the sky.

"Word I need to be at home boning my bitch in this sort of wetta," Lullaby said. Shade was also looking up out the back window at the sky. The rain now began to storm down upon the streets in a great rage. People were running for cover all over the place. It sent a chill down the boys' spines as they rode. They were only a couple of blocks away from their destination. Lullaby turned down the radio and tried to concentrate on driving. The rain was harsh, and he could not see out of the dark-tinted windows. The windows were fogging from the chronic smoke, so they all started wiping the inside glass of the rizzy. The blunt was now a roach. Lullaby turned the shit back up and the Wu-Tang Clan was booming in the shit. "Here Shade, kill this shit," Lullaby said, reaching back and handing the roach to Shade.

"I'm straight with that. I don't need no more," Shade said. Lullaby continued to hold it there despite Shade's denial. It was hard for him to reject the blunt that was right in his face. He stared at the roach which was brown and sticky due to the large amount of resin. "All right, I'll blaze it up," Shade said.

Shade took a long and smooth pull. The smoke would make love to his lungs, and his mind enjoyed the lovely orgasm. He began to indulge in this mind state. He drifted into memories of his beautiful wife. Her smile, her lips, she was one of the baddest bitches to walk Shade's jungle. When he had first seen her he had to scoop her up, and he did. Aww man was she fly. He remembers the way she used to feel, the way she used to smell, and the way her so round . . . "Yo nigga what the fuck you babysitting that blunt for? Pass that shit off bro," Lull said. He was next and he wasn't waiting any longer.

"Hold up one more hit," Shade said. PSPFFFFHHHHHH this shit is PSPHHH crazy. He got a good hit. He not only hit the high the chronic could deliver, he also hit the high from the potent, evil atmosphere that was lingering about in the car. One more pull, one more memory. Shade was once again under the enchanting spell. He still had a mean grin on his face because of the ill shit Lull was talking. His mean grin expressed the way his soul was feeling about now. See, Shade was quick to get mad. Whenever someone would just be playing around with him he got mad. Shade didn't like playing jokes and fucking around. He might bust a cap in yo ass for that shit.

"Here, nigga, stop crying." Shade handed the blunt to Lull. He was still holding the smoke in his lungs. He was awaiting the mating process to bring his mind to ecstacy once again. He was anticipating or remembering something else wonderful about his wife, but because he was still a bit agitated because of Lull's punk ass, he began to have ill thoughts, thus ill memories.

He remembered the time when he had awoken. His wife's arm strung across his chest. He grabbed her arm. He moved toward her. He held her small precious head in his hands. Her hair stringing through his veiny hands. Her eyes were closed and she was breathing delicately. He held her tight and close to him. Out of her mouth and nose flowed a rose-colored river that flooded Shade's weak and trembling palms.

"NOOOOOOOOO," Shade screamed. He buried his face in his wife's bloody bosom. Her chest and cheek had huge steaming holes that were gushing blood. He cried as he felt her body go limp in his hands. He could not do shit. He wasn't no mufuckin doctor. He leaned her back and fixed her up against the passenger door. He propped her carefully, being sure not to reveal her head above the car-door window. He took one last look at his lover and then tried to locate the shiny 9.

He was still in shock. His vision was not yet focused, for smoke was thick in the rizzy. Glass was still falling about. Shattered glass ran rampant through his underwear. The glass was slicing him as he tried to grab hold of his car door. He was weak. The effort drained him and his head fell back down to its starting position. After a few seconds, he began to regain his strength. Then all of a sudden, a soft whimpering cry cut through the confusion. It was his daughter. She was still strapped down in her seat belt. Shade's impact against the tree had dazed her. She was up and moving. At least she had not been hit by the crazy cluckhead fuckers.

"Daddy, Daddy, Daddy," Legacy cried.

"I'm right here baby," Shade replied, while still ducking the open window.

"Daddy, Daddy," she let out again, while unfastening her restraints. She felt safe. She was happy to hear her father's voice. Shade thought he could hear metal fastenings coming loose. He was not sure for he kept his head down in fear. Then he noticed his daughter moving within the car. "I gonna come you, Daddy."

"C'mon baby," he whispered.

As he held out his hand between the center armrest gap, he realized his daughter was just a child. She was unaware of the cluckhead fuckers. This meant that she would stand up and unknowingly become easy sniper prey. Before he could speak she stood up. And unfortunately the gangbangers had surrounded the battered coupe. Shots rang out from every direction. Her little body was ripped apart, right before her maker's eyes. She fell. When her body dropped, Shade let out a thunderous roar that echoed through the concrete jungle.

While busting caps, the gangbangers realized the person they had riddled with bullets was a mere child.

"Let's get the fuck out of here," Shade could hear one of them yelling out. Shade could hear their shoe soles scraping against the pavement while they were scampering away. Shade grew mad with eyes that had become as red and bloody as the sight of his slain family. He began to move his hands in search of a piece of stitching that was open under the front seat.

"Yeah mufuckas now y'all throo," he yelled out once he grabbed hold of the cold steel. The touch gave him an inner strength. He burst out of the driver-side door and started after the fuckers. He took a few steps then fell flat on his face. He scraped his chin and now a new source of blood was staining his polo shirt. He caressed a hurt in his leg. It was then that he realized that he had got blasted in the thigh. The fuckers had blasted right through the door.

Shade realized that he had no time to rest and cry like a bitch because of his wounds. He stood up. The gunmen were in sight and he'd be damned if he'd let them slip away. There were three of them. Shade saw a fourth nigga cutting through someone's yard with a large duffel bag. Before he disappeared, he yelled out a rendevous point. The three brothers had their backs turned to Shade. They were about to turn the corner. Shade was limping quickly while staying low, being careful not to alert the fools of his presence. Shade looked back at his car as he posted behind a tree. People were beginning to gather around it. A friend of Shade's had seen his fucked-up vehicle containing the famous Edwards family. She eyed Shade. She noticed the three niggas trooping up the street, then dashed back into her house. Shade began his pursuit once again.

He began to lose em. They were a block ahead. Shade was bleeding too bad so he sat down and tried to recoup. He could still see those dirty bastards. They had stopped now, and were met by some person. This mufucka was probably that fourth nigga. The heat from the sun made the distant images seem unclear. He could see enough to realize what was going on. The fourth figure was asking them for something. All of them then began to move about as though they were confused. The fourth nigga began to circle the three bastards. A couple of other niggas now began to join the fourth nigga. The fourth nigga whipped out a shiny object and began to fire away while talking shit. His fellow brothers also started to let loose on the fools.

TAT-TAT-A-TAT-BOOOM. The gunfire paused for a moment.

"Niggas, don't y'all know who y'all fuckin wit," Shade could hear one of them say.

And as quick as it had stopped, the gunfire started back up again. TAT-A-TAT-BOOM. One of the brothers must of had a 12 gauge. The gat was dwarfing the merciless and powerful shots from the guns the other kids had. One of the cluckhead fuckers was dipping. He was able to flee the mob. Shade noticed his punk ass coming. He had only one shoe and one direction to run. The mufucka was ass out. He was headed toward the worst death, a nigga that wanted his soul with a vengeance.

"YO, SHADE, BUST A CAP IN HIS ASS," Shade heard a familiar voice scream out. It was that crazy-ass loc-ed-out nigga Bub-G. His fellow brother came to assist Shade like he always did.

The fool was right in front of Shade. The fool tried to do some ole running-back fake, but Shade was no dummy; he popped the nigga right in the chest. He was still in motion because of his spin move and smashed into Shade. His hands were gripping Shade's chest as he slowly went to hell. Shade wanted to hurry him there. Shade stared down at the fool with menacing bloodshot eyes.

"I hope you got a bulletproof soul like me you punk-ass nigga, cause Lucifer is a friend of mine, and he loves to bust shots at bitch-ass niggas like you." BOOOOOOOM. Fade to black.

"Ain't that bitch crazy, Shade?" Bubs asked.

"Huh?! What?" Shade responded. He didn't even realize the music was turned down.

"Nigga, ain't you payin attention?" Bubs questioned.

"That nigga's blasted," Lull said while looking at Shade through the rearview mirror.

"He don't know what the fuck we talking bout."

"I'm straight," Shade said. "I was just thinkin bout some old shit."

"Oh, what you thinkin bout, your ole lady and shit?" Bubs asked.

"Yeah, you know how that shit is," Shade said in a hurt tone.

"Yeah, I hear where you comin from. But at least, you still sitting right here in this caw, hitting this mufuckin bud," preached Bubs.

"Word nigga, I got the mufuckin cure for them ill-street blues right here nigga," Lull said. He reached back and held the blunt in front of Shade.

"Nah yo, I'm straight, and word is bond this time." Shade didn't like the fact that his fellow brothers knew what the fuck was going on in his head. Because they knew what he was thinking, he knew they would begin to show how sorry they felt for him. Shade didn't appreciate their pity. Pity is for punks. And Shade wasn't raised to be no punk. His daddy (the streets) was to blame for his hardness. His daddy was the greatest pimp of them all. He taught Shade not to trust no one. His daddy had always stuck with him through tough times, but Dad was growing old. And this is because he had to act as a savior for the other kids like Shade, who had no other form of guidance. No other figures could or would show them the way.

Mr. Street witnessed many while under his wing get bucked down because of neglectful behavior he administered. Their death was in vain. The cost of his neglect came in the form of chalky outlined blood pools that riddled his entire body. However he was a very wise person. He possessed valuable keys to survival. And luckily, these keys were passed down to the crazy niggas like Shade. They inherited granitelike attitudes from their paved-out father. They were seeds, planted by the ones in power who landscaped the jungle, the Concrete Gardeners (political madmen). And these boys reacted to their hostile environment as if it were the sun. Their roots potted in a cement mixture, their *black* skin *absorb*ing the nourishing ghetto rays of chlorophyll boiling and pulsating within their violently grown bodies. They were like black cactuses. A plant that stands alone, and cannot be touched. It will hurt those who try.

To brighten Shade up, Bubs began to kick some knowledge on their bitch-ass president. "Yo y'all heard bout that bullshit strike-out deal Clinton's tryin to pass?"

"Nah," Lull replied. "Why, what is up with it?"

"Where's the house at? I don't think I got enuff time to explain this shit."

"You straight, we got a few more blocks to go. Go ahead drop your shit, Preacher Man," Lull said. He was teasing Bubs by using his nickname. Bubs looked at Lull like he was gonna punch him in the mouth if he kept acting up. But instead, Bubs began to kick some shit.

"See, Clinton done went and set up some new crime bill shit he tryin to pass. With this bullshit bill in effect niggas would have to do life if they get caught out there committin an act of violence three times. He trying to cut down on crime, or so he says."

"Man, that's cuz white mufuckas is scared of us, brudderman. We smokin each other every day out here. You see what the fuck we bout to do in a couple of minutes, nigga. That shit might keep mufuckas like us from acting crazy," Lull said.

"Nah yo, you need to shut the fuck up and listen. You see, what you just got through talkin bout, right? (See what we bout to do.) Well, nigga, do you think if we were living up in the boonies we would be about to do this shit? Nah nigga, we wouldn't need to. We would already be straight. Therefore we would have no fuckin reason to worry bout this mufuckin bill. But see, Bill (no inhale) Clinton is finally tryin to follow up on his ancestors' first blow. That nigga know that we can't help but to do what we do. He should definitely know.

"That mufucka's great-grandfather stuffed our peoples in the dark bellow of a slave ship, and I mean stuffed nigga. Mufuckas were dying by the thousands. They were rich with filthy disease. They starved, died, then were fed to the blood-hungry sharks. They raped our great-grandmothers. They hung our great-grandfathers."

"So what the fuck are you sayin, man?" Shade asked.

"What I'm sayin is that after all those centuries of goin through this crazy shit, our people are fucked up, and I'm talkin bout mentally." Bubs paused, stared at the boys and then continued. "Peep this: if a bitch was kidnapped, and then raped, beaten, and tortured by a man, and she somehow got free, she would never return to him even if it meant her life. She would be shaky all the time. She would be paranoid and ashamed of her past. She might resort to drugs and alcohol. Any mufucka that grows accustomed to this lady would know that she was in this condition and treat her accordingly. The ho's mind would never be the same, unless she got help or got in touch with her inner self and truly let go of the disaster. She would then be stable once more."

"What the fuck does that got to do with it?" Lull said.

"Well, nigga, Black Americans were raped, tortured, kidnapped, and beaten just like the ho. And I don't know bout you niggas, but a brother like me is frightened of our past. Our great-grandfathers have been through some shit, and I'll be damned if I'm ever coming close to that damn holocaust again. This paranoia is what boosts me into acting all crazy and shit. Man, just remember those racist remarks we heard from our schoolteachers, neighbors, and also them punk-ass Korean store-owning mufuckas around the corner. Cops have been harassin us for ages now. With shit like this going on, I can never let go of our past horror, and we sure ain't receivin much help. We always are reminded of our genocide era, shit, resultin in an unstable and violent condition."

"Muthafucka, this can't be the problem though nigga. The Jews were also once under a genocide era. Most of them niggas ain't running the streets killin. So what the fuck you sayin?" Lull asked.

"Yeah, you're right fool, they ain't running the streets killin each other. This is because they ain't as discriminated against. They have white skin. They are not degraded and put in a position to be p-noid and defensive. They ain't 'Driving Miss Daisy.' They ain't called no nigga, coon, and ape like most of us are. They ain't chased down by cops at an early age and whupped for no goddamn reason. (Reminiscent of the slave and the slave masta.) We always forced to relive and have foul memories placed in our head of our slave history. However, the Jews' wounds were healed by the place we got our necks slit to build, AmeriKKKa. Now Clinton, the great-grandson of them slave-ship captains, is determined to finish off the project that they started. That mufucka knows that we products of the environment.

"He knows we are still recuperatin from our tiring escape. The escape from the clutches of his rapist and battering great-grandpa. He has not grown accustomed to the Black. He don't know how to help. He knows how to forget. His advice to the raped woman I was talking about would be to shut the fuck up when she felt like ex-

pressin her woes. Kiss his ass. Suck his nuts. And if she don't get
her act together and cut out her cryin, he would lock her ass up and
rape her some more. Now do you bonehead fuckas see what I'm
sayin?"

The boys were mesmerized by Bubs's sermon. They didn't know he
had it in him. Bubs became so excited by his own words that he
needed a blunt to cool his ass down. He pulled out a Garcia, then his
pocketknife. He cut the blunt. He rolled down his window. Then he
emptied out the tobacco. He stuck his hand down his briefs then
pulled out some bright green smoke. The perspiration from his
preaching had his drawers steaming, and this made the chronic nice
and moist. He began to break up the bud. It was too silent in the
car. Shade and Lull were still bugging off of what Bubs just said, so
Bubs couldn't help but open his mouth some more.

"How bout them kids who was bustin at us for no reason the other
day? You niggas know I had no choice but to blast one of those
niggas. Now according to Clinton's ass I should serve a whole gang
of time. Then I should have one strike, out of three, toward the end
of my life, just for defending myself. I feel I haven't even lived life.
At least a decent fuckin life. I know I ain't just suppose to be riding
around smokin muthafuckas. What's worse is what if you already
have a record or maybe even two. After two, you already look bad,
so when you at the plate in court, you might as well head for the
dugout (lockup), cause that's definitely where you gonna wind up.

"Look, all I'm sayin is there ain't never been much white mufuckas gettin these violent crime charges, and they ain't never gonna
get em. The shit meant for the Black. This man's game plan is a
basic genocide package. We'll once again be lynched legally. The
only way this shit would even make a bit of sense would be if that
mufucka cleared every nigga's number of criminal records to zero.
And this shit ain't no guarantee, cuz a mufucka like me can't stop
balling. So niggas watch y'all back, cuz they out ta get ya."

"Aww, man, fuck dat. I'm gonna go on over here and smoke all
these mufuckin fools. Fuck Bill and his bill. Shade, is you wit me?"
Lull asked.

"Hell yeah, nigga, you know I'm always down for that ol' 187,"
Shade said.

Even though they were talking shit, Lull and Shade couldn't help
but wonder about Bubs's words of wisdom.

Shade rolled down his window to get some air. The dark clouds
brought wild warping winds. The powerful gusts left Shade breath-

less as the car rode against the hot breath of the nimbus beasts. He rolled the window back up quickly. Lull turned right down a fucked-up street that was full of potholes.

"Yo what the fuck you turn down this crazy-ass street for?" Bubs asked

"Don't worry bout it nigga. I got everything under."

"OH SHIT LOOK OUT FOR THAT . . ." BOOOOOOOOM. PSSSSSSSSSSSSSSS. The tire busted on impact. Lull pulled over and the boys got out.

"Damn this shit fucked up," Lull yelled. He popped the trunk and took out the jack.

"Y'all niggas gonna help right?" Lull asked. Shade looked Lull in the eyes and then gave him a nod. Then he spun around. A car was coming and he could hear the system getting louder as the car crept up on them and then passed.

"Cash rules everything around me. C-R-E-A-M. Get the money, dollar dollar bill y'all. Cash rules everything around me. C-R-E-A-M. Get the money . . ."

"Yo, that's that shit," Shade said, referring to the music.

"Yeah that Clan be booming," Bubs said. He walked over to Lull who already had the front of the Dayton off. Shade was just standing there watching this chick across the street. She was fine. Shade couldn't believe his eyes. He wanted her, and he could tell she wanted him too. She was staring back at him dead in his brown eyes. He started to cross the street. However his path was cut off when a nice-looking truck almost hit him. Shade couldn't see the driver because of the dark tint. So instead Shade eyeballed the vehicle as if it were the nigga driving. The covered headlights (the punk had on sunglasses). The tinted windshield (his dark-skinned forehead). The deep-dish Enkei rims his limbs. The truck was phat. Shade could tell that his brother must have had it going on. Shade grew envious of the fool and his fancy truck. The car drove by slow and interrupted Shade's pimping tactics with its splendor. Shade continued to eye the vehicle while it was in his way. Once it passed, he noticed the extra rim on the back. This meant that the fool inside was a well-prepared player. Shade imagined the fool to be a troublemaker. Shade drifted into thoughts of the fool inside pulling a gun from his buttock region, if it came down to them throwing blows. He imagined him to be a small man. Shade would break his neck if he tried to act crazy. That sucka betta go on.

The Rodeo took a sharp left. It pulled into the driveway of the same apartment complex where the chick was standing. Shade was

looking at the girl again. He missed her smile. It was as if tho he
was her man and he had been away on a trip too long. Shade stepped
up on the curb. He stuck a piece of gum in his mouth and then
proceeded to pimp the ho. His words were smooth. He was feeling
good. The high gave him courage and kept a smile on his face.

"Ay what up, girl?" he asked with a big smile on his face. His eyes
shut a tad. This was so he could appear sexy to her. The trick not
only worked, it left Shorty speechless. He was smooth. He was
suave. He was himself, Shade.

"And what name has God given his most beautiful creature?"
Shade asked her.

"My name is Selene," she replied. Her voice was soft and innocent. She had a Puerto Rican accent that made Shade quiver. He
loved Spanish women. She had long dark copper-tinted hair and eyes
that seemed too beautiful for Shade to stare at. She was indeed beautiful. The gold around this queen's neck would make good conversation for Shade's next move.

"That gold must feel wonderful, being so close to you everyday
all day. What's a beautiful girl like you doing round here in the hood
with all this gold on?"

"I live here," she told him.

"Damn, then I guess it's a good thang I decided to turn down this
street. I just got through having a bad daydream of a pretty woman,
but girl, your beautiful glow melted her image from my mind, as if
tho she was the wicked witch."

"Oh you one of them poem-preaching niggas?" she said. She
smiled. He knew he had her. They sat there staring at each other.
Her eyes broke contact with Shade. Shade grew nervous when he
saw her sudden eye shift. He spun around to watch his back. There
was a girl coming. She was carrying a pullout stereo. Selene had a
smile on her face, and Shade realized they were friends. The girl was
eyeballing Shade. She admired his fly Adidases, his Levi's, his Polo
jacket. She took her eyes off him and smiled at Selene.

"Hey what up bitch?" she said to Selene.

"Fuck you girl," Selene replied. They hugged and kissed each other
on the cheek. Shade knew they were about to start yapping. He was
shy so he tried to avoid the girls by staring at Bubs and Lull who
were still fixing the Dayton.

"Hey hey," Selene yelled out to him.

"This is my girl, Kwestchyn."

"Question?" Shade asked, as if he had heard her name wrong.

"YEAH, KWESTCHYN," they both said at the same time.

Shit Kwestchyn was fine also. Shade wouldn't have minded having either one of em. Kwestchyn looked just as good as Selene, even a bit better. He began to try to pimp both shorties.

"Yo, is that your Rodeo?" he asked her. He was staring at her the same way he did Selene. His eyes still set in sexy mode. A charming smile on his face.

"Yeah that's my whip. You like it?"

"Yeah that shit is phat." He smiled at her, and she began to blush.

Shade took a few steps back and glanced over at the spoiled-down truck. He envisioned the truck in a whole new perspective now that it was motionless. It was trimmed in gold, just like the owner. The shit was bad enough to be in shows and shit. Shade walked back over to the girls.

"That ride is crazy," he said.

"Thank you." She smiled. He knew he had her also. Selene noticed what was going on, so she let Shade and Kwestchyn mingle. She looked over at Bubs and Lull, who were just about done replacing the rim.

"Yo, Shade with some hoes, and one of em is starin at us," Bubs said. He was kneeling down next to Lull, peeking over his shoulder. Lull looked over at the ruckus. He turned to see the beautiful face of Selene.

"Yo, hurry the fuck up with that rim," Bubs demanded.

"Nigga, you ain't even done rolling that blunt yet fool. Back the fuck up off me, and get to yo job nigga," Lull grunted.

"OH SHIT," Bubs yelled. He had forgot all about the blunt. He jumped up and walked around to the passenger side. He leaned in the car and grabbed the sliced blunt. It was stiff now. The air had dried the leaf and made it brittle.

"Damn. Fuck." Bubs was mad. The blunt would be difficult to roll unless he drooled on the leaf again. He checked his pockets. He didn't have any more Garcias. He looked at the stiff leaf and then began to lick. He took a 20 rock out of his jaw and cut open the drippy plastic bag. He shook the bag and out came the transparent pebble. He crushed the rock and mixed it into the weed. He mixed it good. He wanted this woo to be perfect. He looked over at Shade's crowd. The girl was no longer staring at him. She was asking Shade something. She was pointing in Bubs's direction.

"Who's your friend over there?" Selene asked Shade. He spun around. He noticed Bubs rolling the blunt. He smiled.

"That nigga over there rolling that blunt looking at us funny is my main nigga behind the trigger Bub mufuckin G. That other nigga fixing that rim is my nigga Lullaby."

Lull stood up. He walked to the rear of his car. He opened the trunk, and then threw the busted tire in. Bubs walked over to him.

"Are you done with this shit yo?" Bubs asked Lull.

"Yeah, fool."

"Good, lets go ova with Shade, so I can pull that ho starin ova here," Bubs bragged.

"Nigga you know you ain't got no chance once she see a fine-ass nigga like me," Lull said.

"Yeah we'll see about dat nigga." They began to walk over to Shade and the chicks. As they were crossing the street that car with the booms came back around the corner. *"M-E-T-H-O-D MAN, M-E-T-H-O-D MAN, M-E-T-H-O-D MAN, here I am, here I am, the Method Man . . ."* The car cut the music. It stopped by Shade and the girls. A nigga stepped out of the car. The girls had a mean expression on their faces. This meant trouble. The brother had his eyes on Lull and Bubs as they stepped on the scene. The nigga was clean-cut and he wouldn't seem like the type of brother to talk some shit. But looks are deceiving.

"Yo bitch, what you doing out here talking to these niggas?" he said. His mouth was ill, and the boys were aching to bust his lip.

"Who the fuck is this nigga?" Shade asked Selene. She looked at the nigga as if she wanted to stab him in his chest, then she said, "He a punk, a two-minute nigga, a ten-minute psycho, and a lifetime bitch."

"Girl, who the fuck you think you talkin bout?" he said. He started toward her. Two niggas that were in the car with him got out. They stepped up behind the nigga, trying to look all hard at Lull and Bubs. He grabbed her. He spit in the palm of his hand, then smacked the shit out of her. Her gold earring flew off from the force of the blow. She looked stupid. The bitch tried to kick the nigga but he just smacked her again.

"Yo, partna, what up with swanging them thangs over here," Shade said. He could not sit there any longer and watch this ho get her ass whupped.

"What, you punk-ass nigga? You want some of this? You betta mind yo fucking business before you get hurt fool."

Selene and Kwestchyn ran in the building. They knew what was about to happen. The nigga started at Shade. He looked at his boys to make sure they had his back.

"What up, Shade, we gonna do these niggas? This punk-ass nigga just mad cuz we bout to steal his ho," Lull said.

"Nigga, you best back the fuck up off us before it's you who gets hurt. You don't know who ya fuckin wit," Shade said. The nigga pulled out a big-ass machete. He dashed at the boys. Lull was too busy watching the other fools. He didn't notice the nigga coming. He sliced Lull right in the shoulder. The other two fools pulled out gats. The boys dipped and ran for cover. Shade hid behind a car.

He dug into his jacket and pulled out the shiny 9. He cocked the slide back. He already had the gun's safety off. He always left it this way in case of an emergency like right now. Bubs and Lull managed to take cover from the machete-wielding brother. They were across the street from Shade, behind some cars also. The fool let up on his chase. He couldn't decide which one of the niggas to hack down. He walked back over to his boys. They were toting their 22s at the cars the boys hid behind. Their clips emptied out in just a few shots. Then they stood in the middle of the street, and started talking shit.

"Yeah, niggas, what's up. What's up now? Don't nobody say shit to me when I smack up my bitch. Nobody."

As he talked, Lull loaded his Luger. Bubs's gat was in the car, so he was ass out. Shade crept along the line of parked cars, unnoticed by the fools. He ended up a few cars over in back of them. They were still walking in circles, trying to look all tough. The fool believed he had the boys on the run. They were bustas. They don't want none of this. Fuck one of them up, the fool thought. But he was wrong. Lull stood up from his spot, and started bucking. BOOF BOOF BOOF BOOF, the fools ducked, ran, dodged, and slid. They headed for their car. Shade noticed that Lull was busting caps. He decided to join Lull's rhythmic gunfire.

BOOM BOOF BOOM BOOF BOOM, the two brothers that had come with the fool were already in the car, but the fool had a long way to go. His shit talking distanced him from the rizzy. He also was scared and confused. He didn't know where that extra gunfire in back of him was coming from.

"C'mon man, c'mon. Hurry the fuck up," his boys screamed to him. He was trying. He was moving as fast as he could. BOOM, KIISHHHHHH, Shade shot out their front windshield. The fool was a step away from the car. He ducked next to the rear fender. It was then that he noticed Shade busting at him from behind a red Mustang. He tried to reach the door handle. BOOM BOOF, the bullets slammed into his back and shoulder. The force knocked him forward and then back against the car. He was pinned against the backdoor as if tho a thumbtack had stuck him there. He noticed that the door window right above his head was shot out. BOOOM, Shade wouldn't stop bustin shots. The fool stood up, BOOM, staggered a bit, BOOOM, then dove in through the window. EERRRRRGHHHHHHH, the car peeled out quick and took off down the street. The boys jumped in their car.

"C'mon let's get ghost," Shade urged. Lull started the engine.

"Hurry up, nigga," Bubs screamed. Shade took a glance at the apartment building the girl had run into. He punched the backseat in anger. He wanted that bitch Kwestchyn. He looked at the building hoping to see her somewhere. Bingo, she was in the third-floor window.

"Hold up, Lull. Hold up," he said. He rolled down his window. She screamed down her telephone number. He programmed the digits into his faulty memory bank. He blew her a kiss, gave her a nod, and then signaled Lull to pull off. Lull was bleeding. His driving was all fucked up. He ran red lights. He swerved, but they let him drive regardless.

Shade hoped he hadn't killed that woman-beating fool. He didn't want this extra dead body tagged onto his list. For he hadn't even committed the great deal of chaos that he was supposed to in the first place. He knew there were more dead bodies to come. And he already anticipated killing these fools, but the sucka they just shot up was a waste of time. He was just a kid, trying to get a rep. But he was a loudmouth kid who wielded a machete. So fuck him.

Bubs finally lit up the woo. The boys were feining. They all took a hit and relaxed. Lull drove correctly again. He wrapped up the cut with a shirt. Shade stopped thinking about that fool. Bubs was just chilling in his seat. He was watching the clouds, which were black. Lightning slashed through the sky and huge raindrops began to fall.

The rock and chronic smoke settled like volcanic ash on the surface of the boys' minds. It was hard to see out of the car because it was raining so hard. No one was out. They were headed for their original destination. Lull kept an eye out for the fools they just busted. They might gather up some courage and try to come back for round two. Bubs scanned the sidewalk in search of one of the brothers they were after. But the streets were bare with no living souls, except one who Bubs picked up on his enemy radar.

"Look, nigga, my niece. She caught in the rain," Bubs said. "Stop the car fool." Bubs flung open the door. The thick smoke was oozing out the door. "Hey DeShaun what up girl? Come on in up out of that rain," Bubs yelled to her. She ran to the car ducking while running with her schoolbooks over her head.

Before she reached the car Lullaby asked, "Damn Bubs she lookin a little big. What the hell grade is she in now?"

Bubs whispered, "Tenth nigga tenth."

"What up, fellas? WHEW it's smoky as fuck up here," she said. Then she jumped in the back right on top of Shade. Bubs closed the door and Lullaby began to pull off. DeShaun was still on Shade. She had a crush on Shade. Shade knew she had these feelings, which is why he treated her cold. She was a little kid who shouldn't even be thinking about men.

Lull pulled up to a red light. He looked in his rearview mirror and noticed a carload of niggas in back of him.

"Oh shit y'all it's on," he said.

Bubs noticed him looking in the mirror. He knew by the nervous look on Lull's face that something was not right. Bubs spun around and looked out of the back window. Shade did the same. It was those punk-ass niggas.

"We musta killed that fool," Lull said.

"DeShaun get down on the floor," Shade said.

BOOM BOOOM BOOOM. The carload of niggas began shooting. Lull hit the accelerator and was out of there. The car chased after them. Lull dipped down a one-way street and tried to lose them. The niggas weren't buying it though. They followed Lull. KIISSSSHHHH, they shot a hole through the back window. DeShaun was 'noid. Lull's crazy driving was flinging her little body all over the backseat. Shade grabbed a hold of the girl and used himself to cover her. Bubs reached out the window and let loose some shots. BOW BOOW. He hit the driver right in the chest. BOOM. The passenger in the car let off his own shots. The driver eventually lost control of the wheel and slammed into a tree. Lull took a right down another one-way street and was rid of them. Bubs sat back down in his seat. He looked down at his side. He was hit and it looked bad. Blood was pouring out of his side.

"You all right nigga?" Lull asked him.

"Do I look all right mufucka?"

Shade realized the commotion was over so he let DeShaun up. Bubs spun around in his seat to make sure his niece was all right.

"You all right girl?"

"Yeah I'm all right," she replied.

"Take me to the hospital nigga," Bubs said as he reached in the ashtray and pulled out the half-smoked blunt. He couldn't feel the pain once he hit the good shit. He lit the woo and took a long pull. The smoke filled the car almost immediately. Lull whipped around another corner, and DeShaun flew on top of Shade. Shade jerked away in his clumsylike manner in order to move her out of the way. And BLAMM. His 9 mm fired.

Everyone jumped. Lullaby stopped the car in the middle of the street. Time froze and everyone was motionless. They were like statues. Each of them was hurled up in a corner of the car, as if they were trying to escape and the doors would not open. The woo smoke was still thick in the car. No one was able to see anyone else clearly.

"Nigga is you fuckin crazy shootin in my shit, fool?" Lullaby screamed at Shade.

"Word nigga what the fuck is you doing?" Bubs screamed. "Safety nigga safety, you have to keep yo goddamn gun on safety fool," he said in a mean growling voice.

"Yo it was an accident," Shade replied. Shade removed the gat from the inside pocket and clicked on the safety. They all eased back down into their seats. Lullaby began to pull off in the car, yellin about how Shade is gonna have to give up his day's worth of hustling to fix his seat when he was to find the hole. The storm ceased its fury and a ray of sunshine beamed down upon a distant area.

"Those lucky souls. Whoever is under that beam is a lucky soul. That sun must feel good as hell," Lullaby said.

"Yeah ain't that the truth," Bubs said.

Shade was still fucking with his gun. He held the shit in front of his face to check the safety. He then put the gun back in the inside pocket this time on the left side. The right side had a big hole in it.

"Damn niggas check this hole out," Shade said while pulling the right side of his jacket so it was outstretched. Bubs turned around and looked real quick. Then he turned back around.

"It would be crazy if this shit was flesh," Shade said. Lullaby just kept driving and staring at that distant sunbeam. He turned up the system to dispel of all the talk. Shade put his hands to his side and used them to back himself into the corner of the backseat. DeShaun was still in her statuelike position. Shade was itchy as always and began to scratch. He would itch whenever he was high off the woos. He started by scratching his back. He then scratched his chest and then his head. He wiped his face after scratching his head to try to wake up. As his hand passed over his eyes he had a vision of his dearly departed. The dark death vision made him shaky and nervous. His teeth began chattering. He knew something was not right. A few seconds later his face began to feel funny. His eyelids were stiff when he blinked. A force was somehow restricting them. He thought he was bugging off that ol' chronic or some shit. He immediately began to wipe his eyes.

"What the hell?" Shade thought. He couldn't even open his eyes. Something was in both eyes now and they stung like hell. He now began to notice his hands were stiff. When he was able to open his eyes the first thing he observed was his hand was bloodied. The blood was all over him. He began to look around where he was sitting to see where the blood was leaking from.

DeShaun was just motionless and still unsettled in the same funny helpless-looking position. She remained this way as Shade spun around to examine the backseat. He finally fixed his eyes upon DeShaun. He then noticed DeShaun's clothing which was all crimson red. Lullaby suddenly turned down the system.

"DeShaun where the hell you going girl?" Bubs yelled out as if the music was still loud. The silence was disturbing and everyone's ears were still ringing. Bubs figured that maybe she didn't hear him, so he asked again.

"DeShaun I said where are you off at?"

Shade became flooded with paranoia. He couldn't maintain the great amount of weight that was now stacked onto his pile of woe. "Oh shit," Shade said with a high pitch.

"Oh shit, yo," he said again, this time with his normal tone.

"Yo, what the fuck you talking about, Shade?" Bubs said. Then he turned to look at Shade. Shade was a bloody mess and Bubs didn't know how to respond.

"What the fuck nigga? What you do, shoot yourself? What up with all that blood nigga?" Bubs sounded shocked.

"Damn Shade now you bloodying my backseat?" Lullaby screamed.

"Chill nigga the fool is hurt," Bubs said.

"Na niggas I ain't the one hurt," Shade replied. The boys stared at each other as time seemed to stand still once again. Shade's eyes displayed grief and deep sorrow.

"Nigga what the fuck have you done?" Bubs said. He stuck half of his injured body over the passenger seat, hoping he was wrong. Instead he beheld what he most feared. His niece's bloody body, purple-skinned and eyes open. "Ahhh shit nigga!" Bubs screamed. They pulled over into a back alley. The alley was dark now because the clouds were black once again.

The boys all got out of the car.

"Damn yo help me get her out this mufucka." Lullaby and Shade followed Bubs's command. The boys carefully removed her from the car.

Bubs laid her on her back cautiously as if tho the concrete was a soft plush bed. Bubs checked her pulse and tried to listen for a heartbeat. There was none to be found.

"Damn nigga, do you see what the fuck you done did," Lullaby screamed at Shade.

"Ease up nigga you know I didn't do the shit on purpose."

"Nigga you sure about that? Everyone around your ass wind up dead. You responsible for destroying many souls nigga. How is it your soul is meant to survive?" Lullaby asked, all up in Shade's face.

"Don't nobody say shit when you spill all that blood with yo weekly drive-bys nigga, so shut the fuck up," Shade said, demanding respect.

"Why don't both of y'all bitches shut the fuck up and help me take care of this," Bubs said while staring at a fair-sized amount of space behind the dumpster.

"What you mean, nigga? We gonna take her to the mufuckin hospital," Lullaby said.

"Na nigga that some shit we ain't gonna do," Bubs replied.

"Mufucka is you crazy? You just gonna let yo niece die?" Lullaby said.

Bubs walked over close to Lullaby. He stood right up on Lullaby and then said in a tone loud enough to be heard only in their cipher, "Look Lull look over there. You see that nigga over there? That's our nigga. That's our brother. He smoked my niece. Yeah, he smoked her. But it was a mistake. We take her to the hospital and they gonna burn Shade. Now, we ain't gonna let them do that. There is no sense in sending Shade to jail for a mistake, the mistake that only we know he made. The white man wouldn't be able to comprehend the nigga like we can. They would just label him a murderer and send his ass upstate. You hear me, nigga?" Bubs told Lull. COUGH COUGH. Bubs was hurting. He needed to take his ass to the hospital quick. They looked each other in the eyes, then they both knelt down and they each grabbed a leg. Shade came over and grabbed her upper torso, and they all lifted her off of the ground.

"Over here in back of this dumpster," Bubs said. They carried her over, then threw her in the back.

"Come on let's get the fuck out of here," Lull said. They jumped in the car then pulled out of the alley. VRRROOOOOMMMMM. . . . Fade to black.

It was a crazy day, and Shade couldn't believe what had just happened. He knew that he could not get away with living. The fools were trying to kill him. He knew the cops would be after him for shooting that kid. And there was no way he could ever escape the memory of DeShaun's bloody body. He'd be locked up or dead so he could forget about getting with Kwestchyn. He was done, all done. So much mayhem. So much death. What the fuck was he living for? He was tired of always being the sole survivor of deadly tragedies. His rugged and tough soul was now damaged. His granitelike soul sunk into the deep ocean of woe. He imagined himself to be one of those plank-thrown slaves that "Preacher Man" was talking bout earlier. Oh how the sharks would circle your breathless, tied-up, and battered body. He would break free and stroke, but there was nothing he could do to prevent death. He was in their world, so he had to die by their rules.

The car was quiet. Shade leaned back in his seat. A tear rolled down his cheek. The sky was clearing now. The moon was rising in the west. The sun was setting in the east. The stars were twinkling across the orange-and-navy-blue sky. He imagined the sun would be gleaming tomorrow, after he awoke from already having committed the great deal of chaos. He would sit in the shiny and gleaming weather and clean his shiny 9. He would have those thoughts of his slain daughter. And after he was through, he would take one last look around, and then finally give his heavenly loved ones their long overdue visit.

EXHALE. . . .

EPILOGUE: REFLECTIONS ON THUG LIFE BY THE AUTHOR

The Thug Niggas (young Black gangsta-type males) are a batch of brothers that are plentiful on the city streets. They have been demoralized and neglected. Most under this degrading system become full of twisted views aimed at better prosperity for themselves. They are the sole survivors of a holocaust that once destroyed most of their people. They are taught subliminally to be a lesser breed of humans—by education, church, school, and money. It is inevitable that they fall prey to this social trap. The Black male was born in white land so he had to abide by the white man's rules and regulations. He had to take what the white society had to offer. Blacks were different people from the start, biologically, physically, and mentally. Blacks' path to success in life may have been an entirely different path from whites'. Blacks may not want what the whites have to offer. Most feel they got to do what they got to do to make ends meet. Take care of their family using their own special trade. They are rejected repeatedly from prejudiced white establishments across the nation, so they consequently have no choice. They only wish to take care of their families, clothe their woman, feed their sweet innocent children, and last but not least take care of themselves. Shit, ain't that what every man's rightful and inalienable destiny in life is? We should all be free to lead the life we choose.

If they have no special trade then it's off to the kill, the steal, and the drug deal. The life of a rich white gangster is the life these boys admired. Their idols were the Black pimps, dealers, and hustlers who already lived that wanna-be Tony Montana life. Blacks knew nothing of this madness. They did not invent prostitution. They did not conjure up morphine, cocaine, or angel dust. These were acts and materials provided by the white society. Since the slaves' arrival they have observed them performed by the ill society. Blacks observed most whites gaining power, land, money, and most of all respect by using these habits. The Blacks studied the shortcut to power and marketed it in their own mufuckin fashion. The pimp is now bred and raised in Black society. To these boys, this life is the life. It's in their blood to try to reach the goal of living like a *Corleone* or *GoodFellas* character, like white gangsters. The most truthful and deadly fact, which is subliminal and also manages to stay underdiscussed but is alarming, is the breeding of serial killas among the Black race. Serial killas: Bubs, Shade, Lullaby—these boys are all repeating murderers. These boys were taught to kill a fool, while suburban white kids are taught to become cops and kill them. At the same time the Blacks are killing each other and apparently have no control over the situation.

They are forcefully thrust into an unwinnable, incomprehensible, and nonnegotiable battle against all odds, ill prepared. They are in a controlled experiment and their activity is unstable. An experiment that is spearheaded by white political madmen and cunning strategists.

They are contaminated by the plague of racism, which is a word and disease developed by the whites. Racism or communism are the labels usually applied to any minority movement in opposition to white supremacy. The word was barely or never used until Blacks began to hold uprisings because they could no longer withstand the unequal and unjustifiable acts toward their kind by whites. *Racism* is also a word that is deeply associated with the word *stupid*. Our movement is known around the globe. So therefore when young Black males are perceived through the eyes of a neighboring country, we are thought to be incapable of coping with society because we are stupid. Incapable perhaps; stupid no. However we *are* stupid for falling prey to social traps set by the ones who deem us incapable.

Blacks—us, you, me, we—should all take a stand and join as one. Should stand as a class, a new species of man, and put an end to the glorifying of the fools who sold us and condemned us. Our African ancestors had no remorse for their people once they observed the material rewards offered by the white man. Our human lives were bargained for measly fucking material. Now we sit here confused, far away from our motherland. And when the hell is our brave old country gonna save us? Instead, the majority of the armed forces charged with saving America are Black. Some defend the fools who bought us, and some defend the clowns who marketed our ass.

We should cease the evil of racism within the Black clan. Blacks should focus our anger and unleash it when necessary, thus ending the decaying experiment on our people. We should focus on purchasing our own land. Then we should develop our own schools and build our own corporations. The majority of today's teaching methods are designed for an era that is over, that does not reflect the changing American economy. Everybody should know this, but this reality remains invisible to the naked eye of the system. They trick us by not upgrading our school system and continuing to bestow upon us what they deem necessary. *What they deem necessary!!* They are our children. We need to relate to them through our own methods, our own struggles, and our own future. Then we can enrich the minds of *our children*. Whites built an economic structure and are teaching their young how to contribute their share to the structure. We need to gather our own brilliant thinkers and coordinate a masta plan fast. So we can do the same as they did, but within our community. The plan they constructed is a brilliant one. And credit is due to the ones who conceived the structure.

BOOM! Off went the bomb that totally destroyed our inherited traits and filthy diseases. *Obsession* of the wanna-be, *depression* associated with the past, *hatred* of the prosperous, and *oppression* of the unknown are all filthy diseases. These diseases, which are totally interrelated, will most likely lead to the most deadly disease, alcoholism. Alcoholism is one of the most deadly diseases to be inherited. This disease somehow is one of the leading causes of death among Black males. Can't we see this? Can't we see we must let go of this hatred toward the prosperous (whites). Fuck all their restraints. Money and knowledge will pull us through and help us build a foundation, and whites can't keep us from these resources.

It may be hard to gather enough money, but fuck that. Do what you gotta do like that nigga Shade. Just minus the killings. Break this bullshit cycle of depression, oppression, hatred, and obsession, and let's do this. Don't sit around talking shit about whites and the way they got shit hooked up. Don't use their selfishness as a scapegoat any longer. The scapegoat road is now at an end, and a new road must be traveled.

Can't we see we must ignore the intent to cause turmoil among our kind by relying on stories of our past holocaust? Can't we see we must fuck all the dumb shit and get our own shit up in here? That way we can have a say when it comes to the mistreatment of our people. We will soon gain great respect. When we defend our rights we will be defending our people. Our movement toward a better social position will not be associated with "racism" as it has been portrayed through the media so many times.

After a couple of decades in the stupid-ass gangsterlike state of mind that Shade was in, the Black male will certainly begin to feel his sabotage. The monkey wrench thrown in his system by the system. The worm that would twist in his stomach when he realizes his status in the environment, just as it twisted up Shade. It is virtually impossible for Blacks to use the shortcut to success.

Now when Blacks drug-deal, it is blown out of proportion through use of the white-controlled media. The remaining white hustlers hide behind the show curtain of the cop-on-Black male drug war hosted by the media. Most white hustlers were too powerful and now are untouchable. So why do it if your time limit is cut so short and you have a very slim chance of succeeding like the white man? These boys don't know. All they know is "they ain't going out like that."

Some bend to the white survival structure. They adjust themselves to fit the white society. Others like Shade resort to their own Black survival techniques. Shade often thought about his life. He also often thought of lives taken, and when he thought of them he was only moments away from making that thought a reality. This insane thought may never even cross the mind of the (white, black, or purple—what difference does it make?) suburban kid throughout his entire life. This is because the suburban kid is not from a place where violence is exploited and funneled into the young people of the land.

My story, the story of Mr. Edwards, is the story of the *soul survivor* of a murderous spree brought about by a lunatic named Shade. A story of the soul survivor, who survived the evil that claimed the lives of his family. The soul survivor who survived the evil that also claimed and is still claiming the lives of his people. Shade led two different lives. One was the murderous serial killa gangsta life. The other life was hurt and scarred by his past. Either path is painful and painstaking and Shade no longer desired either of the two. Fade to black.

SHADOWBOX

TYEHIMBA JESS

fuck arms too short to box with god we ain't boxin we got 9 millimeter steel sproutin from our hand stumps, blue-blacker than chicago evenin sky screamin into brains like schlitz malt liquor bull
dancin from billboard rooftops on corners made for standin crude
ghost signed bodies crouch the shadows of 71st and crandon, laugh
into bloodstained wind of 49th and federal, mark time in 26th and
california cell blocks tooth and nail knife and gun eye to eye blood
to blood ashes to ashes dust to dust all 17, 19, 21, 23 years of running
from rats roaches and rest in peace, nigga, das my nigga west sidin
folk ridin insane unknown unknown negro male reads the toe tag
but we know first glance from the grin even in death das my nigga
k-bone last of his clan daddy shot mother dead brotha shot sista
crackhead left only this one here wit bared teeth grinnin that crazy
shit he used to pull in playgrounds of broken jumpin mattresses,
classrooms of broken minds, streets of broken women The Hustler
The Mack The Nigga The X-con X-cap wearin excuse for a bullet
bleedin through the back of my nigga das my nigga laid out sunday
best tell us yo secrets from the other side. knowledge us your visions. drop the 411. question: could life ever be like my vcr. just
rewind just hit the double arrows pointin left go to the top of the
story. start over. past commercials past soap opera past ghetto game
shows past the time the hearing on the street the word you was gone
past the liquor toasted to the pavement for you to drink through
concrete cracks past our fruitless search for words our fresh bullets
in the clip as under our breath over our tongues we speak the wine
of dead brothas, lip the substance of our lives to whisper shhhhhiit...

CHICO

BRIAN GILMORE

so i dedicate this
to my dead homie . . .
—ICE CUBE

At last, the killing has become real. The killing of Black men by other Black men. It is real to me now because the only way that the killing becomes real to any of us is when a family member becomes a victim or a friend becomes a victim. In this case, a friend. A good friend from way, way back. A homie.

Lester Paul Martin, Jr., a.k.a. "Chico," one of the closest friends I have ever had, was brutally murdered in Washington, D.C., in April 1993. He was severely beaten, shot in the head, and "dumped" in the back of his car where he was found just down the street from where he and I had become friends by playing in alleys. Chico was one of more than four hundred fifty individuals murdered in the nation's capital in 1993, and one of more than two thousand murdered in the city since 1987 (approximately ninety percent Black men). He was a twenty-six-year-old brother from a middle-class family whom I had known since he was about five. He didn't grow up in a broken home or a housing project, he loved reading books and researching Black history, he respected his parents and didn't "double-cross" his friends, and he, as the worn-out cliché goes, was not supposed to be murdered.

Chico and I were sometimes like big brother and little brother. I was the older, supposedly wiser, big brother; he was the little brother with the golden smile who amazed me with intelligence, wit, and courage. I had other friends murdered in the mayhem that has erupted in Washington, D.C., since 1987, but they just weren't close friends; they were individuals I knew when I was coming up. Chico was a guy I would see or talk to just about every day, a guy who I have thought about every day since the police discovered his body in the back of his car.

Chico loved what I loved—albums by Boogie Down Productions, movies by Martin Scorsese, curry shrimp from Jamaican carryouts, and ice-cold Heinekens. Whenever we had a good time without each other (especially with a woman), we would call each other right away and divulge all the details simply because we wanted to share in each other's joy—true friends do this kind of thing. Now whenever these times come, times I would call him or he would call me, I truly realize that he is indeed gone.

This is the horror of any homicide. The fact that there are those of us who are left behind to deal with the emptiness. To face the fact that someone we loved did not die of natural causes; he or she was murdered. There are millions of people around the country for that matter who are dealing with this drama. They are living my story and I am living theirs.

There is always agony at the wakes and funerals; the services for those who have been murdered are simply not the same as services for those who have lived their life and then died. The participants feel a distinct sense of anger because they know that a life has been "snuffed out" maliciously. In that respect, at nearly every wake or funeral I have attended for a young person who has been murdered, there is always a routine outburst of hostile, uncontrollable rage from someone in attendance, and there is always talk from the young brothers in attendance that this death will be avenged, a life will be taken for this life. So the vicious cycle continues.

But my friend Chico was a lamb. A sacrifice to our neighborhood to save somebody. A message to all the brothers to not think like a fool, it can happen to you. Even if you are middle-class and well-educated, even if you are well-liked and well-loved, even if you are considered honest by nearly everyone who comes in contact with you.

Chico's death made the killing in D.C. an up-close-and-personal event for the brothers on my block; it ushered the reality of the homicide epidemic into our lives forcefully and engulfed us in a cold-blooded reality that insists that we practice survival in the city as an art form. No more arguing with somebody when you get cut off in traffic. No more journeys late at night in the city alone. No more associations with friends in the neighborhood who may have a price on their head. The rules of the street have changed, and until further notice, act accordingly—survive.

Even still, due to the fact that so many people could count Chico as a good friend, his death seems catastrophic. You tell yourself over and over that "it is only a bad dream" or "he's about to call me now" or "he's out of town or something." Only you know this is not true. You were at the wake, you read the newspaper report and the obituary, the homicide detectives contacted you regarding the last time you saw your friend. You hugged his relatives at the funeral and the reception, you were at the grave paying your last respects, and everybody got drunk that night and everyone did it for him, for your "dead homie."

You no longer see any evidence that he has been around: you don't see his car, he is not seen at the barbershop, the dry cleaners, the clubs, the store, the carryouts, and there is no trace of him at any of the usual spots where you always had a good time. You did not see him and have a good laugh about the latest episode of Def Comedy Jam or get hyped about how good the new Tribe Called Quest tape sounds; all of the little things that people take for granted seem huge now in his absence. Things can never be the same and you know it. Your fragile world of innocence and hope has been violently invaded by a random act. Your memories are forever poisoned by the unfathomable, unthinkable fact that one of your best friends has become a victim of a reality that all young Black men in this city want to avoid at all costs.

As if people really believe the present nonsense being proffered that asserts that Black men "just want to kill," or the other position that is presently being claimed, "Black men are just prone to violence; it is in their genes."

It is more like, the Black man is in a strange "survival" mode, and the homicide epidemic across the country just represents a transmuted manifestation of that struggle. At times, he seemingly wants to move forward; he wants to engage his opponents, but he doesn't know how to attack, who to attack, or what to attack, so he attacks himself out of frustration, out of a need to survive. Haki Madhubuti, publisher/poet/essayist from Chicago, describes the present climate in the Black community as "de-evolution." He asserts that Black people are in "survival mode" with a "riot mentality" that "seeks instant gratification . . . [a situation that is] more destructive than constructive." In terms of Black men who are offing their brothers at the drop of a hat, this could not be more true.

But regardless of any political or sociological analysis, the struggle for any Black man is simply not to be next. This is the legacy that my friend Chico has left me. In D.C. and everywhere in America where Black men feel hunted by their own and hunted by the system, thousands, even millions, of young Black men are trying to avoid the destructiveness of other Black men and not be next. The Black man may be marked wherever he goes and whatever he does, but he must overcome these incredible obstacles placed in his path and live a life of dignity and beauty. It is not simply the violence alone which is an obstacle but also this society's growing distaste for his continued presence. This might sound like an exaggeration, this might sound like the Black man's fixation on genocide, this might even sound like a figment of someone's imagination, but go ask the brothers who face it, who confront the racism, bigotry, and dehumanization prevalent in every aspect of American life and who watch the media reduce their lives to silly "sensationalized" sound bites that do not accurately portray the typical African-American male's life. But the daily body count that is presently a central part of that oppressive truth is too real to even for a second suggest that what is going on is not really happening. It was almost "not real" to me too until Chico passed away. Now, it is so immediate that the absence of my brother and friend is almost unbearable to accept. But it is a truth that urges me to go on and make sure that his departure becomes an awakening.

Ghetto Thang

Carlos McBride

Hey there MR. man
walkin all zigzag.
watcha got in yo pocket?
bloodshot eyes, high,
              no one can STOP IT

pardon me MISS,
i wish i could help u out.
3 kids, a welfare check, a run-down house.
i know . . . i know what it's all about

a'yo shorty wop
what's da deal?
packin a 357, skippin school.
i feel 4 u my brotha . . .
              i ain't no fool

there's no escape, no denyin
kids dyin
mamas cryin
fathers tryin
still buyin
gettin high n
babies multiplyin . . .
it's not a

black thang
puerto rican thang
soul thang
funky thang
poor thang
concrete thang
infested thang,

it's a
GHETTO THANG.

VIOLENCE IS AMERICAN

Michael Datcher

You have just walked under the overpass (a place where you can get just below the funk) so Welcome to the Terror Dome. Chuck said it and he wasn't playing. Ask Rodney about Mom, apple pie, and Chevrolets filled with angry officers who weren't asking, *"Can we all get along?"*

Violence is quintessentially American. We have raised it to high art. Those who murder with style and elegance (Bugsy and Clyde) are elevated to legend status. These *auteurs* of misery are afforded romanticized historical interpretations by Warren Beatty and numerous Oscar nominees. They are the Horatio Algier dream in the grotesque. Pulled up, not by bootstraps, but triggers. Steeped in rugged individualism, they are successful. They are violent. They are American. Yet, some have said, "Violence accomplishes nothing." History begs to differ.

When the *Santa Maria* reached the Americas in October of 1492, Columbus was accompanied by a member of the Catholic church. His name was Friar Bartolomé de Las Casas. It was to be a holy expedition. Sanctioned by God. In *Spanish Cruelties* de Las Casas details how Columbus forced the Arawak Indians into slavery on the island of Hispaniola. The island had large gold deposits. Columbus established a minimum amount of gold to be gathered per day by each captive. At the weighing scales, if an Arawak did not reach the benchmark his hand was immediately cut off. This technique was extremely productive, as the coffers quickly brimmed with gold. Violence worked for Columbus.

While still a colony of England, America began to hunger for its independence. Although the patriots ardently harangued the British about their status as subjects of a colonized state, it was violence not rhetoric that brought about change. On Monday, March 5, 1770, Crispus Attucks gathered the townspeople of Boston on King Street and struck out at the English soldiers. The soldiers retaliated with great force, resulting in the infamous Boston Massacre. The American Revolution was born. Poet John Boyle O'Reilly wrote, "And honor Crispus Attucks, who was leader and voice that day / The first to defy, the first to die . . . / Call it riot or revolution, or mob or crowd as you may / Such deaths have been the seed of nations."

In the early nineteenth century, the American economy was agriculturally driven. As the demand for wealth grew, so did the slave trade. The African-American enslaved population were obviously unwilling participants in this "peculiar institution." In order to subjugate and control the burgeoning Black masses and thereby protect American economic interest, whites employed brutal forms of violence during slavery and after. Most whippings and lynchings were made into public, especially savage, spectacles, so as to frighten surrounding African Americans into continued submission. In Walter White's *Rope and Faggot*, a witness recounts the lynching of a pregnant Black woman who had publicly protested her husband's lynching earlier that day:

Securely they bound her ankles together and, by then, hanged her to a tree. Gasoline and motor oil were thrown upon her dangling clothes; a match wrapped her in sudden flames . . . The clothes burned from her toasted body, in which, unfortunately, life still lingered. A man stepped towards the woman and, with his knife, ripped open the abdomen in a crude Caesarean operation. Out tumbled the prematurely born child. Two feeble cries it gave—and received for answer the heel of a stalwart man, as life was ground out of the tiny form.

It is not difficult to ascertain the effects on many African Americans witnessing this atrocity. Michel Foucault explains the function of this type of violence: "The public execution did not re-establish justice; it reactivated power. . . . The ceremony of public torture and execution displayed for all to see the power relation that give this force to the law."

When the cry "Go west, young man!" was first heard and applied, the young settlers did not seem to consider that Native Americans were already living there. Rugged and individual (and defended by the cavalry and broken treaties), the settlers went west and violently took what they wanted. The subsequent interaction with Native Americans is among the most disgraceful chapters in American history. After settlers attacked members of his tribe and dug up their corn crops, Black Hawk, the chief of the Sac Nation, said, "The whites were complaining at the same time that we were intruding upon their rights! They made themselves out as the injured party, and we the intruders! And called out loudly to the great war chief to protect their property! How smooth must be the language of the whites when they can make right look like wrong, and wrong like right." And this is how the West was won—with violence.

Yet, after the first Rodney King verdict, and before the second, many white Americans proclaimed, "Violence accomplishes nothing." This is certainly an ironic ideological position considering that what we know as "the American way of life" was built over a turbulent cesspool of violence. Now that the cesspool is rising, reeking with the noxious stench of burned, castrated Black and Brown bodies, the main beneficiaries of this *American way of life* respond with "Violence accomplishes nothing." It is too late for this refrain. Much too late. Too much water has gone under the bridge, too many bodies have sunk down to the bottom. Too much has been accomplished for the benefit of too few at the expense of too many. The chickens will come home to roost.

If American history has taught me anything it is that violence can start a revolution. In the presence of injustice, violence becomes a viable option. In the absence of justice, violence becomes a necessity. For those who can't dig this knowledge, I suggest you check your history, and watch your back before stepping, here, under the overpass.

PART TWO

LOVING EACH OTHER

FOR THE LOVE
OF YOU

—

HAIKU

In an empty space
shadows born of your womb sing
songs of love, comfort.

In the dark of night
the moon makes our images
my color, and yours.

Lying next to her
intoxicated by her
sweet ebony scent.

Our juices mingle,
combine to create power
that decimates fear.

—JAKE WIDEMAN

A Photograph of My Mother

Jabari Asim

here you are,
on the back steps,
one arm draped casually
across your Levi'd thigh,
the white phone cradled against your ear,
half a cigarette between
your slim brown fingers.
even surrounded by the
cracked and peeling paint
of our porch, you belong.

no pretentious posing for you,
no arching of the back
against an imaginary throne,
for you are
a different kind of queen:
a woman who works with healing hands.
your feeling fingers
belong in soil,
rubbing the roots of tender shoots,
coaxing life from sleeping seeds,
your love blooms endlessly.

COMMUNION

OMAR MCROBERTS

Sister,
listen with both eyes
and feel these words as if
your mind were many fingers
sensitive and probing.
For letters on a page will
never alone express
the mystery of joy and
surrender
which I have known since
I have known you.
Perhaps you have seen these
lines before
in a moment of silence,
our eyes meeting,
burning lamps with
intensity borrowed from each
other's presence.
Perhaps you saw a spark
containing an eternity of words
of thoughts, feelings.
A spark born of countless
copulations between myself and
my wandering goddess of dreams.
The goddess pauses to salute your beauty.

Sister,
I see you wondering if
I love you.
I do
I do.
Never have I desired to be
known so completely.
As Eve knew Adam
his habits no mystery
his origin no secret.
I find myself wrestling with
an infinitude of fig leaves,
now smothering me, my feelings
now protecting my holy of holies
my secret pantheon of gods and goddesses from
the world of laughter, scorn, heartbreak.
I remove one leaf
and the internal temple shakes
but God smiles
as Adam and Eve return to
mutual knowledge despite themselves.

Sister,
listen with both hands
as I speak of making love
as the ink makes love to the
page:
the page becoming pigment
the ink becoming fiber.
Can such a union ever be erased?
Shhh . . .
Listen to the silence make love with your ears.
Has any noise ever filled you so
completely as the silence
that loves you
that is you
that becomes you?

Sister,
I see you wondering if
I love you.
Please, ask again.

Again.
Ask forever, so that I might
answer in eternal words
and that we might become the
silence and enter each other
and worship in the temples of our
personal gods and goddesses.
Never blaspheming. Always offering first fruits.
The silence is eternal, and conveys all
knowledge of otherness.
It is older than change, and will never
be conquered.
I wish that we become silence
and make love
and become the smiling of God.

I'm in Love w/ Jayne Cortez

Tony Medina

I'm in love
w/ Jayne Cortez
cause she's in love
w/ me uh
I'm in love
w/ Jayne Cortez
cause she's in love
w/ me uh
her poetry tells me
this uh
I'm in love
w/ Jayne Cortez
the rockets from her heart uh
the daggers from her mouth uh
the fire on her page uh
super bop Black conscious
boogaloo surgeon
her scalpel is the word
cutting into our dead shit
& madness
relighting the headlights
in our head
I'm in love
w/ Jayne Cortez

cause she's in love
w/ me
her poetry tells me this uh
her poetry tells me this uh
her poetry tells me this

BLACK BOY, BROWN GIRL, BROWNSTONE

COLIN CHANNER

"I wouldn't sleep with you if you were the last man on the face of the earth," replied Nadine to Kenny's wisecrack about having a hard-on. She turned around, giggling flirtatiously, so that he could close up the back of her orange rayon dress.

"What if I was the last woman?" he asked, breathing down her neck theatrically.

"Oh shuddup," she replied and elbowed him in his soft gut. She turned and strode away on stockinged feet out the door and up to her apartment right above us.

Kenny turned around to inspect himself in the mirror. I sat on the bed, which like a lot of the furniture in Kenny's apartment was a carefully selected antique.

I could hear Nadine walking above me. Although she was slender, she walked heavily, and from the locus of the thuds, I could tell that she was headed for the telephone.

Kenny pressed the speaker button as soon as the phone rang.

"Did I leave some earrings there last week?" she asked. Kenny and I laughed quietly because we could hear her faintly through our open door.

He glanced around the room before rummaging through a box of women's things on the dresser.

"I have a couple here," he replied. "What do they look like?"

She described them, but they were not among the bunch. Soon she was thudding down the stairs again.

"Can I see what you have down here?" she asked. Kenny didn't answer. She dug through the bowl of forsaken accessories, while he struggled with his bow tie.

"You've got some really cheap stuff here," she commented, holding a pair of bamboo earrings next to her face. "What can I say . . . cheap women. . . ." She let the rest of her sentence trail off into a chuckle that Kenny ignored.

"Can you do this for me?" he asked, gesturing to the bow tie with one hand and to the world at large with the other.

She took it from him and placed it around her neck, which I admired for its grace and dignity. It turned out that she couldn't do it either, so he decided to go without it, assuming that I was inept.

"How's Bobby?" he asked, as he reached into his closet for a new shirt. The one he was wearing didn't work well without a tie of some sort. At least not with the suit that he had borrowed from his brother. Kenny didn't own a suit.

"You'll see," she replied, screwing up her face to show her disapproval of his shirt selection. "He's going to be there."

"He's meeting you again? How come he's always meeting you? Why can't he pick you up? What? Is he scared to come to Brooklyn? Is he a cab driver or something?"

"He's not scared to come to Brooklyn. He lives in Brooklyn," she said, waving her hand at him as though he were a pesky but harmless bug. "Brooklyn Heights."

I was surprised to hear that Bobby lived in Brooklyn. He just didn't have that Brooklyn thing. But Brooklyn Heights made perfectly good sense. It explained his non-Brooklynness, the residents of Brooklyn Heights being Manhattan colonists in what they perceive to be a third-world country.

That Bobby lived in Brooklyn Heights underscored Kenny's often-expressed opinion that Bobby was not as interested in Nadine as she would have liked him to be. Because it was only a twenty-five minute walk from Brooklyn Heights to Fort Greene, and Bobby had never come to visit.

The smirk that Kenny was holding in must have escaped through his pores, because Nadine told him to stop and she was behind him. As soon as Kenny became defensive, Nadine went on the attack.

"So how's what's-her-name?" she asked.

"Clarisse?" he replied nonchalantly.

"No," she replied, turning to me and preceding her evil comment with a wink.

"Who?" Kenny asked cautiously.

"Yeah, her, Clarisse, a.k.a. Clarence the Cross-eyed Lioness. What eyes. What a wonderful woven mane."

Kenny was offended and told her to keep out of his business. "How do I look?" he asked, changing the subject.

"You look good," I said.

Kenny's brother had nice taste in clothes, and his suits hung better on Kenny than they did on him because Kenny was a few pounds lighter. Not that Kenny was slim. His brother was fat. Kenny had a belly and a double chin and was losing his hair in a hurry. He looked in the mirror once again and adjusted himself. The suit was navy blue. Wool and silk. Five button, single-breasted. The shirt that he had selected went well with it. Pearl white linen with a baseball collar. Kenny had gotten it after a mix-up at the cleaners a few weeks ago. He had lost a shirt in the snafu, but trust me, it wasn't as nice.

"How do I look?" he asked again.

"You look good," Nadine replied with a smile.

She had been busily applying her makeup with a hand mirror when he asked her, and she had not looked up at his pudgy face.

"How good?" he asked, not taking his eyes off himself.

"Let's just say that if you were one of the last two men on earth and the last one was Ziggy Marley, and he wouldn't sleep with me unless I slept with you, then I'd think about it long and hard before turning Ziggy down."

Kenny muttered a lame response and we left.

We took Nadine's car, and we talked the entire ten-minute drive, or more accurately, Nadine talked the entire way.

Nadine is talkative. She'll talk about anything. That's a part of the reason why we get along. Some people say she's giddy, but I'd like to call her expressive. She speaks with her hands, and laughs with her entire body.

Her body is nice . . . depending on one's needs. Her body would be nice for a woman to inhabit permanently as her own, being that it's well proportioned, with good height and posture. It wouldn't be nice for a man to inhabit for a night though. At least not this man. It's not a sensuous body. It is too meticulously cared for. Too gymed and personal trainered. I would feel a need to be on my p's and q's all the time, like being in a Victorian living room. I like bodies that remind me of a basement den. Bodies in which I feel comfortable to just lounge about in and be loose. Bodies that recall shag carpeting and sofa beds rather than kilims and wing chairs. But then, that's just me.

I liked her hair. It was wild. It was too long to be called short, and too short to be considered long. She never combed it, and it didn't seem to grow. It was neither straight nor curly. It was like a big tumbleweed rolling around on the top of her brain . . . and did she have a brain. Nadine was a structural engineer with a doctorate in physics from Cal Tech. She was only thirty-five, and she'd been Dr. Sanguenetti for ten years. She commanded oodles of money in consultation fees, yet she was always late with her rent. I knew because I was friends with Kenny, our mutual landlord. I lived on the ground floor of the brownstone, Kenny occupied the duplex in the middle, and Nadine lived on the top in a sunny apartment with dormer windows. I couldn't figure out what she did with her money. She obviously didn't spend it on cars. We were heading to an elegant wedding on a barge on the East River in a '77 Civic that needed a ring job.

Nadine and Kenny did a lot of things together. She was the closest thing to a best friend that he had. Kenny had few friends. He knew a lot of people, but he usually kept them at arm's length. Nadine however had caused him to relax his elbows a bit and allow her to get close to him. At times she had even leaned against his chest and felt the beating of his heart.

They'd known each other for almost twenty years. They met in an advanced math class in high school. This was 1976. Kenny's family had just moved to America from Jamaica, and he and Nadine were the only two Black kids in that class . . . as a matter of fact, in all their advanced math and science classes.

Nadine's parents were Jamaican, but she was born in New York. So being Black, Jamaican and science-oriented, they fell in together. They felt like outsiders on two fronts. They were bused in to Marine Park from Crown Heights, and the white kids were resentful of their arrival. But then the American Black kids, who were also resented by the white kids, ridiculed Kenny and Nadine because they were different—they spoke funny, and dressed modestly, and were studious. Kenny and Nadine didn't like them either. They resented them for not excelling. The American Black kids were crammed into the remedial classes, and Kenny, especially, felt pressured in his advanced classes to bear the burden of the entire race. I say the entire race, because at the time, these were the only Black people that the kids in Marine Park had ever seen close up and regular.

Granted, the white kids at Marine Park would have foundered in Kenny's math class at St. George's College, one of the most academically rigorous schools in Jamaica. Kenny was an outsider there as well. Free education had been instituted only a year before he attended, so he was a minority among the mainly white, mulatto, Chinese, Jewish, and Syrian boys, most of whom came from moneyed families.

Although Kenny and Nadine were study partners in high school, they weren't really friends. According to Kenny, he couldn't deal with women as just friends. He was in high school, and a lot of guy stuff was happening in his life, so he needed to be around the fellas.

He and Nadine split up after high school. She went to MIT. He didn't do as well as she did, wrecking his average in his final year by hanging out too much, and ended up in architecture school at City College.

He didn't see Nadine for about three years, but then he ran into her on the subway one summer when she was down from school. When she told him she was at MIT, he told her he was at Columbia. She didn't tell him until they saw each other again ten years later that she had seen his mother the week before and she'd told her that he was at City. By then it didn't matter, because she had come to look for an apartment in Kenny's first building, which was in Bed-Stuy, on the border of Clinton Hill. The neighborhood was a little rough for her and didn't offer many services, so she didn't take the apartment. But the two of them stayed in touch and gradually over the years became friends. Then a few years later he gave her a call when he had a vacancy in a building on Clermont Avenue in Fort Greene, and she moved in.

Nadine stumbled as she crossed the gangplank and Kenny caught her. I burst out laughing, and a stern face appeared from over the railings of the upper deck.

The barge was moored on the East River in the shadow of the Brooklyn Bridge, right below Brooklyn Heights. We arrived in the middle of the ceremony, which was taking place on the flat deck on the cabin's roof. The wedding arch framed the bride and groom against the backdrop of the South Street Seaport. And the towers of Wall Street looked like an honor guard at attention. The sky was clear and shaded a deep blue like the color of the open sea. They did a nice job with the place. The railings around the deck were festooned with ribbons, flowers, and balloons. They spent good money, whoever they were. I was just tagging along.

We sat in the last row of white folding chairs. Nadine was nervous, looking for Bobby discreetly, trying not to turn her head too often. She made grand sweeps of the proceedings with her eyes.

I turned to her.

"Where's the food?" I asked.

"Downstairs, I guess," she replied languidly.

Uh-oh. We were talking loudly again. Someone from the front turned around and gave us a nasty look.

"I'm hungry," I whispered. "Let's go below and get something to eat."

Actually, I wasn't motivated purely by hunger. I had seen from the corner of my eye that Nadine was upset. On the way down, I asked her if she was okay and she said that weddings always made her cry. Tears of joy, she claimed. I knew different though. Weddings forced Nadine to reflect on her bland love life.

The caterers were about to move the hors d'oeuvres upstairs for the cocktail hour when we entered the wood-paneled cabin, and they obliged us with a few seafood shish kebabs. Soon the sound of the recessional bloomed and faded upstairs, and the band leapt into some bebop, which was muffled by the sound of happy voices and chairs being moved to accommodate mingling.

The wedding party came in to sign the contract, then disappeared upstairs to hang out until dinner. Nadine descended into silence.

I kept quiet for as long as I could, then I tried to strike up conversation.

"That's the way I'm going to do it," I said, referring to the informality of the occasion. "Quick and simple. See, the bride and groom are up there with their friends, eating up all the food and listening to the nice music and taking in the view of Lower Manhattan they paid for."

We were sitting at a table. The place settings and floral arrangements were exquisite. Nadine shrugged and chomped on her shrimp disconsolately.

She had not had a man for as long as I had known her, which was about eight years, the same amount of time that I had known Kenny, whom I met when we were playing on opposing college soccer teams in the CUNY league. Nadine had come to the match with Kenny, who remembered playing against me in the under-fifteen Colts league in Jamaica.

Nadine and I, both being talkative, became fast friends. With Kenny it came slower, because that was his nature. He didn't make friends easily, especially with Jamaicans of a higher social class. As much as he had achieved—a masters in architecture and a residential renovations practice that had made him a millionaire—Kenny was intimidated by middle-class Jamaicans. His intimidation manifested itself in many ways. For one, he spoke with an American accent. The reason behind this, I figured, was that he was aware that his natural accent was what was called flat on the island, meaning that it did not have the melodious intonation that bespoke education and social rank. This idea was not at all farfetched, as Rudolf Nureyev was said to have had the same insecurity with Russian.

"He's not coming," Nadine said, emerging from her silence.

"Who?" I asked, taken off guard. I had been thinking about Kenny.

"Bobby," she replied.

"Isn't it premature though?" I asked, trying to sound wise. "He's only, what . . ."

"An hour late. He is always on time. He didn't want to come. I'm tired of going to things by myself or tagging along with someone."

Her face was contorted in a frown. I patted her hand, which was palm-down on the table. Her fingernails disappeared into the red tablecloth.

"Why can't I have somebody?" she continued, slipping her hand from beneath mine as though I were a member of the collective enemy. "Men are just so fucked up."

"Come on, Nada," I said jokingly. "Look at me and Kenny. We're men and we're not fucked up. I mean it might have something to do with the fact that we were castrated as children to suit the harmonic needs of the choir master, but . . ."

"Oh fuck off," she replied and began to laugh. "Leave me alone to mope."

I left, not wanting to suggest by virtue of hovering over her that she had a serious problem.

"Where's Nadine?" Kenny asked as soon as I returned. He was leaning against a railing, picking at some meatballs. "Is she with Bobby?"

"Bobby didn't come," I replied.

He laughed snidely and shook his head.

"Didn't I tell you he was a waste of time?" he asked, his eyes ablaze with what I later deduced was triumph. "That boy's a joker. He's playing her."

"I guess," I replied noncommittally, careful as always not to get drawn into even slight disagreements between him and Nadine.

"You never met him, right?" he asked.

I didn't realize until afterward that his question had been rhetorical.

"Once," I replied. I hadn't thought much of Bobby when I met him. We met briefly when I ran into him and Nadine one evening when the Metropolitan Opera was performing in Prospect Park. He was tall, muscled, and handsome.

According to Nadine he was part Hawaiian, which explained his hair, eyes, and complexion. He didn't speak much, to me at least, and I got the distinct impression that rather than being shy, he was impatient, and his silence was a cue for Nadine to stop talking and forget about inviting me to picnic with them. Not that I wanted to have any of their stink food. They were having smoked salmon, whose comestibility, I suspected, had been compromised by the heat.

I took no pains to examine Kenny for a reaction as I spoke. I was distracted by a yacht going up the river, and in any event I didn't think the whole thing was such a big deal.

Kenny's voice however told me otherwise. It was crisp and accusatory. "Why didn't you tell me that you met him?" he asked, attempting to cloak a demand with a question.

"Because I didn't think it was a big deal," I said.

"When was it that you met him? This year?"

"Last year."

"The fuck outta here. Last year? She told me that they had only met this year."

"Why would she do that though? It makes no sense. Maybe you misunderstood her."

He tossed his meatball overboard and sucked his teeth.

I found the whole thing amusing. Nadine and Kenny were so silly sometimes with their territorialism. She more so than he. None of Kenny's women were ever good enough for Nadine, and she did not spare her critical tongue, often giving the girls nicknames based on physical peculiarities, like Lips Incorporated, Mount Everbreast, Horse Mouth, Cow Foot, and Grater Face. But Kenny had had his moments too.

The bride and groom stopped by to greet Kenny. He congratulated them effusively, but turned off his happy face as soon as they left. He turned toward me, his tone somewhat softened, still insisting however that I should have told him about meeting Bobby. I disagreed with him politely. He plucked two glasses of wine from a waiter's tray and downed them like shots of whiskey.

"You should've," he insisted.

"Why?" I asked.

"Because we are supposed to be friends."

"Aren't you and Nadine friends?" I asked.

"So?" he replied.

"So shouldn't she tell you?" I asked sarcastically.

By this point the issue for me had become Kenny's adherence to a weak moral argument, one of his irksome habits.

"She doesn't want me to know," he replied brightly as though he had just produced a response worthy of the dialogue in *Dangerous Liaisons*.

I was so annoyed.

"So maybe you shouldn't know, nigger," I replied.

"So it's like that now?" he said, indicating that I had crossed the divide and abandoned the principles of male friendship, which included among other things lemminglike support during any disagreement with the owner of a vagina.

"It ain't like nothing," I replied. "I just don't like the idea of your asking me to play cock blocker for you. It's asinine and childish."

"Man, fuck you," he muttered, and eased his way into the crowd. "Get a regular job and stop this free-lance shit, so you can pay your rent on time at least some of the goddamn time."

"Lose some weight, you fat motherfucker," I muttered to myself. "You could smuggle drugs in the folds of your goddamn neck-back."

He stopped and turned around. "I heard that," he said.

"Good. Learn from it."

I looked away. Kenny went home.

Nadine surfaced about fifteen minutes later, and when she asked where Kenny was I told her that he had left. She wanted to know why, and so as not to upset her, I made up what I thought was a simple story.

Big mistake.

I told her that Kenny had run into an old girlfriend whose presence had been making him uncomfortable.

She pounced on me.

"Who?"

Not wanting to be caught in a lie, I pointed in the general direction of Manhattan, and, unbeknownst to me, at Trudy Cohen, a pretty woman with dark, curly hair, a well-sculpted nose, and a deep tan the shade of batter-fried shrimp. Her breasts and legs were working a low-cut, powder-blue minidress to exhaustion, and a gaggle of middle-aged men were hanging onto her every word.

"Trudy Cohen?" she asked incredulously. "She is such a whore. Your friend Kenny is so fucked up. All along he has denied being involved with her. Just friends, he always says whenever I ask him about her. Just friends. Why did he find it necessary to lie to me? How long did he say they were involved?"

I quickly considered what to do.

Tell her that it was a lie? No, because knowing her, she would press me for the truth and would be dissatisfied with whatever response she got.

Continue with the story and allow it to die a natural death? No, because this would be unfair to Kenny.

End the conversation on the grounds that I didn't want to get involved with hearsay, then explain the situation to Kenny later?

I took the third option, but it did not have the desired result, which was for Nadine to respect my wishes and change the subject. Rather than shutting up and leaving me alone, Dr. Nadine Sanguenetti proceeded to treat me to a smorgasbord of innuendo and slander, low points—or should that be high points—of which included the tidbits that Ms. Cohen, a vegetarian, was nicknamed the Kielbasa Queen, and that she had trained her German shepherd, Lolly, to provide cunnilingual satisfaction on demand.

In contrast with my annoyance with Kenny, I was mildly amused by Nadine. Her reaction was cute, almost. Here it was, this grown woman weaving these stories without pausing to reflect on their outlandishness . . . like a little girl. (And if you think that's sexist then beat me with a pair of pumps.) But, unlike Kenny, Nadine didn't press me for information when I refused. She simply tried to pollute the knowledge that she thought I had. And in the process she regained the energy that had left her when she was sitting downstairs, depressed by Bobby's no-show.

Nadine and I spent the rest of the time in high spirits, cracking jokes on Trudy Cohen all through the cocktail hour and dinner. Why did Trudy Cohen scale the top of Saint Peter's basilica? She wanted to use the dome for a diaphragm. Why was Trudy Cohen mumbling in the line at the sperm bank? She was going to make a deposit. What is Trudy Cohen's favorite kind of sex? Doggy-style.

We saw Kenny on the way home. It was almost midnight, and as the Civic burped before attempting the slight gradient on the Myrtle Avenue side of Fort Greene Park, we saw him jogging under the trees that line the cobblestoned sidewalk, drenched in sweat, his buttocks rolling around like wet clothes in a washing machine and his flat feet falling like stones. He was so predictable. He was jogging because I had called him fat, and, as I divined to Nadine, he pretended not to see us.

Nadine and I were a little charged from champagne.

"Let's yell 'Trudy Cohen' as we go by," she whispered.

"No," I replied, "let's slow down to his pace and make him miserable."

Nadine slowed down and I turned and folded my arms on the windowsill, daring him to keep running while ignoring me.

Driven by pride, Kenny gritted his teeth and began to run as lightly as a Kip Keino.

Kenny and I didn't remain upset for long. As a matter of fact he knocked on my door the next morning and asked me if I wanted to go to Sunday brunch at Two Steps Down. We didn't apologize to each other, but I knew that the smirk on his face was telling me the same thing that mine was telling him, namely that we had been acting stupid the night before and that it was all over. I showered, got dressed, and went up to Kenny's apartment. The door was open, and some reggae was skinpoopalicking from the speakers.

I called out Kenny's name when I entered the room, but there was no answer. As I walked toward the back I saw him though.

He was standing in profile at the window, staring outside . . . transfixed . . . one hand in the pocket of his khakis, the other resting on the marble mantel. Curious, I walked over to him.

I was almost upon him when he became aware of my presence. He spun around quickly, startled and confused, his face contorted with guilt, and tried to steer me away from the spot where we stood. Being a nosy bastard, I pretended to not notice his not-so-subtle effort and sauntered over to the window to see what had been so interesting.

It was Nadine.

She was sitting out in the back garden on a bench beneath the pear tree reading the *Times* with Bobby. He had his head in her lap and she seemed to be reading to him, as her mouth was in motion. What was indisputable though was that she was feeding him cookies from a tin, daintily placing biscotti between his parted lips.

As I watched her stroking Bobby's hair, I felt happy for her. Just the evening before she had been so down about things with Mr. B.

As I watched her though, a funny thing happened, and exactly when it began I wasn't sure . . . it might have been when I heard Kenny suck his teeth while fumbling with the cassette player. The sound made me shift from thinking about Nadine and Bobby to thinking about him and Nadine. And as I turned around and looked at him, then out the window again at the spectacle of Nadine with a man, I was embraced by the obvious truth . . . slowly . . . like dawn rising over the mountains.

They were in love.

I turned away from the window. Kenny was standing over by the stereo, doing his best to appear unfazed.

"You're in love with her, Kenny," I said to myself. "You and Nadine are in love."

I thought about the day before. About Kenny's interrogation and Nadine's smear campaign. About their interaction up to the present. And it was clear. They were in love.

Kenny began to smile sheepishly as I looked at him. Before I could say anything though, a question floated out of his mouth.

"I wonder if she loves me too?" he asked. His face was blank, bringing into question the genuineness of his curiosity.

"I think so," I replied. Then I told him about the Trudy Cohen story.

He was flattered by Nadine's reaction, but being Kenny he didn't say that. He went about it in an emotionally circumspect way. He just kept asking me to repeat the story, on the pretext of wanting to get the facts straight. Of course he neither admitted nor denied being involved with Miss T.

"Nah man, nah man, she's not in love with me," Kenny said, referring to Nadine, after hearing his fifth installment of the Trudy C. tale. "Nadine just doesn't want me to give my time to anybody else. She's jealous of me like a girl with her brother. She's not jealous of me in a boyfriend kind of way. Nah man. She doesn't feel that way about me . . . I don't think I am her type. She's not really my type either."

I went back to the window and called him over. He stuck some Sugar Minott into the player before coming. We stood next to each other watching the lovers with undisguised excitement, like schoolboys.

"Is he Hispanic?" Kenny asked.

"I heard part Hawaiian," I replied.

"Hawaiian and what?"

"Black."

"From here?"

"California."

"So what does he do?"

"Personal trainer and sailing instructor. He used to be on the U.S. swim team when he was at UCLA."

"Did he make the Olympics?"

"I don't know. . . . I don't think so though."

"So it doesn't mean a fucking thing then."

"So how long have you been in love with her?" I asked, changing the subject.

"Did I say that I was in love with Nadine?" he asked.

"Yeah."

"Look at her," he said through clenched teeth, "feeding that punk cookies. I couldn't care less what she does, much less be in love with her. I mean, what would be the use?"

I resisted the urge to remind Kenny that he had admitted to being in love with her just a few minutes earlier. Experience had taught me that the conversation would have turned into a heated disagreement mined with charges and countercharges of ignorance. Kenny is fucked up that way. He will say one thing today, deny it tomorrow, then cling to his original statement three days later if it suits him.

He doesn't do this because he is a liar. He changes his opinion in good faith. These shifts reflect his inability to accurately gauge his emotions. He doesn't measure them directly, you see, but rather, through the walls of a steel safe. In other words, Kenny keeps in touch with himself by eavesdropping, and he isn't getting a clear message. It is always jumbled, mumbled, muffled, and soft.

As I stood with Kenny by the window, watching Nadine and Bobby, I was overwhelmed by the notion of seeing Kenny and Nadine together, of at least seeing them make a try at it or discuss it even. But I realized that there were mitigating considerations, such as Kenny's many women, the existing landlord-tenant arrangement, and the fact that I knew it was probably easier to convert a Soviet arms factory to civilian-commercial use than to transform a platonic relationship into a romantic one.

The reason is that the lifeblood of a romantic relationship is mystery. And the essence of a platonic relationship is openness. In their pure states, the two are diametrically opposed.

When we say that we love someone as a brother or a sister, we are saying that we love them in the form that love assumes when generated by people who have limited privacy—as is often obtained with siblings, who hear each other's farts, know each other's histories, habits, and routines, and have grown accustomed to each other's plainness.

A romantic love however is different. In a romantic relationship, because we do not know as much about our partner, we project. And we project the ideal, which we then try to prove to be true. Mystery is the fuel of romance. And even a handmade Bentley can't run without gas.

Kenny interrupted my thoughts.

"That's her type right there," he said to me, pointing at Bobby. "Doesn't he just look like a George's boy though?"

"Aren't you a George's boy, Kenny?" I asked, playing devil's advocate.

"You know what I mean," he replied. "A typical George's boy . . . good hair . . . fine features . . . kinda Syrian-looking . . . middle-class type."

He spent the next five minutes trying to define the type, misting the glass in front of his face with the humidity of his breath. His voice was steady, his eyes set on the scene below.

I could tell that he was getting ready to unload something big, and that it would appear without an introduction, like a shooting star. It was not his way to give a preamble to an important statement. He just made them, seemingly out of the blue. If you knew him though you could tell when they were coming. Friends have this kind of intuition, like guys in a band who sense the imminence of a chord change. Nadine and I had often discussed this tendency in Kenny and had come to the conclusion that he didn't give a pre-amble because he was so out of touch with his feelings that he didn't know when they were on the rise.

"I've had feelings for Nadine since I met her," he said as we stood side by side at the window. "But I knew it would never work. Nadine is an uptown girl and I am a downtown guy. She is from Cherry Gardens and I am from Waterhouse. The two don't mix.

"I remember the first time I went to Nadine's house to study. The family had a nice enough place in Crown Heights. I lived right down the street from them in a nice enough place too. But when I stepped into their house there was a difference . . . in tone . . . in feel. That was the day I decided to stop speaking like a Jamaican.

"Mr. Sanguenetti, it turned out, was a George's old boy, and you know what he said to me? And he wasn't trying to be offensive . . . he was making a casual observation. He said that I didn't 'sound like a George's boy or look like a George's boy.' I read between the lines. He was telling me that no matter how far I climbed in America, my speech and features marked me as inferior to him and his daughter, so I shouldn't even think about checking her. All this based on a life that was so far behind us in Jamaica.

"I felt so self-conscious. Embarrassed. All the things about my life in Jamaica that I had told Nadine about—racing skates in gullies and all this—were so alien to her parents. It was not their reality.

As a matter of fact, when I mentioned I was from Waterhouse, Mr. and Mrs. Sanguenetti told me that their maid used to live there and that she lived in a little shack near Binns Road, and asked me if I knew her. When I told them yes, the father remarked that people like me must be really glad that they left Jamaica. People like him, though, he said, had made a mistake because they had taken a step down in life. Later on when Nadine and I were discussing my visit to her house she couldn't understand why I was upset and didn't want to go back there ever again. As a matter of fact she called me hypersensitive and thin-skinned.

"Class was and is a barrier between me and Nadine, star. I've suppressed certain feelings for her for so long that I don't care to deal with them anymore. I will take an American girl over a Jamaican girl anytime. An American girl deals with me in the here and now. A Jamaican girl always wants to know my past for social reasons— where I lived in Jamaica, what school I went to in Jamaica, who I knew in Jamaica—so she can peg me. Class, in their minds, is fixed. But what can I say, it is a slave society still built on the same economy from slavery days . . . sugar fucking cane . . . so what can you expect. I am a loner, star. I don't need Nadine. I don't need you.

"When I went to George's, free education had just started in Jamaica. There were only a few Black boys there, and most of us were from the ghetto. The redskin money boys didn't like us. When we tried to be friends with them they used to patronize us. They would take us for a ride on their trail bikes . . . but just so we could watch them when they parked them. And they would be friends with us at school, but then Monday morning would come and we would hear them talking about a Saturday-night party that we were not invited to. So I just learned from that experience to keep to myself. You and Nadine are the only two new friends I have in this country. Nadine wouldn't want me. I am not her type. That's her type right there."

The pane was cloudy when he was through, making the scene below us seem impressionistic.

I didn't respond to Kenny. I couldn't. I didn't know what to say.

"She didn't have to lie to me though about how long she knew him," Kenny continued. "How do you figure that?"

"She wanted to feel like she was cheating on you," I replied, trying to sound inspirational. "Same reason why she was upset about Trudy Cohen. She loves you man. She wants you . . . but you have to do what's best for you. And if you don't feel the same way for her you can't force yourself."

Kenny turned to me and shook his head as convincingly as Olivier or Depardieu. "I'm sorry for Nadine, but I can't force my feelings," he said. "What can I say? She's a nice girl. I'm sure somebody wants her."

We turned around and watched Nadine and Bobby again.

"You, Kenny," I said to myself. "Kenny, it's you."

WINDOW-FRAMES

IRA JONES

through window-frames without glass
your cat stares and hazel eyes glare
with thorn-like splintered affection
of an Aretha Franklin love soul song
sweetly smelling up the room
("there's a rose in south St. Louis")

softly, opening the shades, letting the sun shine
gently, cracking the misty windows open
in pollinated springtime air
your hazel eyes flirtatiously dancing 20/20
alone in the powder-blue solitude of distance

as we move closer, gazing into the whites of each other's eyes
blues are reflected beneath glass
in an old broken wooden window-frame
through climatic change, with weathered paint
peeled back in jaded shades of green
cracks sign the time and winter season's seen
you break into my midday work, meet and greet me
smiling with hazel hush-puppy eyes
titillating my soul with emotions
enter my inner sanctum
cotton stroke my peace of mind
with a presence that invites me

to walk barefoot across your spring-green grass
with neatly red-painted toes, you point to the yellow dandelions
passionately, showing me the earthbound hidden purples
inside of you

there are sculptured door-frames
waiting to be unhinged from a falling house
filled windowpanes with your mother's lace chiffon dress
torn into black-on-black silk swatches

sensuous semi-anonymous woman with three faces
wrote me a perfumed love letter in the air
swirling with icons of Voodoo thrills
said *i want you to get to know us better*
have dinner with us Friday at six
i'll curry some vegetables and for dessert,
you can dip my cream with your spoon

conversation alone with you, the cat and the dog
Saturday morning 'til two
with the lure of a budding rose
your lips bloom in red and call me closer

you let me see your soul with a microscope
nakedly framed beneath cut glass
passionate pleasure is your possession
interweaving polyphony of treasure troves
prettified to my desires

bare your open pages to me
sculpt me with your love
mold me with gentle word songs
let me be the one to enter your basement workshop
create us a multicolored masterpiece
give me a hot lemon pepper birthday present
hand me the key that unlocks your doors

the rapture of your hug
the bliss of your kiss
an unbroken cycle of passion-marks and pleasure
jeweled belly button

framed in windowpanes
your soul is a work of art

breathe breath into my being
tie your flesh around my bare bones
moan poetry with your horn-shaped lips
embellish me in the cotton softness of your touch
call our unborn children into the womb

take these uprooted trees and make them live again
make a nest for the tired eyes and flapping wings to rest
when the stolen doors return instinctively
like our stolen moments together
to roost in your backyard again
like birds coming home for the summer

look to the northern sky and hunger for my gentle words
like i hunger for your teasing girlish laughter
i've heard . . . that silence is golden
but not in my house

why not answer, when i call . . .
why doesn't the phone ring like it did once upon a time
in this story, have you painted the windows open
or angrily slammed them shut
or has your ex-lover made you paranoid about what's outside
in the darkness of not knowing, we hold the key
with our minds
love will unlock the door and we will both
come inside from the cold
gently open and close the windows together
feel the fresh cool breezes on hot nights

the cat and the dog have come to passionate peace,
if i could touch you without making love
i wouldn't have the strength
if i could make love without touching you, i willfully wouldn't

your fire-tongue burns my earlobe
deeply throbbing into my brain cells
as i lick your dripping pecan ice cream breasts

i promise you, none of your sweet love
will ever fall onto the ground
especially the pecans

what a sweet surprise
we meet at a dreadlock art exhibition
you hold my hand and take me to church
halleluJah halleluiah

THE JAZZY JAZZ

LENARD MOORE

Heat. Lightning zigzags
the tavern's tin roof.
Rain backlashes
against the diamond-
shaped pane on the door.
My honey, Sweetback sings,
jazzy jazz
setting my baby on fire,
a match licking a candle's wick.
I keep thinking
about our syncopated nights of love,
shadows grooving a muted funk.
I want to snatch her off that stage,
take her home,
jazz her into midnight
and see her in my dreams.
Our bones whisper on wet sheets:
jazzy jazz,
the heartbeat
of a slow hourglass night.

THE POET MAN/SPIRIT WOMAN

LENARD MOORE

Spoken words speak now
speak the unspoken words.
Inner ear hears the drumbeat.
Sacred woman speaks
sweet spirit healing song—
love taking the heart-flesh.
His pounding song, like the night's
dark city heat, infuses
the infinite stillness.
The song turns back into itself,
only to surface again
into resonant silence.

Let these words stoke, join
this poet-man/spirit-woman,
break the blues song.
Here where there is harmony,
anonymous light lingers,
revises silence
clearly in the darkness.
And the spirit again unfurls
while the soul whirls.
Pure as magic,
love's long night
unreeling in the bones.

EENIE MEANY MYNIE MO

GLENN DAVIS

PART ONE: JUMPING THE BROOM
This is a story, a story of Black men. It's about how we think and
live and love. I'm Eldridge Green and it's important I tell from the
jump who we are not. We are not drug dealers or gangsters. We are
not dope fiends, psychopaths, vigilantes, or martyrs. We are not boys.
We are not homicidal, suicidal, or genocidal maniacs. We are not
rapists. Nor are we movie stars, professional basketball players, talk-
show hosts, rappers, comedians, police officers, politicians, "intel-
lectuals," Republicans, or Democrats. We know and have known all
of the above and that's not us.

We are your brothers, your sons, your husbands, and fathers.
We are your neighbors, co-workers, lovers, and cousins. We're that
guy sitting across from you waiting patiently at the traffic light
with the look that tells you something is on his mind, or the
brother on the subway, that handsome well-groomed brother on
the subway that you made brief eye contact with this morning on
your way to work. We're never invited to appear on "Oprah,"
"Donoho," "Donohue," or whatever the fuck his name is. They
never make movies about us. Rappers don't rap about us and we're
definitely not on TV shows or the news. But we've got stories to
tell. DO I HAVE TO KILL SOMEBODY to get to an opportunity to
tell my story?

WE ARE REAL MEN. We laugh, we cry, and we make mistakes.
But we make this world a better place. We hate and we love; in fact
I'm in love right now and I'm getting married tomorrow. I know it's

the last minute but you're invited. Please come and meet my wife,
Toni, and my lifelong boooys Chester, Robert, Richard, and Leroi.

Robert

*Robert Smith is in bed with his wife, Nikki, in suite 616 at the
Ramada Hotel, Westchester, California, at 7:00 A.M. on Friday,
April 15, 1994.*

My boy El is about to jump the broom. And if I wasn't in L.A. for
his wedding I wouldn't believe it. The last of the Sterling Place homies is getting married. So she must be fine. Knowing picky-ass El,
she must be superfine with a corporate position. She's probably making more money than he is, in her late twenties, wears a size five,
has a high IQ, rich parents, and a low-mileage coochie. Yeah, she
can't cook, doesn't have OR want any kids, and I bet she's into that
multiculti shit. What got me was when El said they've never lived
together. That's some of the craziest shit I ever heard of. I always
test drive a car before I buy it.

But I'ma give El the benefit of the doubt. He's waited so long she
must be Miss Right. She better be Miss Right! Anyway, this is a
good age for him to get married. It was for me, cause I don't think
with my little head anymore. My little head just INFLUENCES my
decisions. Now, I can make decisions based on more than a big butt,
a pretty face, and a snapping coochie. Me and Nikki are making
marriage work this time. My first marriage was a coochie marriage.
I had to put my name on that coochie. It convinced me to marry
Sonya. I can admit now my motives were all wrong. I wanted a
woman to obey, get my slippers, cook dinner, raise the boys, go
shopping, worship me, and drop that coochie-coo on me every
night. When I was hitting it I loved the way she said, "Oooh Paapi"
with that sexy Puerto Rican accent. I had my cake and was eating
it too.

Then I got caught and did a two-year bid in the penile. When I got
out I could tell someone else had been hitting it. But, I couldn't
blame her—two years is a long time and she was really mixed up.
Then out of the blue, the bitch up and moves my boys to Puerto
Rico. My boys, damn, I ain't seen Eddie and Steven in over five years.
I might never see them again. Fuck that, I'm gonna find them. That
bitch got me good. If I know one thing about marriage it's you've
got to pick the right person. Damn that sounds simple. I hope for El
sake he knows what the FUCK he's doing.

Richard

Rich Edwards is seated on Continental flight 169 with his girlfriend, Lisa Samuels, on Friday, April 15, at 7:00 A.M.

I've finally made it to Los Angeles. I've heard Eldridge talk shit about L.A. for years: "L.A. is fake city, fake eyes, OW's (obvious weaves), fake tits, fake bank accounts, fake people, all front and no back, and thousanduplets—everybody looks the same. El also said more than once, "Fake country-ass L.A. niggers are why the L.A. women are so phony." He might be right because everywhere I've been, the women are a reflection of the men. Now I can see for myself. Because, I've also heard Los Angeles is the place—"cars, bars, movie stars, trend setters, and go-getters." I know L.A. looks good on TV and in the movies. While we're out here we might as well play the tourist role. Lisa and I will go to Venice Beach, "home of butt-floss bikinis," to Spike's Joint West, and to Compton to see if it's all that. El says Compton "ain't shit compared to 'Do or Die Bed-Stuy,' and 'Shoot to kill Brownsville,' or the 'Nickel' in Houston." Lisa and I want to see Hollywood, Melrose Place, and Beverly Hills.

I hope El's marriage works. Mine didn't. At least I have two good-looking children. Cheryl was a good wife but I wasn't ready for marriage. I sabotaged the marriage with drugs, alcohol, and other women. I wasn't ready for commitment to anyone, not even myself. If anyone else would have done half the things to me that I've done to myself I'd have had to kill them. But hey, that was then and this is now. And now Lisa wants to get married yesterday. But, I'm not in love with Lisa and I'm not even thinking marriage, except to avoid it. I'm young, I'm good-looking, from New York, clocking nice dollars, got all my faculties and parts working. I got the heart of a burglar and as much rap as Iceberg Slim so women are on my tip HARD.

And now I'm supposed to put my mack book on the shelf and go into retirement. I think not. I'm still blowing up. I might look like Jordan but don't have to act like him too. Every time we go to a wedding it gets worse. Lisa intensifies her "marry me" manipulations. That's why I had to move out. Lisa would "punish" me by withholding sex. I remember one Friday night I came home and met her in the kitchen and started rubbing up behind her and kissing her on the neck. I was ready. Something from who-knows-when was bugging her. So Lisa gave me an angry look and said, "We won't be doing that tonight." I said, "WE? Who the fuck is *we*? You mean YOU won't."

I left and didn't come back until the next day. That's when she said, "We-got-to-talk." So we sit down and she says, "Richard, where is this relationship going, and what are you afraid of?" Then we went over the same old stuff—AGAIN. The difference this time was we finally decided I should leave. The reality is I don't want to get married, to anyone. Unfortunately for Lisa and a whole lot of other sisters there is a shortage of us and their options are limited. That's not my fault. But hey, my options are limited too! What they don't realize is there is a shortage of available quality sisters. Most of the ones who "got it going on" are already married or in relationships. The quality sisters available are usually "recovering from their last relationship" which means I've got to pay for someone else's mistakes—the ones with potential young girls who aren't ready or are so wrapped up in their careers they don't realize success means nothing if you have to live a warped, unbalanced life to achieve it.

That leaves me with these country girls who are a good fuck and that's it: Miss "I-want-a-real-man" who doesn't have a clue what a real man is, and Miss "Divorcée" who has a problem with men but needs some occasional dick. I'll admit there are plenty of fine sisters out there but to be my woman you got to bring more to the table than just good looks and good sex. I need ambition, independence, heart, and smarts to go with beauty. Sorry, I'm not ready to settle for less. Even though Lisa isn't all of the above, I'm going to cut her loose. I like our relationship just the way it is. She must like it too because she's still here.

I'm glad El finally found someone. He said she's from Queens and I've met her, but I don't remember her. I'm happy for the brother. That's great. I was getting tired of listening to him talk about his problems with L.A. women. I was just about to tell him to look in the mirror, that's your problem. I hope he knows what he's doing. He's waited too long to make a mistake now. God is in charge; I just do the best I can and leave the results up to Him. I hope El does the same. I'll be praying for him.

Chester

Chester Washington is going northbound on the 405 freeway in his '87 Acura Legend coupe. It's Friday morning, April 15, 1994, at 7:00 A.M. and Zhane's "Sending My Love" is playing on the radio.

Why is it that when people come to town they never take into consideration how their arrival time affects the person picking them up.

All they're concerned with is the price of the damn flight. I told my staff if I come in at all today it'll be late.

Rich thinks El is going to pick him up. I can't wait to surprise the motherfucka! It's been almost twenty years since the whole crew has been together at one time. A lot of shit has happened since the last time I saw Rich. The most important thing is that we've stayed alive. When you're from Brooklyn, reaching the age of thirty is an accomplishment and being a successful thirty-plus is a motherfucka.

My father always said, "Boy, keep some money in your pocket at all times. It's always better to deal with the white man with some money in your pocket." Yeah, Pops. It's also better to deal with the Black woman with some money in your pocket too. And if you're out of money you better have much game. Cause between the white man and the Black woman a brother has got to have his game tight or chunks of his ass are going to wind up in somebody's stool.

That's why I'm with Teri cause I know she's got my back. I'll admit she ain't all that in the looks department but she LOVES me and that's the most important thing. She's got my back one hundred percent and that's a miracle in the nineties. I've been with attractive, pretty, beautiful, and fine women. Shit, I married one of those motherfuckas and now I know that beauty ain't shit to be getting all bent out of shape about. Especially when these fine motherfuckas want you to play Santa Claus just cause they're fine.

Ten years ago I went to hear the Minister Farrakhan and he said, "No one affects a man more than his woman. If she plays her cards right she can get him to do and achieve anything. . . . The Black man will never be all that he was created to be without a loving partnership with his beautiful Black queen." When the minister says *beautiful* I know he's talking about inner beauty like my Teri has. Farrakhan knows what he's talking about and he's got the smoothest rap this side of Jesse.

But fuck all that, I'm picking up my boooy and have big. And see who has the most juice, cause I'm like Tropicana, one hundred percent fresh-squeezed juice. I ain't one of these Sunny Delight ten percent juice-from-concentrate motherfuckas. I heard Rich is going bald. I wonder if he's getting fat or developing a little gut like me. I wonder how many kids he has and if he knows about mine. We got some catching up to do. Wonder what his girl looks like. If I know Rich she's fine. Rich always was a sucker for a pretty face.

Leroi

Leroi Miller is home at 670 St. James Place, Crown Heights, Brooklyn, on Friday, April 15, at 7:00 A.M.

"Yeah, baby, I'm up, I'm up, I'm up!" OK, let's see, I've got a 9:30 flight. "I'm up, I'm up!" I'm glad Gwen is on maternity leave. I know Gwen and the kids will be OK without me but I sure hate to leave them even for a few days. I hope everybody shows up, cause I'll be in DA HOUSE. El's bachelor party better be dah jooint. And he better have some light, bright, damn near-white honeys too. Fuck it, go for the gusto and get some white freaks. Oh yeah, I almost forgot El is scared of white freaks. B.Y.O.C., bring your own condoms.

I got the lubricated jimmies with the nonoxynol-9 for boning and some nonlubricated joints for the big slurpie. I need to get away from work and the family for a couple of days. This is going to be a good change of pace. It's been a hell of a year for me. Boom, I become tri-state manager, Gwen gets pregnant, and we shack up. *Bam*, we get married and Natasha is born. Boom, in no time Gwen is pregnant again, and *bam*, Roy is born. A year and a half ago I was a bachelor. Now I've got two kids, a wife, and I'm tri-state manager. Is this "Leave It to Beaver" or what? Sometimes I don't believe that my life has changed so much in such a short time. But when Roy starts crying at two, three, and four in the morning, I believe it.

Our house in Westbury should clear escrow soon. Then all we'll need is a dog named Spot and it'll be "Leave It to Beaver" for real. I grew up in a "Leave It to Beaver" house and I was the Beav. But "Leave It to Beaver" was over when my dad died. Then I had to figure man-type shit out for myself. When it was time to get my shit together, asking myself what would Dad do in this or that situation worked most of the time. My dad left me a clear example of what a real man is. I've got to do at least as much for Roy and Tasha.

Oh yeah, the bachelor party. We're probably just going to look at some fine honeys, give them our money, and get the shit teased out of us. Fuck that—what did Richard Pryor say? "Just let me smell the pussy." Gwen has been stingy with the pussy since Roy was born and that was almost two months ago. I could use some strange pussy. Shit, I NEED some strange pussy. It's been years since I bumped anybody else. We'll see. I guess I'll get up. "See, I told you I was up."

Eldridge

Eldridge Green is home at 10101 Cedar Avenue, Apt. 248, North Hollywood on Friday, April 15, at noon.

Twenty-four more hours as a bachelor. A quick twenty-four. This is one of the times I really wish Pops was alive. I wonder how he felt before he married Mom. Was he as nervous as I am? I wonder if he was second-guessing himself. I don't know what I'm so nervous about. I love Toni, she's my best friend, our friendship has spanned twenty years, three thousand miles, boyfriends, girlfriends, marriage, my drugs, and her illness . . . but I'm still nervous. Man, I wish Pops could see me now. He would be proud and real cool about it. Tomorrow he'd tell anyone who'd listen, "That's my boy. I taught the kid everything he knows. It was hard work but I did it."

The bottom line is I'm living swell. I'm a computer network analyst with a major corporation. I've got skills and I'm getting paid. I don't live in the city but my heart is in the inner city, the "community." Pops would be proud of the way I'm living even though he never thought much of the West Coast. He'd especially be proud of the fact that I'm holding my own in a world that's unkind to Black men.

Being educated at predominantly white schools (I even went to a Catholic university) had its ups and downs. While I was going to St. John's he thought I might become an INCOGNEGRO. But I ain't going out like that. I'm a Black man in love with a Black woman. I love myself, my history (African and American), my creator, and my culture. Every day I wake up I'm batting a thousand, cause this country has been built up by chewing me and brothers like me up and spitting us out. But me and the crew are getting ours. It's a real blessing having my buddies even though we're spread all over the country. My boy Robert turned his life around in Atlanta. My boy Rich is coming off big in Houston. And Lee is living real fat in Brooklyn. I wonder how I'd be living had I stayed in New York. And my ace Chester is doing good here in L.A. with me.

Mom is real happy. She probably thought I was never going to get married. I know Mom was praying for me. When your mom is "all that" it's hard to settle for "part of that." Beauty, brains, ambition, courage, sophistication, spirituality, and humor—that's my mom. That's one reason why it was so hard to find Miss Right because my mom has always been the model of what I want and I would never settle for some, part, or half.

It's hard to believe this will be my last day of getting up alone.

But the cool thing is I did it like Frank Sinatra—my way. I'm glad WE didn't try living together. It seems all these shack-up-then-get-married marriages are folding up like paper bags. About eighty percent of the marriages I know of are over. And these divorced motherfuckas always want to play the marriage-counselor role. Everybody wants to tell me the right way to do things. Ask me anything but don't tell me shit. They've missed the whole point. I've tried on her mind, her humor, and her anger. I've tried on her love, her cooking, and her personality, her body and her spirit. And they fit. Not living together was the right thing because otherwise I would have found a reason NOT to get married. This way our marriage will be a real adventure. I'm prepared. God, are you listening? I'm prepared to do whatever it takes to make this marriage work. I'm in love. I know it's going to work. But, if for some reason it doesn't work I'm not gonna call Dr. Kevorkian.

Chester

I'm pulling into LAX in my car, listening to "Equinox" by John Coltrane on KLON, L.A.'s "real" jazz station. It's 7:30 and it's already seventy-one degrees so it might be a hot one. I'm glad LAX is a lot more modern and organized than that motherfucking zoo called Kennedy. "Yo, bitch, stay in your lane. Fuck, are you looking, white ho? I swear motherfuckas in L.A. can't drive." I throw my licorice root in the ashtray and light up a Newport. I let the windows down so it doesn't get too smoky in here. Ahh! Nothing like a cigarette to take the edge off, except for a joint or a blunt, as the young boys say.

I'm looking for Rich and the airport police as I drive my lode on LAX's lower arrival level to Continental's terminal. I haven't seen Rich in the flesh in over twenty years. But thanks to video technology I did see him last year. Flight 169 should have landed twenty minutes ago. I always try to work it so they're waiting at the curb with luggage when I pull up. I can see the Continental sign fifty yards ahead. Naturally all the parking is taken. I'm just going to have to go New York on these motherfuckas cause I . . .

"Yo, Rich! Yo, Rich! Whaaassssuuup!!"

As Rich turns to spot me I double-park and jump out of the car. As I walk toward them I'm so excited everything seems to go into slow motion. Rich hasn't changed much. He's an inch taller than I am at five ten. He's wearing avocado slacks, blue shoes, a white polo shirt, and a plaid single-breasted jacket. From the neck up he resembles Michael Jordan except he's not completely bald. He has a sunny-side-up haircut.

His girlfriend is a crucial brown-skin sister with short fine hair, shorter than mine, brushed back. She's wearing a two-piece yellow, orange, and green African print pantsuit. She standing with the posture, figure, and demeanor of a model. I'm glad I decided to wear my blue pinstripe Zanetti db, with a white shirt and a hand-painted tie, cause I hate to be outdone. When I'm real close, I see Lisa sizing me up. Rich and I make eye contact and we embrace in a I-haven't-seen-you-in-twenty-years hug.

"What's up, Ches! I thought El was coming to pick me up."

"I talked him into letting me do it. Surprise."

When we finally stop hugging I say, "Introduce me to your lady."

"Lisa, this is Chester."

"So you're the Chester I've heard so much about. It's a pleasure to meet you."

"You've heard of me?"

"Are you kidding? All Richard talks about is the 'Sterling Place crew.' I feel like I know you. I do know you! Let's see, there's Eldridge, Lee, and Robert"—Lisa pauses to think, then continues—"And Billy. No, No, Butch. Did I miss anyone?"

"That's it except for Dale and Harold but they weren't all the way down with the crew. Lisa, you know you just made my day. And Rich, I gotta give you credit. You still have excellent taste in women. I don't know how you ugly brothers be pulling these fine women."

"Don't start, Ches," says Rich as Lisa smiles. Good, I try to keep the honeys cheesing.

"I'm just joking. You look good, Rich, damn good!" I say. "But what's up with your haircut?"

"Ches, you just set a record for 'quickest person to talk about my head.' It's hereditary, my brother. I'm going bald just like my dad, Ralph, Ronald, and Reggie. Rod still has his hair but it is just a matter of time."

"Goddamn, relax, Rich, I'm just fucking with you." I grab Lisa's bags and tell them, "Let's get out of here. It should all fit in the trunk."

I'm driving down Century Boulevard past all the big-name hotels with Lisa up front and Rich in the back, when Rich says, "Ches, it looks like you're doing pretty well for yourself. El told me you were, but it's always good to see for myself."

"I could have told you that."

"Ches, with you seeing is believing. Lisa, Ches could always talk a good game."

I turn my head around, make eye contact with Rich and ask, "So what are you saying?"

Rich answers, "Sometimes you stretch the truth, exaggerate, and blow things out of proportion. That's what I'm saying. Relax, I'm just fucking with YOU. Next subject! How's your family?"

As I'm thinking about whose 411 I should drop first, I notice Lisa has some serious legs. "Moms is hanging in there but Pops passed away three years ago. How's Mr. Edwards doing?"

"My dad's been battling prostate cancer for the last five years but he's still in the game."

"You're lucky. Everybody's else's pops is gone. The rest of my family is doing all right. Claude is out on parole and my brother Ralph is still a businessman, if you know what I mean."

Rich says, "Yeah, I know Ralph."

Damn, Lisa is fine. "Rich, when's the last time you been to New York?"

"Man, it's been three years. You?"

"I was just in New York February. I've buried three relatives there in the last year."

Rich asks, "What's up around the way, in the old neighborhood? What's up with Ghost?"

"Rich, he's doing bad. I don't know if it's the pipe, the bottle, or the needle, but he's gone. He looks like he got the virus."

"AIDS?"

"What'd I say? The VIRUS!"

"OK, what about my boy Harold?"

"Harold is still Harold, in fact, with all the brothers in jail, on that shit, or getting with each other." Lisa's cracking up at the way I jerked my pelvis when I said "getting with each other." "Rich, Harold's having a field day with the honies. He's got about five baaad ones and they know all about each other. Well, not ALL about each other. But they know he's got other women."

Rich adds, "Nothing Harold pulls off surprises me. What's up with Butch and Dale?"

Rich can see it in my eyes and says, "Uh-oh."

I respond, "Damn, you have been out of touch."

"Hey, my family lives on Roosevelt Island now. So when I go home it ain't really home anymore."

"I can dig it. Butch has been dead for three years, the VIRUS . . . shooting that dope. Dale's OK even though I know they must have shared needles. Dale's still around the way drinking his ass off, talking about what we used to do."

"So Lisa, how did Rich luck up and meet you?"

"Chester, are you trying to imply that . . ."

"Yo, Rich, shut up and let Lisa answer the question."

Lisa's face forms a warm smile then she says, "Chester, we've been together so long I haven't thought about it in a while. But this is what happened. A mutual friend introduced us at a party, and we vibed immediately."

Rich butts in. "Actually, Lisa tried to make me beg for her phone number. And she never did give it to me."

Lisa retorts, "That's because Rich came on a little strong. Plus right when the vibe started getting good he called me 'baby' and ruined it. That's when I started having second thoughts about Richard because I also felt a playboy vibe. So I had to test him. He passed, and we've been dating ever since."

"Dating? I thought y'all were living together, one step away from marital bliss." Richard looks at me like I said the wrong thing.

Lisa answers. "We WERE living together but not anymore. We decided it was best to live separately until we figure out where this relationship is going and . . ."

Rich gives me a pissed-off look and butts in again. "Next subject! What part of L.A. is this?"

"This is Westchester and . . ."

Now Lisa's pissed off. "Richard, PLEASE don't cut me off like that."

"I'm sorry, baby, I just don't want to get into that right now."

"Well, say that then. Don't just cut me off like that. You need to grow up, Richard. Chester, you've just seen ONE of the reasons why we don't live together anymore."

Rich winks and gives me a sly grin through the rearview mirror before he says, "Ches, I need Lisa cause she keeps me in check."

Lisa ends the little disagreement by asking, "Chester, what were you saying about Westchester?"

"I was saying we're in Westchester, but now we're in Hawthorne."

Lisa asks me, "Where do you live?"

"In Torrance. We'll be at my place in about five minutes. You know when I first moved to L.A., Blacks weren't allowed in Torrance."

Rich laughs. "Damn Ches, you make it sound like Alabama, with what's his name? Bull Conner and George Wallace."

"No, not Alabama—Calabama, with police chief Daryl Gates. The police out here had a charge called N. I. T. The radio would go off. 'One Adam Twelve, One Adam Twelve, N. I. T. in progress. I repeat, N. I. T. in progress, NIGGER IN TORRANCE, apprehend immediately.' "

Lisa says, "This doesn't sound like anyplace I want to live. California is pretty and everything but if we move it'll probably be to Atlanta."

Rich says "Ches, you had me going at first."

I respond, "I'm not bullshitting. That's the truth, Ruth. Now that we have a brother in charge the police treat us like men. It's a damn shame we had to have a rebellion in order to get rid of Gates and get some R-E-S-P-E-C-T. Now even Mexicans can live in Torrance. It's still very white but it's changing."

This is the kind of day that makes people want to move here— bright, sunny, and hot, but not crazy humid Houston hot. My section of Torrance has an even mixture of ranch-style homes, upscale apartments, and condos. Each side of the street is lined with forty-foot-tall palm trees. The streets are clean, there's plenty of parking, and all the buildings are less than five years old with that "Miami Vice" style of architecture. If you like to see people walking up and down the street, you are out of luck. Nobody walks around here.

My cell phone rings as we turn the corner. "Hello . . . yes Hauser . . . yes Hauser . . . YES HAUSER! Why do you ask me the same questions over and over again? If there is a discrepancy in the bill and you can't find it on the day log, pass the customer on to the business office and they will handle it from there. Then e-mail them a memo explaining the nature of the problem. Wait a minute! Did you try the tel log? Always try that before you call me! If that doesn't work THEN do like I just said. And, Hauser, don't call me back. You're going to have to start making some decisions on your own, immediately. Are we clear? You're sure now? OK. Bye!" I hang up, then say, "They'll put a white boy, an UNQUALIFIED white boy, in a position in a heartbeat, then expect me to train the motherfucka so I don't look bad. But yo, I ain't havin' it. What makes it so fucked up is he's a stupid-ass nigger. But I'm pencil-whipping his ass so bad I might get him and my manager fired for promoting him. Lisa, don't mind me, that shit just pisses me off."

It's time for another Newport. "Do you guys mind if I smoke? I'm assuming y'all don't smoke."

Lisa says, "Go for it, Chester. I used to smoke. It doesn't bother me."

Rich looks like he minds but he doesn't say anything. I tell them,

"OK, people, we'll be at the crib in a couple of minutes. Yo, Rich, remind me to document that call when we get upstairs." As I walk through the master bedroom into the bathroom I yell, "I'll be right back."

I feel something and I don't know what it is. But whatever it is, Rich is the reason. I'm not sure what he's been through since we left Sterling Place, but I've been through more shit than I ever thought I'd have to go through when we were young boys running the streets.

It's miraculous for all of us to be coming together like this, cause the streets broke a lot of niggas up like motherfucking fortune cookies.

In the other room a phone is ringing, HER phone. That's it! That's what it is. I feel God. God has been watching my back. Don't get me wrong. I'm not religious but I ain't an atheist either.

Teri knocks on the door and tells me she's buzzed Robert up. I finish handling bi-nes and walk into the living room just as the doorbell rings. "Yo, Rich, that's Rob. Answer the door and surprise the shit out of him."

Rich walks to the door, hesitates a couple of seconds, and then opens the door slowly like he is afraid of what he might see. Once he completely opens the door, they just stand there looking at each other like little kids who've just seen something for the first time. Just as I am about to say something they yell each other's names and hug each other so tight they'd crush a gorilla. They keep hugging for about two minutes but it seems like fifteen. All the while Lisa, who is seated on our eggshell overstuffed sofa, and Teri, who's on the loveseat, are smiling and on the verge of laughter as they alternate looking at each other and me for a clue to when the guys will stop hugging or an explanation of this display of unbridled emotion.

While the lovefest is going on a short healthy woman squeezes between the fellas and the doorway and says in a classy southern drawl, "Hah, I'm Nikki."

Nikki's voice brings them back from Lovetron.

Rob says, "Man, I never thought I'd see you again, Rich."

I yell, "Yo, what about me?"

Robs says, "What about you! Nah, I'm just bullshitting. What's hannin bruh. I wasn't worried about you cause El is always talking about you. But Rich moved to Houston and don't call nobody."

Rich replies, "I don't know about you but my phone works two ways."

This is my house so I take charge. "Yo, don't even try it, Rich.

You never returned my calls either." I call my girl Teri next to me and continue. "Teri, this is my boy Rob, and his wife, Nikki. Nikki, I'm Chester. I know you've heard nothing but wonderful things about me. This is my fiancée, Teri. And that's Rich and his girlfriend, Lisa. Everyone, this is Rob, who still needs to brush up on his etiquette, and his wife, Nikki."

Rob looks at everyone and says, "Yeah, yeah, yeah. What's up with breakfast, y'all? I don't smell no breakfast jumping off."

I laugh and say, "Guess why? Because you're not cooking it. Get in the kitchen and do what you do best." I've never tasted Rob's cooking, but I know he's a chef. He used to eat his ass off back in the day. And judging by his just-under-six-foot and a-little-over-two-hundred-pound frame he ain't missing a whole lot of meals now.

Rob says, "I cook for a living and I ain't about to cook a damn thing. I'm on vacation. Let's go GET something to eat. You know what happened the last time Ches took me to a restaurant? He took me to a damn Sizzler, you believe that shit."

"You're lucky I took you anyplace."

Nikki says, "Chester, Robert takes his food real seriously."

Then Teri comes up with a good idea. "Let's do a late breakfast at Roscoe's."

Sounds good to me. I say, "Good choice, honey. Since we've been together, Teri makes the little decisions and I make the big ones."

Teri replies, "It must be a coincidence. Mr. Big hasn't had to make any big decision yet."

Lisa laughs as she extends the two long fingers of her right hand toward Teri who does likewise, then Lisa gives her a "high two," the female version of the "high five," and says, "Same here girl. They talk that talk, but we know what time it is." Nikki says "Yes, Lawd" and gives Lisa and Teri each a "high two."

Roscoe's House of Chicken and Waffles on Pico Boulevard is made up of booths and a few tables for larger parties. The clientele is almost entirely African American and it looks like a sixties diner, with a lot of pictures of famous Black actors, athletes, recording artists, and Afrocentric art on the walls. We arrive around eleven A.M., which is a good time because we're between the breakfast and lunch crowds, so we're seated immediately in the largest booth located in the corner. This is the place I usually take the family on Saturdays. I like Roscoe's because the food is slamming and usually a celebrity or two in the place. In fact Franklin Ajaye, Keenan Wayans, and David Allen Greer are at the booth across from us under a print of Malcolm staring down at their food. Today I feel like talking MUCH shit. Everyone winds up seated across from their mate, Teri and I the long way.

Teri starts the conversation by asking Nikki, "Have you ever been to L.A. before?"

"No, this is my first time. L.A. looks great and I wish me and Robert could have gotten here a lil earlier, but I've got the kind of job that's hard to get away from."

Robert is staring at Keenan when Teri asks Nikki, "What do you do?"

Nikki replies, "I design clothes. I specialize in Afrocentric fashions but I do it all. The problem is, it's almost summertime and my clients want their summer outfits a.s.a.p. I don't blame 'em. Have you ever been to Atlanta? It was eighty-five when we left yesterday. This is mild to us . . ."

Lisa butts in. "It was eighty-eight and humid in Houston yesterday so I'm loving this. Go ahead Nikki."

Nikki resumes. "What was I saying? Oh yeah, I've got a backlog of summer orders to keep me busy for months. But I put my foot down and came out to the coast for the wedding because I need a vacation, but I'll settle for this little getaway. Plus, Toni made me promise I'd come to the wedding when she was in Atlanta."

Lisa says, "Nikki, that's the kind of problem I need: too much work. When are you going back?"

Nikki replies, "Sunday night, and you?"

Lisa says, "We're leaving Monday afternoon."

Nikki is dressed in a black bodysuit topped with a long white blouse with kente cloth patches and trim and a red crown. She's a peanut-butter-colored sister almost the same complexion as Robert, just a little lighter. I don't know if he's changed, but in Brooklyn he never fucked around with females darker than he was unless they were the bomb. It's ironic that Robert, the least stylish dresser of the crew, would marry a designer. I guess opposites attract.

Teri asks, "Is everyone going to have the chicken and waffles?"

Rich says, "Yeah, in Houston lots of people are into gourmet waffles, like cinnamon pecan waffles, banana raisin waffles, and stuff like that."

I chuckle as I say, "Guess what, Rich?"

He laughs and says, "Yeah, I know this ain't Houston."

Everyone except Rob goes with the house special, chicken and waffles. I tease him. "I see you still love that swine, my brother."

"Sheeiit, swine is divine and boss with hot sauce, nigga."

The food comes while we're engaging in small talk. Rich says the grace. Just as I'm about to dig in Nikki asks us, "Is Eldridge having one of those bachelor parties with naked or half-naked women that have you guys doing all kind of stuff I don't even want to MEN-TION?" We all look at each other to see who is going to answer. Rob and Rich are looking at me, so I step to the plate. "Our boy has never been married, he's thirty-five years old, and he wants to go out in style. His exact words were, 'I want to do something special with my boys on my last night as a bachelor.' We can't let our home-slice down." STRIKE ONE.

Then Robert says, "I'm not into this striptease thing. I can go for the strip part but the tease is out. I hate being teased. I don't partic-ularly like it but I'm going to do it for El." I look at the women. STRIKE TWO.

Rich says, "This is . . ."

Lisa cuts him off. "Stop, Richard. Girlfriends, I know you don't believe this noise I been listening to. And Richard, don't EVEN try it cause it's not going to work."

Nikki says, "Lisa, you should have let him continue. They were getting funnier by the second."

Rich reasserts himself. "As I was about to say, this is the brother's last night as a bachelor. If he wants some vicarious pleasure so be it. We men like bachelor parties, and I assume strip joints cause I've never been to one, for the same reason women watch soap operas and read Harlequin romance novels. It's make-believe. When I'm at a bachelor party I can fool around, with my eyes. I can talk and lust, but I'm not going to act on it. I'm just going to look at 'this here' and 'that there' and imagine what I could do, just like you women imagine you where married to Dr. Parsons of 'One Life to Live.' Then I'm going to come home, wake Lisa up, and tear that stuff up." STRIKE THREE.

Lisa says, "Nice try, Richard. You don't have to go through all that. I can live with the bachelor party idea. I just want to know if you guys are going to have any white women there."

Teri says to Lisa and Nikki, "Oh no, girlfriend, you mean they have WHITE girls at those things?"

A surprised Nikki says, "Where have you been girl? Sometimes that's all they have. Lots of Black men are crazy about white women, especially blondes. That's probably why so many sisters are dyeing their hair blonde. If you can't beat 'em, join 'em. Some Black men's only chance to fool around with some 'pink toes' is at bachelor par-ties. Isn't that what you guys call them, 'pink toes'?"

Robert says, "Who is 'you guys'? You must be talking about your brother."

Now I've got to say something. "Hold up, hold up, hold uuup! I don't know what Black men you're talking about, but none of them are at this table." Then I realize I don't know who Rob and Rich have been knocking the last ten years.

Teri says to me, "Honey, I see brothers with white girls every day. YOU'VE sampled the merchandise yourself, so don't even try and be Mr. Innocent. What about you, Richard and you, Robert? Have you ever slept with or dated white women?"

Now Lisa, Nikki, and Teri are energized and focused intently on Rich who says, "Of course I have. But it was just natural curiosity. I was in my roaring twenties and I was hitting almost anything with a heartbeat. But that's ALL it was, CURIOSITY. And it was a valuable experience because now I know for sure that that's not for me."

Lisa asks, "What's not for you?"

Rich says, "White women, snow bunnies, or what'd you call them Nikki, pink toes." Lisa's smile says one of us finally got a base hit. I could tell Robert was uncomfortable and I wondered who else picked up on it.

Teri says, "What about you, Robert?"

Robert hesitates, looks around the table and then says, " 'There's nothing more beautiful than seeing the white woman's hair blowing in the wind. The white woman is a goddess to me and my love for her is religious and beyond fulfillment. . . .' "

The women appear stunned, especially Nikki, who seems embarrassed. I'm tripping because I know he's paraphrasing a portion of "Allegory of the Black Eunuchs" from Eldridge Cleaver's famous book *Soul on Ice*. Robert hipped us to it in our late teens.

" 'I worship her. There is no such thing as an ugly white woman. Even if she is bald-headed and has one tooth she's beautiful to me. I love white women. It's in me so deep I don't even try and fight it anymore.

" 'It's not just the fact that she's a woman. I love her skin her soft smooth white skin. . . .' " Now the women realize Robert is reciting something and they have a puzzled look, except for Nikki, whose embarrassment appears to be turning to anger. " 'I like to just lick her skin like sweet honey flowing through her pores, just to touch her soft silky hair. My desire for the white woman is a cancer eating at my heart, my soul and my brain.' Eldridge Cleaver, *Soul on Ice*."

Nikki looks like she needs to vent, quickly or else she might explode. She says, "ROBERT, what the hell was that all about?"

He coolly states, "That's from the 'Allegory of Black Eunuchs.' In it a brother, a sick brother, explains how he feels about white women."

Nikki asks, "Why would you even memorize that sickness—that's what I want to know! You seemed to get some kind of sick perverted pleasure from reciting that garbage in front of us. Are you sure that's not how YOU really feel about white women?"

"No, baby. I memorized those words because they fascinated me, still do. It's hard to believe a brother could say that shit. I know some brothers feel that way but saying it is something else. I was only sixteen when I read that. Brothers like that aren't an accident. It's all part of a plan.

"I . . . I might as well say we grew up watching those 'blondes have more fun' commercials, Samantha on 'Bewitched,' Jeannie, Ellie Mae, Ginger, Mary Ann, and Marcia on 'The Brady Bunch.' I didn't see no Nikkis, Lisas, or Teris on TV. OK, there was Julia but she didn't even have a man.

"The moral of the story was nobody wants a Black woman. One of the book's messages was that the white woman is the white man's last trick to fuck brothers up in the head. Obviously it's working, ain't it? Love of the white woman is in a lot of brothers. It's even in me, a LITTLE bit." Nikki is looking at Robert REAL crazy now. "Seriously, I don't love white women but I love me some light-skinned women and I am not attracted to those dark Whoopi Goldberg–looking sisters."

I ask him, "Yo-yo-yo Rob. What about my girl Angela Basset, and Sheryl Lee Ralph? You telling me you ain't with that?"

Robert collects his thoughts and says, "Yeah, they're fine but they're exceptions. I like light-skinned women like Nikki Smith, Vanessa Williams, and Lonette McKee."

I ask, "What about Halle Berry?"

Rob smiles and says, "You know it. OK, now let me ask you this. What makes Black women light-skinned? White blood! That's what! I like what I like because I like it. And I prefer light-skinned women, so go ahead and burn me at the stake."

PART TWO: ELDRIDGE—BUMPIN IN L.A.

While I sat in the terminal looking at people coming and going I thought about Lee and the changes in his life. Finally the monitor showed the flight had landed and was at gate twenty-three. I hadn't seen him since his marriage. We'd been pretty good about staying in touch, usually a couple of times a month. He said marriage was treating him well. I believed him. That's why I was curious about Gwen, who decided to come to the wedding at the last minute, probably to keep an eye on Lee. She had to be a hell of a woman to tie him down, because as far as I knew marriage wasn't a part of Mr. Morgan's busy agenda.

Then I saw them. I could spot Lee a mile away. He may have gone corporate, but he still walked like he was going to cop a nickel bag in Brownsville. And his wife is . . . No no no no, she's not . . . she's just light, extremely light, but she can't be, I hope! What the fuck is she? She IS . . . I don't believe this. Lee would have told me if he had married a . . . wouldn't he? Then my conscience spoke. "It's his wife, Eldridge. What difference does it make to you if she's Black, white, or green as long as he's happy? Shut the fuck up!"

They walked right past me to carousel number four, and PA-DOW! Gwen was definitely black. There are certain ass formations that are distinctively Black. If you've got one, you're BLACK. White girls, Asians, Indians, and others just don't have them. If they do, check their blood line. Some Puerto Ricans and Cubans have them because there's a lot of Black blood in Cuba and P.R. And Mexicans? Hell no!

Let's start with the half-a-basketball butt. That's all the way Black. Every now and then you'll see a three-quarter basketball butt, but that's a rare one. They say you can sit a drink on one. There's "donkey backs"; that's about as Black as you can get. Donkey backs are firm, shapely, almost disproportionately large buttocks. Donkey backs are the unofficial ass of choice of Black men, followed by butta—Gwen had butta. Butta is a variation on the half-a-basketball butt with less bubble action plus hourglass hips added for good measure, literally.

I caught up to the Morgans at the luggage carousel, we exchanged hugs, and I met Gwen. She had sandy brown or dirty blonde hair depending on the lighting and your angle. Gwen had a Whitleyesque southern accent. We grabbed the luggage and jetted to Roscoe's.

"So, El, are you ready to get married?"

"I better be!"

Lee said, "You know I was at Toni's first wedding."

I snapped back, "Now, that was a fucked-up day. Pardon my language, Gwen. The hard part was seeing that nigga, Greg, marrying MY girl. . . ." Gwen winced as the word "nigga" left my mouth.

Lee said, "Yeah, El, I don't know how you sat through that one."

"Lee, have you hipped Gwen to communication Brooklyn-style?"

Gwen shot me a perplexed look while Lee replied, "Yes and no.

I've schooled her to a certain extent but she's straight out of New Orleans and . . ."

"N'orlans," Gwen corrected him.

"See what I mean? We've only known each other three years and been married a year and a half, so this trip is going to be very educational for her."

"How so, honey?" Gwen asked.

"You are going to see my past, and you're going to hear stories about me, from way back. Mind you, the fellas like to exaggerate."

"Gwen, you know Lee wasn't always this smooth, professional Black man that he is now."

"El, come on now, it's not like I was a thug."

Gwen's taken Lee's educational spiel seriously because she's looking at me like I'm a professor and she's about to take notes. "So, Lee, do I have your permission to tell Gwen anything?"

He smiles and replies, "Of course, my brother" as he flicks his forefinger across his nose, our old bid whist signal for I'm bluffing. "We'll have plenty of time to get into me, but what were you saying about the wedding?"

"I'm ready."

"No, about Toni's first wedding."

Now I'm wondering why he keeps bringing that shit up. But I go with the flow. "That was a bitch of a day. I shouldn't have went. That was the worst kind of torture, self-inflicted torture."

"You should have yelled, 'I have a reason why they shouldn't get married.' "

"I don't think so. 'Tis better to be silent and thought a fool than to speak up and remove all doubt.' Actually I missed the ceremony. I arrived just as the wedding party was walking out. I walked into the chapel and Toni stepped right to me. Damn, she was beautiful in that dress. I hugged her. She was so excited I don't think she sensed how hurt I was. After we separated, Des, Sylvia, and Monique were looking at me. It was obvious they had read me like Dr. Seuss's *Cat in the Hat*. I even shook that nigga Greg's hand and congratulated him. I KNEW he could tell how much I envied him!"

I felt Gwen's compassion come through in her large puppy-dog eyes. I'd never seen eyes like hers. The color. They weren't blue. They were more like teal, or a greenish blue. They were different.

Lee said, "Deep. You sure fooled me. I didn't know you were going through all that or I wouldn't have brought it up. You deserve an Oscar."

"Yeah right, motherfucka!" I said to myself, but I told him, "Don't sweat it."

"El, didn't you try to pull Greg's sister at the reception?"

"Nah BABY, she was on MY tip. Gwen, why are you looking at me like that."

"You just called my husband 'baby.' "

"And? Only Black men can call each other 'baby' and make it work."

Gwen smiled, and her smile said a lot. It told me she understood. It told me she liked Lee's street-smart edge wrapped in its corporate package. It said she was an upper-middle-class southern girl in love with a lower-middle-class Brooklyn boy named Lee Morgan. You can tell a lot from a smile, especially if you from Crooklyn.

I continued, "The thing I love about slang is its versatility. . . . OK, so I scared whatever-her-name-was away when I told her I used to bump Toni."

"Ti-ti-ti-ti, you guys never cease to amaze me. How low you'll stoop to take your frustrations out on the Black woman I'll never know."

We pulled to a stop at Santa Monica and Vine, as two Black home-less people were struggling at a bus stop. When I made out a male and a female figure, the man socked the woman twice, wrestled a bottle away from her, and turned it up to his mouth. After a nasty wino-style chug-a-lug, the ho said, "Fuck you, you stupid-ass bee-itch." We all watched, frozen. Nobody said a word. It wasn't so much what we saw—hell, they live in New York. It was the timing.

The green light snapped us out of it. I pulled away and Gwen continued. "That poor woman didn't do anything to you except ex-press some interest in you. Then you guys want to know why we give you a hard time. It's not that we want to give you a hard time but we've got to protect ourselves. Nobody else will. For every Lee out there there's ten Mike Tysons."

Lee says, "Here we go again. Mike was framed!"

I put in my two cents. "I think they both lied! But you're right, Gwen, I was out of line. My ego had been smashed so I took solace in the fact that I had sampled the bride's goods."

Gwen gave me a look reserved for your distraught daughter the first time she skins her knee, followed by "Poooor baaaby! I bet you never told Toni about that."

"Of course not. What kind of fool do you take me for? Don't an-swer that."

———

We arrived at Roscoe's about forty minutes late. Our friends were at a table kitty-corner from some of the cast of "In Living Color." Ninety percent of communication is nonverbal, and I picked up some serious nonverbal coming from our table as soon as the waitress pointed it out to us. They were really into Robert's conversation. The scene looked like court. Robert was facing us and perspiring. He was the defendant and apparently his own counsel. Robert wasn't talking in a confident Jesse Jackson manner. He was nervously using exaggerated hand motions while looking furtively at the "Jury." I led Lee and Gwen across the restaurant. No one at the table noticed us until we were right in front of them. When Rob saw me he said, "Yo, the man of the hour is here. What's up, El?"

Then Rob, who was real tight with Lee in high school, recognized Lee and shouted "Ohh shit, what's up BLACK . . . BLACK what's up!" Rob hopped up and hugged Lee, then Gwen. Then he stepped back from Gwen, gave her a quick once-over, followed by a big smile. Then he nodded his approval, and said, "Lee, you're a lucky man." Nikki's expression never changed. Rob was still on trial, and had probably just picked up another count.

Chester looked right past me to Lee. "MY NIGGA, whaaaasss-sup!" Chester and Lee were never real close back in Brooklyn but fifteen years will make it seem that way. Chester's screaming snapped the others out of their trances and caused a lot of heads to turn throughout the restaurant.

Then Chester's face turned from elation to, I don't know what it was. It wasn't anger, it wasn't fear, it wasn't sadness. It was shock. It quickly spread to Lisa and Teri's faces. Rich, cool-ass Rich, got up, gave Lee a hug, and said, "Aren't you going to introduce us to Mrs. Morgan?"

While this was going on everyone was looking past me and through Lee at Gwen, staring and waiting, staring, waiting. Lee looked nervous like the first time you introduce a woman you really like to your mother. "Everyone, this is my wife, Gwen." Gwen stepped forward, said hello with a big smile.

Boom. Nikki mumbled something back barely audible. Lisa looked the other way. Teri was the only one of the ladies to actually smile and greet her with a little warmth. Tension was in the air. Nikki looked at Gwen again. This time she sucked her teeth and rolled her eyes. Lisa was looking at Lee with a disapproving frown and subtly shook her head no. Lee said to everyone, "What's UP?"

Nobody said anything. Then that quiet voice said to me, "What did you think at the airport?" I wondered if I should tell them she's

Black. Too late! Lee became furious. "I don't believe this shit, what the fuck is wrong with you motherfuckas?"

Ches says, "What's wrong? Bad timing, that's what's wrong. Don't take it personal." Don't take it personal, don't take it personal. . . . Most of Roscoe's was watching this little drama.

Chester says, "Lee, it's not like it seems. You guys just came in at the wrong time. Look, we got a scene going on here. Let's get out of here and I'll explain everything then."

"Yo El, you are still coming to my crib right?"

"Yeah."

"OK, we'll see you there."

Gwen, who's been looking at the menu, says, "Honey, we can't leave now. I'm starving. Look this menu: pork chops, chicken wings, grits and gravy, homemade biscuits and syrup, Alaga syrup, salmon croquettes. I'm in heaven!!"

Nikki and Lisa did double takes. It was like Gwen said, "Excuse me! Excuse me! I am BLAACK. I might be light with bluish eyes and sandy brown hair but I'm as BLACK as anybody here, OK?"

Nikki and Lisa sniffed her out like wolves confronted with a new member of the pack. Gwen passed. Nikki said, "Girlfriend, the waffles, whatever you eat, try something with a waffles or have one on the side." Then she smiled and said, "Trust me."

King Bee Blues

George Elliott Clarke

I'm an ol' king bee, honey,
Buzzin' from flower to flower.
I'm an ol' king bee, sweets,
Hummin' from flower to flower.
Women got good pollen,
I gets some every hour.

There's Lily in the valley
And sweet honeysuckle Rose too;
There's Lily in the valley
And sweet honeysuckle Rose too.
And there's pretty, black-eyed Susan,
Perfect as the night is blue.

You don't have to trust
A single Black word I say.
You don't have to trust
A single Black word I say.
But don't be surprised
If I sting your flower today.

VIOLETS FOR YOUR FURS

GEORGE ELLIOTT CLARKE

I still dream the steamed Blackness, witness, of you in rain;
I talk about that—pouring living fire on guitar strings,
And suffer Cointreau's blues aftertaste of burnt orange,
The torturous, bitter flavor of the French in Africa,
The crisis of your long, black hair assaulting your waist,
Your small, troubling breasts not quite spoken for,
Your spontaneous mouth unconsummated with kisses,
'Cause you cashed in your pretty *négritude* and gone.

Ah, you were a living *S*, all Coltrane or Picasso swerves,
Your hair stranded splendid on the gold beach of your face,
So sweet, I moaned black rum, black sax, Black moon,
The black trace of your eyelash like lightning,
The sonorous blackness of your skin after midnight—
The sadness of loving you glimmering in Scotch.
Now, this sheet darkens with the black snow of words;
In my sheets, a glimpse of night falls, then loneliness.

I can't sleep—haunted by sad sweetness outside the skull,
The hurtful perfume you bathed in by the yellow lamp,
Three-quarters drunk, your rouged kiss branding my neck,
The orange cry of my mouth kindling your blue, night skin.
The night blossoms ugly, I down gilded damnation.
I've been lovin' you—more than words—too long to stop now.
What will happen next? I can't know, you should know:
The moon tumbles, caught in fits of grass, seizures of leaves.

TRIALS TOWARD TRIUMPH

—

SOME DAYS ARE NOT AS LOVELY AS LOVE

BROTHER YAO

you get to singing to yourself
rocking the baby a little fast
but still slow
close your eyes
don't speak
drift beyond me

our daughter cries

you struggle to keep
her body still
be calm
be calm
aching love
betrays you

you join her

and i want both of you
to fit into my arms
so i can cradle you

but you know every inch
of this day came like a mile
each moment a mountain

four murders, two fires—six dead
three children dead in another and it
appears racism is on the rise

a horn
a siren
two bouncing checks
our smiles on the decline
unemployment
a stray dog who follows us
everywhere we go
this snug house of closed doors
and bolt locks
is in a haunted country
our life
reappearing
disappearing
damn
ghosts

Can't move no stone

George Elliott Clarke

Can't move no stone
to let my savior out.
Can't move no stone
to let my savior out.
Can't move your heart
if I start to doubt. . . .
Can't move no stone
if you won't help.

Can't find no love,
gotta find my Lord first.
Can't find no love,
gotta find my Lord first.
Can't get your love:
I damn well must be cursed!
Can't find no love;
things can't get no worse.

Can't drink no wine
without my savior's bread.
Can't drink no wine
without my savior's bread.
Can't make no love
without you in my bed.
Can't drink no wine,
might as well be dead.

Chimp Shrink & Backward

Marc Nesbitt

Abacus clacks of vertebra beads when I turn in a chair; spinal cord in a phosphorescent red shiver. My organs sleep on top of each other. Lungs reach for ribs, warm against the rest. I hear my heart walk slowly, smack heels on a flight of stairs; I feel all the soft hardware run uninterrupted, without clicks or whirs or gas or batteries or blue-greenpinkredblackwire or bytes or chips or bolts or pain or smoke in the suburbs like commuter cancer quilts on a windshield, dying sponge deaths in a polymer soup next to ass in the air and Aerosmith squeezed out the holes in a cheap radio, white July fourth and so forth.

I'm black and I own a black suit. Wearing it right now. Wear it on skin on muscle on bone around fluids and crap that covers what I felt a minute ago. Black shirt. Black tie can't be seen, people think I'm not wearing one; think of the fat guy with the sucker quote. The cops call my build athletic. Heard attractive before, who hasn't?; everyone's found attractive by someone.

Across the table sits Joan talking.

The place I sit is tin-can architecture, sit where the beans used to be, a cylinder, a crop circle, a whirlpool of tables around a stage sits round in the center; disco decorations clutter dark ceiling like dead satellites. *Everyone black*, everyone smokes, the bar curves around the back. The stage in a spotlight, lighthouse in deep fog: thick poisonous kind, scares the sailors in the shine-yellow rain gear holding splinter-wood steering wheels with hands sting from seawater.

See Joan again, black in a black dress and she could be better looking than me. Face long and carved into a warrior's mask. "You're not listening to me," she says somewhat slowly, addressed to a foreigner perhaps.

"No," I say. "No I am not."

She looks across the room, down at bony fingers tap the tablecloth. Her hand jerks like a leather spider. "Goddammit Simon." Almost a whisper, her voice rolls around in a pocket. Now rises, "The only couple you're capable of is you!" Her mouth held smaller than usual. Right eyebrow bent. Down. "Conversations aren't one side over the other. They're not competitions. You don't get prizes for winning. They're supposed to be expressions of possibilities." She said something else. Something about monologues.

Look, poet on stage, thin like pipe sculpture, dark-skinned Ivy brother, even bought the costume: Bill Cosby sweater, popsicle-stick color pants. He wears glasses for personality. "An original piece entitled 'Washing the Furniture,' " he says, can't pronounce his own language (warshing). Begins. More feeling in his reading than his writing ever had, behind it even he doesn't care. Bad posture. He sways in hula-hoop-hip-slow motion, drunk because he heard it gave poets a bad name. "I knew a bitch named Cunt Mantrap," he says, swaying still, more, "And she was a *whore!*" He laughs occasionally; the words *dig* and *me* bounce black on the floor in brand-name letters fit right in your wallet. Lower lip pulls speech off the bottom of his teeth, flicking Italian hand abuse as he reads. "In the store and *more!* Can't see the end of *your!*" He points while he talks, talks while he points. His forehead folds. He launches small spit particles that blink in the light.

"Simon?" she says. "Simon," she says. "Simon!" Smacks her palm on the table, rattles the fork and knife against themselves, spoon left lonely.

"What?" I say.

"God," she says to me, "you're worse than a chimp."

"Why do you always bring your work into everything?" I say.

At work she talks to monkeys with her fingers, watches them bang blocks of balsa with heavy rubber mallets. Watch twenty, watch a hundred, watch a thousand monkeys; one beats Macbeth into the air on a wood square. They run around, smile long bone, signal touchdown, hop, shake things. She shorthands character traits. She names them. She says she's a scientist of the psyche.

Joan has been talking, reciting, list poem I've heard before, "Like picking the dead skin off your feet when you're on my sheets in my bed. I never see you pick your feet when we're at your house. You won't even let me fucking eat toast in your bed," she says.

"I," I say.

"Shut up," she says.

I grab edges of our round table like a bus wheel, door-lever calluses bleed the smell of smacked gum and armpits. Clench my teeth and settle in for silence.

Joan faces me, watches pipe sculpture poet with disgust in the corner of her eye. His current poem is jokes about fucking. "So I stuck it in the one side, and it came out the other!"

Weight surrounds my table. Minutes of noncommunication. Pores in our tablecloth expand; ice melts; food ages; around me people change position with a *shish* like they're made of corduroy.

A tall black man in an all-tan suit passes us through water darkness, self-satisfied. Other side of the stage, look at his table just left: his date sits alone; she stares at Pipe Sculpture.

I look at Joan. She looks still to the stage. Still. "Yeah," I say, "I got to go to the bathroom." Stand up. She is behind me. I slip my crotch between shoulders on the way between chairs. No one blinks when I pass.

Through the crowd (whirlpool braved), the bar distracts me in an aforementioned fifty-yard curve. Two bartenders man twenty yards of filed booze sitting on glass shelves; the remaining thirty shelf-yards run empty along broken mirrors with a million fractured reflections each. The bar is glass too. I lean on it. Look down the row of belly-ups, the row of other places' regulars, drunk soloists with their freedom and their liver problems. They sit on stools that turn and drive drinks into their teeth, wait for the end of the night. They fell from the colander crowd of round tables pinned to the floor with couple weights, crashed stomachfirst into the back.

"Can I help you?" a bartender asks me.

"Yeah," I say. "Yeah you can. Get me an Old Number Seven with ice. And a glass of water," I say.

"You know, we sometimes have seven bartenders behind here," he says.

"Is that so?" I say without enthusiasm. I have ways to make people stop talking.

He rests his chin on his chest, dries a glass, and speaks softly, "Yeah," he says. "Just not tonight." Pours my drink in the glass just dried. "Five dollars." Forgot the glass of water.

I pay. Take my change. Parts of the bar are broken also, foot-long sections spiderweb in white shatter lines. I carry my drink and step across the carpet, listen to the ice bells chinking in the liquor.

Arrive at the bathroom, open the door (squeals because it has to). See: lime-green walls like a meat locker I read about; white from three feet down to the black-and-white floor. Checkered: the floor. Sweating urinal silver. Yellow crack cheap sinks with rust drips beneath the faucet. Chipped paint claw-marks stripe the stall doors. The light fuzzes perception, hums buzzing. The tall man in the all-tan suit stands with his back to me, with his hips square, legs slightly bowed, one foot in front of the other, poses dumb gunslinger. Suit nicer than mine. Bought it with money I don't have. We both glow in the soft whites like aging actress close-ups on television.

He has the black head of a grasshopper: compound eyes, large, oval, tops pointing slightly toward each other; antennae, short. He admires it in a full-length mirror. From high between the shoulder blades begin stained glass wings green, rearranging; two pairs, all for himself. The suit is custom-made. Confidence keeps him company. See a wine stain on his back, above the wings.

He grabs his lapels with the thumbs up, an astronaut. Adjusts the jacket. His lower lip and chin are a section in itself, moves like a dummy, moves like a proxy. He speaks to me. "What do you think?" he says. He turns around, my jealousy replaced with veneration.

"That's a hell of a suit," I say. I mean that. "It's khaki."

"Not sure I follow you, young man," he says. "It's tacky?" Glowers with the low section.

"No," I say. "No, not at all. It's *khaki*. I mean, it's nice," I say.

He nods, sizes up my suit, considers a comment. "Ah yes. Well of course." Turns to the mirror, grabs lapels again. Looks at himself at a three-quarter angle. Wipes the sleeves with his arms straight out, steal third—wait, no indicator. "They call it the Café au Lait," he says. Turns to me again. "Armani, you know." Turns back to the mirror.

"I did not know," I say. "How can a guy like me get a suit like that?" I ask. Serious.

Turns around to me for the third time. Smiles with the low section pushing the upper. Looks at the floor. "I'll show ya," he says.

He starts tap dancing. Humming. Singing an occasional word, words. "My love . . . around . . . to see ya . . ." Arms swing in front of him in mocking pendulums, legs snake around and across each other, feet spin in vibration. Tippity-ka! Tippity-ka! Loafer morse on the bathroom tile, he tells his life story to fingernails melting behind the radiator. I listen too and I hear it, the tapping always there, sometimes it fades a little and I can hear his orgones.

Still taps. Wipes sweat from his head with a bony middle finger or something else—four of them, wiping. A separate audience of automatic dryers shine fifty-car optimism from a foursome on the lime wall, reflect round his sideways face in fidgeting fat buttons of fender-glint metal. His joy is in his insistence; his consistence; his existence. Grasshopper grunts, twitch, soft-shoe Grasshopper. He slows it to a smooth finale, shuffles three times sideways, stamps his left foot on the floor in conclusion.

"That's a long story," I say.

"I know it is," he says. "Follow it step by step and you'll be in my position someday. Suit and everything." Turns for a last look at his head in the mirror. Around again. He walks toward me, pats my shoulder on the way past. Heads for the exit.

"What about women?" I say to his wings walking away.

"They feed you crap and expect you to shit steak, boy," he says to me. "They've got *everything* backward." He waves with the back of his hand on the way out the door.

"Backward," I say to myself.

The door squeals closed, imitates itself in opening again. Grasshopper head poked into sight. "It's just that," he says, "*that*," points at my navel intending to mean the whole suit, "makes a bad impression on people."

I look down at my body.

"Understand?" he says.

"Yes," I say. "Yes I do."

He nods, leaves, hear the door again.

Admire myself in the mirror with a tan suit reflection. Three-quarter angle. Grab my lapels. "It would be nice," I say, "to have a suit like that. It would be nice."

Turn on hard heels and step across the checkered floor; the taps of my walk drown out the liquor bells. Listen to the door and its noise.

Walking now on the carpet in darkness; looks navy, purple, brown, no, not brown, black, like me, no, black like blood, maroon maybe. Look up in time to see the row all drinking, winking at me without looking, like they're my pops, like they understand things, all things, cauldron blisters on their fingers from the witches of their past. I turn to the swirling crowd and, centered in a cone of light, raised on the stage, Pipe Sculpture reads a blow-job poem.

"Blow me on me in me in you you on me it jussssssssssst keeeeeeeeeeeeeeeeeps commmmmmmmmmmmmmmmmming."

I tack through the crowd and again no one blinks, busy with the back-forth hissing and moaning of small words. At my table slowly approaching, Joan still watches the stage with a face of impending spit.

On the opposite side of the stage Khaki Grasshopper sits at table seven, no, three, one knee over another. It isn't seventh or third from the front or the back; it feels three. He raises a drink. "Understanding what needs to be done," he doesn't say.

I sit down, raise return.

He laughs hard with his low section, smacks the table.

Across from him, his small date slumps depression. She smiles when he points at her, resumes her previous activities: napkin fold, fingerprint wine glass, sigh flares shot toward the chandelier. Let an insect shrink your person. . . .

He points at me now, still laughing, winks a compound eye.

"Who's he?" Joan asks me.

"Nobody," I say. "Nobody. Just some guy."

Mouth held smaller than usual and right eyebrow bent return to her face, never left, always there maybe, like the sweater she's wearing, same maroon as the blood-pool carpeting; wore it first time I saw her, she walked through the crowd at the man-made lake fixing her bra strap and she never meant more. "I have a question, Simon," she says. Whispers her interrogation. "Do you know what I do for a living?"

"Yes," I say. "Yes I do. You are a psychologist of chimpanzees," I say.

"No, Simon," she says. "I'm not. That was over a year ago. Remember that one month when you were woken up before noon every day because I didn't have a real job either? Did you think I was just skipping my work to help you find something?"

"I," I say.

"Chimp shrink was just the first thing that ever stuck in your mind and you haven't paid attention since."

"But," I say.

"No," she says. "No but." She grabs her side of the bus, looks for the blue route signs, *make the drop-off politelike*. Rolls her finger around the rim of her wineglass. "I'm an animal trainer now. I train chimps for the movies. You could've guessed that, Simon. After all, what's always been my lifelong dream?" she asks.

Years of conversation at a glance, high-speed microfiche, overhead transparencies, Post-its, planes dragging nylon letters, crystal-clear images of high school textbooks and the theory of photographic memory. "To have twin boys?" I say.

She puts her elbows on the table, rubs her eyes with the butts of her palms. "No," she says. "No, that definitely was not it. It's to be in the movies, Simon. That's the answer to the question. That's the answer to the fucking question." Pause, looks at me, bites one thumb in silence.

"Well," she says, "at least my goddamn chimps'll be on the screen. What the hell've you done, Simon? Huh? I'll tell you: shit." She holds it in the air two-handed, like a postcard. "Shit is exactly what you've done," she says. "You're an English major who never graduated and I'll tell you something else; they got a name for people like that, Simon. And it's *a fucking bum*," she says to me. She hasn't been drinking. She puts the bus in fifth. Catch your stop on the fly.

I'm not getting off. Grab the metal bars by the door, never served a purpose before. In the undermowed lawn next to her bus stop, see: dead black Nova, weeds growing in the seats; knotty pine fence the same weathered stained white as a hundred years of piss on an inbred's crooked teeth, a couple slats missing; Loneliness sitting alone as a pit bull bitch, white body tattoo stamped like a cartoon suitcase with marine slogans and beer logos, writhing at a chain, hanging herself in horizontal leap-jerks, bust the chain when I step in the bus stop, canine canines all along my flesh, pain as opposed to death.

"Well, Joan," I say. "It's the whole situation. Nobody's read the books I have and I've never heard of the books they've read. Not to mention the timing," I say. "Yeah, the timing. And the monetary issue." I say other things I don't know the meaning of. "You know what I mean, baby? There are things I got going on. Things I can't control. Things I can't control." She doesn't hear me. She doesn't care. I'm not listening either, my part of the conversation is a formality. The words keep coming. Somewhere toward ceiling I see flake rust-bolts keep spotlights from smashing poet skulls. I watch myself from above, an absent talent in the bad-color shaky film of my teens; every word was a birth, days spent searching for speech through a dirty attic brain of dust-covered donkeys and dinosaur frames; stuff needed cleaning, step over look under, stuck, nothing, resort to the construction mud-boot words of everyday conversation; they sit in the closet next to the door mouth. Everyone has them, uses them; the sound they make is *clumpf*. Now the search is left unbegun and I fling boots out the door without effort.

She listens to the sound of humans sitting. To everything else in the room.

To the stage, filibuster finishing, "You're a little cunt just like the rest of them! Thank you!" Hear: Grasshopper cough from across stage, people's low babel, man in the back clap three times. Pipe Sculpture Poet walks off while no one pays attention. Takes his place next to the rest of the poets in a line of folding chairs.

"Just shut up for a minute, Simon," she says.

A woman replaces the place on stage, rolls across in folds, in unfolds, stands straight. Shaved head beautiful, thin, dark-skinned. Tall in a blue dress, she colors the light. I'm sure she used to high jump. No atom cage of grief around her, no; *the poems* are grievous. Maybe she met somebody. She reads eulogies to herself but she's ecstatic through the middle with a flagpole spine of perfect posture. Her head spits her colors and I love her like a country; I have a heroine habit; she could make me do anything. And now she points in no direction (at me?). She speaks, "Open to show with your dirty nails. Who put the thumb in your brain, Erebus ersatz?"

Silence.

Joan clears her throat. I hear that. Joan's mouth begins to move. Fade back to black silence of alley corners yet to be constructed. I can still see the poet, sometimes talking.

I look back to Joan's painted mouth spasms. Her lips extend and open and slide across in sea-floor mannerisms. At the bottom of the water, spread across miles of Paleozoic parade grounds and darker places where fossils swim around with dangling headlamps, are creatures like her lips, mouthing her words to the top of the waves.

Sound becomes a record slowly backward, fits like a helmet: water in the ear; deep slow vowels for seconds holding changing holding more; short hisses; *zup; zup.*

From right to left her volume returns, firm now, constant, in the middle of a sentence, "to think about me. What you do is not enough. Look around you Simon, we're not satellites."

Cold craters in blue rock orbit.

"I bet you don't even remember what I ordered," she says.

I don't.

"You know what I think about a lot?" she says.

I don't know that either.

"What I want. I didn't use to do that, Simon. Like when we first met. Remember?" she says. "The man-made lake?" she says. "That's not me anymore." She barrels the bus between houses that start looking familiar. Bus stop blocks away (I can see it). She can't wait for formalities, door hiss, construction boot to the chest. "It's oooooooooooovvvvvvverrrrrrrrrrrrrrrrrrrrrrrrrr. . ." voice redshifted in slow motion, I'm out the door in a Nestea plunge towards the tarred-together.

I see her face. I see her foot; her mud print on me; bus side too blurry to read; exhaust ball; bus back reads, "Play lotto!". Hear a chain break. I smack the macadam. Bounce. Bounce. Roll, roll, roll. I lie and melt. Hold my grated head together. Bleed. I hear claws on concrete, barking getting louder. Loose rocks the size of M&M embers burn holes in my cheeks.

Dog pads skid to stop and I can hear her tattoos standing over me. She hot-pants on my neck, aims slobber-drip into my skull cracks. Eyes on my thighs and she's drawn away. Bites halfway through my leg, muscle safe in jaw force furious shaking feeding shark-headed demon pulls, she pulls, she pulls until it gives, *bwang snap*, piano cord or a fat man's fat suspenders. She chews. She swallows. She hacks up hamstringy pieces. Bites the other one and pulls, she pulls, and she pulls again until one side snaps *bwang*, tears it in half; the rest rests warm on my calf. She walks into my sideways sight, yawns a bloody dog smile with a mouth full of muscle pulp. Jumps over my head. Claws on concrete going the other way. She heads back to Nova, bowlegged strut with blood on her chest.

"Did you hear me Simon?" Joan says. "Did you hear what I said?" she says. "We're done."

"Yeah," I say. "I mean, yeah, I heard you." I clumpf paraphrases of movie scripts to her. "You can't make it without me, baby. You'll be back. You'll be back. I'm all you got."

On stage, Flagpole Poet wraps up, "Sliding the backside of time, the past is shit. Underneath, none of us matter. belong. to anything. but ourself."

The entire can stands ovation: claps, stomps feet, whistles, screams, shakes the picture. Khaki Grasshopper looks confused. Pipe Sculpture sulks and scowls at other poets. Flagpole Poet walks off-stage slow, succinct, smiles through the noise in a crown: she's convinced the crowd to be more like her.

"Why aren't you saying anything?" Joan says.

"I thought the conversation was over," I say.

Two men who said who went when sit fat by the front and the coat check, on stools that turn, smell of wet wool and wire hangers. They say a woman won't be last; being last is important.

Standby Poet stops pulling on his cigarette, turns metal gray like his chair. Thin already, loses weight instantaneously. All set to go home, thought he had an excuse, grabs his belt to hold his pants, makes for the door, stiff-arms Sheila (organizes the readings, clipboard, bolt-straight back, legs folded on a folding chair, sits at the end of the row, and knows she's in charge). He makes it to the coat check where the two fat men jump off stools to grab him by the throat.

Sheila sprints through the tables screaming, "Don't hit him in the face! Don't hit him in the face!" She weaves through chairs dropping clipboard papers on the floor, one in a wine slick. "Do you hear me! Don't hit him in the face! He's on next!" Strains her neck. "Don't hit him in the face!"

One fat man hits him in the face. Fat man number two in a sweatshirt too small; his bottom belly sniffs a moose nose over his belt. He beats repeatedly on Standby's chest. Hear moan bursts of pain from all the meat in his body.

The men drag Standby to the stage; he limps to the microphone a stern joke, moves like beef jerky. Standby's life has always been day-old bread in a fat baker's shoe tread, seven in a six pack, February thirtieth. Now, here, a lifelong quest in the happening. Finally stuck in the rotation, part of the act; trapeze artist psychology numbs the pain. He has the face of four elementary school classmates never remembered. Body the height of a human, nothing unusual, noticeable, freakish. Dressed in denim.

He bleeds internally, coughs into his hand; motes float in his head gravity. I forget him as he reads, voice evens out into dull smooth dial tone slides through my brain in a see-through slide show; words appear. "I would," I see him say, "murder my *self*. if I were stuck with you. Only, I'd die slow. painful. make sure at least *that* would be interesting."

Joan leaves the table and I do not notice. I know that because Khaki Grasshopper sits where she was, stares, reflects me in a million mirror chambers for each oval black eye.

"Where's Joan?" I ask.

He drinks a vodka cranberry, smokes handrolls like a girl. Of course pause before answer, "If you're talking about the person who was sitting here," pulls tobacco off his tongue with a hand or something else, looks at it, "she's on her way to the bathroom, with all the other women in this goddamn place."

This is true. All the women make deliberate for the door in a suppressed rush. Joan in front. They zig between numberless tables, zag around chairs; put their hands on the backs on the way past, warm from the woman just left.

Some of them pause, take a knee like lost something, serious profile against the now-curtain side of a tablecloth, let a few women pass, up, zagging again. They file stoic around the stage, quiet as s.w.a.t. A couple wear blood-pool maroon sweaters and they never meant more to me either. A few leave as couples. Three do. Their backs in coats, backs in dresses, backs in backless dresses, jagged lines toward the doors, and hit it, sun in their hair seen across the room. Watch them run across dead leaves and election flyers before the door closes and I miss the embrace with the brothers who were waiting for them.

Standby notices nothing; everyone sitting watches him.

"Why are they all running out the front doors?" I say.

"I told you," he says. "They've got it backward. Like to make things harder on themselves." He laughs to himself. Tan suit folded hard sharp line at the knee, like cardboard. "You should certainly know that by now, boy!" Now he laughs loud square noises on my face, slaps his top knee with his hand or something else.

More words appear from the direction of the stage. "Mary had a little dog. So I ate it. We were in a fight, I mean, you would too, right? Dial toooooooooooooooooooonnnnnna(e)," in slow motion it ends like *tuna*.

"They'll be back?" I say. Think of backs before; shoulder blades bending skin from behind.

"Sure." He drinks, sighs with a wet lip. "Maybe."

"You ever done this before?" I say.

"Oh, absolutely. I'm a regular," he says still khaki, still sharp-folded, yacht chair posture position (an attempt at least, he slightly slouches). Bug smile fades. "I read here once." Rolls a cigarette in his lap, wipes tobacco from a suit fold. "They didn't . . . appreciate it."

"They ever come back?" I say. "Tonight, I mean. The women. They ever come back?"

His hands around a new drink dropped by the waitress slides away before seen. "No," he says. "But that doesn't mean they won't." He drinks, throat pieces move to make way.

"No," I say. "No, it doesn't."

His face odd-shaped, being insect, his eyes glitter black lake rain. "Let me tell you something," he says. "When the bomb goes off boy, all that's left are the insects." Drinks, gasps at the liquor burn, signals distant waiters for another round. "And when the sun explodes, I'll be around then too."

"We have to worry about that?" I say.

"Everything is a possibility," he says.

Standby continues to read to a half-empty room. Voice slides slower now, some squares blank white, some upside down, some gone too quick. An occasional sentence crammed onto one, read fast: "Andthepersonality!Ratscanhitapelletbutton,I'mnotimpressed."

Around the room men sleep with heads in their arm laps; others, head back, mouth in a hang. Standby continues, no longer words, just white light and a deep hum lapping, lapping, lapping, against the walls, against the doors, against the bar in the back where the belly-ups are smiling. Against my temples. My eyes are half-open. Across from me, Khaki's eyes don't have lids, open while he sleeps. He nods without consciousness, neck snaps, drools on his hand or something else, on his suit, on the carpet, dark without color. Everything's that color; I can't see.

LOVE NO LIMIT

KEVIN POWELL

VERSE ONE
My girlfriend is moving out. She told me two days ago and I am still
in relative shock. It's not that I didn't expect it; we had agreed it
was the thing to do given how rocky our two-year-old relationship
(we've dated and lived together an equal amount of time) has become. But her departure is like going to trial, being forced to come
to grips with the circumstances which provoked our often heated
arguments. Was it my fault? Was it hers? Is there really blame or
just confusion?

My editor asked me to write this essay nearly three months ago:
*Kevin, you're in a relationship, you've dealt with some relationship
issues publicly before, and I think you can do it justice.*

But how can I tell an editor that, at twenty-eight, I am grappling
with (holding on to, really) whatever definitions of manhood I've
managed to obtain over the years, which means I, too, have much
to put into practice in terms of my relationships with women?

VERSE TWO
My mother and I have never really talked about the male-female
thing. The best I got as a child were snippets of my mother's conversations with my aunts Cathy and Birdie (all three ran single-
parent households): *Girl, these men just ain't no good* or *I can do
bad by myself.*

I heard these and other feelings and often wondered why women
felt this way about men. Was it some ritual that men—specifically

Black men—father babies, then split the scene, leaving the child-rearing to the mothers? I just didn't get it.

Of my father: I saw him intermittently until I was eight, then one day he declared boldly to my mother, *I ain't gonna give you a near-nickel for him again.* And I haven't seen him since. But I do remember my mother telling me not to grow up to be like my father over and over again. That has stuck in my mind.

VERSE THREE

I am like my father in more ways than I care to admit. My girlfriend is moving out. Our relationship has been good and it has been bad. It was, like most relationships between Black men and Black women, built upon someone else's definition of what a relationship is supposed to be—in spite of the fact that the last few years have witnessed me struggling with men's often obsessive desire to dominate women (i.e., sexism) in all spheres, in spite of the fact that my girlfriend is a fiercely intelligent, articulate, and independent spirit.

The main problem (and we discussed this last night) is that our relationship has never had clarity. That is, what is a relationship? What is my role as the male partner and what is her role as the female partner? How do the twin issues of racism and sexism affect Black people in this society and how do they affect our relationships? Are we merely boyfriend/girlfriend or do we envision a long-term future together?

Confused about all these issues, we often fell into the roles prescribed by this society: I became the breadwinner, the man of the house (my artistic career is a bit further along than hers); while my girlfriend, out of guilt for not being able to help more with the bills, ultimately began cooking and cleaning the house.

But this is not what I wanted. I never asked or demanded to be the breadwinner, nor has she expressed the desire to be a domestic wife. But there we went participating in the age-old and sexist definitions of what men and women are supposed to do. And the resentment built up time and again and we would verbally lash out at each other and cry and make up and then repeat the process again and again and again.

VERSE FOUR

I once believed that women were inferior to men—that women were toys to be played with, sexed, then discarded. I learned these things when I was a little boy growing up in Jersey City, New Jersey. Older boys would brag to my ten-year-old ears of their sexual conquests, of gangbangs, of how "girls liked to be treated that way." My imagination would run wild, my body pinned close to the most beautiful girl in my class, squeezing her still-developing butt, my lips parting hers, making way for the french kiss I had learned from my baby-sitter's granddaughter.

I wanted to talk to my mother about girls and sex but my mother, being the conservative Southern-born Black woman that she is, was not trying to hear it. Matters of sex were taboo in our house, so I stole books about human anatomy and read as much as I could understand. Feeling quite prepped, I hit the adolescent world ready to wreck shop and get me some.

VERSE FIVE

I pushed an old girlfriend into a wall. That incident will always be with me. I cannot forget it. As I said at the time, that incident forced me to see my lifelong behavior as a man for what it really was: sexist and utterly dangerous to women. But it is one thing to reflect on an experience such as that and a whole other matter to put into practice what I was feeling.

So, to be totally honest, I acted as if I were now the authority on sexism, from a male perspective. I gave female friends advice, lashed out at young Black men who committed similar or worse crimes than mine, and foolishly believed that I was healed of any sickness.

VERSE SIX

I saw my girlfriend's new apartment last night and I felt good for her. She doesn't need me. No woman, contrary to what society tells us, needs a man. It is her space, defined by her and for her. In the space we shared, rather than opening up and defining and sharing with her, I was, as she put it, "unpredictable," with one foot in the relationship, it seemed, and one foot out. Part of that has to do with the fact that I don't have a desire to be a breadwinner or the man of the house. That much I know. But that position, the resentment I have allowed to seep into my mind, doesn't excuse any sexist behavior I have exhibited.

VERSE SEVEN

She is moving out and I am not by myself but with myself. And forced to examine myself. My girlfriend is doing likewise. Whether or not we will be in a relationship much longer remains to be seen. We both claim we are exhausted by this two-year roller coaster ride. I'm sad because beneath all the negatives are some wonderful and positive experiences. I've learned more about a woman, her body, and her soul than in any prior relationship. I listened more. I participated more.

But the question lingers in my mind. Was I really serious about being in and sustaining a long-term relationship? Or was I, like so many men, merely committed just enough to receive the nourishment and emotional support that Black women have historically given to Black men?

VERSE EIGHT

This essay is late because the patterns of this relationship have changed from week to week, month to month. Who am I, really, to talk about and offer advice to other people about Black relationships? Yeah, given the racist and sexist nature of this society, Black-on-Black love is a necessity, a political act, if you will. But can healthy Black relationships exist where a Black person doesn't love him- or herself enough to evolve?

My girlfriend has moved out and the issue, ultimately, is not whether or not she and I will be together but what we have learned from this relationship and how we will apply that knowledge to future situations. The clichéd response from me would be that I should never resent a Black woman, that I have to learn how to control and channel my anger, that I have to redefine myself as a man.

But the deeper, more concrete answer lies in creating a love (for self and for others) which transcends petty differences (class, likes or dislikes, etc.) and fosters relationships based on mutual respect, trust, and unconditional commitment. One day, I assure myself often, I will be in that type of relationship.

A TICKET 'TIL MORNING

A NOVEL

DANIEL J. WIDEMAN

MORNING

It is morning many places at once. An arc of light through blue sky or sun cleaving dusk-colored clouds. Somewhere a dream bursts. Elsewhere another begins. Coffee and storms are brewing. Each will quench peculiar thirsts and drown certain vistas, certain pains and memories.

Nat runs arpeggios, runs his life out along the piano. His fingers black and white like the keys, transparent as they dance up and down with all the capriciousness of children skipping through hydrants in summer. But the notes released are heavy like leaden boulders. Deep within the piano, which sits hunched like a hibernating bear, the felt heads strike the delicate wires with the force of sledgehammers. Hands dance an ethereal ballet across the keys. Sparks glinting off rail ties as John Henry, shirtless and glistening, pounds away.

Saunders runs his hands across the map on his neck. He traces history and rivers along the scarred ridges and soft pockets of flesh. The Mississippi meanders around his esophagus and runs straight past the Euphrates into Da Nang. Many mornings his hands raft down these waters and come to rest in the hollow at the base of his throat. He is patient then, waits for the beat to begin, waits not for the comforting rhythm of a pulse but for the thrill of feeling his heart spew blood and silt up into the tributaries he has traced, valves pumping in time with the memories, and some days, creating new tempos, new currents to carry him along.

Rhodessa runs her hands across the bare canvas each morning before she begins. The texture tells her a story. It reminds her of the innocence she longs to feel. The language of colors is the language of guilt, and she wishes more than anything for the easel to remain clean. For it to frame a nothingness, a whiteness that will not betray her life, her sins, her pain. She looks out on the new dawn which is never quite new enough. No matter how early she rises, browns and reds and indigos have begun to run through the horizon, watercolor trails of tears, and so Rhodessa sighs and after a last lingering caress takes up her brush and begins.

Erned runs his hands along the smooth brown leather cue case. He has replaced the case countless times—as soon as the creases of age begin to groove and wrinkle the hide or the glossy luster begins to fade, as soon as it begins to betray any signs of a history longer than the moment, he exchanges it for a new one. The stick inside holds a life etched like Braille along its length. Were he to go blind he could run his fingers along the nicks and carved ridges the colors of beer and blood and recover all of his life he cares to remember and probably more. So the comfort of cradling that life within shiny new leather is enough succor for Erned. It means if he can make himself resist the zipper, can keep the shell around his life intact, the past will remain soft and new and redolent of the luxury that is brand-new leather.

Morning and hands, water and memories, many places at once. Fingers, hands running as fast as any legs across flesh, running away from time, into shadows, toward a dark green–shaded grotto where the bending branches of pines are like dark arms in church swaying over brown heads, limbs swaying in witness, arms that wave at Jesus and wipe away the demons always floating just above our heads. Can I or you or anyone take these hands into our own, turn them palms up, and find in the streams and crevices, in the sweat and calluses, fossiled testament to lives? To theirs? To yours? To mine?

RHODESSA AND EKELLE

She rolls fitfully through cotton, through parched bedding poised to ignite, flaming with the blue gas heat of her dream. The darkness cannot keep the room from rolling sharply, it is angled atilt like quarters at sea. Rhodessa buries her head beneath the pillow but cannot escape the rushing sound of waves breaking just above her head, water surrounding her in sleep, dragging her down, freefalling and weightless. She clings to sleep though the dream terrifies, wallows in the drowning depths she despises for she feels the voided pit

inside, the chasmic space where heart and hope should be, knows
by the torrents and pulling currents plaguing her sleep that she is
still empty and not yet ready to swim out of her dream and *somehow
begin the measured rise*. . . .

Valentine's morning. Ekelle. Wrenched awake before dawn, velvet
blackness of the sky her cushion, softening the rabbit punch that is
light of new day without Ekelle. Birthday Valentine morning again.
Ekelle. Rhodessa curls up tight beneath the covers, folds in upon
herself 'til she is nothing and listens for the sound of her daughter
entering the room. She wonders if this year she will finally be able
to disappear, relinquish the small space her crusted soul occupies
crushed into the corner of this dark room, evaporate into the charged
air and if she does, will Ekelle come? Stock-still but for the fluttering
hummingbird beat of a dead heart. Ekelle. Are you coming today
sweet one? She struggles each morning with the decision to rise. If
I don't get up, don't pad quietly into the bathroom, will there be no
room for Ekelle? And if I do, will she know I am not abandoning the
vigil, will she understand when I leave it is not from lack of faith
but because the day approaches, inexorably, and I cannot face the
colors of the river in the light? Is this the day, sugar plum? Sharp
arc of magenta cuts through the raven sky outside the window.
Morning leaks its first watercolor trail through the night and she
knows she must get up. Bathroom. She leaves water as empty as the
transparent liquid in the bowl and wonders why she bothers to flush.
Back in the indigo haze of the bedroom she stumbles and cries out.
Ekelle. The quilt she left immaculate and taut across the bed now
twisted into a serpentine curve, charting a sinuous course from tail
to tongue, Ekelle, a brown, beautiful python curled across her
mother's bed.

Why you name me for a snake, Mama? I'm scared of a snake,
ain't I?
No, baby, how can you be scared of something you never seen?
I saw a snake.
Hold still lil bits.
Hot comb a loom shuttling through knotted morning hair.
That how come you be keeping my head like this alla time?
What you mean, girl?
Little snakes hanging off my head.
Stop squirming around why you got to fidget so Ekelle?
Why then Mama?

Why what?

Why my name mean snake in bobo . . . in . . . how you say that African word?

Igbo. The Igbo people come from Nigeria.

Eebow. They be calling snakes Ekelles over there?

Burnt strawberry smell of grease on warm hair.

Fingers flying and colored beads snapping in the air.

Eke. They call a certain kind of snake *eke.* And that snake is the symbol for daughters to them.

Which one? Which kind, Mama?

The python.

They the ones that squeeze you right? And eat up them mice without chewin.

Plaits alive and warm, limpid across her palm.

From the roots, left over middle, right over left. A three-snake dance.

Who taught you about pythons, baby?

Nobody. I seen it on Channel Eleven.

Saw it. I saw it. You speak properly when you can help it, girl.

I saw it on the TV.

That's better. And you're right. Pythons are constrictors, which means they squeeze their prey.

I can squeeze real tight Mama.

Small brown head cocked to the side.

Smile wide as pie beggin for trouble, grin on her baby melts Rhodessa through.

You think so, huh? Come show your mama how strong you squeeze.

Sprung from her lap, skinny wires flung tight around her neck Ekelle hanging on for dear life and faces cheek on cheek strawberry and musk and morning breath hot head baby-soft skin tight together Mama love you love you too Mama squeeze again don't let . . .

That why you give me a snake name cause I squeeze so tight?

Rhodessa laughs, takes her daughter's hands in her lap.

They do much more besides just squeeze. The python is a sacred animal to the Igbo.

What that mean sacred?

Special. Very special.

Why a python so special?

Well, for one, did you know that the Igbo say a python should never be killed?

How come, Mama?

Well, the python stands for life, for daughters. They are the only
animal that can turn itself into the shape of a circle, like the circle
of life. The only time a python is killed where the Igbo live is when
a girl-child is born. Then they sacrifice a snake so that its sacred
spirit can enter the newborn child and keep her safe.

They say every little girl got a snake inside her?

Sort of. What they mean is every little girl has the magic of the
circle in her.

So if I got my magic already inside why I got to have snakes hanging off my head?

Quicksilver flash and she's gone. Halfway across the room, burst-
ing with giggles before Rhodessa drops the comb, gives chase, calling
to the wind:

If I catch you you gonna have more than snakes upside your head!

Strawberry grease, snake hair, time, whirring through shuttles in
a loom, beads and laughter the color of dew, all that's left of the
weaver and her child who've left the room.

How to paint a picture out of pain. How to blot out the pain with
love. Easy as laying a coat of color on top of the rough beige puckered
skin of canvas. That was how it began. She woke up the morning
after putting her child in the ground and knew she had to give life
to something. She needed a birthing to make her whole again and
didn't have time to wait. No time to grow a child. No love in her
heart to make one even if she had the time. Rhodessa woke up that
morning in the pitch-black just before dawn believing the day itself
was refusing to get born. She knew then she had to paint the day
into being or else it wouldn't come at all. Ripped the wrinkled sheet
off a sleepless bed and went searching for color. House empty as a
shell after what's inside crawls out for good. What's left then doesn't
even look like it was ever alive. More husk than shell. The luster
and gloss faded; shed skin is dead skin, desiccated bone, brittle like
plucked twigs in winter.

Out into the cold and down the street and still no color to be
found. Not the kind you could grab hold of, anyway. Yellowed porch-
lights gleaming like rheumatoid stars, sterile neon bar light a garish
red zebra stripe through the night, but no real color, none thick
enough to carry home, hot enough to burn the violet breath of dawn
into the longest night in the world.

Somehow her feet carrying her toward the lake. The last place in
the world she wanted to be, but her feet knowing she has to step

into that water, stand on the bank, close the circle, bring the snake-tail around to the head before she can walk anywhere else. As she slips quietly onto the shore, the water shivers and trembles, lets go its first ripple of the morning which quivers in the middle of the lake and then sets out undulating toward Rhodessa, a waterline. As it moves it changes from obsidian to silver to gold, then shimmers with the possibilities of all colors, touched by the sun peeking over the trees on the far bank, a ripple stretched out into a rainbow. She lifts her head and watches as its path becomes an *S*, then another, cutting perfect letters into the still slate of the water and racing toward her, spelling out a story in its wake, a serpent in the desert leaving fables and colors in the sand.

She gathers up this scene, a shawl she cannot quite stretch all the way around herself, and carries it home where she paints the world awake so she can breathe again, can hum the tune she always used to rock Ekelle to sleep.

NAT AND SALTY JOE

Satchmo in the house.
A fierce whisper, then a light swell.
Ain't that . . . Naw, can't be . . .
Damn straight it's him.
Satchmo be at the bar.
Smoke haze hangs like dream fog in Small's.
Rustle of silk and seersucker,
spray of fine oil as greased
coiffs whip and crane toward
whispered rumor.
Flash of gold through cigar cloud
an aureate pearl in an ivory smile.
Louis.
Satchmo's here.

Chokecherry cheeks of the women flush
their bodies draw taut as bowstring.
Languid smoke sizzles away
air suddenly too pure to breathe
currents of heat float stageward
waves wafting from deep beneath
carefully pressed folds of Saturday-night clothes
that got to be home in time for Sunday morning.

Nat alone on stage but
it is before so he is not sealed up
in soft silks
is not wrapped like a secret
gift not held
together by a shiny black bow tie
his flesh hot tonight beaded and wet
but it is before so it has not yet begun to melt.

Nat alone for these precious minutes
Salty Joe slinking away.
"Intermission," he announces the
parched crackle in his voice,
the deep wink and sloppy grin telling all
about where he's going; telling
everybody who's anybody who's woman and
don't mind sweet lemonade whiskey breath and
five minutes then nevermore.
His swagger says he needs more than ice water to
cool his lips
lips still hot from the honk
searing with hornjuice and weatherworn from
two hours of making trumpet love
need me a taste of mama now
little dark honey to sweeten my pot
ain't got another set in these chops
till they beef up on home cookin show me
the bull's-eye in your black-eyed bean, baby
this ham hock don't stray better
believe it, better believe in me now
    believe . . .

Nat's solos are soft riffs that make the bed
nimble neatness as he tucks hospital corners,
quiet and busy on the keyboard then he tiptoes
out the room, makes way
for Joe's raunchy rump busting;
horn a woman he rides to the upper register
all squeals and peals, hollers and wails.
He likes to sweat all the way through the sheets
make her come three or four times
remove all traces of angles and order before

he rolls over breathless and calls the butler
in to clean up,
Nat brings cool linen and the chorus
rolls out a blanket for the hot cascade of stars
to settle upon
the shards of flesh and wrung notes falling
like shrapnel around them.

Joe offstage, "busy out back" to anyone
not a sweet young thing that wants to know.
Nat can close his eyes now
he can breathe
feels the air clear around him when Joe
steps off the stage into the cologned
smoke funk of the club his silver
sword mute now, lying quietly on her side
light bouncing off the rim of the bell and
disappearing down that cavernous mouth
that bellows Nat into the background
when Joe puts it to his lips.

Nat's lids nictitate, then close over
smoke-burned eyeballs he sees
better this way Joe gone he can
breathe he lets his thin shoulders,
hunched against Joe's notes as
if braced for blows,
slump back now, arms poking further
out his sleeves, the bunched muscles
in his neck relax, begin to slew
to a new rhythm Nat unfolds
himself like a dark turtle emerging from its shell
his bald head effulgent in stagelight
brighter now that it is not fissile.
Salty Joe gone now so for a while
Nat need not play cantilena
to Joe's insouciant caterwaul he
can shed the sequacious style,
Nat can breathe now, he can hear,
he can close his eyes and remember the
rattling of gourds and curried goat
can breathe

can remember
can begin to
play.

Why you wanna work for free?
They ain't payin you to play intermission, man.
Don't know about down the islands brother
but up here we got a union.
You flash that cabaret card they got to
give you a half-hour break per set.
New York state law.
Half off your drinks too.
Panama don't take no liquor.
Yeah, he play clean and sober.
Wish *I* could do that.
He high and dry.
He got to be high to sit up there
doodling through the down time.
Got to be dry too—when that boy think he gonna piss?
Leave him be Joe.
Fine by me. Nigger wanna spend his break
feelin keys stead of honeys he can knock hisself out.
Ain't nobody listenin, Nat, give it a rest.
Let's go man.
Don't pay him no mind. He lost in the music.

VIOLATIONS:
EYE OF THE STORM

IS NOT A KNIFE

Omar McRoberts

Penis is not
Penis is not, brother
  is not a knife, not
  an instrument for cutting or killing, brother
Penis is not,
Penis is not, brother
  is not a skyscraper
with glass and steel
scraping atmospheres with foolish pride of Babel
  is not sanctuary wherein
capitalist imposition is schemed
Penis is not
Penis is not, brother
  is not a gun, despite
R. Kelly's album cover, despite
its dark casing, despite
its frequent use as weapon
  kept near the pelvis
Penis is not a knife, brother
Penis sends messenger of life
  is sensitiveprobing
  awareinquisitive with
a million nerves listening attentively, as if to
Jazz, or
  Sunshine, or

    a Rose
Penis is not, brother
    is not a knife, urgent and jagged tool
Penis gently waits
listening . . .

a prayer for Peace.

TRUST (THE RAPE OF)

TYEHIMBA JESS

on the day she tells me Black men ain't shit at first there is si-
    lence, there is us
sitting there with only circuit noise of television tuning in to the
    both of us.
there are her children and the patchworked furniture living room.

and clarence and anita.

better than "geraldo." better than "current affair." could even
    compete with a bulls game. it is a tv nightmare of dirty, dys-
    functional, dangerous, and confused laundry in which we are
    dress rehearsed for destruction. comes for three days and nights
    complete with eight white men sitting there with questions fol-
    lowed by the questioning of the questioners in news articles and
    headlines. and amid all the shuffle and commentary and opin-
    ions and rerun after rerun in the news something lies dying in
    the family as you wonder is its presence as tangible as coke
    cans, propositions over law books, and porno tapes?

it is something called trust.

question: this airing of dirty laundry. whether you choose clarence
    in long dong leer-crusted underwear, or anita clad in low-down
    schemin designer garments tailor-made for rolls in the burning
    bed of lies: is this a step toward building trust?

in our house that was the issue. it started when kennedy was on
trial. the senator's nephew the rich and powerful on Miami Long
Beach shores gettin his piece of the american dream as defined
by Playboy Mansion and uncle president and uncle senator.
Playboy legacy continued in the parted seam of her groin.
but this time all of america watched on cnn.

and america' watched. on tv monitors and front-page photos and
court tv we watched as a jury decides not guilty leaving the rest
of the country to debate and take sides. and then the flashbacks
started to happen. the rapes of days past stalked the earth again
in the flesh of wounded women trying to heal, who had thought
they were healed, but rape doesn't go away like a bad cold. it
lingers like a virus for the rest of a lifetime and is dealt with at
every depiction and mention of the deed. and that is why the
phone lines were so busy at the rape crisis center on an evening
of jury decisions, a night of rapes remembered, a night of kay being more and more stressed, the two rapes from her past tearing
out of her eyes and the face of the taxi driver, and the ex-boy-
friend's visage thrown on top of my shoulders as i try to lift the
burden of her ripped and throttled insides off of me trying to
stop the midnight sobbing as we dial the rape crisis center and
finally get through and she talks for over an hour. but it is over
two days before we really touch again, before we really love
again, before we really talk again without the lingering echo of
my denial:

no.
i am not a rapist.

as i search my mind for the times it came close, when eighteen
and horny and backseats and deserted parking lots mixed like
dynamite in my probing fingertips pushing back barrier after barrier of bras and blouses. and when there were no's and then hot
skin embracing mine mocking the sound of no. and i end the
search for rape in my past as i say it again i pray it again when i
tell her:

i am not a rapist.

are you sure?

what do you mean am i sure? i think i would know if i raped
someone.

but how do i know?

i don't know how you know. have i ever tried to rape you? do i
look like i would even try that?

i don't know.

what do you mean you don't know?
you're sure you've never raped anyone forced someone coerced her?

well i've been persistent, i've kept tryin' before but i've never taken
. . .

what do you mean you've been persistent?

shit you know, pleezbabypleezbabypleezbabybabybabypleez, you
know, all that shit. handseverywhereandallthat. you know.

yeah. i know.

no. not a rape. i am not a rapist. how could you know me for so long
and / i mean damn / i mean yes, i do have a dick / yes, i do listen
to Ice Cube / but i am not a rapist. that is not the sure sign of a
rapist goddamn you've known me for over a year shit do you really
think i would

howdoiknowhowdoiknow how do i know?

trust me
trust me
and believe in me
and please. i love you.
and i am not a rapist

and tv circuit noise tunin in:

in 1991 the fbi reported 106,593 rapes. that's 292 rapes per day, or 1 rape every five minutes . . .

hey, kay

from 1991 to 1992 there was a 128 percent increase in rapes. . . .

hey, it's me

thirteen percent of all women in a recent study have been victims of rape. . . .

it's me jess

twenty-nine percent of them had been raped more than once. . . .

remember me?

only sixteen percent of rapes were ever reported to police. . . .

hello?

strangers committed thirty percent of all rapes. . . .

i'm here.

acquaintances were responsible for fifty percent of all rapes. . . .

really, i'm here.

while lovers, friends and relatives committed twenty percent of rapes. . . .

> howdoiknow
> howdoiknow
> do i even know you did you ever feel the hands were
> you ever thrown to the floor and then knowing what's
> going to happen trying to put yourself a million miles
> away pretending it's happening to someone else cause
> it can't be happening to you, it can't be happening
> just praying for it to end soon cause now they have
> you pinned and now you even have to pretend like you

want it so it won't hurt so bad on the dirt of the
concrete of the floor of the empty warehouse hopin it
will be over soon closing your eyes clenching your
teeth and hating him cause he could be your brother
your cousin your daddy your son because he shares your
skin and hair and was cut from the same Black bone but
now is a hand on my throat a knee in my stomach and
an intruder in my womb as i wish to hate him hard as i
ever could and it would be easier if he were white but
no. before that night i would have called him brother.
and now i look at you and

are you really

my brother?

my brother.

i wonder have i met you before.
and have we ever together grasped the three-move
double-clasp handshake in passing or did we just
nod in slidin by each other down these south-side
corner-stood streets. have i sat next to you in
the bar or on the bus and laughed at our pussy-
laced jokes without realizing the hands you hold
the mouth you wear were hooks, claws of wrenched
fury on my lover's outstretched skin and mind.
you and i have traveled the same landscape of
browned breast and thigh but you rode through on
hooves of steel and razor in hand and i am here
now standing awed at the pain you left behind
years ago now rearing up again to stare at a life of
opened wounds. i mean i wonder: have i ever seen
you and what and what would i see? do your hands
still bleed pain of her thighs? hips still sound
of hammers pounding nightmare into midnight? lips
still feel torn flesh of her mouth? painter of
legacies of scream in the night, sculptor of
ripped flesh memories to reincarnate with mere
mention of the word *rape*, do you ever wake from
the nightmare that is yourself? like my lover
did, does, may always do?

and before i would call you my brother
  i would call you homeboy
  i would call you man
  and now i call you
  screamer into a music called woman
  mark of cain on Black man's brow
  breaker of trust we must break before we call you brother again.
  and
  would i call you miles.
  would i call you tyson.
  would i call you ike.

and would your fraternity of fools extend to clarence?

clarence this bullfrogged-looking man with an occasional cigar and
  full-time white wife and reagan appointments pushing him up a
  golden ladder for ten years and now talking about long dong silver,
  gritting his teeth, eyes bulging from electronic lynching as he dangles dangles dangles.

anita. shown in the daytime so only the unemployed and night shift-
  ers can see her straightforward glare into the tv high voltage bulbs
  flashing each second of videotape into our nation of a million
  minds searching for the slightest crack, the smallest flinch, the
  blink to send her to instant infamy.

and of course we are all sitting and watching and dangling along
  with him, flinching for her, watching the best tv show on. and the
  worst. and the two of us clinging to every word and occasional
  burst of emotion that frames the tv senate hearings in our living
  room late-night discussions all crammed into the tiny four corners
  of our tiny space as we listen and hear her saying it, the lines of
  her face drawn into revulsion and hatred like i can taste the words
  coming from her inner depths of betrayal she has felt, she has lived
  as she spits

"Black men ain't shit"

and the only thing i can do, almost as if i was waiting for that response, as if i had heard it before and this was only the refrain in
  an old and empty song, as if my tongue were on autopilot and my

hands on remote i utter the words and pointing to the five year
old playing on the carpet with

"tell that to your son"

i am not clarence thomas.
  i am not willie horton.
  i am not ike turner.
  i am not mack daddy.
  i am not absentee father.
  i am not drug runner.
  i am not child abuser.
  i would still have hands that do not hit.
  i would still have mouth that does not call you *bitch*.
  i would still have arms that hold you in love and not in anger.
  would our home be a temple. a shrine away from terror of no-
trust.

and i am looking at your son and seeing him as more than ever a
  link in a chain of unbroken minds reaching to tomorrow of un-
  beaten women and men satisfied with loving them and the sound
  of trust in the air like laughter and laughter and laughter.

and i am still cut from that same marrow of bone that you are cut
  from.
  i am still ancient flesh of your ancient flesh.
  we would still be one family.

tell that to your son.
  and let me tell him too.

Rio

Tony Medina

When I was young
it didn't use to be
like this
my brother didn't
always use to
smell like glue
Mama never had
to worry about
him being caught
by the cops
for stealing
or finding his
body in the
street with
his head
cracked open
by a bullet.
When I was young
I think I remember us
having food
& my hair
& my feet
being clean
& stroked
to sleep

by my mama's
hands
& not the fat
white ones
of the tourist
asleep in the
bed who'll
wake up any
minute and
pay me
with his drunken
breath
and turn me
out into the
cold waiting
for another john.
When I was young
I hated the
tourists
now I need them
& there's more
to choose from
tho I have no choices.
Some of them
want to make it
with a pregnant
girl
but I can't
go on like
this
I'll soon have
to find someone
to give me
a "heavy one"
one with big shoes
& strong legs
one that'll make sure
that it'll only take
one kick.
I can't afford
another baby.
Two years seems

so long.
When I was young
life was less
complicated.
I'm twelve.

Fist of Blues I

Ira Jones

why a man want'a screw every woman he sees
why my man's fist of blues want'a hit a pretty good-lovin' woman
  like me

fists filled with blues hit hard and low
his blues knocked me down to the floor

won't let me go no more
blues won't let me go no more

one day death gonna snatch his life right out the door
one day death'll knock and i won't see him no more

when he's dead and gone i ain't crying no bucket of tears
he's on his way to hell and i ain't drowning no sorrows in my
  beers

SELLING SHORT

CHARLES W. HARVEY

He say, "Hey, Nigguh,
Brown clay, red wine for blood—
Come here. Let me look at you.
Let me kiss yo' lips."
I say, "Hey man,
Alabaster skin, flax hair
Red wine for blood—
Ain't you talkin' about my momma?"
He say, "Oh no.
It's you, man. It's you."
I say, "A fag live down the street
With his daddy ina yellow shotgun house."
He say, "I don't like no fag.
They got too much of their momma's soft ways.
I like muscles, the hard edge of a man
His dark solitude, closed mouth."
I say, "Let me close my door."
He say, "Please, please, please!
I can do the James Brown."
I say, "I don't like James Brown.
Do you know William Burroughs?"
He say, "He's a fag writer, no I do not know him.
But I know Little Richard. I know Angel Face."
I say, "I know William Shakespeare
And what the Ides of March mean.

I ain't no nigguh."
He say, "Oh you one all right.
And you swallow men's babies."
I say, "Take your foot outta my dark door.
Ima call the police!"
He say, "I like police.
They so blue, cool, crisp, and kind."
I say, "Man, where you get your fantasies—
from the back end of Venus?
He say, "I get my fantasies
from looking at you, boy—
Your sleeping eyes, your hair soft
and black like the baby Jesus',
Your mother-of-pearl teeth, hard thighs,
heaving ribcage—
The smooth back of your adolescent neck,
Your hot testicles swimming with future generations,
And that rhinoceros horn there
that makes you shiver all jazzy—
You are where I get my fantasies, nigra.
And here is three hundred dollars."
I say, "Man, I ain't selling no black jazz to you."
He say, "Humph, uppity nigra.
There's plenty mo' where you come from."
I say, "A fag live down the street
With his daddy ina yellow shotgun house."
He turn his corpulent fat face to leave.
I say, "Hey Joe, ain't information worth a hundred dollars?"
He say for me to kiss where the sun don't shine.
I say, "The sun don't shine
In Cicero Illinois or Queens New York."
I close my dark door and lock away secrets.

WHEN DOGS BARK

CHARLES W. HARVEY

"New York's got two bad, bad habits," C.C. had said, standing black, naked, and wet next to me as we showered off dirt and chemical residue from our jobs at Baytown Exxon. "She'll trip your ass up and she's one long stinking fart." So far he's right about one. I've been here three days and this place never stops belching and farting—buses, sirens, taxis, trucks, subways, jackhammers, mouths yelling "fuck yoooou!"—so much noise. New York sounds like it's been eating beans all its life.

I'm here with Eartha Pearl visiting one of her relatives, the cousin with the buckteeth. She wants to be an actress. But between me, you, and the woods I think she's only cut out for beaver movies. I mean that girl can stand toe to toe with any beaver who decides some damn forest is in its way.

Eartha and this cousin get on my nerves after a few days of sitting in this tiny apartment—they doing that girl talk about men and me in particular—dishing up men's shortcomings. Stuff like "I don't know which is uglier, a naked man or a baboon turned inside out."

EARTHA PEARL: Some days I think I married a baboon . . .
COUSIN: One man can outstink a whole herd of goats . . .
EARTHA PEARL: I know one who can outstink two herds . . .
COUSIN: And honey, not a brain in their heads . . .
EARTHA PEARL: Lord, the biggest muscle *some* folks got is in their heads . . .

I growl softly at Eartha. She looks at me and hushes. Her cousin keeps jabbering away—those big teeth sawing the air as if it's wood. I begin barking.

"Oh Diane, I picked up a cute Butterick pattern for a pantsuit. It's virgin leather or something. I wish I could sew," says Eartha Pearl. Eartha's cousin looks at me like I'm queer.

"It's just his nerves when he gets angst out," Eartha says, smiling as if she's explaining a puppy's bad habit. I get up and put on my shoes. Eartha Pearl tries to establish her ownership rights to me.

"Who you know here? Where are you going?"

I say, "I got eight million friends here and ain't a damn one in this room!" I slam the door behind me.

Now by the time I get from the eleventh floor to the first, my mind kicks in. It must have been the blood on the wall on the fifth floor. My mind says, "Now Jethro, this is a crazy city. All of these eight million people ain't your friend. One of them will kill you if you let him. Go back!"

Naw. I ain't going back. Eartha Pearl and her cousin will just laugh at me. And I'd have to kill them to prove I was a man. I peep out the door and it looks innocent enough outside. Men and women passing by. Trash blowing in a circle. The sky looking like faded blue drawers. So I venture out and sit on the stoop. I look east and I look west. I look east and I look west. Then I look west and I look east.

I say, "Now wait a minute, Jethro, you ain't gonna have no cultural experiences stuck scared here on this stoop. Suppose Columbus had just sat on a stoop all his life. Just suppose. Shit. A man must take action!"

While I sit debating, this big white dude in chains and leather walks toward me. Now these chains ain't dainty little things you get from the Spiegel catalog. These chains come from the navy yard. I mean these chains can lift submarines. He wears three around his neck, five on each wrist, and two on each ankle. Now the chains do not bother me. The fact that he has on funky raw uncured leather does not bother me. Even the glass eye—I hope it's glass—dangling from his left earlobe on a chain does not bother me. What bothers me is when he turns in my direction, and grabs his grapefruit-sized crotch and smiles—that's what bothers ol' Jethro here. I say, "Uh-oh Jethro, somebody wants you to swing a certain way. And I don't swing that way." I wonder why he picks on me? So what if I do have on these black hightop sneakers, shorts with Texas bluebonnets all over them, and a pink T-shirt that says I BRAKE FOR MOONERS—that don't mean I'm gay. Shit. I'm just a colorful dude. Well okay if you want to count that time when I was in the eighth grade and me and Johnny Scardino grabbed each other's rods behind the gym bleachers. I wouldn't have gone back there with him, but he told me he had *two* and he would show me if I showed him mine. Okay it tickled and I got a hard-on when he grabbed me and I grabbed him out of reflexes, but I haven't *seen* Johnny since the eighth grade. I dreamed about him once since I been married to Eartha Pearl. But I woke up and made love to Eartha real quick.

So anyway I hang my head and growl softly at the man in leather. He must think I'm calling him to dinner cause he moves a little closer. When I see him step, I bark louder. And not yap yap like a poodle either. I'm Doberman and Great Dane combined. I rattle nearby windows. New York people stare at me as they walk by. And they tell me you're doing something when you can get a New Yorker to stare at you eye-level on the street. The dude slinks away like he's carrying a tail between his legs.

I say to myself, "Damn Jethro, my barking stuff is right on time. Damn if I'll ever let a head doctor take it from me." Fuck Eartha Pearl's suggestion. I get off the stoop and walk down the street barking my ass off. Nobody messes with me. Not even that gang on the corner with bones sewed to their leather jackets want a piece of me. I'm free as a pigeon. Do *I* stand up on the subway? Hell no! Sometimes I have a whole car of seats to myself.

Eartha Pearl and her man-hating cousin never want to go nowhere. When it's daytime, they say it's too hot. When it's evening, they say they don't want to get caught out at night. And when it's night Eartha and her cousin share the bed and give me a rug on the floor with my feet in the bathroom and my head in the kitchen. So I spend most of my time riding the subways and checking out the humanity that rides with me: brothers singing opera or preaching Malcolm X; cripples on crutches hustling dollars—throw a dime right back at your ass; folks changing clothes—stripping down to their swiss-cheese drawers and looking indignant at you for looking at them.

All Eartha Pearl experienced was that suicide that jumped out the window of her cousin's building. Of course that was something to see. We hear this screaming in broad open daylight and look out the window. There's something spread out like a bloody chicken on a car's roof. Downstairs in the middle of a circle of people, a young white boy lies naked on the roof of a black Cadillac with cow horns on the hood. His legs are spread as if he's relaxing on a bed instead of frying in his own hot blood. The car's owner stands with his arms folded across his chest. Every now and then he kicks a tire or fender and yells, "Goddamn!" In a window above us, an old woman waves and screams like a hawk.

"Goddamn! What she want me to do? Throw him back up to her? Who's gonna pay for my car?" the car's owner asks as he kicks a fender. Eartha Pearl has to have two valiums and a bottle of beer to make her eyes stop bugging out and her hands stop shaking. So maybe that's enough excitement for her. But I have to have something else. Something to make the blood rush through my heart like fire.

One day I'm sitting on the subway barking softly, but loud enough for people ten feet away to hear. I look up and see this sweet white chick in a pink leather miniskirt so high up her thighs she has to cross her muscular legs three times to keep out any drafts. So I stop barking and growl softly at her. I had heard that New York girls are the freest, and I love free samples. C.C. said all you have to do to get a New York girl is say, "Hello, I'm straight and AIDS-free." I growl at her again. She looks at me. I see her glance down at my legs and look off, slightly cutting her eyes at me. She plays with a lock of blonde hair that's curled behind her ear. I look down at my legs and have to admire them myself. I mean I'm no freak who stands in the mirror looking at my buck-naked self and saying, "Oh Daddy-o what a sweet daddy you are." But these legs always catch women. (They caught Eartha Pearl who, when she isn't mad at me and when we're in the bed, runs her hand up and down my smooth brown thighs calling me "doll legs.") I ask the chick what time was it.

"Tony," she says in a husky voice.

"Tony?" I ask.

"T-o-n-i," she spells out slowly.

"Well hey, forget about the time. All I got is time. I'm Jethro from Houston."

"Soho?"

"So? Baby, Houston is the baddest-ass city in Texas."

"I went to Texas once. Nothing was happening. Everything was flat and brown as a mud cake."

"Well, you see, you hadn't met me . . ."

"I've met every man, Mr. Dogman."

My brain searches for something clever to say, but my eyes stay on her smooth white legs twisted around each other—two long loaves of sweetness. I can see my legs twisted with hers—locked like a pair of brown-and-white fingers, soft, warm, and sensual. "What part of Texas was a chick like you roosting?" I ask her.

"Dalhart."

"Dalhart? Where in the hell is that?"

"You're from Texas. You ought to know, Mr. Dogman." She flutters her lashes.

"What were you doing in Dalhart?"

"I was stationed there in the army."

"Baby, you don't look like any kind of army girl I ever seen."

"I'm not." Her answer is sour as a lemon. Something tells me I have parted my lips before I listened to my brain. Damn Jethro be yourself, cool, man. You don't want the pussy to turn cold before you even get to the front door. What would C.C. say? Shit he even gave you some of his glow-in-the-dark rubbers that he uses for special occasions like birthdays and Christmas. Can't let C.C. down.

"You look like a nice man." Toni's voice brings our eyes together. There's a flutter in her lashes as if she's lying or has specks in her eyes. Her teeth are too big and her chin is too square for a woman's, I think.

"Well, I think I am. I mean I am nice. God knows I'm nice," I say. The sweat of my thighs glues me to the subway seat. A young woman the color of ebony sitting in front of us glares at me. She has been reading a book, but the nervousness in my voice makes her look up. Her gold earrings shaped like Africa tremble. She looks at Toni and goes back to her reading. Suddenly she slams her book shut and folds her arms across her chest. When she gets off the train I see her look into the window at us and shake her head like we are to be pitied. She then makes an ugly sign at me with her forefinger. Before I can make one back at her the crowd swallows her.

"Don't you scare off my cat, Mr. Dogman," Toni says as she opens the door to her apartment. She led me to her place—inviting me to smoke some herb and have a little drink. These New York girls!

I step into a pink zoo. Pink stuffed animals are all over the couch and chairs—elephants, turtles, bears, lions. Two pink alligators perch on her bed, mouths open waiting to bite my buck-naked ass when I get down to business, I think.

"You sure have lots of animals, baby," I say stroking her for-real white cat with pink ears.

"I like all kinds of animals."

"I see," I say, looking at myself in the huge gold-framed mirror on the ceiling above the bed.

"Pull your shoes off and relax. I'll get us a little smoke."

"I'm cool as a cat," I say, clearing my throat. For a moment I think I see Eartha Pearl staring at me from the ceiling. I bend over to pull off my shoes and my eyes fall on a small photograph in a gold frame. A square-faced white boy in an army suit smiles a toothy grin at me.

"Is your brother still in the service?"

"Who?" Toni looks puzzled as she hands me a bubble-shaped glass of amber liquid. She sits a flattened beetle ashtray on the table and lights the twisted end of a cigarette. She puffs on it and holds her breath. Toni thrusts the cigarette out to me.

"This dude here," I say. Toni looks at the guy as if she doesn't know him.

"Oh yes. I mean, I don't. . . . He's dead."

"I'm sorry. You got other brothers and sisters?"

She doesn't answer. She gets up and puts a Jimmy Smith record on the stereo. "This chick knows what's happening," I think. A white girl in Houston had tried to entice C.C. with Clint Black singing "Them Ol' High Alabamy Trees." C.C. said he couldn't make nothing happen.

Toni takes the cigarette from me and takes a hit. She smiles and asks me to dance. I take her hand and put my other one around her waist. Her back feels tight and muscled. It isn't fleshy like Eartha's. We rock back and forth like a pair of old people. Jimmy Smith's "Midnight Special" and Toni's intoxicating weed soon put me in a traveling mood. We start to glide all over the room. The organ's rhythm pulsates through me and moves down my thighs. Toni puts her face next to my cheek and cries softly.

"My whole family is gone away. I'm all alone, Jethro. I'm all alone. What can a nice man like you do for a lonely one like me? Can you hold me? Can you squeeze the loneliness out of me?"

I want to scream, "Pussy, here I come!" But I say quietly, "Yes baby, I can hold you." We sit down and she sits on my lap. She feels heavy. How can a little woman feel so heavy? Her wrists are thick, not thin and feathery. Her lips are rough as work gloves. The whiskey and the weed soon lighten and smooth all of Toni's rough edges. Her skirt and legs have the same velvety tickle. She brushes my hand away from her crotch. I pull down Toni's bra and caress her small breasts.

"I'm so lonely. Are you a nice man?"

"Yes, baby, yes. Let me show you how nice I am. I'll take you to Kilimanjaro and we'll smoothly ride down the Nile. Just let me get on the train, baby. Just let me ride." That Nile and Kilimanjaro works with Eartha Pearl, unless she's in her hurry-up-and-get-it-over mood.

Toni reaches up and pulls a cord. The lights go out.

"Can you put on a condom in the dark?" she asks.

"Baby, better than the queen can put on her gloves. I got my own." In the dark, my rod glows like a bright yellow banana. Toni's deep laughter fills the room. I curse C.C. under my breath. The cat's bright green eyes move side to side as he follows my swaying rod. Toni and I bray like mules. Then I smother Toni's laughter with kisses. I take another hit off the weed and the wheels of the train start to turn. I become Casey Jones. I can hear myself make train noises in Toni's ear. Suddenly I jump.

"Damn! I got two rods. What kind of herb is this making me grow two rods, baby?"

Toni throws her arms around my neck and kisses me.

"Just drive your train, Daddy. Just drive it. Just drive it Daddy. Ooh Daddy just drive. Lord have mercy. Drive me, sweet Daddy," Toni screams in my ear.

A sweet-tasting bug nibbles on my lips. I look up into the powder blue eyes of a nurse who's feeding me grapes. She places them one by one on my lips and I suck them into my mouth. There's a badge pinned over her left breast that says "Eartha Pearl" in small red letters. As I look into her face, a beard appears around the edges of her jaw. My eyes open. Toni stands over me with a bunch of cherries taped above each of his nipples. The cherries dangle juicy and red by their stems. He straddles my body. I pucker my lips around one of the cherries and pull it. Toni giggles like a young girl.

"Oh you're so much fun, baby. You're so much fun." I pull another cherry off Toni and eat it. I spit the pit toward the ceiling. It scatters to the floor.

"Ooh you animal," Toni softly scolds me. I pull a handful of cherries from Toni and stuff them in my mouth. "Ooh you big bad baby," Toni croons to me. "Give me the pits." Toni holds his hand under my mouth. I grab his fingers and put them in my mouth. Toni squeals and I pull him down next to me. We kiss.

"What do you want to eat?" Toni asks, slipping into his short silk kimono.

"Pancakes and eggs," I answer.

"Again?"

"I like the way you lick the syrup off my chest."

"I like the way you like me to," Toni giggles and bounces off to the kitchen.

I look up at the ceiling at me staring at myself in the mirror. You don't look like no punk, I say to myself. You don't wear lipstick and false eyelashes like Eartha's "aunt" Don. That fat sissy with his big feet jammed in pink high-heeled slippers. I spread my legs and look at the outline of my sex under the covers. Shit I'm a man, am a man, am a man! I fuck. I like the Celtics. I work my ass off. I made a baby once. So what if he trickled out of Eartha Pearl in the middle of Woolworth's like a bottle of cherries? I still made it. She the one who couldn't keep him. Toni Toni Boboni! Why didn't I knock the hell out of you? Got a rod bigger than mine. Fooling me up here. And I can't leave. Why can't I leave? I'm not a punk. I don't walk funny. Johnny Scardino walked funny. Johnny Scardino kissed my thigh after he blew me. I just stood there. Just stood there like a statue. I'm not a punk. Lots of men take a side trip now and then. I can leave. Just get up and toss Toni a dollar or two and say later alligator. . . .

"Sweet, sweet honeydew," Toni sings from the kitchen. "I can't get over this pageboy haircut you gave me. Are you sure you're not a hairdresser? The girls at the ball tonight are gonna flip when they see me dressed like a man."

"I don't know about that bullshit," I answer.

"Are you still sore about the leash? I told you it wasn't racial."

"Always a nigger got to have a chain around his neck," I answer.

"I wasn't thinking anything racial at all. I was thinking of your barking dog routine. We could really work those girls' nerves!"

"Well you're not putting a chain around my neck. You don't have to remind me I'm a nigger."

"Oh Jethro, for the last time! That's not what I meant! If you hadn't given me such a hairdo, I'd shoot you!" I can see Toni staring at his hair in the reflection of his coffeepot. I look at the nightstand littered with marijuana roaches and condoms. I look at the gray tube of K-Y Jelly squeezed violently by my own hands. I hate Toni and I want to beat him lifeless.

Toni brings the breakfast tray to bed. The fat pancakes are as smooth and brown as Eartha Pearl. "I can't wait to go shopping for our tuxes," he says. "Imagine me buying a tux! Me in pants. Girl, my friends . . ." I spit a mouthful of pancakes at Toni.

"I told you not to call me that." I grab Toni's arm and twist his wrist.

"Oww baby! I'm sorry. I just forgot."

"Just don't forget again." Toni wipes the pancake from his cheek. He tries to kiss me.

"Let me eat."

"But you've got syrup all over you."

"And you've got shit all over you. So beat it!"

Toni bursts into tears. "Oh Jethro! Jethro, don't be so mean to me."

"Shut up acting like a sissy!" I shout at him. Toni stops crying. A tear rolls down his cheek. He sits with his cat in his lap. They both stare at me as I eat—Toni as if I'm a god. The cat looks at me as if I'm a piece of shit.

"Sit with your legs apart!" I bark at Toni. "Men sit with their legs apart!" Toni parts his knees as if I've tossed hot coals between his legs. The cat falls to the floor, clawing Toni's thigh as he tries to hang on. It looks up at Toni and hisses before walking away. Toni shivers in the chair with his knees apart. I brush past him on my way to the kitchen. I stand for a moment at the sink and listen to him whimper and sniffle. A wave of sorrow washes over me. I want to hold him. (I'm the same with Eartha Pearl. When I hurt her and make her cry, love and remorse come up from the pit of my stomach. I get on my knees and beg her to forgive me. I kiss her thighs and hands until she rubs the back of my neck softly.) I walk over to Toni and put my hand on his shoulder. He stiffens his body at my touch. I gently soothe him.

"I'm sorry, baby," I say. "I'm so sorry." I wipe away the blood from his thigh with my fingers. He leans his head on my shoulder. His tears flow down my arm. I kiss him and coax him back to bed.

"Jethro, you've got to hurry! Will you come on! It's four o'clock and the stores close at five!" Toni races ahead of me wearing a pair of red platform shoes. His bell-bottom pants hug his ass and dangle like loose pajamas around his ankles. His shirt with red and pink roses squeezes his body like a sausage casing. His steps are short and prissy as if he's stepping on spit. People raise their eyebrows at us. I try to walk far behind Toni, but he turns around and pulls me next to him. My head swims. All I see are flowers and eyes circling me —frowning eyes, arched judging eyes, eyes burning us like hot coals.

"C'mon Jethro, c'mon," Toni sings to me over his shoulder.

Three young men dressed in gold chains and baseball caps pass me and Toni. I hear them snicker like mice. "C'mon Jethro, c'mon," one mimics Toni's singsong voice. I look around at them. The darkest one tugs at his crotch. I start toward him. Toni grabs my arm. "No, baby, you'll get us killed!" Toni pulls me away. "Ignore them, baby. Ignore them. . . ."

I snatch myself from Toni. "Stop walking so womanish and don't lean on me! Don't even talk to me." We walk on. Toni's shoulders are bowed. I've hurt him again. But all of this shame I feel. I'm hurting too. All of these eyes on me. "I'm hurting too, bitch," I shout at Toni. "Look what you're doing to me—dragging me through your fucking gutter! I don't want to go to some punks' ball. I don't want to bark my ass off for a bunch of queers. I want to go home, watch the Celtics, and play with my wife. She's got real knockers. She can't have a baby, but she's got real knockers!" I can see Toni shuddering like it's zero degrees. I feel a sharp pain in my tailbone. I grab my back.

"Hey faggot, that's how my ten-inch dick will feel up your ass!" I look around and a shower of glass and rocks rains toward me and Toni. We turn and run. I feel the needle-pricks of glass pierce my legs. I run fast and hard until I feel I'm reaching the edge of the world. It's not the bottles I'm running from. A voice screeching like a wounded animal chases me. "Pleeease stop, Jethro! Don't leave me, baby! Pleease! Pleease!"

Honking horns drown the voice in a noisy sea. I stop running. My legs feel as if they're wrapped in thorns. Every building is the same —tall, gray, and ugly. I imagine there are spirits flying out the windows and bumping into me on the sidewalk. Where in hell am I? I stop. There is something familiar about this block. In front of me leans a Cadillac with the roof dented in. I look into a window into the faces of Eartha Pearl and her cousin looking out at me—mouths open like two screaming cats.

"And you just walk in from nowhere and don't say a word about where you've been. Just walk in like King Jethro and don't have to give nobody an explanation. Ha! We owes *you* an explanation about why we standing there with our mouths open. Lord have mercy," Eartha Pearl sung at me all the way to the airport in the taxicab. "Legs all bloody. And then insulting my cousin the way you did.

Lord have mercy. I know it'll rain ice cubes in hell before she invites us up here again. 'Did you screw my wife while I was gone?' What kind of question was that to ask my cousin?"

"All of y'all know she's a dyke," I say smugly.

"It's nobody's business what she is. And how dare an ingrate like you call her names. She was the one on the phone all day and into the night calling hospitals, morgues, city police, transit police in every county in New York."

"Boroughs. New York has boroughs."

"Bastard, don't you dare correct me! Girl crying herself to fits being put on hold, hung up on, and screaming into that damn phone and here a son of a bitch like you call her a dyke and try to correct *me*! If I had half the guts of Momma's aunt Carrie, I'd gut you like a pig. Just like she did that husband of hers. Cut his roots off too! That's what a nigguh like you needs!"

The cab driver laughs. I know what he's laughing at. Some vision of me running down the street without my "roots," blood running from a hole beneath my belly. I try to kiss Eartha Pearl. But she's on fire with anger.

"How can you kiss me after what you've done to me and my cousin? When I let you kiss me again you'll be so old and senile you'll think I'm a man," she says with a sharp jab in my ribs.

Back in Houston a few months and the dust has settled, almost. I've gone back to work. The pain is gone out of my back and legs. Eartha Pearl has let me make love to her once. I've worn out my tongue telling C.C. about the hot chick I met on the subway, how she made me buck like a wild horse, and her fairy brother.

"Yeah man, her brother wanted to give me a blow job—but I drew the line there."

"Shit nigguh, uh-huh, I bet you did," C.C. says back to me. "I'da took him on and I know I ain't no punk, but turn down a blow job? Shit . . ."

Yeah I'm almost back to normal. If C.C. had said those words about punk and all to me a month ago, I would have barked at him. But those words don't trouble me so now. It's just, it's just that damn piece of paper that troubles me. I wish C.C. had thrown it in the trash instead of hollering out, "Well looky who's got them a letter from New York! Mr. Jethro Green, Manager, Exxon, Baytown, Texas, United States of America—Lord have mercy! Manager? Nigguh, what you tell them folks in New York you a manager of? You manages that shovel all right though!"

I snatched the letter from C.C. The first word I saw on the envelope was *Tony*. I jammed it in my back pocket. "It's just that chick's nutty brother," I said to all the laughing faces around me.

"Ha! I knowed you was lying about that blow job," C.C. bellowed.

That damn piece of paper—I crumble and toss in the trash, then sneak into the kitchen late at night and wipe the coffee grounds from it—I place it next to my heart.

Dear Jethro:

Please baby, Jethro, please call me. I love you. Here is some of my hair that you asked me to cut. Remember? I made it into a little bracelet for you. Don't that prove I love you? I thought you were going to be my life. You mean so much to me. Can you see the red tearstains on the letter? My heart is so broken my tears are red. I thought you were going to be my life. You loved me so and made me love myself. Why did you run away? Please, please call me.

Love,
Tony
your love

Some nights after I read that letter, I go out on the back porch and I bark and bark until the far-off sky turns red like a tear-filled eye. And Johnny Scardino's phone number rumbles through my head—all sevens and a zero.

PART THREE

BROTHERTALK

Rappin' with John Singleton

The following is an edited transcript of a conversation between John Singleton, Daniel Wideman, and Rohan Preston which took place on March 28, 1995, at Mr. Singleton's office in Culver City, CA.

PRESTON: We were saying beforehand that we don't really have an agenda. In many ways our project is just what you're doing, you know, in a different medium—we're writers, you're a filmmaker. . . .
WIDEMAN: We're trying to use this book as a forum. The subtitle is *Young Black Men on Love and Violence*, and we have people from the whole spectrum. I mean we have people who've never been published, we have people such as yourself who are in the public eye, and what we're trying to do is basically have an open discussion around some of the issues. By the way, I'm supposed to pass greetings to you from Patrick Day down at Texas Tech who was part of the *New York Times* piece.*
SINGLETON: They left a lot of stuff out.
PRESTON: But your voice came out of there real clear.
SINGLETON: Not as clear as I wanted it to be. One of the first things that I said was that America has traditionally made an industry out of the destruction of Black people. An industry that could be tan-

---

* "Who Will Help the Black Man?" *The New York Times Magazine*, December 4, 1994. This was a symposium moderated by Bob Herbert which included Mr. Singleton, Patrick Day, Ken Hamblin, Hugh Price, William Julius Wilson, and Joseph Marshall.

tamount to the industrial revolution where American industry learned how to make shoes quicker, how to process meat better, how to make products quicker. The whole supply-and-demand thing. To support this country, an industry has been created from the very beginning supported by institutional racism and the destruction of Black people. They didn't write that. *[Laughter]* It's very clear, you know.

WIDEMAN: Initially, one of the things that we ran up against [while writing this book] was [the publisher's desire] to get a little more gangster stuff, more [entries by] brothers in prison and drug dealers. . . .

SINGLETON: That's the effect. We have to get to the root of the cause. Those people are only acting out the social dysfunctions of society. Make no mistake about it. A Black man, and Black people in general in this country since the first Black person set foot in Virginia of his or her own unfree will *[laughter]*—we've been at war for our survival in this country and our survival is a miracle in itself. We're at war with our oppressors, we're at war with each other. Black men are at war with our women, Black women are at war with their men. Black women are at war with each other, Black men are at war with each other, and this has been going on for centuries.

It's created a climate in which we have a whole population of people, whether they know it or not, who are living out their own social dysfunction of being displaced. [But] we've made out pretty well over the centuries, by trying to create roots for ourselves, by creating foundations where there were none. When our language was taken away from us, we had to adopt this language and we've made it our own in terms of Black English. Our music was taken away from us, but we retained our rhythm, and we created jazz.

PRESTON: All of American music.

SINGLETON: Yes. So the thing is that Black America lives under the auspices of being a population whose survival is a miracle in itself, but a lot of people are running around thinking that they are not really at war, they're not really aware of the fact that they're at war, and they don't understand why so many things happen. Why Black men are killing other Black men, why everything in this society's institutions works against them. It's amazing how many people just don't understand how clear it is. You know, you could turn back the clock a hundred years and you could say, "Oh wow, they *did* have segregation, they *did* have Jim Crow, they *did* have public lynching," and then ask yourself, Do these things still exist today? They do, in other forms.

It was outlawed a hundred years ago for Black people to even learn how to read. [Now] everybody has the opportunity to learn how to read, but not everybody is—how can I say it—"encouraged" to because of the way that certain sections of society are set up in the inner city. People say, "Oh, there's a conspiracy," this white angst, this white contingent, and Black people always say, "There's a conspiracy to destroy Black people." It's *not* a conspiracy to destroy Black people; it's a very natural part of institutionalized racism to destroy Black people.

WIDEMAN: It's organic to its structure.

SINGLETON: It's not like they have to sit up and write a plan, because if they had to write up a plan then maybe there would be a chance. It's more dire and more evil in the sense that it's very natural for them to make us feel less than human. Right now there's something going on in the country with the so-called Contract with America. It's actually a contract *on* America.

It's amazing how continually, over the centuries, Black people have been used as scapegoats for the problems of the country as a whole. We're a very convenient scapegoat. It's almost as if Black America is treated like that pet that you stole off the street. When you walked up the street you thought it was a very cute pet and you kept it for a while and you fed it for a while, you have it around. . . .

PRESTON: You put it in the yard.

SINGLETON: Then you get sick of it and you put it in the yard, you don't want to feed it, you don't want to nurture it, and after a while you just send it off to the pound. That's why you have a large amount of brothers going to prison, you have a proliferation of drugs in this country, that's why that will never stop. There's an interest in keeping things very chaotic, so that certain social structures can come up to control that chaos.

If there is more violence among certain sectors of the urban population, if there is a need for more prisons, a need to subjugate the masses, the state and the government can say, "Oh well, we need more police, we need more government control over this." It allows people's rights to be taken away from them. It allows them to continue to lessen our humanity.

WIDEMAN: One of the insidious things about institutionalized racism is that precisely by making the decision to build more prisons as opposed to more schools, for example, you make a deliberate political strategy of oppression appear preordained. Because then what you're doing is saying, "Well, we're only building more prisons cause y'all are killing each other," and it doesn't go to the root cause.

SINGLETON: I think we're a step away from being where we were a hundred sixty-five years ago. They are making it possible for more Black people to go to prison, so there could come a day where at least fifty to sixty percent of the Black population in America is in prison, and somebody up there is going to think, "This is a labor force, an unused labor force." So what do we do? We don't want unions, we don't want to pay for unions, we don't like unions anymore, we're trying to get all these Mexicans out of here, why don't we just, you know, use Black prisoners as free labor? Which is back to a hundred sixty-five years ago. I mean, they do that right now in the South—they're called chain gangs. Chain gangs and those prison farms that they have.

WIDEMAN: They do it all over.

SINGLETON: But it's about to become more widespread, if you see my point. Because that is a labor force. They're gonna take away any rights that they have as human beings while they're in jail and give them only this: "You plant crops, you plant this." Then they can loan labor out from this prison over to the Dole corporation to pull up pineapples in Hawaii, or they can loan other prisoners out to plant tomatoes or plant cotton.

WIDEMAN: And the power of the media is so strong that they'll be able to put a spin on it so it seems this is legitimate . . .

SINGLETON: This is something that needs to be done . . .

WIDEMAN: This is rehabilitative.

SINGLETON: Yes. And there will always be a contingent of Black people that will look the other way and say, "Yes, that's right, that needs to be done."

PRESTON: I agree that it's not a conspiracy where someone's sitting around the boardroom saying "Let's kill the Negroes." But what's remarkable about how organic it is is that when Susan Smith, who's crazy—clearly beside herself and couldn't keep two and two together—ran her two little children in that lake, she knew in her unconscious that it was a Black man who did it.

SINGLETON: Yes.

PRESTON: And everybody believed her.

SINGLETON: And everybody believed her.

WIDEMAN: It's so deeply ingrained in the mind. As my father says, look at the three countries with the highest percentage of their populations incarcerated—South Africa, Russia, and the United States. Look what happened in Russia—revolution. What happened in

South Africa—revolution. What do you think's gonna happen here? And when you say that to people they turn it around and say, "Well this is a different case. It's not our 'population'; it's a certain 'segment' of our population that's incarcerated." But the facts remain the same, the portrait of Black men as inherently pathological remains. To me, that is declaring war, because if Black people are out there swallowing these images . . .

SINGLETON: Then it helps to create a cycle of delusion. It helps to support our dysfunction. That's one of the reasons why right now I'm leaning more toward not dealing with contemporary subjects and am trying to find other subjects within history to focus on that are relevant to today.

WIDEMAN: I'm working now on a project about the legacy of the African slave forts.* And I'm going to West Africa to research [this period] because I think you have to go back that far to find a time when our lives were in as much peril as they are in right now. A lot of stark parallels exist: brothers selling each other into slavery—whether it's actual physical slavery or mental and economic slavery is to me a moot point—for trinkets, for gold, for drugs, you understand what I'm saying.

So there are parallels but people don't learn the history, and it's not brought out in such a way that allows people to make those connections. You're not going to get a fifteen year old from South Central or the South Side of Chicago to sit still and study that history unless he perceives its connection to his reality.

SINGLETON: That's right.

WIDEMAN: And that, unfortunately, can only come through the popular culture. We're not reaching 'em through the books. We *can* reach 'em through the movies, we *can* reach 'em through the records, and that has to be the hook. Pop culture has to be the hook so that a kid who goes to a movie comes out saying, "I now have to go and do my homework, learn the real deal." But the question is, Are we gonna be able to make these films? Are we gonna be able to make these records? Are we gonna be able to create a hook that will do that?

SINGLETON: Not everybody's gonna be responsible enough to do that, though. Not everybody's thinking about the fact that a large segment of our population looks to these different forms of media for information.

PRESTON: Connected to the imagery is voice. When Black people are

* Simon & Schuster, January, 1997.

seen in film, there are expectations. With the nature programs, [Blacks] are presented in the same way that the animals are presented, and their languages are not translated.

WIDEMAN: You see Africans babbling next to chimpanzees, next to baboons.

WIDEMAN: When you turn on the "National Geographic" programs, the nature specials, they hardly distinguish between the animals and the people.

PRESTON: Because we are so "separated" from them we can't understand or hear the voices as language. Another image is the Black male on the news. We're so conditioned to see Black people with say, weapons, or to see Black people as automatically guilty that the most someone on the news walking by in handcuffs can say is "I'm innocent," you know, and we laugh. But in both of these situations, and in others as well, there's no voice.

WIDEMAN: You take a brother like O. J. Simpson who makes a living for twenty years speaking to the public. Now he's silenced. They're creating whatever image they want of him, and he has no voice.

It's a problem that cuts much deeper, not only in terms of silencing voices but of which voices are allowed a forum. I was watching *Poetic Justice*,* and it's clear to me why the critics reacted the way they did. This is a film in which you were trying to deal with the complex forces at work in Black male-female relationships. What does that have to do with . . .

SINGLETON: They know nothing about that. It has nothing to do with their lives.

WIDEMAN: What does that have to do with the pathological image of the Black gangsta? That's what they want. Not that they understood *Boyz N the Hood*, but they praised that because it let them point to the pathologies in the culture.

SINGLETON: And also, that film [*Boyz*] didn't point the finger at any larger [aspect] of white America. That film was all about the internal struggle within Black America. If you notice, *Higher Learning* is the first film I've done that actually says white male supremacy is the root of all evil within Western culture, so it's like, "How dare you!" But that's the truth.

WIDEMAN: It's amazing how people will deflect it.

SINGLETON: Because the large majority of white Americans are in denial about their past, are in denial about what they feel organically about anyone different from themselves.

* Singleton's second film.

PRESTON: And at the same time, they will gladly take all the privileges that come with it. There's such a tyrannical stereotype—I would even say a psychological violence—against Black people to the point where we're hobbled. We don't have full humanity. I know that you're struggling with that in your work and you've offered alternatives. How far are we on the road to getting that sort of voice? And in terms of Black male-female relationships, what can we do to forge a more unified approach to our problems instead of being so much at war?

WIDEMAN: We were talking about the fact that Black men and women are at war with each other, and we can point to all sorts of reasons. You have brothers actually believing the recent garbage about the "success" of Black women in white corporate America. When white people say, "Black women are taking your jobs; it's Black women who are taking those high managerial positions," you get Black people thinking we need to fight each other over one slice, or a few crumbs, instead of fighting together to eat the whole pie. People internalize that and it drives a wedge between them.

When people started sending in submissions for the book, we sat down and looked at them and said, "Wait a minute . . . where are the young brothers talking about Black women? Where are they talking about love and positive relationships with Black women?" We didn't get a lot of that at first. One of the things that strikes me is that in our field, in literature, Black women have made almost a cottage industry out of talking about Black male-female relationships. You have Toni Morrison, who deals with it from a historical perspective . . .

SINGLETON: Terry McMillan.

WIDEMAN: Terry McMillan, who deals with it from a contemporary perspective. Where are the brothers? Do we not love? Are we not in constructive, positive, affirming relationships? It's been difficult to get people to talk about that. My wife loved *Poetic Justice* precisely because she hadn't seen [those issues] from a young Black male perspective. Are there other male filmmakers trying to do that, and what about the Black female filmmakers you know? What sorts of issues are they dealing with?

SINGLETON: Well, I don't know. There really aren't a lot of sisters that are making films that are promoted in the mainstream. You gotta go to a Black bookstore and get the tape, you know what I'm saying, on the underground. I think the Black woman's voice is more prevalent in literature than the Black man's voice, now. The voice of Black men [can be] heard in films now. But it's very much a muddled voice. There are very few people speaking with any clarity in this medium, in filmmaking.

PRESTON: Can you elaborate on that?

SINGLETON: Well, it's just to say that nobody's dealing with anything real in film. But the sisters are dealing with real stuff in literature.

WIDEMAN: Let's discuss class for a minute. It seems to me that the Black middle class is growing, and the only way that it's going to continue to be allowed to expand is as long as the people in that class believe that their success is directly proportional to how far away they get from the hood. Psychologically, economically, in every way. People are swallowing that.

I hear constantly that what white America really fears is the Uzi-toting banger. And I say, No, what they really fear is a Black man who's come through the system and acquired wealth, status, etc., goes forward and mobilizes those resources (because the Black middle class has an enormous pool of resources), and commits them, stakes it all on a unified struggle for liberation.

But it seems like these people's words and works never come to light. They can never find a forum. We can turn on a TV and see bangers all day long, but you won't see that other side because I think that's where the *real* fear lies.

SINGLETON: I'm concentrating not on the urban stuff anymore, because I can do that with a grain of salt. I wanna do films about our historic struggle within this nation.

PRESTON: Nat Turner.

SINGLETON: I'd love to do a movie on Nat Turner. I'd love to do a movie on the Middle Passage. Films about the red summer in 1919. The door of no return.* You know the island dungeon you want to go in? Don't pay to go in. They use it as a tourist attraction. And they make you pay to go in.

WIDEMAN: I know. They did that in Ghana.

SINGLETON: I said, "I ain't gonna pay to go in. My ancestors paid too much to go in. I'm not gonna pay for it. I'ma *walk* in here." I walked in. They had all these Dutch people there. But we already paid the price. And there's a sign over the different doors when you go there. They separate the men, they separate the women. They have a sign for what are called "recalcitrants," the rebel groups, and then they have a place for the children. They used to pack 'em in like sardines.

---

* This was the "door," really nothing more than a hole in the stone, through which the captives passed to reach the slave ships. Locals called it "the door of no return" because those who went through it were never seen again.

And there's a sign that says, "Oh weep, young children, your cries are far from your mother's eyes and arms," something like that, and you go in there, you feel . . . you just feel the souls of these people, the souls of your ancestors. And it's so humbling. So much energy is just taken away from you; like your life force is just pulled away. I went there and I looked around and I just had to sit down. I didn't have any energy. That's one of the most significant experiences of my life. . . . That's the kind of stuff I'm leaning towards right now.

WIDEMAN: Well, if we can get that history documented, more power to you.

SINGLETON: They don't even want you to think about it.

WIDEMAN: They say, Go do that for PBS, right?

SINGLETON: No, man, this will be on the wide screen. *[Laughter all around.]*

PRESTON: I'm writing a book on the current Black arts renaissance. And in preliminary research for the book, I've found a pattern emerging. At the end of World War I, when Black men returned after performing so valiantly against all odds at home and abroad, they came back to a more hostile nation that created the red summer in 1919 and basically increased repression. But that was met by Garveyism and the Black arts renaissance. At the end of World War II a similar kind of thing happened with increased McCarthyite practices and oppression of Black people—we have all the FBI files . . .

WIDEMAN: We responded with the Civil Rights Movement.

PRESTON: We responded with the Civil Rights Movement and the Black arts movement. At the end of the cold war and the war against apartheid in South Africa we have a similar situation with the Contract *on* America. We have a similar situation in terms of the number of Black men who have been killed by each other, by the system, by whatever, the last five years, rivaling the number of people who were killed in Vietnam. Some people want to think that we're definitely gonna emerge out of it in a similar way based on these historical parallels.

WIDEMAN: But we don't have the institutional structures in place to ensure survival. That's what's frightening. As you're saying, we have voices that are muddled, that are all over the place, but we don't have ground-level organizations. Those movements in the forties and in the twenties grew out of a very strong community base. You had the church, you had . . .

SINGLETON: We also picked up people of different classes and status living within the Black community because of the color of their skin. They've tried to mute the class barrier within America, but at the same time they make people believe that if they make a certain amount of money they can be a part of the accepted norm.

It's a battle that I've been fighting constantly in the sense that I can never be deluded about the fact that no matter how much money I make, no matter how popular I am, no matter what the hype is—I'm still me. I could still get stopped on the street by two white cops and get shot in the head and nobody will ask any questions.

WIDEMAN: You're still one trip to the 7-Eleven away from getting humiliated.

SINGLETON: That's right.

WIDEMAN: And the problem is the allure, the attraction, and the power that comes with that success has corrupted so many people.

SINGLETON: Yes. I still live in a Black neighborhood because I'm really more comfortable living there. I can afford to live anywhere in the world but I'm really more comfortable living around my own people. In the sense that I know, strategically, what's going on. If I lived anywhere else in the city I'd run the risk of coming home one night with good intentions to my family, to my children, and having somebody stop me and say, "Hey, boy, what are you doing in this neighborhood?" I've grown up around only Black people, all my life. Inglewood, South Central L.A., Vermont and 101st. Only because I do business with different types of people am I now becoming more comfortable with them.

WIDEMAN: When you were coming up in that community even fifteen years ago, were the strongest male role models people in your family, or was there still that sense of successful brothers living in the area?

SINGLETON: No, I never looked up to drug dealers or nothing like that. I looked up to my father cause he was the strongest Black man that I knew. His name's Danny Singleton and he would always read his books called *Think and Grow Rich* and *The Power of Positive Thinking*, and he always used to tell me to say to myself that today is a great and a beautiful day in America and I'm the master of my destiny. And I would say that like a mantra when I was a teenager, you know, "Today is a great and a beautiful day in America and I'm the master of my abilities and my destiny." That became internalized. My father, he was the kind of man that would never let anybody Black or white disrespect him. It's like in *Boyz N the Hood* when the guy breaks in the house, you know, my father was there with a magnum to take him out. I can remember being in a theater with him, you know how we are when we're in a theater.

WIDEMAN: Loud!

SINGLETON: We get real emotional and loud and everything. We went to see this movie, *The Island of Dr. Moreau*, and he was real emotional and laughing out loud and this white man in front of him said, "Could you keep it down?" and my father kicked his chair and said, "Don't you ever tell me to be quiet! Who the fuck are you? I'll kick your ass! Shut the fuck up." He was that kind of man.

WIDEMAN: And he did, I bet.

SINGLETON: And the man was quiet. It's funny cause that happened to me one time when I was in film school. There was a movie that was showing at school called *Colors*. It was about two white cops, and they were billing it like it was about the gangs in L.A. as a marketing tool to get butts in the seats. I was so incensed after seeing the film and there was the producer up on the stage. They didn't let any Black people in except for a few film students, so there were five hundred white people around and just me and this girl that I brought there.

I was so incensed I was talking while the guy was talking on the stage and this guy in front of me was like, "Hey, could you keep it down?" and I kicked the back of his chair. My father in me kicked in at that point, you know, cause this guy was telling me to be quiet and I kicked his chair and said, "Don't you ever tell me to keep quiet!" And I stood up before everyone and I told the producer of this movie that the movie was bullshit, that it really was about two white cops and not about what's going on in South Central L.A. and that someday somebody was gonna come along and make a real movie about what it is to grow up in L.A., and within two and a half years I did that.

WIDEMAN: So much of our motivation comes from the anger and frustration that builds up and people don't understand—"Why are you angry at me? Why'd you kick my chair?" So often people say, "Why do you take it out on me? I didn't do this, I didn't do that," but I say to them, "Your sin is one of omission. If you didn't do anything, the fact that you're not doing anything is *more* infuriating to me." I'd rather have somebody come up in my face and call me all kinds of names because then you know who you're dealing with. I can deal with that. My parents taught me how to deal with somebody who's confrontational. When we were talking about the blindness of white America, the myopia is the most infuriating thing. That gets you more angry than anything.

I had a similar experience when I saw *Mississippi Burning* at Brown University in an auditorium full of white students. They came out, and what's funny is they all came up to us seeking the

Black students' approval: "Wasn't that good? Did you like it? We *loved* it."

I said, "Well, I've seen movies about cracker sheriffs before. This wasn't anything new." When they bill it as a movie about the Civil Rights struggle, it's not only that it makes us mad, it's that that pre-empts another movie, a real movie about the Civil Rights Movement, from getting made. They are not gonna bring one out next month because, "Oh, no, *Mississippi Burning* was about the Civil Rights Movement." So here comes John Singleton or Julie Dash or anyone else and the studios say, "Sorry, we just did that, we had that already." So it's a way of preempting us from telling our own stories. When we stop having the capacity, the ability, and the forum to tell our own stories, that's when we get in real trouble.

SINGLETON: That's right.

WIDEMAN: It's the power of stories that sustains a culture.

PRESTON: Can you tell us about the little boy John Singleton?

SINGLETON: The little boy? What do you mean?

PRESTON: As a child, your models of love?

SINGLETON: My mother and father, they never married. My father was seventeen when I was born and my mother was eighteen and she left home cause she got pregnant with me. I grew up a large part of my life shuttled in between my mother and my father. Even though they weren't married they lived within miles of each other and I could always catch the bus to see my father, or he would pick me up on weekends and we'd go to the movies and the park.

I'm very much a product of my mother's humor—and my mother's love and nurturing—and my father's intensity. My father has a great sense of humor too. I don't really understand how he became a man because his father was not around. But he did become a man. He says the army made him a man; he was in the army, in Vietnam. A lot of the man that he is, I've learned that I am very much a product of that.

My father told me at one time that he would never work for a white man. He'd sell pencils before he worked for the white man. After he left his job at Drug King as a manager, he got into sales and real estate and insurance. He didn't want his destiny determined by somebody in a company. I feel that I'm a very proud person. No matter what my decisions are, my decisions are based on that pride. I can't make a decision that would take away from me as a man— that would make me feel less of a man. I can't do a movie that I feel

I'm just doing to be doing, I can't fade myself like that, you know?
WIDEMAN: It seems somebody taught you love of self.
SINGLETON: I've learned love of self, love of my people. Everything else comes from that.
WIDEMAN: When you look at your children—how many children do you have?
SINGLETON: Two children.
WIDEMAN: When you look at them and how they're coming up . . .
SINGLETON: *[holding up their picture]* These are my babies.
PRESTON: They are beautiful.
WIDEMAN: When you look at them, obviously from a material standpoint they're gonna be taken care of, but in terms of looking into the future, what is the thing that you fear the most? In terms of your son, what do you fear the most? What can't you do for him as a father that frightens you?
SINGLETON: I can't protect him. At a certain point I can't protect him from everything, from forces of institutionalized racism. But what I can do is give him a foundation to fight that battle. The same foundation that my father gave me.
WIDEMAN: I think one of the biggest challenges is how to instill in children who are looking at the world we're looking at that sense of pride and self-love in the face of what's going on now. Throughout time it's been one of the biggest challenges, but I think now it is especially difficult given the increasing power and enlarging influence of a media equipped to project devastatingly simpleminded and debilitating images of us across the globe.
SINGLETON: I think that my children will be more prepared for that than many other children, as I was very much prepared for that. I felt that there was no way I was gonna let anybody make me feel less than I was because of the way I looked. I make it a point to exude that. I can look someone in the eye and just [intense stare] . . . you know. *[Laughter.]*
WIDEMAN: In terms of teaching love of Black women . . .
SINGLETON: Oh, that comes from me but that also comes from his mother.
WIDEMAN: How are we gonna prevent our kids from going to war with each other the way we are at war with each other?
SINGLETON: I'm really worried about my daughter and the world that she's coming into. The things she will have to deal with, conceptions of how to look and how to act.
PRESTON: How is parental love different now that you're on the giving end?

SINGLETON: I'm very much more at their mercy than I am at anyone else's. I take my daughter to school three times a week, I make her breakfast give her a bath, and clean her up and sometimes I get so tired I don't want to get up. So she comes in the room and she's like, "I want milk!"—She's two and a half—"I want milk!" and I get up and give her a bottle and get back in the bed and she'll jump up on me and put her feet in my back and look at TV, and I'm like, "Get your feet out my back!" and then she'll put her feet back on my back. Because she wants that closeness, just to put her feet on my back. Then she'll say, "I'm hungry, I'm hungry." And I have to get up and make her food, I have to feed her. I can't just sit there. The baby, he just cries and makes a certain noise when he wants food.

PRESTON: How old is he?

SINGLETON: He'll be a year this week.

PRESTON: What are their names?

SINGLETON: Masai and Justice.

WIDEMAN: After this upcoming tour of southern Africa, where *Higher Learning* will open, are you at work on other things?

SINGLETON: Several things. You know how a person can look at their work over a period of time and find reccurring themes? I think the predominant theme in my films now, if anything can be said about this, is the state of the Black man in America. This is not to exclude Black women, because they are all a part of it, but it's very much the state of the Black man in America from all different angles. It's a subject that I think I'm going to end up exploring through the course of my career as a filmmaker, depending on how long that is.

WIDEMAN: You mentioned going into a more historical mode.

SINGLETON: History has always fascinated me because truth is much stranger than fiction. Fiction is only a reflection of the truth, usually an aberration, and so I've really been concentrating on historical things.

PRESTON: Is there anything you can tell us about?

SINGLETON: I don't like doing that. Everybody I grew up with was all about, "I'ma do this, I'ma do that," and I'm the kind of person . . . I'm just gonna do it.

WIDEMAN: Which of your films is your favorite and why?

SINGLETON: I can't say that. I've done every film for different reasons. Each one of the films I've done has reflected a period in my life. I do films from an emotional standpoint. Whatever I'm feeling emotionally at that time I just do.

PRESTON: How is it working with Ice Cube?

SINGLETON: It's great working with Cube. He's just a soul brother.

WIDEMAN: It seems, from watching the end result, that there's lots of power. . . . You get people together and I'm sure half the best stuff happens when you turn the camera off.

SINGLETON: Oh yeah. We sit around just happy to be doing what we're doing and we know that millions of our brothers and sisters are gonna be seeing it and feeling the power of it.

PRESTON: My wife and I recently saw *Higher Learning* and the first thing we commented on was the caustic criticism it drew from people who didn't understand it. Most of the critics are white and coming from a much different place. But my wife said that to get to where there may be some understanding you had to go through this transition.

WIDEMAN: She talked about survivors. About how there was a crucible of violence and one of the statements the film was making was "Here's who made it." You know what I'm saying?

PRESTON: My wife said that as a Black woman, watching the ending where you have the brother and the white woman arriving at a better, or a mutual, understanding . . .

SINGLETON: It's not an understanding, they just meet.

WIDEMAN: I thought her issue was more, why did the sister get killed?

SINGLETON: Because she was the brightest and most significant thing in his life. Take that away, and he's lost the shining light in his life.

WIDEMAN: I didn't even think of it that way, which is interesting because when my wife and I go to films and we come out I'll say one thing and she will say, "Really? I didn't see that at all!" I think it's important that we dialogue about these things. Especially given the paucity of serious Black films, we're forced to look for all of our issues in one movie. Nobody reads Faulkner and asks why he didn't talk about the state of electoral politics—he's doing what he's doing and he gets respect. But I think there's such a hunger . . .

SINGLETON: For serious work. And it's not being fulfilled.

WIDEMAN: What steps can you take, given where you are and what you're doing now? What fronts are you at battle on?

SINGLETON: I can continue doing what I'm doing in terms of my film work and I can also try and support and help other people realize their visions. That's all I can do.

WIDEMAN: I think it's important that everybody recognize their limitations. If you look at some of our revolutionary heroes, they failed when they spread themselves too thin.

SINGLETON: Yes. Yeah.

WIDEMAN: If you do too much, you sacrifice.

SINGLETON: I'm just gonna try and concentrate on being the best filmmaker that I can. That's all.

WIDEMAN: Who do you like to read?

SINGLETON: Contemporary? I used to really be into Toni Morrison.

WIDEMAN: What was it that attracted you to her work?

SINGLETON: She has a very lyrical, poetic style to her work. And Langston Hughes, who I think is the best Black male literary poet of this century. If you're gonna point to anybody, Langston Hughes is the dude.

WIDEMAN: So much of how we learn is not only reading the work but meeting the people. That's an African thing. We are a people-centered people. It's not enough to read on the page. My wife's African; she's from Sierra Leone. Whenever she reads a book she asks me to tell her about the writer, what his life is like. When I was coming here she might say, "Well I wonder what his mama is like?" We need people's cultural background to contextualize what they are doing.

SINGLETON: That's right.

WIDEMAN: What we have to get past is allowing our culture to be demonized.

SINGLETON: By other people. And ourselves.

WIDEMAN: And ourselves. To me that's murder, because that person who swallows a demonized version of himself is doomed to destroy himself and probably three or four others.

PRESTON: What's that Maya Angelou quote? " 'You better create yourself . . .' "

WIDEMAN: " 'You better create yourself before somebody else creates you.' " And I think those are words to live by. There are people who make millions of dollars off inventing us. Further, they have positioned themselves to have the resources to be able to beam that image out to the world. That is one of the main battlefronts. Everybody talks about the arts being removed, where I think the arts are the heart of culture. No matter how corrupt popular culture may be, it's the most powerful tool we have.

SINGLETON: That's right. We can reach anybody.

WIDEMAN: And it can't help but be a corrupting power. But the struggle is not to allow that power to corrupt your work.

SINGLETON: That's good. It's a struggle to keep it from corrupting your work. At all times. A constant struggle to keep from being corrupted. I do what I gotta do. And if they come at me, I tell them to get the fuck out my face. There's a lot of money at stake, and I do what I do anyway. They're not gonna tell me how to make a movie. That's *my* movie—What you gonna do?

PRESTON: What's your favorite music?

SINGLETON: Black music. Nothing really contemporary. I love soul music from the mid-60's to the mid-70's. That's my thing. I love soul music in that period. I just love it. The Stylistics, the Dramatics, the Delphonics, and I love Diana Ross and the Supremes. I met Diana Ross personally for the first time recently.

PRESTON: Do you remember your first love?

SINGLETON: Love of what? A woman?

PRESTON: It could be. It could be anything. The first time you felt the capacity to love.

SINGLETON: I think my first love before I knew about women was film. Was being in a theater and feeling a film. Feeling the power of cinema. It's funny because that's something I'll always have to deal with in my relationships with women. How much I love movies in comparison to a particular person. I tell any girl I'm with, "I love movies," and they say, "Do you love me more or do you love movies?" and I always say, "Why you wanna ask me that?" I think it was the first time I was in a film and I felt something.

WIDEMAN: So you knew that's what you wanted to do very young.

SINGLETON: Yeah. And that's the only consistent love that I've ever had throughout my life outside the love for my parents.

A TALK WITH MICHAEL FRANTI

Rohan B Preston rapped with Michael Franti, the lead vocalist, composer, and band leader for conscious hip-hop, funk, reggae, and jazz outfit Spearhead, on Saturday, March 11 and Sunday, March 12, 1995, and Thursday, April 20, 1995. This transcript distills those conversations.

PRESTON: Big up the man named Michael Franti for staying conscious, staying positive, staying up, and for dropping some serious rhymes. Bup-bup!

FRANTI: Riiight! *[Chuckles.]* Respect to you, man, for being out there and staying up. I've been on the road awhile now and I'm just getting over strep throat and bronchitis at the same time. They put me on thermonuclear shit, so I'm feeling a little better.

PRESTON: I was talking with my brother, Lee, a couple of days ago, about growing up in America, man, and catching hell everywhere and from everyone, and how we were not prepared for it because our immigrant parents were sold on the American dream. Do you remember the first time you realized that you were adopted, and did your parents prepare you for the American reality?

FRANTI: I was pretty much a kid, about a year old, when my mother gave me up. I was in the foster-care system for a while—shuffled around from home to home. I was born in Oakland but when I was a kid I lived in Berkeley, Albany—all around the Bay, except for San Francisco. It was a good home environment. The family that raised me adopted another Black kid after me but my parents were both white. Although they did the best to raise me, you can't really teach culture, you have to experience it.

PRESTON: There is a broad discussion going on right now on the subject of interracial adoption. Did you have an experience which crystallized your position on the subject or did you just evolve into it?

FRANTI: I remember coming home from school, in kindergarten, when these kids called me a nigger. I got home and told my family that some kids called me the N-word (because we weren't allowed to curse at home). My parents told me about how sticks and stones can break your bones but words can't hurt you. As somebody who deals in language now, I know that definitely not to be true. Words do hurt people, sometimes more than they even realize. It wasn't until years later, in the fourth or fifth grade, when I began reading deep stuff like [Alex Haley's] *Roots*, [Eldridge Cleaver's] *Soul on Ice*, that I began to wake up, that I came to a different way of looking at white people, including people in my family. It clicked that there were people around who shared this hate, there were parents and whole families with this venom, and that changed the way that I walked through the neighborhood. It made me become a soldier, made me know how to balance things and what was necessary in different situations—how a sense of humor works, how being bad works, how being nice to people works. I really knew what it meant, then, to have other kids on the playground calling me "nigger." I felt it. And my parents didn't know how to deal with it. It can't be buried under the rug. My parents hadn't really taught me that white people can hate, so reading the stuff about the Panthers really spoke to my Black reality, really affirmed me.

PRESTON: Was that the first time you had heard the N-word?

FRANTI: No, but that was the first time somebody had hurled it at me in a hateful way.

PRESTON: Was that the beginning of your own awareness of your identity?

FRANTI: Definitely. That and other experiences began to form and inform me. I was a very rebellious kid—never felt like I could fit in the mix. That led me to have my own notions about race or whatever.

PRESTON: What were some of those notions?

FRANTI: Nothing in particular so much as how I viewed the world. I was always on the side of the underdog, whether in sports, arguments with friends, or whatever. I always chose the side that was supposed to come up short.

PRESTON: Was that also because you were adopted?

FRANTI: As a kid, I always wondered who my birth parents were. I never really felt that I fit in with my family, even though they tried to provide a good environment. When I went out in the world at twenty-one, I started looking for my birth family. It took two years, but I finally located them in 1989.

PRESTON: Where did you begin the search and how did you conduct it?

FRANTI: When I was adopted, they gave me a number. I went into the Oakland birth records and looked up that number in a microfiche file. There was a number that matched mine, without a name, just a number that said a baby boy was born to Ms. Lofy and Mr. Hopkins on my birthday. I then checked out the tax records and found that there was a woman who had had that name years earlier, and since "Lofy" was so unique, I figured it had to be my birth mother. No one lived in the area with that name, so I checked out the marriage records and the California tax records. I found her married name. She owned some property in California and the tax bills were being sent to Massachusetts. I got the number and just called her up.

PRESTON: Do you remember that first conversation?

FRANTI: Yeah. I called her and the first thing I said was "Let me give you my phone number, because I have something really important to tell you." I asked her if my birthday meant anything to her. She said, "Yes," and there was a long pause. She knew. We talked awhile but it was hard, you know, like you would imagine it—tight breathing, some awkwardness, and inexpressible emotion.

PRESTON: There must have been some serious hurting there?

FRANTI: It's like when somebody dies, except in reverse. You go through a grieving process. You want to know why—you're sad, you feel joy, you cry, you wonder. It's still an ongoing thing. I met my birth mother at the airport in Boston in the summer of 1989. When I saw her, it was how you would imagine a homecoming to be: you hug, there are tears and silences. But we really don't look alike. You can tell that we're kin if you look hard enough. Man, it was a heavy experience. It's a constant sorting through—some days I am energetic about it, other days I can't deal with it at all.

PRESTON: How did you feel then, and how has knowing more about your family affected your sense of who you are?

FRANTI: The white side of my family is still not able to grasp it, to embrace me. I am not able to fully grasp, as a father myself, how you could give up your child. My birth mother introduced me to my father and my paternal grandmother, who was raised by her grandmother because she, too, was given up—left on a doorstep by her mother. My grandmother was raised until she was twelve by her grandmother who was a slave. So, just like overnight, I came in contact with five, six generations of my history. Yes, that really transformed me in terms of the way I see myself, how I relate to people, everything. I'm very close to my [paternal] grandmother—she's a big source of strength. She told me that in life, you can't always be in a hurry; that's one of the things about my grandmother, who has taken care of other kids, raised them, and worked as a domestic: she instills in me great strength.

The first thing my grandmother said was, "Why didn't your mother bring you to me? I would have raised you." And she would have. When I look at my own life, I could recognize when I was a teenager making the decision to play basketball instead of continuing to hang out with fuck-ups; another turning point was deciding to find my birth parents.

PRESTON: I admire your integrity and honesty—that you're able to deal with this and other aspects of your life so openly. What happened the first time you met your birth mother?

FRANTI: When I met my birth mom, she said that the reason she gave me up for adoption was that she was moving back into her family and she didn't want me to grow up in that environment. I've had times when I really can't see or speak to her—it's too difficult to go there. At other times I force the issue, and say, "Yo, Mom, we're gonna talk."

PRESTON: And where is your birth father in all of this? You seem to have less anger for him.

FRANTI: Well, my father is another story. I am not close to him at all. I have less contact with my father, so because of that I have less anger. He had five kids with three different women. Now, at seventy-four or seventy-five, he is finally coming to see what it means to have all these kids. But the Black side of my family is more accepting of me—every aunt, every cousin was immediately there for me, inviting me to meals, and I have a greater affinity with them, a more natural vibe. The white side is just a little more white, and I don't mean that in a bad way but culturally. They are not as open to things and not as creative or expressive. And that was always hard for me growing up, especially now that I'm a musician and my whole world centers around expression. I see now that I'm an expressive person.

PRESTON: In my own life, I spent some time away from my parents, and that created some distance between us. Even now, I am not as close to them as I would be in an ideal world. Did you grow up with resentment because you did not know your birth family right off? How did you come to know and show love?

FRANTI: I had a very hard time expressing appreciation, expressing love for people. I loved basketball and I loved music, but it was awkward to express appreciation for other people. You got to get in your rhythm, your vibe, to do what you're put here to do. And that's where my spirit is, that's where my heart is, that's where my head is. The stuff that you do here and there, it's like trials to find yourself. I found it in basketball and music. Like if I started playing this "Stalag 17" riddim, it's simple, people can feel it riddling through, can feel what follows next. "Dum-dum, ta tada dah dah, dum-dum . . ."

PRESTON: "Ring the alarm, another sound is dying!" *[They break into Tenor Saw's "Ring the Alarm" and Franti freestyles.]*

FRANTI: That is why I love music—the poetry of the music, the soul expression. And you can reach people with funk, with reggae grooves that you make funky and sexy. People are beaten down daily everywhere they turn. They don't want to hear Spearhead hit them over the head with didactic lyrics. I didn't like most of my teachers for that reason. That's why I sometimes stop the music, reload, and come a little funkier. . . . But back to my own behavior. It wasn't until I had a kid when I was twenty years old and started looking at the example that my own family was for me, since my adoptive parents were alcoholics (they quit when I ran away at seventeen), that I began to really understand. That's when I saw clearly the things I didn't want to repeat and realized that I had to snap out of crazy behavior. So my son is growing up completely different from me.

PRESTON: Your dislike of school must have also shown up on your report card.

FRANTI: I used to get A's and F's. I liked English, history, art, and writing. I hated chemistry, biology, and math, although now I really like them. Just the other day I was talking to a friend about how we invented math in Egypt and we've gotten so far away from it, so far away from what we've created, from what we used to know.

I had lots of fights as a kid, and they weren't always about race. People knew they could always get into fights with me. So I was in the after-school problem-child program all the time, always in detention after school. The shit that's tripped out about it is there would be all of us Black kids and the Mexicans on one side and on the other side, the white burnouts. We were the minority, but they came up with some names for the white kids who were fucking up, some more clinical names, whereas we were problems.

PRESTON: When I see you in concert and look at your audiences, I think, If you had been a youngster, you would probably be kicking more than lyrics to them. . . .

FRANTI: Even though I was a big kid, I probably got my ass kicked as many times as I kicked ass. But I also learned the limits of my own strength and learned that I could cause hurt. I remember grabbing this kid's collar, holding him until he turned blue and purple. And people were yelling, "Yo, Mike, you're gonna hurt him." That's when I realized how I could hurt somebody. At another time, I was reading this book on some gangs when this kid threatened me. I said that I was gonna stab this country redneck. I brought a knife to school and put it in a wine bottle. It's like the teachers knew where I was headed. They threatened to send me to juvenile hall. It really began to dawn on me that there were other ways to solve conflict. After that, I was always a class clown.

PRESTON: What do you say to your son about school?

FRANTI: He loves school, he is into chess, his nickname is Genius. He's on a different level, thinking about stuff that I could not have thought about when I was his age. He told me he wants to be a judge. And Cappy loves chess. So he brings home chess homework, you know, because he's in the chess club. Normally, I try to let him win fifty percent of the games but two nights ago, I was on the phone while I was playing, and he goes, "Daddy, checkmate!" That's the first time he really beat me. I am proud of him. Sometimes I look at my life and ask, How could my mother have done that (Give me up for adoption)? I love my son dearly. I love my girlfriend, Tara, and I love the people who love me.

PRESTON: And your parents—birth and adoptive?

FRANTI: [Pause.] I have love for the people who raised me and for the people who brought me into the world. But as you get a little bit older, you realize that love is not the infatuation that you have with your girlfriend; it's that energy, that force that pulls you into the conflict, into that struggle, that makes you say, "We have to get through this, whatever it is, if we have to fight, to cry, to fast or purge." Love is that intangible thing.

PRESTON: Sounds like courage and stamina.

FRANTI: Yes, courage, stamina, and energy. I have to want to, have the energy, drive, honesty, and courage to work it through, to work it out.

PRESTON: How do you deal with anger or frustration? You have said that you couldn't focus in school because that was not the thing for you.

FRANTI: "Every man thinks that his burden is the heaviest . . .

PRESTON: "But who feels it, knows it, Lord."*

FRANTI: I may not have suffered more than anybody else, but I know my own struggles and achievements. And I am thankful. Things might have been completely different for me.

PRESTON: In many ways, your background and hardships helped create your dynamism as an artist.

FRANTI: The fact that I grew up as a Black person, living around white people, and at the same time I saw both sides of the fence, spent my life with one leg on one side and the other on the other, trying to make sure my nuts don't get squashed. At the end of the day you're still Black.

If I didn't get involved with basketball, I don't know what I would be doing. School was boring, not fun at all. And I didn't agree with the authoritarian nature of school—the teachers would say shit like "A civilization is a culture with a written history," and you are supposed to accept it. I remember arguing in fifth grade with teachers. I argued that white people didn't read history until they invented the printing press. And what about oral history? Those types of questions weren't supposed to come up.

PRESTON: How did you get to where you are today?

FRANTI: I was at the University of San Francisco, home of Bill Cartwright and K. C. Jones and Bill Russell, all my heroes. I was studying communications and playing varsity basketball when my son came. I was going out with his mom, about eight years older, and after six weeks, she said, "I'm pregnant." It put a halt to my studies. I transferred schools, went to San Francisco State, and started studying in interdisciplinary arts programs. I made up my own program, combined the film and music industries. After a while, I realized that I was already doing all the shit I was studying. I took time off to work and became a bike messenger, which allowed me to do my music. I was a bike messenger for about two years. I used to love it because when you're out there on your bike, you don't have any boss. Once they tell you where to go, it's just you. It gave me a lot of time to think, to sort out stuff and still be real physical, get all that frustration, that energy, out of my system.

PRESTON: Are you on good terms with your son's mother?

* The Wailers, "Who Feels It (Knows It)"

FRANTI: We don't hang out today and we're not exactly friends and buddies. But we're coparents. Like when I'm on tour to Japan, she keeps him. She's a great mother. And we have a terrific child together.

I got to break, got to go pick up my son. My birthday is tomorrow and we're going to see the Warriors play the Kings. It's a total b-ball birthday.

PRESTON: Well thanks for your time, man.

FRANTI: Peace.

PRESTON: Peace.

FATHERS AND SONS:
PASSIN' IT ON

FOR MALCOLM

You taught us to stand
when lying down was easy
we've fallen again.

—Jake Wideman

April 3-4, 1968

George Elliott Clarke

A century of rain smoulders in luscious,
Stark richness. He meccas through wet lightning
To the church to chant his death. He feels sparks,
Something torching the tindered, fissile air.
To the pulpit he ascends, thundering
Justice, Jesus, and John, because God
Mapped the Promised Land; his voice splinters,
Lightning rives the rapt church:
I've been to the mountaintop. Tomorrow,
After the rain, he steps into the cool
Dusk, into the cool, wet, Tennessee dusk.
   Andy dreams he hears an engine crackle.
Ralph jumps *instinctively*, then turns, then turns,
And sees King, his arms outstretched, blood blazing
From the hole the bullet's punched through his neck.

The Martyrdom of
el-Hajj Malik el-Shabazz

George Elliott Clarke

Like bees scenting the myrrh and frankincense
Of his flesh, bullets congregate around him;
Blood honeys at the entrance-wounds in his heart.
Smoke—the nepenthe of his own death—staggers him;
He falls, becoming a garden of perfumes.
The faithful swath him in ivory muslin,
But his flesh goes farther, straining into starlight.

Days Ahead and Journeys

Jabari Asim

(for G'Ra)

on a Saturday,
amid push and yell,
you arrived:
a dreamlike thing.

wet, cold, and cautious,
aching for the absent, blood-warm womb,
you peered through narrow eyes
into harsh lights, deep darks,
shifting shadows.
how strange the world must have seemed!

absorbed in the navigation of this newness,
the sound of your own excited voice,
the pumping in and out of air,
you could not have noticed
your father carefully counting
the ten tiny fingers,
the ten tiny toes.
he, too, was absorbed,
pleased by the perfect completion
of your voyage.

he removed himself
and left the life tending

to more experienced hands,
reluctant, but secure in his knowledge:

there will be time enough for touching
there will be days ahead and journeys.

Night Vigil

Jabari Asim

(for G'Ra)

my eyes focus and blink tightly:
once, twice, like a camera shutter,
wanting to take a picture of this moment
and commit to memory
you lying weak and silent,
the too-sweet smell of sickness
seeping from your skin.

i will want to tell you
about nights like this,
when you were too tired to lift your head
and i sat like a stone beside the bed
feeling your pain,
close enough to hear the roaring
in your thunderstruck stomach.

my mind's eye takes snapshots
of you stretched out and struggling
to breathe,
embracing your old striped shirt
like a favorite friend.

my eyes blink again,
once, twice,

seeing your fingers reach out to rub
the comforting cloth.

i hope to have many pictures
in the days to come
when i am old like your shirt,
and you have learned to stroke women
with that same soft touch.

DEEPER THAN MEMORY

JABARI ASIM

(for G'Ra)

I

your second year is a series of trials.

this time our test takes the form
of three little lumps
suddenly seen
swelling like bad magic
against the tender curve of your skull.

II

surgery on so young a child
is such a shame;
each incision is a sharp pain
that cuts deeper than memory.

while you lie spellbound
under the ether,
your mother and I wait
and hide our heads in books
as if words could shield us
from howling doubt.

afterward:
your bald patch so surprisingly brown,
the strips of stitches like tiny teeth,
leering grins that mock our love.

SPITTING IMAGE

JABARI ASIM

(you know who)

they think one good whipping is what you need
to tame your too-quick tongue, but
your sass is safe with me. once I
suffered the same condition: a trickster
trapped in a four-year-old body.

your movements are mirrors
freeing memories long locked under skin.
you bring music with each step,
shedding seasons as you go.

G-man
Ra
Hannibal
Babe Boy
Special One
these are affirmations,
songs I chant to name my renewal.

who would think you'd be this tall?
"high waters" is your middle name.

there's a great growing up going on.

DADDY

ANONYMOUS

Dear Father,

It has been seven years since I last saw you. I believe it was Thanksgiving 1988, but we may have even seen each other briefly around Christmas of the same year. None of those encounters were particularly memorable and I would have avoided all of them if there was somewhere else for a college senior on break to go. Anyway, although I want to, I can't say that I have missed you much. These seven years have been ones of intense growth, soul searching, and honesty. I am developing integrity and know how to be faithful— how to tell the truth, how to love my mate and remain true, and how to be of genuinely good cheer (grandparents taught me that). I am also trying hard to trust people, although it's very difficult and I automatically cut off anyone whose bad ways remind me of yours.

Although you did not come to my wedding (you said that you never received the two invitations we sent), I plan to have children soon and would like them to know their paternal grandparents. I would also like to get to know you better, to understand you more, and to purge this bitterness for you in my heart. And though I still have reservations about your honesty, and had vowed to myself that the next time I saw you would probably be at your funeral (even though I might very well go before you), I am willing to work on it with you. I am willing to forgive you for your physical and psychological mistreatment, although it's impossible to forget your brutality.

I wish I knew how you came to be the way you are. As you know, your five children and daughter-in-law recently gathered in a prayer circle—the first time all of us had been together since 1988—and we thanked God for bringing us together, for helping us survive and thrive through all the things that we have been through with and without you. And we were a teary-eyed motley lot of joy and sadness. It is hard to think of your transformation from how you were in Jamaica to your station here. How did you turn into such a person? What happened to the hero of my youth?

After you and Mummy left Jamaica for New York in the early 1970s, my sister, Winsome, and I stayed there with Mama and Papa [your in-laws, Mummy's parents]. I knew you then only as a faraway myth a Foreign. I knew you then as "Daddy." You were the one the people of our district spoke of in hallowed terms—even the elders whom you could call by their first names. You were the one they pointed to often, of whom they said with longing, "Bwoy, Mas P—— is such a wonderful man. You have the best father anywhere, Chaplin." Oh, yeah, they greeted me after you, even though I cracked no jokes. And sometimes they even hailed youngster me as "Mister," pronouncing it with delight and saying that they wished Winsome and I were their grandchildren.

Naturally, the other children had red eyes, envy, because of all things we had. When they came by the dozens to watch television at our home on Saturdays, when they came to ride my tricycle or play with my remote air planes (which you sent down), I (through you) was the apple of their eye. And the adults too—family, district people, but also strangers in then far-away places such as Galina, Annotto Bay, Oracabessa, even Kingston—strangers who had heard of you and Mummy would swoon over Winsome and me, calling out our pedigree of brains and character.

Everyone kept reminding us that we had to live up to great parents a Foreign. We were expected and encouraged to excel, and sometimes did. You and Mummy were so well regarded that even though you had left Winsome and me with Mama and Papa and we did not really know you, we were very proud and happy to be your children. Teachers encouraged us in school by reciting your test scores, accolades, and other educational achievements. They pointed to the way you treated everybody in our family as lessons in virtue and generosity (and you often played gift-giving father to the whole district). They pointed often too to your great promise, with frequent (and idle) talk that you (the accountant) and Mummy (the teacher) would be prime ministers one day, that you would come back to help early-seventies JA and stop the "fingerings" (killings). That was when I started saying that *I*, after you, would be P.M. too.

When you and Mummy came out once or twice a year, those were the most highly anticipated events in the district—after Easter and Boxing Day. Everyone wanted to be the first to look in the barrels of foodstuff and clothes and gifts that you brought. Remember the food and music and dancing? My guardian grandparents would kill a ram, make mannish water (soup), jerk some pork and chicken, make sour sop juice and carrot juice, cook run-down. . . . Lawd. And Uncle C—— and Uncle P—— would set up the sound system out a road—skittering but sweet tweeters and heavy, liquid bass—and many people from district and town came to the ram-jam session.

And Winsome and I could even stay up later than usual, eating with both hands, drinking put-it-back [dragon stout and condensed milk with a cracked egg and nutmeg], romping and making merry with our playmates, all the while staying away from the adults holding their corners. And when you entered, everybody welcomed you. There were broad smiles all around and the deejays sent nuff respects. And people beamed at me too, your firstborn son, the firstborn of all my grandparents and great-grandparents. If I could have bottled my pride and joy those days-into-nights, I would have had enough to last a lifetime.

After playing with my mates and leaving the dance to the big people, Papa, our late but dear grandfather, would begin his horror storytime in moonshine—the crickets, pattoos, music, and occasional dog bark mingling in for good effect. He regaled and frightened us with rolling-calf duppies which dragged chains around like clanking innards, traipsing up and down in their satanic chariots. And then there were tales of immense snakes which swallowed goats and cows, and eagles so large they could snap up teenagers.

That's when we wanted to put those questions to you—because those big snakes and eagles could only be found a Foreign and you were fresh out of New York. We needed to know more. But I don't remember ever sleeping with you, Daddy—those nights or ever. Did you stay in the district then or did you go to the next one and rest with your parents, or at your home across from theirs? (I liked that big house, the envy of your parents' district, and the cars you had, but none of that ever felt like home. In fact, the last few times that

I have gone home to JA, I have barely recognized what used to be a fine place.)

Do you remember the first time we had some real time—several days—together when I was big enough to understand? I was on the cusp of ten. We went to Little River to bathe that June day in 1976. I wetted the tip of my towel and snapped it in excitement—the crack sounding like a little version of Papa's Winchester. And you told me true stories about Foreign—about how there was no need to fetch water because it was in your house and how you could get anything you wanted as long as you had the money. You told me about how there were many colleges and they were better, and education would be free if I worked hard enough.

And when I told you I wanted to fly planes, you even told me to become a barrister instead because a legal accident was less likely to result in death. Besides, there were many attorneys in positions of leadership, but not too many pilots. I always answered "lawyer" when people asked me later what I wanted to do. (Still later, you filled out "physician" in the career goal section of one of my college scholarship questionnaires, remember?)

A few days after that river romp, we played cricket in the yard, with real cork-and-talk and regulation lignum vitae instead of the tennis balls and coconut-stalk bats we boys had been using to practice. (The good gear, including leather balls, was reserved for test matches.) And while other adults took care to bowl slow balls to your son, you said then that I was your youth, and should be treated like a man. I remember swelling with pride. Then you came in hard with a pace ball that mashed up my too-too. Everyone had to take a look at the inflamed gonads, the sting and fire swelling your youth's little wood. I was out of the game, but pretended not to be too hurt.

Years later, after going through a couple of junior high school blood brawls in Brooklyn—I learned to never surrender from you—I can say with certainty that your pace ball had hurt me dearly. Anyway, I don't hold that against you. Besides, when I got licked later in a championship match, it didn't faze me—I had already been there, and your cricket-captain son set a good example by not being bowled out.

Those are the only memories I have of you in my childhood. And I did not mean to reject you when I recalled with fondness things done with Papa or Mama or my great-grandmother.

When Winsome and I, twelve and thirteen, finally joined you and Mummy in 1979, leaving a JA burning with gunfire and rumors, New York was quite a culture shock. We had come from a familiar community of several hundred, where the worst thing people did was susu-susu pon each other, to a glistening, artificially-lit megalopolis of ten million where I was to witness and experience harrowing muggings. I still can't forget how New York looked from the air that night, endless pulsing lights as if all the world's chandeliers had been lit there. Winsome and I chewed gum like you and Mummy had told us to keep our ears popping. And then you picked us up in your leathery car, dragging on a Winston and explaining what all the lights were.

When we got to your apartment, our new home, Winsome and I rejoined our younger kin—our brother, Clive, and sisters, Sandra and Millicent, who were born here. We did not know them well but it was not a big deal because our grandparents also reared our first and second cousins whose parents were in England and Canada. Besides, we were all blood of the same blood, flesh of the same flesh. And Winsome and I were also older than they were.

After forcing ourselves to, Winsome and I got used to Mummy's bland chicken and fried plantains. We started spelling it "Mommy" since, you said, the other spelling was an eye rhyme with an Egyptian cadaver, even though we pronounced the *u* with a cushion. I even stopped eating bun-bun, because you said it was unbecoming and "bush" to eat from the bottom of the rice pot.

But it was hard to get used to not having a yard to play in and not being able to go outside. Even then I could see why you wouldn't want us to wrap up with what you called the streetside streggae and hooligans of Prospect Heights. I resented, and still think it was wrong, that you simply cooped us all up except for visits to the market, school, and the library. We barely even went to church. True, you worked at least two jobs—doing books, driving cabs, and other odd jobs—and were redoing your degree. (Mummy worked and went to school too.)

But after our schoolwork was completed, what then—television? more reading? I had studied all the state histories, music this and that, calculus, sciences, and was tired of the encyclopedias. And whereas we always played village host in JA, you didn't allow us to have friends over since the three-bedroom apartment-home wasn't something (large? clean?) enough. It became more immediately obvious that to you "parent" was synonymous with "owner." And your uncompromising strictness—compounded by your temper and paranoia—ultimately began the unraveling of our relationship and our family.

"Let me say that I do believe that, in your hard-driving way, you honestly wanted the best for us, even if it seemed at times like you simply wanted to be a boasty parent. And I had a hint of some of the stresses you faced as a proud, accented immigrant man in Brooklyn who had known a much better life back a Yard and had been accustomed to much more respect, admiration and fairness, socially and at work. Maybe if you had walked us through some of your challenges and had shown a little more respect for us as individuals, my relationship with you would be different. But you released the pent-up pressures (caused, I now acknowledge, by your descent into a lower social class, your lack of community and your lower-than-deserved station at the job) on those who loved and admired you the most, even if you doubted the sincerity of that love.

You have left me, my brother, and my sisters, with layered, deep scars all over our bodies. And our psyches are really a moonscape, though various forms of therapy have helped some. The hurt sometimes feel like tufts of needles beneath the skin. Even though my body carries the memories of your beatings, I think that I got off fairly easy, with only a few welts on my thighs. Winsome, Clive, Sandra, and Millicent were not as lucky.

Father, do you recall the time you busted Winsome's eardrum when she was only fourteen—she spent eight hours in the emergency room? We had just come back from visiting Aunty C——, then our only family in New York, and you said that Winsome had done or not done something or another. She had to have treatments for six months to retain her hearing. I picked up the pattern that whenever we visited Aunty C——, the only place we were allowed to go for pleasure, we came back to certain beatings. I don't agree with you that she was part of a conspiracy to destroy your reputation and career. We only saw her as our aunt like all of our aunts and uncles. We only saw encouragement (and joy) in her small gifts. I don't believe she was showing that she had more than we did.

There are so many memories of you thumping Mummy in her stomach and face, of you breaking her ribs with the wickets from the cricket gear I had. That is how I know of the scars all over her body, not because Mummy and I are lying down together, as you continue to say, but because I witnessed it. And, instead of defending herself, she made up excuses about why Babylon [the police] should not be involved.

When I went on spring break to Jamaica in 1987, you beat Mummy till she couldn't move, couldn't turn, because you said you were the one who should have gone, that I was probably down there telling them lies about you. You crushed Mummy's left ankle and foot with the car in 1988—remember her screams and the black-blue-purple of her internal wounds? And in March 1992, after you had moved to Maryland, you locked Mummy out of the house, accusing her of having a man. When Millicent couldn't tell you where Mummy was, you bloodied your youngest daughter with keys in your hands, busting her face and leaving that inch-long high-rise slash she still wears on her right cheek.

When Sandra and Millicent refused to stay in the house at all times, you would wait until just before ten P.M., then report them to the Oxon Hill police as missing or runaway juvenile delinquents so that they could be locked up. And after they refused to give you the money that they earned baby-sitting the little boy next door, you told the neighbors that your own daughters, fifteen and sixteen, had AIDS and that they were running a prostitution ring in the neighbors' place. You always told my sisters, for as long as they can remember, how they would become nothing but prostitutes. Fortunately, none of them fulfilled your bad blessing. You told even them, as soon as they developed any friendships, that their girlfriends were their lesbian lovers.

When I worked summer jobs, beginning at fourteen, you and Mummy would take my paychecks, saying I was impertinent and facety to object. My "impertinence" made you come after me with that knife in August 1985, remember? After the police came, you called your brothers in Canada to let them know how terrible your children were, how they were conspiring to destroy you. Your ransacking of my belongings got worse. I could never find any of my own things because you kept searching for evidence to show that we were plotting to destroy you. And as if you hadn't stripped me of my privacy then, you always came into the bathroom when I was in there. Always.

And then there were the other things: I kept meeting half-sisters and -brothers whose birthdays are quite close to ours. We now know of five, scattered from Hartford to Jamaica and Canada, including one who is younger than I am by only a month or so. (You gladly claim her now that she has won a national beauty pageant.) You cheated on Mummy during your very first year of marriage—how could you? At various points, you even introduced your firstborn son to your lovers.

There were times, after your heinous verbal and physical punishments, that I would think of boiling you in the hot oil which lapped at chicken on the stove. Indeed, I began to develop (in my teenage head) many exquisite tortures for you. There was the vat of curdling acid over which you were suspended on a fraying rope—you wouldn't die right away, of course, your skin would just peel away gradually. And after any of the times you draped me up and put a belt to my backside, there was the ratchet in your throat and you bawling like a billy goat. After you decked me in summer 1985— blacked me out as I sat up on my bed, with a left to my right jaw because I hadn't signed over the check from my summer job—I began thinking of guns.

But instead, I moved out—ran away, really—down the block to a friend who was only a few years older. He was living with a girlfriend and a roommate who also lived with his girlfriend. And there I was, sleeping on their living room floor. For two weeks. And, to me, it was heaven, even though I can now see the perspective of my hosts. I was finally free of your terror, your stubbed cursing.

The things that really stuck with me, more than the beatings, were your words. I had tried to please you academically, even if you kept reminding me that you were and would always be smarter. And physically, I tried to be manly by building up muscles, even if you said you would always be stronger.

But your lying to and on me, from China to Chicago, that I was smoking ganja, that I was a battyman, that I did not love you and was not proud that you were my father—those words really hurt. I began to see your hatred. I will have you know that I was more receptive to those things—ganja and homosexuality—after that.

I have never really apologized for calling the police on you that summer night in 1985—after years of your daring me to. I knew what it meant when I did it—to call the New York 5-0 on a Black man—but you made it out alive even though I had hoped otherwise. I had come to the decision after you had boxed me down that you were worse than the wicked people you said were holding you back on the job. I had come to the conclusion that it might have been better for Mummy to try to raise us solo or for you to put us in orphanages. I know that I did not want to remain in any way close to you, and that is why when I got a chance to go to college, I jumped and have never looked back, at least not to you.

And it's not my fault that all my siblings left as soon as they turned sixteen. I know that you haven't seen Winsome, now twenty-six, in four years or Millicent, now nineteen, in two. I am the only one to finish college so far although I know that my brother and three sisters are strong, beautiful, and talented and will do so some day, despite your bad blessings. It would be great for the family to get together again, you together with Mummy and then all of us together. But it would only be surface, unless you have really changed. I know that you are against therapy but it will help us all.

Today, I know you as the man who sired me, my biological father. But it is difficult to say "Daddy," because the affection, respect, endearment, and love in that term wore off long ago. The myth of you is manifest and I am no longer a child.

You are with me in ways that I do not care to acknowledge. The two people who I have genuinely loathed in my life, Dick Pritcher and Fuba Somting (not their real names), have replicated to a tee the traits in you which I abhor most. Both are lying, dishonest, and deceitful samfi men who gained my trust only to try to undermine me. Even though I have not seen these two in years, I recognize the suggestions and declarations of their presence and yours often enough and, deny as I might, these deceits always call out your name. They tell me that I cannot run away from you.

Worse, I do not want to become what I fear in you. Whenever I find myself blowing up or wanting to tell a lie or put someone down, I try to catch myself, to remind myself of broad human genius.

I am writing now so that I may purge. I have been afraid of writing a letter such as this to you and certainly would like to have some sort of redemption.

When I first heard that some Jamaican man had shot up a train on Long Island, I prayed that it was not you. When I saw Colin Ferguson, I was struck by how much he resembled you and talked like you.

I have called up many things in this letter which you, no doubt, can explain, even point to as more evidence of the conspiracies against you. You say that the whole family is at war against you. I disagree. All I know is that it's unhealthy for me to carry around all this toxic and noxious stuff.

I hope that you are willing to make a good-faith effort to heal. I want to embrace you, to say and mean "I love you." Most of all, I hope one day, once again to call you Daddy. One day.

Song for Father

Omar McRoberts

Long ago, a father or fathers
would take sons into
dark trackless woods and ruff
them up a bit, teach them laws of
Society and Universe, teach them
Mysteries of Manhood. I
remember no such night journey, yet I
know that over

years I
have undergone silent powerful
initiation with you, Father.
For in your example I
have found seed of mysteries.

You have shown
Paradoxes of Right Action and
Selfless Giving. You have given gentle
Wisdom and Peaceofmind.
And you have shown hidden art of
Introspection:
only art which can
save world from Itself.

Father, you offered truths to me in a
night journey of years and I
emerge from darkness with thirst for
Mysteries
more awesome consuming than even Manhood.
Father, you have shown sacred art, and I
thank you.
Father, you have put seed of Thirst in me—
and for this, Father,
I love you.

No Character

Charles W. Harvey

My father was no character.
Simply a man who ate a lot,
Loved the Tropicana, jumbo shrimp in crispy skins,
Stood on the cut in sharp-toed orange shoes
Outside of places where cue balls
Cracked like knuckles,
Answered the "Whys" a little boy rushed
To his ears like rainwater pouring, as he steady
Piloted the red-and-white winged Plymouth.

He was the one I conned into
Buying me candy at the market—
A bear in yellow hard hat
Taking me for rides in a big-mouthed truck,
Dozing in church, breathing heavy,
Flicking a napkined breeze toward his face
Like you bat away a fly,
Leaping over fences before lying
Gray-skinned and still in his casket.

This, the only time I feared him.

EDDY

CHARLES W. HARVEY

Our Fathers who art not of heaven
But who reside on earth—flesh, bones, and death—
Sometimes they do not know love.
They know women. They know sex and baseball.
To them a "thing" between men
Must be hidden in smoky bars,
Shielded by amber bottles of beer,
Backslapping brotherhood, and dark shades to hide soft eyes.
Touches must be shoulder-level.
Comparisons are allowed over restroom urinals.
But then they quickly say, "My *woman* likes me this way."
Hand squeezings are allowed for dying buddies—
Hugs for brothers, sometimes.
Eddy, you must resist kissing your mother—
This is what our Fathers mean
When they say, "Act like a man."
Yes you can cry on a battlefield
As you place your comrade's severed hand
In a body bag.
But you can't keep shedding tears the day after
And the day after . . .

When you learn you are no longer the lighted vision
Your Father had when he lifted you and saw his symbol
Between your bowed legs, and named you his name—

When he knows you'd prefer to love the sun
Than battle the wind,
When he sees your mother in your walk
When he knows you will not be another
Dark shaded MacArthur who walks on water
And spits out the bones of men,
When he knows all of these things
And gives you his raised eyebrows—
Dance on like you dance,
Like a man stepping on burning tongues.

REBELLIONS, REVOLUTIONS
AND OTHER RIGHTEOUS ACTS

———

HAIKU

A revolution
without vision duplicates
present misery.

Pure white princess, kiss
a frog, make a prince, kiss a
nigger, cause a lynch.

If peace is the end
of resisting status quo
I am a warmonger.

Can a people thrive
with its values exploited
merely to survive?

What is the difference
between rusted, black shackles
and an untrained mind?

—JAKE WIDEMAN

WHEN NIGGAS LOVE REVOLUTION LIKE THEY LOVE THE BULLS

TYEHIMBA JESS

When niggas love Revolution like they love the bulls
youth will wear red, black, and green patches
over the emblems on their starter jackets.

When niggas love Revolution like they love the bulls
brothas will gather regularly at barbershops and cornerstops to
discuss george jackson, the handbook of revolutionary warfare,
and people's war before they go home to take care of their
children each night.

When niggas love Revolution like they love the bulls
playground basketball courts will become paramilitary training
grounds where we learn to shoot guns at the enemy
                                     not baskets for bets.

When niggas love Revolution like they love the bulls
we will spend hours and hours watching our children grow into
soldiers, not basketball players.

When niggas love Revolution like they love the bulls
We will know cia stats
                 fbi stats
                 infant mortality stats
                 police brutality stats
                 political prisoners and prisoners of war

       and literacy training techniques like we know
paxson's shoe size
pippen's rebounds
grant's salary
and all the intimate details of michael's last gambling spree.

When niggas love Revolution like they love the bulls
you will be able to ask any youth on the street
who is angela davis?
who is sundiata acoli?
who is assata shakur?
who is mutulu shakur?
who is queen mother moore?
and they will be able to tell you without skipping a beat.

When niggas love Revolution like they love the bulls
you will go on to ask them about michael jordan
and they will say: *who?*

When niggas love Revolution like they love the bulls
masses of us will go down to tear up a carolina coroner and his
office to find out what *really* happened to james jordan, instead of
waiting on the word of newspapers and sheriff's offices.

When niggas love Revolution like they love the bulls
they will start to seriously wonder why one negro putting a brown
ball through a white net makes more money in one season than
they will make in an entire lifetime . . . and *do something about it.*

When niggas love Revolution like they love the bulls
you will see phil jackson running up and down an empty court
minutes before game time screaming:

              WHERE ARE MY NIGGAS?
              WHERE ARE MY NIGGAS?
              WHERE ARE MY NIGGAS?

as those niggas leave the stadium to
go build schools in their community.

When niggas love Revolution like they love the bulls
all niggas will refuse to shoot ball with the president . . .
with or without their dashikis on.

When niggas love Revolution like they love the bulls
swisshhhh will become associated with the sound that cia agents
and drug dealers make when they are thrown gracefully face first
into open manholes.

When niggas love Revolution like they love the bulls
nike will no longer be able to sell hundred sixty dollar basketball
   shoes
in our community because
we would rather spend the money on liberation, thank you.

When niggas love Revolution like they love the bulls
they will love it   more than chitlins
                      more than all my children
                      more than jheri curls
                      more than permanents
                      more than cadillacs

cause
When niggas love Revolution like they love the bulls
When niggas love they family like they love the bulls
When niggas love they children like they love the bulls
When niggas love to be free like they love the bulls
When niggas love struggle like they love the bulls
When niggas love dignity like they love the bulls
When niggas love niggas like they love the bulls

we will become Black people

and the bullshit will hit the fan.

South Central Olympics

CHARLIE BRAXTON

it's happy hour
here on d-day of
decision for
the masses of
south central
los angeles and
the son of man
stands still
at the blazing edge of night
his hand tightly
clutching
a molotov cocktail
shouting:
"no justice no peace
no peace no justice
you y'all it's on
strike a match and
let the flames begin"

THE FIRE THIS TIME

MICHAEL DATCHER

fire *vb* 1: kindle; ignite 2: stir; enliven 3: shoot

When I was eleven, a policeman yanked his gun from his holster and pointed it directly at the bridge of my nose. He yelled, "Freeze!"

I was shaking so violently that he yelled, "Freeze" again.

My four preteen friends and I had found an abandoned newspaper machine that someone had forced their way into. There were a few more coins in the machine. We were trying to shake them out. Someone called the police. Three police cars rolled up, sirens off for the surprise attack. Out of the police car closest to me a white policeman jumped, his arms fully extended, both hands squeezed around his pistol's handle (just like on TV). He had to squat down to line up the bridge of my nose. I have heard it said that when a person is extremely afraid, or near death, his whole life flashes before him. This is true. My eleven years rushed by as if they were being chased by time itself. He had his gun ten inches from my head. I was eleven. He called me a nigger. I am from L.A.

I was a Lakers fan when Paula Abdul was a Lakers Girl. Before Jack Nicholson began sitting courtside. I fluently speak Lakers announcer Chick Hearn's frenetic language; I have spoken to Lakers owner Dr. Jerry Buss about the menace that the Celtics are, met his unsettlingly beautiful wife, confirming once again that money talks. I played ball at Venice Beach, knew white men couldn't jump long before larger than lifesize images of Wesley Snipes and Woody Harrelson began to appear in the innards of our nation's dingy cities: on the sides of dirty buses, on the tops of yellow taxis that would never stop round midnight to pick up a man of Wesley's jazzy complexion.

I was at the Compton club, Dootos, when rapper Dr. Dre was judging a rap contest. Seemingly to my surprise alone, a five-foot five-inch, S-curl wearin, nonlyrical brother with a Raiders cap squeezed around his oily locks won first prize. Women (fine women) were ecstatically releasing screams, like orgasms on late-night cable. I finally asked the brother next to me, "Who is this cat?" "That's E, man," he replied. A few years later, E and his curl would become Easy E, leader of N.W.A. . . . I have known, lived next to, played with, admired, and feared Crips, and seen Crips kill two Bloods at a party in Melody's Dance Studio. I lived in Crip hood. "Wassup cuz" was the greeting of choice and necessity. It showed, at the very least, tangential allegiance to the gang that controlled our Long Beach neighborhood. The Crips commanded more respect then the peace officers, who routinely stopped Black males and beat them. Beat us. I'm sure this is why my mother, like most mothers raising their Black sons in the ghetto, taught me at an early age how to deal with policemen. How to call them "sir" and feign respect for the badge that has, historically, given them license to beat on people who look like me. Just like the white skin of their ancestral fathers served as a license to inhumanely hang Black men from the limbs of Georgia peach trees, like sticky rotten fruit whose nectar, no longer sweet, was discarded.

Randy Newman is also from L.A. We, however, do not share the same reality. His point of reference emanates from a different experience. The product of a soul treated differently. He is not from my L.A. When he sings his song, "I Love L.A.," he is really singing, "I Love My L.A." (I didn't see any people I knew in his video.) It is Mr. Newman's choice to sing what he wants to sing. However, a problem arises when people begin to sing, or discourse, or report, on places and people and cultures about which they are unfamiliar. Unfamiliarity with one's subject leads to a superficial understanding of it, which results in its misrepresentation. An especially heinous and dangerous act when the subject is a complex race of people.

During the rebellion, some people came up to me to express their "outrage" at the verdicts. Each seemed surprised by the ensuing violence. None thought violence an appropriate response to violence. All were white. They do not know L.A. My L.A. The L.A. that is not seen on "L.A. Law." They do not know, intimately, the long history of police brutality inflicted on our community. They have not seen a white policeman pull a Black teenager from his car in front of his girlfriend and force his head to the curb with a pistol seemingly made just for this purpose and these people. They do not know who Ron Settles was. Do not know he was a bright student and star tailback at Long Beach State. Ron was stopped by Signal Hill (a Long Beach suburb) police because he was driving through their city in a nice car and it was dark and he was dark. That night Ron Settles was found hanged, suspiciously, in the Signal Hill police station. I was eleven. He was my role model. There was an investigation because there had been other "incidents" involving Black males and the Signal Hill police. No policemen went to prison. The Signal Hill jail was simply closed. The building shut down. Lights snuffed out. Just like Ron Settles's life. It was not a fair exchange. Ask his mother. Ask me. She lost her son, I lost a role model.

Mrs. Settles knows L.A. My L.A. She knew and experienced the hope created by finally capturing on video, for the whole world to see, that which had become a daily part of our lives. A video that would give insight into why some Black men are so angry. A video that we anticipated would elicit justice and understanding, not pity. What man does not want to be understood? Appreciated? His perspective proven valid? We really believed justice would be roused from L.A.'s somnolence, loosing the chains of its pathetic antecedent.

Not guilty.

Not guilty.

Not guilty.

Not guilty.

I got the same sinking feeling I got when King got shot. I went to work. Left. Couldn't be in the same company with white people. I went to a bar. It was on the news already. I felt nothing for that white truck driver. When that cat came back and snatched his wallet, I said, "Right on."
—*Norman, 49, former history major, currently manager in large automotive chain*

All of the guys I know round my age don't have nothin to do with white people. Been round too long. Seen too much. Been lied to too many times. Don't trust 'em. Can't trust 'em.
—*Frank, 52, retired truck driver*

What did those white people who walked up to me expect me to do? Analyze the situation? "Now what went wrong here?" "How can we constructively respond to this amazing injustice again?" "Where can we possibly find another cheek to turn?" Black people are tired of being treated with heathenish moral imprudence and then being expected to respond like Jesus. Historically, this expectation has not been loaded onto the shoulders of any other people. No one could or should bolster such a pledge. This unfair burden of passivity was only exacerbated by the rebellion's television news coverage.

The visual image, especially when buttressed by sound and constant commentary, is unmatched as an agent of influence. This is corroborated by America's parasitic relationship with its televisions. Usually, the people making decisions about what images are transmitted through this powerful medium are not Black people. Nor are they people who have significant insight into Black culture or the condition of Black people in this country. Nor, based upon their track record, have they shown a meaningful desire to learn about our culture or condition so as to present a more accurate and complete picture of my people.

This shirking of responsibility was made manifest, ultimately, in the media's presentation of the Los Angeles rebellion from the mind, soul, and experience of a person who is not from our L.A. Instead, a debauched voyeur, sensually aroused to passionate masturbation by large burning fires, and hot pistols and long rifles.

This rakish display dominated the television coverage in the first twenty-four hours of the uprising. These first hours were critical because they defined the tone of the coverage to follow. More significantly, they left a lasting first impression, an indelible brand, on the minds and souls of white Americans. White Americans with a previously established, superficial knowledge of Black culture. White Americans in a position to hire and arrest, and jail and fire and judge a great multitude of my people. Thus, the media hindered an already troubled relationship, embedded deep within the densely tangled forest of frustration, distrust, and fear.

The news focused on the peripheral: fires, looting, and violence— without delving into why. During those initial hours, no news team interviewed Black men from the community about their personal experiences with police harassment and how it made them feel. No news team tried to tap into the pulse that drives these brothers. Instead, they focused on fires and how Black people breaking into stores taking milk, VCRs, diapers, and clothing had nothing to do with the Rodney King verdict. In the crucial first hours, no news team talked to Black children, to Black boys, the next generation of would-be angry Black men. No news team tried to gain insight into how social and economic conditions affect our youth. No news team asked Black schoolchildren, "How did you feel when you saw all those police beat on that one Black man?" "Why do you think they beat him?" "Do you think they would have beat him if he was not Black?" "Have you ever seen the police beat a Black man?" "Do you believe the police are there to protect you?" "Do you think, one day, the police will beat you?" "Does that make you afraid?" "Does that make you angry?" "Was it right and fair for those officers to go unpunished?" "Do you think the fact that Rodney King was Black, like you, influenced the jury?" "Does that make you sad?" "Does it make you angry?" "How does that make you feel about America?" "When you go to a baseball game, and the national anthem is played, are those words true for you and your family?" "How does that make you feel?" "Does it make you angry?"

Black children represent the Black future. At an early age, they are acutely aware of the breach in the American moral contract that supposedly governs human relations. On June twelfth, forty-four days after the rebellion, I visited Ninety-ninth Street Elementary School in Watts. I wasn't sure if the school was in Crip hood or Blood hood, so I dressed in the most neutral browns and tans I could find. I left my sister's West Hollywood apartment, walked up to Sunset and Crescent Heights, five minutes from Beverly Hills, and hopped on the number two RTD heading southeast. As the bus rambled east, then south, I was struck by the gradual change in skin complexion of those riding the bus. By the time we passed the first burned, Black soot–covered remains of a former business, the only white face I saw was on a campaign poster next to the decimated building, ironically urging South Central to "Vote Lyndon Larouche." I exited the bus in front of a large dark power plant and walked next door to the school.

The two-hour trip provided me with ample time to confront my fears of returning to an environment that I hadn't dealt with in six years. An environment that I felt fortunate to have survived the first time through. On the evening of the day that I received my acceptance letter from graduate school at UCLA, I had a haunting nightmare that my first night back in Los Angeles I was murdered.

I walked through the school visiting classes with the principal, Ms. Althea Woods. I was quickly convinced that she was yet another strong Black woman, in the tradition of the African sisters preceding her. I met with six young Black boys for a closed-door roundtable discussion. Their ages ranged from eight to twelve. I asked the group, "Why do you think those policemen beat up Rodney King?" Derrick, the biggest and most aggressive of the group, talking fast with a slight stutter, jumped in with the following:

Because he was Black, and maybe they thought he was high cause he was driving fast. They [police] don't like to see Blacks driving fast. They stopped him. Beat him because he was Black. One time, this man was walking down by the power plant. A policeman rolled up on him, and said, "What are you doin?" Then two more police cars pulled up. The first policeman pushed his [the Black man's] head against the [police] car for nothin. Then one of the other policemen came up and started hitting him with his baton.

I asked the boys, "How many of you have personally witnessed a policeman beating a Black man?" Five of the six boys raised their hands. I posed the question, "Are you guys afraid of the police?" Nine-year-old Gregg, chubby, with dimples and wearing a Jheri curl, looking like a midget Ice Cube, raised his hand and slowly said, "I'm afraid of them."

I asked, "What would you have done if you were older, and the police beat someone in your family, or in your community, like they beat Rodney King?"

Steve, eleven and startlingly intense for his young age, responded very matter-of-factly, "I'd take the police off." His frankness, and the seriousness of his tone, revealed that the seeds of rage had begun to sprout. He was one of the five who had witnessed a police beating of a Black man.

There was one dissenting voice throughout the discussion: Donte, a thin, soft-spoken, but very confident twelve year old. He confronted Derrick and Steve's opinions with an agenda of peace. His view, his voice, were like someone calling out from deep within the tangled forest of frustration, trust, and fear. Donte calmly but firmly spoke of patience, hope, and love. When I raised the question of what they would have done if they were older and witnessed a police beating, Donte replied:

I would have been mad, but I wouldn't have done a Rambo like you [*talking to Derrick*]. I would have made sure my family was okay. Then went and passed out food [if stores were closed after looting] to people without cars, because my family has a car. Ain't no need for all that killin. Ain't gon change nothin anyway.

As Donte presented his nonviolent agenda, for a moment I felt ashamed of the anger and rage that had become so much a part of my being. Ashamed because I felt as if I had given up hope that the racial hatred I had been exposed to could be overcome by love. My Judeo-Christian background will never allow me to be comfortable with relinquishing my belief in the power of love as the agent of change. I want to believe. My mom believed. She was born and raised just outside of Birmingham, Alabama; the heart of Dixie. She has intimately known racism; deep hatred has been her companion, but she raised us to treat everyone equally, regardless of race. To love. She taught by example. She still believes. I don't know how she does it. However, I too want to believe because I know the anger that breathes just beneath my skin is desperate like a cornered beast; it is turning inward on me, making me a masochist; it's destroying me.

When I was an undergraduate, I applied for a job as a police aide, trying to directly confront my hatred for the police. An opportunity to know them as human beings, as opposed to what I had experienced them to be. I frankly told the oral board that interviewed me why I was applying. They hired me. I was there thirteen months; it was like therapy. Although many of the officers I encountered were insensitive, simpleminded motherfuckers, there were a few who were genuinely wonderful people. Thoughtful and sincerely concerned with the citizenry they were protecting. The experience affected me deeply. A new seed of understanding began to sprout and fragile petals of hope emerged where fallow earth had been before.

The Rodney King beating, like the harsh realities of midwestern winter, destroyed my garden. The ensuing verdict roused my weary beast. I was in a café when the verdict was first announced. I stumbled out of the café, literally in a state of shock, then walked directly to a computer center on campus and wrote the following letter to a colleague in New York:

April 29, 1992

Dear Kevin,

It's 3:56 P.M. on Wednesday, thirteen minutes after the white judge read the four not-guilty verdicts handed to him by the white bailiff, who carried it from the white foreman, leader of the all-white jury that just set free four white police officers who beat up yet another brother (on film) and I'm surprised at myself for being so surprised. Something has fallen off the shelf inside of me to disturb the calm that I was allowing myself to enjoy these last few weeks before I leave for graduate school. I really don't know what to do man. I am so hurt. I am so disappointed. I feel betrayed.

I know there will be riots in the streets of L.A. tonight. I know that people will die tonight. I want them to be white people, Kevin. I want white people to die. I want innocent white people to die and experience injustice. To experience the land of equality like we experience it. To experience America the Beautiful like we experience it. To experience the melting pot when the heat is up and they ain't the ones stirrin. I'm sick of this shit man.

I can only imagine what I must have looked like as I walked down that crowded sidewalk, my facial expression. I needed any white person to bump into me or just stare at me for too long, so I could unleash my beast outward, for Rodney King and Dr. King and Medgar and Ron and slavery. I just wanted to scream. I wrote instead and I write now, everyday, because it keeps me sane. Tames the beast. Mine, however, is only one of many beasts living in a people, in a city, that feeds the raging beast a steady diet of bloody, stillborn hope covered with the afterbirth of despair. A city that ignores all the signs that say Danger: Please Don't Feed the Animals.

AMERICAN DREAMS,
WAKING NIGHTMARES

———

I Dream of Jesus

Charlie Braxton

last night i dreamed
i saw jesus pimp strolling
peacock-proud down crenshaw blvd.
looking for lost souls
in the concrete valley of the damned

for forty days and forty nights
the son of man sought souls
in south central l.a.
home of the body bag
the bloods the crips, the pigs
and the inner city blues
only to find shell-shocked soldiers
raging over the rock of caine

last night i swear i saw jesus
dressed in black khakis cracking
a 40 and shooting the dozens
while hanging with all the homies in the hood
just cold kicking it
things were smooth until some fool lost his cool
and shot another
jesus tried to save the brother
but couldn't
that's when all hell broke loose

tempers started flaring
gats started cracking
caps started popping
and niggas started dropping
like flies
the body count read twelve injured
three dead
crucified on the cross of ghetto life

Rock-Star Savior

Charlie Braxton

and on the third night
jesus wept
his tears a bittersweet
mixture of blood & sweat
flowed like the river nile
staining the urban concrete
streets crimson-red
with the anguish of his undying love
screaming
    "Father o father why
    have you forsaken them
    in their hour of dire need?"
but there was no answer
coming from the cool cruel streets
of south central
only the faint sounds of
gunshots and broken glass
echoing faintly throughout the city
so the son of man turned his back
on the night and took a hit
from a glass dick
now jesus is a rock star touring
the ho stroll
looking for a strawberry toss-up

to wash his weary feet
before his next craving
comes crashing down
like the wailing walls
of jericho

Ruminations on Violence and Anonymity in Our Anti-Black World

Lewis R. Gordon

**for Lisa, Mathieu, and Jenny,
and in memory of
Grandma Ellene, 1942–1995**

I have been spending a great deal of my time recently on philosophical questions of anonymity and violence. In the process, I've found myself delving more deeply than I ever expected into the work of Frantz Fanon, the philosopher, psychiatrist, and revolutionary from Martinique.

Fanon was a humanist who believed the most basic human problems to be linked to the question of humanity itself. For him, violence is fundamentally a form of dehumanization; any effort to create a human place in response to violence is inevitably caught up in a swirl of continued violence. This is because inhumanity—dehumanization—forces human beings into unavoidable cycles of action and reaction and dirties everyone's hands.

To grow up in a world in which this cruel reality keeps asserting itself, marks the core of oppression. Fanon is right when he says in *The Wretched of the Earth* that oppression constantly forces us to answer, "In reality, who am I?" And more, "What am I?" For in a brutal environment, one slips into invisibility like a mouse when the lights go on, leaving only droppings. But sometimes there is identification—"Look!"—although such occasions are loaded with a rancid odor of sadism. For there are many ways to look without seeing, and for those caught in the web of oppression, not being seen is so familiar that it feels ordinary.

I've been spending a lot of time on the ordinary. To be ordinary is to be hidden in the bosom of anonymity—the word means to be nameless. But we live in an anti-Black society. The result is a violent namelessness committed against Blacks which transforms the protective dynamics of anonymity itself. But anonymity is not the cause of this violence.

In a humane world, anonymity offers us an understanding. For as we go about our business and interact with each other, we remain aware of the limitations of such encounters. For example, I can see that the fellow across the way is a custodial worker, a father with his children, an African American, a baseball enthusiast, as he shares a moment discussing baseball cards with his children. He is all this, but above all he is someone whom I do not know. To know him requires effort on my part, and my need to make that effort reminds me that his humanity goes beyond my assumptions about him.

Not so in the violent world of anti-Blackness. For an anti-Black racist, to see a Black as *Black* is to see enough. Nothing more needs to be known. All else will follow like effect to cause in the mechanistic world. What's more, an array of endorsed institutions and prevailing ideologies discourages many efforts at human contact. The same oppressive one-dimensional identification is made, over and over, to the point of limiting the options of a Black man in an anti-Black world. This limitation is unleashed with bitter, sadistic irony. For after all, in the midst of all this, is the prevailing, existential reality: "Well, you always have a choice . . ."

Choice. It teases, caresses, punishes, and intoxicates the oppressed individual. For he knows that no matter how many limited options are thrown at him, he faces the bitter reality of always having to choose among his options. Does he live them as defeat or victory?

For my part, I've always tried my best to refuse to surrender. But there are times when I wonder. . . .

Bad faith is a expression which lurks in the undercurrents of philosophy, a form of lie to oneself about the effort to escape one's freedom, one's choice. Can I choose not to choose? As I face all those limited options thrown at me, telling me each day what I cannot be, telling my son each day what he cannot be, telling my daughter what she cannot be, telling my brothers each day what they cannot be, telling my sisters, aunts, mother, telling members of the community of Blackness in which I am but a cell each day what they cannot do, as I face all these, don't I, in my effort to make sense of it all, find myself constantly facing the questions "Who am I? *What* am I?"

ONE

I received a rather brutal welcome to the USA in 1971, at age nine.

"Don't you know you're a nigger?"

"Nigger." Sounded like the Jamaican word, *neayga*, which meant those other, those "dirty" lower-class types who were always the darkest. "What's a nigger?" I asked.

Eyebrows rose as smirks filled the classroom. I asked around until one boy, Black like me, explained. It is a bad way of saying Black person. So I returned to my seat.

"So, what's up, nigger?" repeated the little white boy who sat next to me.

My fingers pressed his throat when I grabbed his neck. I beat him twice that day. The first was at that moment; the second was after school.

Everyone was shocked to see a white boy running from a Black one, especially into an Italian neighborhood in the Bronx. I was chastised by my teacher. "I didn't expect this from you," she said. I didn't expect otherwise.

Still, neither *neayga* nor "nigger" became standard speech in that classroom again. But outside, it was everywhere, assailing me from every direction across the full spectrum of color. Not only did everyone become "nigger," but it also seemed that everyone was convinced that *others* were "niggers."

So later that year, I was caught by another surprise.

"Get out of the park, you fucking Puerto Rican!"

I looked around and saw Black and white boys with sticks and pipes in their hands. I could have told them that I wasn't a Puerto Rican. I could have told them lots of things. I could have run. But at that point I thought I had had enough. Against whom was this encounter—the "Puerto Rican nigger"?

I hadn't realized it then, but I had decided to *be*, for that moment, a Puerto Rican, whomever *they* loathed—"they" (to this day, I still don't know who they are) whose consciousness is saturated with false American ideals holding out a promised land of "us" at the end of all the misery and suffering. Through the years, I've made sure never to apologize for their limited perception of me, since ultimately the sickness is theirs, not mine. So, I was blackest when they hated my Blackness, Jewish when they hated my Jewish ancestry, Jamaican when they were troubled by my accent, a question mark when they were curious about my sexual orientation. Whatever they were attempting to evade by making me what they wanted to see, hear, or smell, I refused to oblige by escaping into whatever identity was convenient.

But such a battle is tiring, is it not? As I looked around me at all the hostility, it became apparent that I needed rest. Somewhere out there, there must be space for an everyday, a place simply for living.

But therein is the dream, is it not? I remember lying on a park bench on a hot summer day, closing my eyes, and simply taking a moment to sleep under the warmth of the caressing sun. I woke to wet tar burning through my skin, and I looked over at the fleeing, laughing agents of the "they."

"They" come around when you least expect them. "Come on!" I sometimes hear. "Why are you people so sensitive?"

I remember being an adolescent of thirteen standing at my school door with three other friends as we stared at the white members of the community who had gathered at the edge of the school to deal with our Black presence. They filled about three blocks. Their ages ranged from ours to elderly. Some had bats; others, chains; some, metal paddles; others, pipes—all had hatred in their eyes. We were bused into that neighborhood. We had missed the announcement of an early departure. We were alone.

Yeah, many of us are very sensitive people.

Two

"Ricky, please call. C——s has left us." Ricky, my childhood name. It was as if hearing that name, my name, was a way of calling me back to the past. The message on the answering machine was toned with gray, as all things seem when steeped partially in reality and partially in the unreal.

My wife looked at me, her eyes swelling.

"No," I said. "He must have moved out."

C——s was my best friend of fifteen years. We had met as early adolescents wrapped in a shared world of jazz. We played music together under the most arduous of conditions, and we embraced each other's joys and sorrows. Eventually, we formed a close-knit group of five friends: a bassist, clarinetist, saxophonist, trombonist, and drummer. C——s played the bass. He was a somber soul with whom I shared everything. But over the years, his life slipped into violent inner turmoil. He saw a woman for a while who reminded him of his mother. He beat that woman incessantly. We parted company with a great deal of pain, with my urging him to seek psychiatric help, with his disgust at my interference. Eventually, he and that lover parted after having a child, and he found himself twisted with shame and a desire to "fix" himself. He was never going to be abusive again. He met a woman to whom he gave and gave and gave.

So I approached the message on the answering machine with great trepidation. "No, you know he must have just broken up with his recent flame. He must have . . . he must have . . . he must have . . ."

The phone rang. "He's dead. He died yesterday from a bullet wound to the heart."

So began one of my worst years' encounters with violence and death. I received the news of my friend's death after a day spent cleaning up for a community rally to retrieve a neighborhood park from the crack dealers and give it back to the children who used to play there. The year was 1991.

At first I refused to deliver the eulogy for my friend. I took his death harder than any death I had ever experienced. It seemed surreal; there he was, stiff as dried wood, his face so swollen and full of anger. But worst of all was the moment of placing his coffin into the ground: there, in the earth, was a line of other coffins. In the midst of all that death, my friend, with all his unique talents—a would-have-been architect, a would-have-been famous bassist, a would-have-been who-knows-what else—was laid to rest as a dull, blank, anonymous nothingness. Beneath the earth, sealed in their coffins, the dead were all reduced to the same thing, all ripped out of the drama of life. It became clear to me why tombstones are so important; they are cries against the nothingness, cries to be cherished in the heart, cries to be remembered.

As the tears flowed down my face in that August heat, a friend of the family walked up to me and said the most asinine words, which I shall never forget, words that revealed the degree to which understanding of the special connections between human beings is being submerged in a mire of a society that is practically brain-dead: "Don't worry. You will have other friends."

THREE

I find myself sitting down three years after my friend's death with the question "What have I to say on violence?" At the time of his death, I was a graduate student in New Haven studying philosophy. I had gone there to delve more deeply into the dynamics of human evasion. Today, I find human evasion to be such a mundane feature of our world that the possibility of its being extraordinary seems an extraordinary thought.

I now stand as a Black man of thirty-two years. As I walk through the world, I find myself suppressing each day the gnawing sense of being an existential anomaly advancing farther and farther across enemy lines.

"Why are you still here?" the voice asks.

To have survived this far!

Many others have fallen along the way. I remember a friend's older brother—a tall, dark, handsome fellow who loved to play basketball. He always gave a kind hello in the afternoons as he passed our building, which he did as regularly as the famous philosopher whose strolls helped villagers set their watches. One day he didn't appear. Stabbed in the chest. Lost into the bleak nothingness that grows with obscene familiarity.

The bodies are mounting up. Our clarinetist, my friend S——n, beautiful S——n, whose smiles were so bright and full of cheer that we used to call him Jaws.

"Did you hear about S——n?" He's gone. AIDS.

"We're dying," the trombonist, R——d declared. He and the saxophonist jumped ship to the Netherlands. But he's returned. Now, the thought gnaws. Two of the five haven't reached thirty. Who will reach forty?

P———kin', the drummer who sold me my first set of Zylgian cymbals; saw him on "Soul Train." AIDS. Gone.

Community activist. Came up to Yale to study ministry. Dropped out and became a dreadlocked community preacher. Was to show up at a rally for the community group Brothers Getting Busy. Heart attack while watching television the previous day. Gone.

A brother went nuts the next week. Shot his wife in the face and then himself. Craziness.

Then there was S——z, my comrade-in-arms in the streets of New Haven. The hours he spent on the streets, in the prisons—many hours, for the sake of what? One day he showed me. He lifted his shirt.

"See this?" he asked, pointing at his stomach that bore horrible, violent scars, a great deal of missing flesh. "This is from my gang days. I crossed enemy territory. They caught me and tied me to the bottom of a car. Then they drove down the street as fast as they could. Good thing I was wearing a thick coat. I felt it peel away until my skin began to go. They stopped the car and set it into reverse. But they got stuck. I hollered and hollered so loud that finally some people came out. Fortunately the gang got out of the car and ran. The people who came to help me picked my insides up off the street and got me to the hospital."

The phone rang on a Sunday morning that was so gray that it felt like twilight.

"Did you hear about S——z?"

A drunk white lawyer ran into S——z's van on the highway. The engine of the car broke through the front and crushed his wife. S——z and his wife had been together since they were twelve years old. They had five children, all boys, and another on the way. Their eldest was twenty.

S——z suffered an understandable deterioration from that point onward. I would visit him and the boys and talk with him as his face trembled with pain and sorrow. We became family in a way until I left New Haven. S——z was left always on the edge. I think his family had been prepared for *his* death, but not his wife's. There isn't much in the way of resources and moral support for widowers, particularly Black ones. He was feared, he was pitied, he was supposed to be able to work and provide as though a world of great, patriarchal opportunities were available to Black family men. Had he died, there would have been a community on the alert with a great deal of practice dealing with a widow and her children. But not a man who suffered from an accident.

"No one stopped as I flagged for help. I had to ask the white man who knocked us off the road to flag down help. That's when someone stopped," he had told me. S——z was such a man, who suffered violent intrusions into his skull, operation after operation.

Recent news. "Did you hear about S——z? He's accused of stabbing to death a man who shouted insults at him while waiting to use a phone at a public booth."

FOUR

Yeah, I've been studying Frantz Fanon quite a bit of late. Fanon was a firm believer in social illness. In his resignation letter from the colonial hospital in which he was directing physician, he declared that the very notion of well-adjusted human beings under oppressed conditions is equivalent to the accomplishment of happy slaves. He considered that an obscenity. I agree.

We live in a sick society. I have always known this, as we theoreticians say, "theoretically." But over the past year, I have had the opportunity to travel a bit and gain a different way to situate the reality of our disease. Perhaps the most vivid for me was my recent trip to Cuba. I was invited to the University of Havana to present my work on Fanon, and to learn about the Cuban dimension of Caribbean philosophy. There, I saw many things that left a mark on me. One of the most significant was the scarcity of one kind of poverty there, poverty of the human spirit, though spirits can of course be broken.

There, there was constant talk about the children, about the importance of leaving the legacy of a human project for them, a legacy that Cubans hope will be able to beat the effects of what Fanon would identify as the liberty without freedom they are sure to experience when the U.S. affirms its hegemony *within* the island again. Whatever one thinks of the Cuban people, whose racial constitution was debated in the U.S. Congress at the turn of the century, or of Cuba, whose division into a white and a Black side was once proposed by the U.S. Congress—whatever one thinks of what Cuba represents today, there has always been one uncontested feature of the world as lived on that island, and that is the ever-present question of a human agenda in its public sphere. Whatever happens to Cuba politically, its judgment rests, ultimately, on the degree to which it has been able to forge a human agenda in the face of the war against it by the U.S. and by Cuban Americans who encourage the continuation of those hostilities.

History does not forgive failure.

I landed on U.S. shores again. (When all is said and done, after twenty-three years here, I am from the U.S. just as much as I am from other shores.) And here I was greeted by a hurricane of madness. Here, on a television screen, was a white Bronco being followed by a team of black-and-white police cars. On both sides of the highway's divide were people of color cheering on the Bronco. Inside was a Black man with a black shotgun, a man whose name is also a nickname for orange juice.

The running commentaries, like frequencies caught through a roving tuner on a radio dial, offered rationalizations and irrationalizations. Antimiscegenation snippets here and there gave way to an opportunistic district attorney "speaking out" against domestic violence at the kind of news conference where it would be standard to say "no comment" until the suspect has been apprehended. Here were carefully guided efforts to avoid the race-word as the image of a dead white woman and her dead white male friend permeated television screens, newspapers, and magazines. Editorials on women, mostly white and battered (which raises questions about the Black face of the batterer versus the battered), everywhere; and on and on.

Switch the channel, turn the page, turn the dial, and yet we find that one cannot simply turn off reality, however surreal it may be.

Then there are the constant explanations here and there for complicity in oppression. This stuff is marketable—a *Time* letter from the managing editor states that no offense was intended in the "blackened" mug shot of the Black man of the week.

The Black man never seemed so Black until he was so obviously down. It was absurd for me to try to say something now, say something while I searched within myself for a response to the questions.

"For what reason?"

"In reality, who/what am I?"

"Who/what are *we*?"

FIVE

Nothing can be said against a businessman in a world in which business rules. I am told, and am expected to believe, that there is a world of difference between the businessman who swipes his profit off the backs of underpaid and malnourished laborers in other countries and the businessman who makes his profit off the local exploitation of vices. The Philip Morris corporation makes money off cigarette addictions, legally, but homie on the corner makes his money illegally from illicit addictions. How can anything really be said to homie? Isn't there a great deal of moral bankruptcy here? For homie knows that he is not even close to the reality of Bob and John and Henry and Tony's profits on illicit vices, but he bears the face for the crime. He knows as he raises the question of who he is that he constantly encounters what he is. He is crime.

I am a crime. I have known this from my encounters with the police—their attacking me while I was defending myself against a group of adult whites; their stopping me on the New Jersey Turnpike for driving too slowly after a drunk driver nearly knocked me off the road; their accosting me and my friends while we moved our instruments into our rehearsal place; their pulling me over (again on the New Jersey Turnpike) while I was driving to North Carolina to see my brother who was losing his mind after the absurdity of "our" second intervention into the Persian Gulf; their sadistic grins as they attempted to confiscate my car in a frigid Connecticut winter while I held my four-year-old son in my arms; and on and on.

Hot pursuit is their rule of thumb. What can I think when I am pursued because I am seen, when what I have supposedly done is determined by police officers after I have been stopped? What can I think but that they lie in wait, confident that there is a problem with my very existence, which will emerge and provide them with what they already know, and that problem is that I exist?

SIX

The Black man's everyday in the U.S., if he ever really has an everyday, will be an extraordinary achievement. Think of it—to face social problems purely and simply because they are realities that humans have to negotiate their way through, not because of a rote response, a decline in understanding, that emerges when the weight of problematized Blackness has been imposed on everyday experience.

I've been hearing of late that I, by virtue of my race, am a violent being. Bigger Thomas lurks within my veins, and my cowardice forces me to live out my fantasies against "them," whites, in mad barbarism against my brothers. I don't have mere disputes. If against whites, they are racial; if against Blacks, they are Black-on-Black violence. I stare constantly at an exclusively racial explanation of what I do, where I'm from, and where I am going.

In the eyes of those who fail to see beyond the thing whose anonymity has been perverted, I become the problems I face instead of finding myself facing the problems. So the communities in which I live become Joseph Conrad's Congo—stared at from without, defined by the garbled imagination that hears only gibberish from my mouth, and condemned to the sublime rhythm of natural forces against which our punctual eighteenth-century philosopher once suffered and trembled. Oh, yes, it is the violent din that claws at who I am that makes me constantly the anomalous "survivor," yes, violent with fury, violent with that ever-present call to *destiny*.

They are waiting. For they know that I have to be on the alert. I have to be on call—no respite, no letting my guard down. Somewhere out there, until the day I die, there is the weight of the fuck-up.

I have seen many a Black man struggle, struggle hard, and then just when he is about to achieve his goal, he goes to pieces. He slips into a horrid absurdity.

"What's up with that?" a friend once asked.

Yeah, what's up with that? But he himself knew what it was to be the exemplification of sin, to be, that is, guilty in advance. Guilty of what? Time will tell. It lingers out there, hooking an index finger, calling us into full view of the storm, calling us to explode.

"Yeah, violent, criminal, sexually deviant Black man, come to me, I await you—yes, me, your *destiny*."

We've seen the explosions. We've seen the eruptions of "destiny," of Blackness in its fusion with black death through black guns in the night, of even shiny knives taking on a promise of permanent darkness. Oh, yes, of the thickness of a racist cloud hovering in the skies and swooping through windows, into lungs, into hearts, with a promise of violent destiny.

Yes. "Who am I?" "Do I mean all these things—do I?"

SEVEN

So I, like many before me, reach out, an act of faith. There are Black people in the U.S. and other affluent parts of the world whose cushioned lives protect them from the experiences I have been describing. Perhaps, even, their access to a seemingly safe world has enabled them to imagine themselves protected by their own *accoutumance* of class or ethnicity to avoid, or at least to evade, the lurking anti Blackness that simmers in distant places. But to them, I do not know what to say.

I suspect they will be willing to listen when the weight of "destiny" invades their sanctuary. Even they will discover, albeit occasionally, the importance of being alert. For there is a form of groping going on, and in the midst of it nothing falls but crumbs.

I return to anonymity, for it taps me on the shoulder now and then when I realize how extraordinary it would be to be extraordinary in an ordinary way. But in the midst of all this, there isn't much time, like life during wartime, to sulk. "Destiny" must be destroyed, and in that victory will stand the possibility, albeit fragile, of a wonderful affirmation of our strength and willingness to love.

ELECTION DAY: U.S. OF A.—U. OF S.A.

Tyehimba Jess

Welcome to our garden grown.
Welcome to our home in this new day, today, our minds poised to
    embrace in double clasp
                      fingersnap
                    soul-baked
            handshakes on soil of new tomorrows.

Here, where we stack centuries of children filled chains in our
    hearts as dynamite in our skins.

Where we have 4/4 timed our thoughts to explode in shouts of
    blue seekin spears of warring eyes and clenched fists.

This day, today, where we watch 6:00 eyewitness to your long-
    lined lumbering the one-day, two-day, four-day journey to the
    nearest village of voting.

Where we visioned a medgar evers spirit fly through three decades
    and two thousand miles to land in the spring of your massive
    toi-toi.

Where we could've sworn we heard fannie lou hamer's voice
    rippin sweet from the patchworked, million-lunged, unchained,
    boldened tongues singin
    "nkosi sikelele afrika."

Homeland. Our land. Carved from lifetimes countin up legends of
   alabama dogs and nataal sjamboks
   projects and bantustans
     rikers and robben
       freedom fighters labeled terrorists
   and terrorists labeled freedom fighters
of fury-fisted fingertips bathed in soweto-chicago-alexandria-
   philadelphia-johannesburg-pittsburgh nappy-headed soul-footed
   black-boldened blood-burnin in policeman's paws.

Where biko bloodied cells—malcolm murdered halls —trees of
   broken necks and horizons of black hands stretchin out to grasp
   themselves forge a territory
we have called fight
   called struggle
   called war for survival
     called self-determination
      called collective
       called nationhood
        called any which way *you can*, brotha/sista
                 And
       when cbs calls it "victory for capitalism,"
      when mcdonalds calls it mcbusiness venture,
     when clinton calls it photo opportunity,
    when diamond mine owners call it political party,
   when tourist agencies call it gold mine—

We say: *Welcome to our garden grown.*
Welcome to our home.
Kinder, gentler warnings from your cousins in the western sun,
   where we pitch tent in the shadow of glass-and-steel canyons,
furrow the asphalt, and dig ourselves a meaning somewhere
   between the cracks in a concept called america:
some call it democracy, but somehow, that small word doesn't
   seem to capture the countless generations in your soil you toiled
and now can call your own—without argument.

And somehow, those four syllables would leave the size of our
   lives' purpose half-naked and trembling—all the warrior tongues
   that have tasted your/our struggle cannot be contained
by a single nine-letter word.

We done seen this brand of democracy and can tell you to beware
   its legacy of counting firsts:
First mayors, first congresspeople, first representatives, dead last in
   justice.
First fired, last hired.
First in jail, last paroled.
First in sickness, last in care.
A democracy where ballots are the size and weight of dollar bills
can only buy a freedom with the taste of dry coins.
And the stomach grows weary of promises and promised lands.

So on this day, we know that forging new gardens is the work of
   many hands growin tall in the heat of ourselves in the day we
   create for ourselves on the back of the fading cusp of midnight
   called today.

When we art us when we grow us when we love us
we will say it like the old-time greetings from our backyard home-
   grown turf of our lives:
Welcome to our garden grown.
Dig our fruit we shall grow unstranged from itself, tree of hands
   holdin hope, roots of arms ripplin roarin waters underground
families bendin only in the light of the sun of our resistance . . .

Welcome to our garden grown,
where we taste a freedom that don't spring from nine-letter
   grecian words,
when our mouths are full of *amandla* and *fight the power.*
where we throw our hearts full of our minds full of our backs
full of our sweat on the plow
into the sun of the day when we own our gardens and sow seeds
   that kill canyons—
and we continue to call those seeds our blackness in the soil when
   we say
welcome home. luta continua.

The Screaming of the Silences

KERRY RILEY

The scene is familiar; the personalities are the same. The images, though shadowed, are still revelatory of a horror of unspeakable magnitude. Slowly, a Black man, dark of hue, struggles to recover a shaky composure. Meanwhile, white blows continue to rain down upon his eventually prone body. This videotape "seen around the world" mesmerized an unbelieving global humanity—witnesses of a technologically captured temporal brutality which has been perpetuated for centuries. In the videotaped battering of Rodney King, African-American men believed that finally our communal cries of violent injustice and oppression had been vindicated. Of course somehow twelve "peers" managed to confuse the victim with the victimizers; the deadly results proved catastrophic to the city of Los Angeles, as well as to humane and compassionate souls worldwide.

Yet, while I was devastated by the verdict and its aftermath, I also sensed an incompleteness regarding the videotape. With repetitive viewing, I recognized the absence of a crucial sensory apparatus: THERE WAS NO SOUND!! And as I pondered this loss, I began to reflect upon the position of sound in our lives. During the beating, we could not hear the screams of Rodney King, but neither could we experience the crunch and thud of steel baton upon human bone and ligament. Missing was the zapping of stun guns and the "coaxings" of surrender from the Los Angeles Police Department. We never heard the words of the fourteen other officers at the scene, nor did we hear the roar as King's Hyundai raced through the suburban Los Angeles landscape allegedly at one hundred fifteen miles per hour. In fact, we heard absolutely nothing. However, I believe the silence heightened the brutality of the scene. In fact, it was the silences which screamed the loudest.

The Screaming Silences—an oxymoronic metaphor and yet an absolutely apt description of African-American men in American society. Daily, our screams emit from numerous bruised and abused bodies and can be heard from the depths of the most hopeless ghetto to the fax-filled heights of corporate boardrooms. While aspects of our plight are captured on newsmagazine shows and talk shows, it is the Screaming Silences that have become deafening. Across America, African-American men are being systematically exterminated, thus creating a devastation equivalent to the perpetrated during the worst periods of enslavement. Witness these statistics: one out of every four African-American men between the ages of twenty and twenty-nine is incarcerated; one in twenty-one African-American males is a victim of homicide, usually perpetrated by another African-American male; homicide is now the leading cause of death for African-American males between the ages of fifteen and forty-four, followed by accidents and then *suicides*, a recent addition to the list; more African-American males also have more cardiac arrests, hypertension, and alcoholism than any other group, a development which has led to a *decline* in life expectancy. In fact, one report from the Centers for Disease Control states that, if preventative measures are not applied quickly, by the year 2000, seventy percent of African-American men will be addicted, incarcerated, or deceased. These frightening statistics have led many social scientists to refer to African-American males as an endangered species. These proclamations of genocide are creating a situation in which a silence can scream.

The Screaming Silences are ubiquitous; they can be found in neighborhoods, schools, bars, homes, churches—arenas whose hallowed spaces echo the consistent anguish of genocide. They are within the screams of parents who are constantly burying their sons and the screams of children whose daddies will not return home. They are the screams of voices which have been silenced by a genocidal rage perpetuated by the behemoth of insidious racism, both overtly and covertly. As a child of the sixties, I grew up during the "age of Aquarius," a time of turbulent protest yet of racial progress. I was told that life in America could be summed up by such popular musical offerings as "You've Got a Friend" and "He Ain't Heavy, He's My Brother." Therefore, the discordant strains of segregation became but a murmur in a distant newsreel. I and others of my generation were promised the fulfillment of Martin Luther King's dream—that things would be easier for us and that oppression would be eradicated during our lifetime. Naïvely, my integrated mind swallowed the vacuous rhetoric which hailed the arrival of an egalitarian society. The voices of protest—Martin, Fanny Lou, Malcolm, Rosa—urged us to "Keep Your Eyes on the Prize" and I, highly educated and fairly assimilated, foolishly believed that I had very few obstacles to overcome.

Yet no one predicted the eighties and the "Reagan revolution." This led to a "kinder, gentler racism" which undermined our progressive movements and peeled back the materialistic layers of our complacency, leaving us with the rawness of our reality. One by one, our prophetic voices ceased, whether because of death, apathy, or infiltration. A segment of the population moved forward to accept the bones thrown from the master's table and refused to share the spoils of victory with their peers. I found myself to be a victim still—by police escorts who've searched me on the shoulders of dimly lit highways; by white women who nervously clutch their purses when I enter their presence; by shopkeepers who insist upon escorting me through their stores; and, most tragically, by my own brothers in the justice struggle, who see myself and others similar to me as *their* prime enemy. It is the traumatic carnage typified by this final group which compels the silences to scream.

I know the piercing sounds of these screams. I've been there. Five years ago the phone continually rang with disastrous news: "Papoose passed away today"; "Howard passed away this morning"; "Joseph is dead"; and so on. Within one and a half years, nine people died in my family, seven of them men. Tragically, we experienced death via murder, AIDS, alcohol—indeed, via the entire litany of maladies which are causing the genocide of African-American men. In the wake of a destruction which snatched three generations of men in less than eight months, I was compelled to ask: "How could this have happened? Why aren't all the resources of the country being utilized to cease this bitter destruction of life? Why are we fighting wars in other countries if we cannot deal with the bloodshed in our own? How did the lives of African-American men come to be so trivialized, undervalued, and worthless?" And as I sat amid the eternally departed in the ironically named Harmony Cemetery, I wanted to scream, to cry, to grieve, to throw a fit; but all I could do was to sit in a stunned silence. However, it was not a passive silence; quite the contrary. As I sat witnessing a family of dead men, suddenly something began to swell and surge within my body. This intangible feeling grew louder, louder, and louder still until the cacophonous symphony rang throughout my body as though I were directly underneath a pealing church bell—an existential pealing which created the bodily spasms of a mournful soul captured within an abyss of eternal agony. I clutched my ears, but the screaming silence within and without grew to a deafening roar which clung to my every movement even as I left the place of Harmony. Wherever I went, these overwhelming sounds penetrated my entire self, disrupting my daily routine and forcing me into an obsession with these noises to the exclusion of all else. In vain, I sought to be liberated from these deafening silences—appealing for aid or support for the achievement of peace. But others—they heard nothing. My testimony became lost in the self-serving rationales of those who were convinced that I was paranoid, that I "was inventing it," or that I simply wasn't "trying to love myself."

But I knew what I heard. I knew that these Screaming Silences were emanating from the spilled blood of my forefathers. These Screaming Silences were the cries of broken male spirits appealing for justice. But it was not my family alone that I heard. These Screaming Silences also emanated from the lynching trees of the South and the crack houses of urban America, from the city of Birmingham and the back alleys of East St. Louis and the plantation walls of yore. Indeed, the screaming emanated from all the places where men of African descent and others have been silenced by the racial injustice and violent hatred perpetuated by a dominant European caste. And what is our crime? The fact that we are truth tellers. Yes, our beleaguered voices confront and illuminate a patriotic America with its deceitful character and ignominious history. African-American men stand as irrefutable proof of the falsities of American cultural appropriations. We expose the shallowness of "the land of the free and the home of the brave," and we loudly denounce its trite morality which echoes within walls of hatred and desolation. Most people were horrified by the Rodney King beating *not* because of its brutality, but because of its truthfulness. White America was horrified because of its identification with the officers, *not* with the victim. *All* of white America was on trial during the Rodney King trial, and this confrontation with savage reality was unbearable.

But most important, America could not bear the silence. Due to the absence of sound, it was forced to hear the screaming of a silence too long ignored—a silence which will only disappear when we undergo a "revolution of values." It is highly unfortunate that the deafening silences led to the death and destruction of Los Angeles.

However, white America was finally forced to listen. There have been attempts to rebuild our cities. There are a plethora of mentor programs designed to strengthen the character of our young African-American males. There are interethnic and crosscultural colloquiums designed to destroy the barriers which exist across racial lines. There are various economic cooperatives which are being utilized for economic empowerment. Through dialogue, discussion, and sharing, numerous attempts are now being made to heal the broken spirits of African-American men and their families. The greater the optimism and success, the quicker the screaming subsides in my soul. My life, my love, my passion, and my goal will be to silence the screams forever.

BLACK ALLEGIANCE

Michael Datcher

You have just walked under the overpass (a place where you can get just below the funk) and, down here, we have a difficult time pledging allegiance to the flag. "I pledge allegiance to the flag of the United States of America and to the republic for which it stands, one nation, under God, indivisible, with liberty and justice for all." These words are predicated on constitutional language, proclaiming self-evident truths: that all men are created equal. The logical progression is that all men should be treated equally. This is where we get lost because equality has not been our truth. Our truth has made us question the full value of our humanity. When we kill each other, our truth is self-evident. This is why it's so hard to pledge allegiance. Our voices are raspy with discontent. The verbs get caught in our collective throat, the nouns block our breathing. We cannot speak.

It would be unfair to call us unpatriotic because we do believe in defending the place where we live. We do believe in the red and the blue (if not the white). We can be proud of the most desolate stretch of land, willingly giving up our lives to protect it. We even carry our red and blue flags on our persons to show our loyalty. We wave our flags proudly before TV news cameras while engaging in urban patriot games. We have no shame. We compose anthems about life in our homelands and blast them from our car speakers. We want everyone to know where we are from. It would be unfair to call us unpatriotic.

We would like to have the same kind of passion for the flag carrying the stars and stripes. In theory, those stars and stripes represent the inalienable rights of life, liberty, and the pursuit of happiness. Historically, those rights have been difficult to obtain, so down here, under the overpass, we have come to value them. We love freedom. During the most trying of times, we *will* find a way to pursue a little love and happiness. We believe in those American principles. For years, we have been trying to make others believe that we believe. We longed to engage in the ultimate patriotic act: to lay down our life for our country. We fought in WW I even though we were fighting for freedoms that we didn't have at home. To show their appreciation upon our return American citizens lynched us in our uniforms. Undaunted, still trying to impress, we returned for duty in WW II. Again, we played liberator, emissaries for a president who we couldn't vote for. There were more wars and movements and police dogs and turned cheeks and turned cheeks and turned cheeks. We have been so accommodating. We have tried so hard to stand up and show our desire for full acceptance in the American citizenry. We ached for America to pledge her allegiance to us. We wanted to be loved.

This has been our story, but now we are tired and frustrated. Many have forgotten our years of struggle and accommodation. Many have forgotten the patience and turned cheeks. We see our anger, but refuse to acknowledge the pain that caused it. We gave and gave and still were rejected: our heart has been broken. We have become the spurned lover. Hell knows no similar fury.

Down here, under the overpass, we are tired of reaching out, so now we have begun to strike out. Across socioeconomic lines, there seems to be a resurgence in Black antagonism toward white Americans. I hear the anger in line while shopping at the grocery store. The old brothers who spend their retirement days playing dominoes in our neighborhood park routinely begin references to whites with "Those mothafuckas. . . ." During a casual party conversation, my multidegreed friend suddenly turned to me enraged. "I can't stand white people, you can't trust them. They smile all up in your face but as soon as they walk away, you know you're just another nigger to them." It has not been just talk. A year after frustrated black New Yorker, Colin Ferguson, killed six whites on a Long Island commuter train last December, a young brother in Washington, D.C., smuggled a 9 mm pistol inside police headquarters. He did not come to pledge his allegiance: he killed two white law enforcement officials.

What is causing all of this? The country's conservative mood swing, general white backlash against Blacks, and the resurgence of white hate groups are significant factors. To many African Americans, these factors coupled with the two-pronged attack on affirmative action and civil rights legislation are tantamount to a slap in the face. Now, however, few cheeks are willing to be turned. That accommodating, assimilationist spirit has not maintained its appeal, even among the old guard. *Integration* has become a bad word. Call someone an *integrationist* and he might scream, "Yo' mama!" With progressive Afrocentric thought beginning to permeate our communities, we seem to be less consumed by trying to seek affirmation from white people. Instead, we are trying to learn how to affirm ourselves. Trying to build bridges of understanding between disparate groups within our community: between men and women, straights and gays, Muslims and Christians. We are working on our communal infrastructure, circling our cultural wagons, pledging allegiance to ourselves, here, under the overpass.

BEYOND BORDERS,
BEYOND BOUNDARIES

—

THEIR STORY

THOMAS GLAVE

And then in those afternoons that were yet to come after so many
other events of that time and our days too had passed over into our
dreams, even after all details and memory had merged into those
rivers of our nights, you would see the two of them there walking
together, past our windows, past our front porches and our doors,
through Sound Hill: Mr. Winston and Uncle McKenzie. In summer,
the trees fluttering down their eyes and watching so quietly the heat-
drowsed life along those streets, the smell of the Sound (the water
only yards away behind the farthest of our houses) hanging heavy
through the air as first one pair of dark hands from behind a fence,
then another, and then still another, waved at them in greeting, and
large, heavy, dark eyes all along that street—through the heat,
through our dreams—looked out from every other memory with
easy smiles of recognition.

You will not see them walking quite that way now, and our summers too have grown more silent. But even then, as starlings chat-
tered overhead and our backs strained over hedges and coaxed
geraniums to turn their hands to the sky, you knew that it hadn't
always been that way: that the faces of those two, and later our own,
had not always borne that sadness; that once, you remembered, there
had been more of a lift to those old shoulders lately so rounded and
a spryness to the step that no winter of the heart nor mind could
remove. Some of the older folks, like my grandpa, remembered that
time so many years ago when Mrs. Winston also had walked through
our streets: the iron-gray hair framing the heart-shaped face, the

heavy body that had known many years of difficult labor, the pair of long brown legs ending in bright sneakers beneath a flowered dress; remembered (and carried into the dreams) that voice singing away the long hot days in her garden down by the water, where, among those hydrangeas and the peonies that had done Sound Hill proud, she had worked tirelessly in a relentless quest for color. And memory of her could not be summoned without bringing to mind Uncle McKenzie's wife, Icilda, and the smells of curried goat and ackee and codfish that had always breezed out of her kitchen. In that time, when the world still allowed those of us who were young to be children, scraped knees and pop-eyes turned up without fail at Mrs. McKenzie's front porch for Jamaican bun-and-cheese not even the best of the Jamaican bakeries in Baychester and up on Boston Road, even years later, would equal. There, between taste-swallows of an island of whose mountains we knew nothing, we always greeted Uncle McKenzie, who inevitably found time to put himself all up under Mrs. McKenzie in that cluttered kitchen—"a goddamned kitchen jack!" her voice shouted as her always-crisp house-dress rustled in ferocious blue; as, softer, came, "Here, pickney, take it, nuh?"—and we felt the caress of rough brown hands we also carried later to our dreams.

Uncle McKenzie was play uncle to all of us. What you Americans call play uncle this or that, we in Jamaica call pet name, he said, and that is mine. And so, without fear of what was to come later, reaching up to those hands and running back out into that time of protected ignorance, we called him Uncle, for the rest of his life, in fact, as we ate bun and hard dough bread and gizzardas conjured out of that distant unknown place called Trelawny, from where they both had come and where, they always told us, lived creatures called duppies—ghosts.

Ghosts in and of themselves wouldn't have been enough to scare us in Sound Hill. In our isolation in that forgotten and far-off North Bronx part of the world, so far removed from the churnings of a city whose streets permitted their prisoners no real vision of the sky or light, we had already known them. We had learned long before that even the vaguest rustle of a bedroom curtain on nights of the most abject loneliness only betokened—in most cases—a visitor of the gentlest and most yearning benignancy, longing from so far off (within that other darkness, emblazoned by that light we couldn't yet see) to share and comfort our solitude and theirs. We knew they came and went as surely as the summers came and went until our fire-shadowed days of autumn; there were beneficent ones and those troubled and—depending on how one had treated their personages in life—those who could bring terrible dreams and vengeance. All of them, if permitted by us the living, possessed the power to access and decipher our thoughts, appetites, memories, devotions, regrets, and even our most secret and thwarted obsessions, mostly when we walked those night rivers of painful remembrance, which was often. So that even many years later, when so many of us had moved out of our parents' homes in Sound Hill and into (smaller, lonelier, meaner) apartments in the city, leaving behind the lilac fragrances of those ghostly night walks, we would summon again to the rushings of our own shame just what had happened with Mr. Winston and Uncle McKenzie, as we learned the truth.

When Mrs. Winston died—Miss Ardelia, we called her—all of Sound Hill turned out for the funeral. Because we had no church of our own, it was held at a church way up in the Valley. Midway through the service, all the ladies, my mama included, bent low over their knees and raised their palms high up in the air—supplicating that light which had never been kind but which they so devoutly believed would someday fall from the unyielding sky and maybe even now, especially now, bring Jesus down into their reaching hands; as their men, like my daddy and grandpa, sat like stalwart sphinxes in silence beside them—afraid more then and always of the silent storms building within themselves than they were of the future explosions a lifetime of such storms could cause at any moment to rip open the tender flesh of their hearts. Mr. Winston was the worst. His daughter and son-in-law came all the way from San Francisco to see Miss Ardelia put to rest; they had to help him into the church because his own knees would not. That last week of spring he had turned sixty-six, and last June he and Miss Ardelia had made forty years together. "A man can't take but so much," my mama said. "Taxes, killing, young people dying, social security that don't feed nobody. That's all one thing you could put into a box and just say God help you try to sleep at night. You'll lay off worryin and go on to sleep when you get tired enough. But a wife sick so long and then to go off like that and leave him, sweet Jesus. A man can't take but so much. Especially a man like him."

Mama was right. That day when we were all in the church up in the Valley feeling the spirit and Miss Ardelia's spirit too with Mr. Winston bawling and then being real quiet and then the light that wasn't ever kind falling over us and us listening to the preacher's words about how Miss Ardelia was now with the Lord our shepherd in the sight of all His goodness and His grace, I watched Daddy holding on real tight to Mama's hand as he looked straight ahead and held me too and I knew she was right. Everybody's mama knew and everybody's daddy—those who were there—knew too. Mr. Winston was a soft kind of man, good soft—the kind you had always seen on those later spring and summer and even winter evenings walking down past the fences and the lawns with Miss Ardelia almost tall at his side—walking, you remembered, a little stiff; joking with Noah Harris and Hyacinth-who-danced about how that lawn sure enough looked like the ragged-torn side of some trifling nigger's head, hadn't they never heard of Bill and Acie's Lawnmower-U-Rent on Gun Hill Road?; greeting the Walker twins, Timothy and Terence, telling them apart only because of the fiercely protective look and arm-about-the-shoulder Timothy always had for his born-twenty-six-minutes-later brother; making Yvonne Constant, the quietest little girl in Sound Hill, look up for more than a second and even smile; with Miss Ardelia not humming quietly then to herself as she often did but just smiling and laughing softly once in a while; admiring O. K. Griffith's irises or Johnnyboy's front-yard eggplants; putting a hand now and then again to that white straw hat she always wore on warmer days; then the two of them walking down to the Sound, when you would hear the man's soft voice telling her how someday when they had not three but four grandkids he would build them all a sailboat and take them up off over the water, past Westchester and Connecticut on one side and Long Island on the other, and wave to all the rich whitefolks who'd be watching with the same wideopen eyes they'd always imagined us to have, and say, Hey y'all looka here!—I got my family out with me for the day.— So whyn't y'all let them maids and chauffeurs free for a day so they can come on with us for a swim? Hush up, Win, would come the woman's voice then: very like a flute, more light than sound; as you imagined her resting a thin hand on his thin shoulder still moving with the laughter he had learned to embrace as joy—a small, pithy sort of joy, but the form and shape of joy enough. The hand would remain there then, moving over the joy, as the curve beneath it leaned slowly into the arm and hand, feeling it long after eyes and flesh and desire had joined and gone home to watch the nightly news, watch the outer darkness descend, watch the inevitable. There, where eyes mattered less than touch, the feeling continued, you knew, as we felt the hint of it or the breath or the moment among ourselves, even long after everything had happened.

How, then, did those future events come to occur? Some would say later, after they were over, that they had begun with a sort of

blindness. Uncle McKenzie's blindness, after Icilda McKenzie's
death a few years before from a cancer that in her earlier years had
begun gnawing away at the smooth flesh of her breasts like a tenacious but unasked-for lover, been arrested by several pairs of surgical
hands, savage machines, and scalpels, and skulked in her body for
twenty years until the tenacious lover finally turned vengeful, silently exploding into her brain on that gray morning none of us
would ever forget. After the explosion and the memory, Uncle
McKenzie did become blind. From that morning on, he had been
able to see nothing except that long dim pathway leading yet further
down into a valley of utter silence, where all trees and even the most
humble ground-dwelling creatures had long ago learned not to weep,
stricken with the knowledge that all about them grew the most un-
imaginable sadness which no tears could redress. So that, as our
restless spirits showed us, it wasn't quite a literal blindness. And
then some of us thought that actual no-sight might have been almost
a blessing on those nights we dreamed Icilda McKenzie's ghost came
back in her aching grief to wander past our sleeping houses, past the
house of her dead friend Ardelia Winston and so many other passed-
on or sleeping friends who wept and reached out to her from the
endless sorrowing rivers of their dreams, until she found that particular green house down by the water she was looking for: where the
kitchen still smelled of bun and curried goat and calf's-foot jelly, and
pictures of Discovery Bay and Port Maria hung on those weary walls;
yes, that house, whose structure was of slight wooden frame like all
the rest; where the walking shadow paused for a moment to embrace
those summer-night delights of ripe apricots still hanging on the
front yard tree her own living hands had planted so many years ago,
the dark man with that bit of the sea in his voice laboring not far
from her. Then, like that which she had become and which the object of her eternal searching desire was fearsomely becoming, she
entered the house—patting the clay-potted geraniums on the front
porch to make sure they were still properly dry in that season of
frequent thundershowers; as she drifted upward into the room whose
walls had watched her die, where the mirrors had watched her
watching herself making love throughout the years to him whose
sleeping, trembling cheek she then, in the dark, began to stroke;
caressed the grieving forehead; kissed, with the fleeting touch of
ghost-love, those lips so lately useless throughout the new appalling
silence of so many sightless days; as he, mired in the mud of that
dream-riverbank that continued to hold him fast in the wretchedness of his own despair, called out to her from a place she could not

reach him, to save me, Icilda, help me, Icilda, I'm ready to go now, Icilda, I'm ready. I'm ready. She would calm him then. For while she could do little or nothing to lighten the blindness of his days, which she anyway spent on the banks of a distant shore he wouldn't know for some time, she was able at least to quiet the ceaseless fury of his nights. When, in that dark solitude, he awoke sweating and fever-pitched, grasping the air wildly and crying out for her, feeling the pounding of his heart and thinking, praying, that this might be the heart attack at last, Heavenly Father, O Jesus, that would finally bring him closer to her and allow him that sweetness of resting his fevered head in her cool lap once again, forever, she was there—just behind him, out of his sight but close enough to lay her hands on his neck and rub him there, pulling him with that gentle ghostly insistence back down into the twilit country of sleep and the river where, at least for the space of time within earthly boundary, he could rest his fatigue on the shore and listen in peace to those rushing waters.

In those hours of silent immeasurable time between two worlds —one raging, the other in the most unknowable and confident serenity—what secrets, we wondered, what wisdoms did she share with him? Our own dreams never told it all, being currents allied with the nocturnal unspoken mysteries of death. But we learned then, as everyone gradually discovered, that only those ghosts we knew among us were capable of telling the complete truth, unencumbered by twitching lips or the diurnal cutting of an eye. They alone possessed the fortitude and the power, buttressed by the breadth of eternity, to stare down the remorseless intelligence that outlined and directed our destiny. Fearing death—perhaps because we did fear it—we knew that their knowledge was infinitely greater than our own not only because they had already faced what we feared—loss of life and the awful pain-resonances of human grief— but also because they had long gone on to whatever it was our surviving hopes, wisely or in pathetic human foolishness, insisted we continue to believe in. Our spirits, like Icilda McKenzie's, had only to face the circular time of what to us for our time on earth would remain unknown, as we yet walked through our days and nights in constant fear and avoidance of the certainty and ostensible closure of death. So that when the living, fretting Uncle McKenzie stuttered out the pain that had so tightly coiled about his heart and spirit, protesting the entry of yet another presence into his dreams, wanting only her in the flesh, in his arms again, or himself with her on that farther shore, she the wiser spirit would shush him who was still her husband and lover, whispering to him that he must allow what was beyond his power to alter; that, soon, some night, they would again be joined in always-time; and that, for those moments of his continued suffering, he would do best to listen to the sounds of all those other wandering spirits, who—for all he knew—might be bringing him news of her sojourns on those quiet shores along which she had so lately walked. Oh, she was strong, our night rivers told us; she would never allow him to descend of his own miserable willingness into the deeper parts of that current from which, for him, at this moment in his destiny, there could be no return. In her patience, and from within that firm and infinite resolve deepened by the requisites of death, she soothed the bitter maledictions of his raging heart until the restorative river melody sighed once again in the more steady sound of his breathing. It was then—only then—she knew that she could (as she must) remove her hand from the relaxed grip of his and, just that way, a vision diminishing, a force once again released, make her way once more out of that bedroom and down the stairs, out into the sleeping world so uneasy from its own day terrors, to walk again in her own aloneness until the unrevealed hour when their separate courses would again meet for all time in that other world of light.

Thus, in that way, until the end, some of us thought, Uncle McKenzie's nights gradually came to be illuminated by those private moments of transcendent vision even as his days began to descend into that most terrible form of blindness which preys on the living bereaved. It wasn't long afterward that we saw how he began to stumble, not walk, through our streets he knew so well. When, one evening, he fell down on the sidewalk in front of O. K. Griffith's irises, O. K.'s boy Walter R. later told his daddy that, as he'd reached out to help the old man to his feet, Uncle McKenzie had looked dead straight up at him, right through and past him, as if seeing a sunset world behind and beyond Walter R.'s nappy head, and in the most terrible earth-filled voice had whispered, "Icy. *Icy*. Got to get home to help Icy wit the curried goat. She waitin pon me, you no see, pickney?"—so that later Walter R. would tell his daddy too that the look in Uncle's eyes—that vacancy which saw nothing in this world except those sunsets laying waste desolate fields beyond a river which in daytime did not exist—had terrified him as much as the hopeless weight of those old, fragile bones held up in his arms. Later that summer, when the police brought Uncle McKenzie to Noah Harris's doorstep with the news that he had been frightening women at the Pelham Bay bus stop by asking them through his tears if they had by any chance, please, seen his wife, Icilda, walking through the river, several of us wept into the most private spheres of our own hearts, feeling the dreadful certainty that, from all appearances Uncle McKenzie wouldn't be with us much longer. It was as if, seeing what was to come even very much later in the ashes of tragedy and reborn gods whose acts would forever terrorize our survivors, and not having the good sense to run even then from what would be that later horror, we sought in both Uncle McKenzie and Mr. Winston a glance of the forever-survivor, who might lead us into a possible future and more fearless resketchings of ourselves. In our sorrow for him, we were obviously feeling also a prescient sorrow and fear for ourselves, sharing the knowledge that even more unnerving than the final rivers of our dreams were those inescapable deserts of our surrender to the ashes of the future.

But then—thank God and the spirits—through the workings of unseen guiding hands, it came to seem an almost natural occurrence that, neither too soon nor late, the stronger of the two old survivors' personalities began gradually, cautiously at first, to guide that one who had fallen to his knees with the scent of a dead woman's curried goat still in his nostrils up to his feet and to a place where, far above that night river, two old wrinkled men could begin to weave out the intricate patterns of their common distress; as the trees in that place gazed down upon them with wise and silent knowledge of the miracles humans yet might achieve after so much time of blinding loss.

And so it happened. As the hazed languor of those late-summer days crept into the cooler fires of the coming nights, we began to see them—bent-backed, shuffling, wary of step—more together: in the steady company of shared grief, perhaps, but also in the occasional slow surprises of that elusive light that children, and all others who find they still have much to discover in the world, know. Thank Jesus, our mamas murmured, because a man at that age needs someone he can slap thighs with and trade jokes with about the good old days that were already past most of our recalling and about which practically no one wanted to listen anyway beyond the necessary polite smile of one minute or less. So that, even years later, well into the time of our own separate and lonely autumns, we would think back on our surprise and pleasure at the sound of their mingled voices, low music frosted by age, as Mr. Winston guided Uncle McKenzie down to the Sound they both loved; relating to him over their slow steps the joke about rescuing the maids and chauffeurs from the whitefolks. It began there—the slow unraveling of the tale of his grandchildren in San Francisco, who knew only what the evening winds and their parents' whispers told them of their grandfather's distress, were sent by their mother and father to "quality" schools where they were taught nothing about themselves, and—most unforgivable—had been raised by the lawyer his daughter had become and the architect his son-in-law had always been not to believe in spirits. That was why, he told Uncle McKenzie, those two children had learned all about the lives of so many important people and all the gleaming cities they had built in the snowy wastes, the anchors they had tossed on the coral reefs, the radioactivity they had brought to sun-scorched deserts high above the secret lairs of scorpions, and even the luxury housing developments they were planning to erect on all the bright planets still reflecting the moon's ageless light on the earth, yet to this day could not have midnight conversations with their departed grandmother, who, like Icilda McKenzie, also walked steadily between this world and that one. None of his living people knew how to listen to the older spirits, Mr. Winston said, nor to those tall trees in the South he remembered that still brought the tortured last words of so many skeletons that only some years ago, and even yesterday, had swung in white silence from those long branches, a length of charred bleached bones and shame drying in the sun. So what kind of way to raise children was that?, he asked; and Uncle McKenzie only shook his head and said that it was no kind of way at all, Massa God, for pickney must raise up to know the spirit and true. Amen, intoned that other, thinking again of Miss Ardelia; and they would stand there for a while, looking out at the glistening waters of another vision, another dream, as the hushed waters of the Sound lapped up at their feet on shore.

The days grew chilly; the light thinner; late flowers offered up to us their resolute and noble last, falling fast before the proud marchings-in of our stately chrysanthemums. We returned to the dreaded boredom of school, weekend leaf raking, honors projects; our grandmamas again turned to preserves, worryings about the world, and scoldings; our parents once again every day rode the Sound Hill bus to the Pelham Bay station to their jobs in the city and back again. Between these dull, regulated spaces in our lives and nights of TV telling us how not to think and feel and what winter would bring, we heard: Mr. Winston, with Uncle McKenzie at his side, leaning on O. K. Griffith's fence; regaling his companion, O. K., and Walter R. with that long-ago truth he had never forgotten, about how the most persistently disapproving eye to his marriage had not been Miss Ardelia's mama or daddy but her grandmama, who had died six years

before the marriage yet had insisted from that calmer world on making an appearance at the wedding of her beloved third granddaughter,
and who indeed on that hot South Carolina June day had appeared
in her cream linen suit—spanking new as forty years before—that
had matched her cream high-heel shoes and the yellow-cream flowers on her hat. Settin up there big as day, Mr. Winston said, and
didn't leave off bugging 'Delia bout what her duty as a wife was til
two weeks *after* the honeymoon. Even then they'd still been aware
that she had been lingering, a presence, carrying her aroma of mint
jelly and beeswax through the big new house young Mr. Winston
had moved into with his young bride; a presence gently ruffling
lemon fragrance through the bed sheets before the newlyweds turned
in for private hours of love; plaiting Ardelia's hair with gardenias
throughout the night as the bride slept in her husband's protecting
arms; dusting off the kitchen table, always leaving behind her beeswax scent; scolding Ardelia for walking around like a love-struck
rabbit instead of with a broom in her hand; until, on a gray humid
afternoon which promised a cooling absolution of rain, the old lady
felt the ponderous weight of an earlier rain in her soul, and, her face
wet with sudden tears, cried out, "Your grandfather's calling me! It's
time to go home for good! He's calling me!"—and, bestowing one
final kiss on her granddaughter's stricken face, disappeared into that
seamless memory of rain, drawn back into the embraces of a lonely
husband awaiting her at the edge of the world. In that moment the
young bride put a hand to her own cheek and felt her grandmother's
tears there, which would remain there and bring to her face a glow
of supreme life touched with an implacable sadness her husband
would not be able to caress or kiss away until eleven days and twelve
nights later, when Ardelia would sit up abruptly in bed to cry out,
"Nana's home! She's with him!"—and sink with a sigh of deepest
relief and contentment, yet edged by a lingering melancholy which
would never completely leave her, back into her husband's waiting
arms. The earliest dreams began then. Late one night, the elderly
couple returned to the newlyweds from an uncharted place on the
other, broader side of the world, where, nightly, it had been said, the
sea crawled with a maroon skin beneath a ceaseless moon and in
every tide carried back to shore the intoxicating unmistakable scents
of beeswax and mating crabs. "Me and 'Delia never was much for
writin letters," Mr. Winston said then, "but can't nobody write letters to folks passed on no way. But with the dreams at least we could
see em." It had remained that way always, he said, as O. K. Griffith
snorted and said he didn't believe in no ghosts comin back like that

and leavin tears and whatnot on people, especially on people that young; Mr. Winston just came right on in with Hush up, boy, letting O. K. know he hadn't hardly lived his life yet and probably still didn't know the difference between a real live ghost and a baby coon's fart.

A shining then. Uncle McKenzie's face. Almost wet with the memories that until his last hour on earth would call to him from the framed photograph of Icilda as a young girl, kept on his night table, close to his heart. With those elbows easy on fences, at the side of his indomitable-spirited and trusted friend, what occasionally came close to the surface in him was clear. And, watching as we did, you would feel as we did that gladness for him in the something—a flicker of that other, deeper knowledge he hadn't yet named or uncovered—that, anticipating the gift it would shortly bestow upon him, had for the immediate present transported him, too, back to those days of his youth.

So, then, should any of us really have been surprised to discover that—quite suddenly, almost forever—all memory of the present was swept up into that slow breeze's beginning and the signaling thereafter of evening's arrival off the Sound, as that other aged voice we knew so well began recounting once again the events of that time of the relucent miracle of the dolphins, who, in a sadness so grievous it couldn't be shared even by the spirits of countless other creatures long ago hounded to extinction, and bearing in their eyes the foreknowledge of an impossible destiny even the most self-aggrandizing marine biologist couldn't explain, had begun to wash up and suffer out the last days of their stricken dreams on that long, thin, palm-lined strip of land Uncle McKenzie's countrypeople at that time called the Palisadoes, which years later would be renamed for one of the nation's most illustrious and forthright heroes, whose name, even in times of willful collective amnesia, would never be forgotten by the wisest. No explanation ever emerged for the dolphins' appearance on those shores, nor for that deep lingering sadness in the eyes of so many once-sleek sea acrobats which, particularly in that part of the world, had been known to chase sharks to the farthest ends of archipelagic exile, rescue children from foreign ships in distress, scratch their own backs on the spines of silent sea eggs in that tropical midday heat, and—most astonishing—balance in perfect stillness on their fins in the undulating open sea, bottlenoses stiffly pointed toward shore in upward-facing attention, when, at events of great historical moment, the anthem of national pride and independence was sung by uniformed schoolchildren at the prime minister's residence. They had faithfully guided fishermen at dusk past hordes of camera-wielding tourists out to the deepest, bluest waters where green-dreadlocked mermaids and their seaweed-bearded lovers (the older, oceanic true brethren of the Maroons) forever sang the wistful political songs they would later bequeath to the beloved dreadlocked singer who, until his untimely death some years later (attributed to cancer of the brain because of his love of that special weed, but strongly suspected by the informed to have been engineered by predatory northern intelligence agents) would, with the peerless talent bestowed upon him by the sea and the sky, sing those sunset chants of hunger, suffering, and triumph over endless mockeries of justice, with a style that would catapult both him and that green island of blue mountains into fame throughout the world which nonetheless would continue to insist that what the poor everywhere really needed was charity, only charity, don't you know.

The dolphins continued to suffer. The wails of their dying young could be heard all over the tin roofs of those shacks in neighborhoods on the other side of the harbor, in the western part of the city, and even up in the hills, in the larger homes of those who blocked their ears with mango leaves to keep out the suffering creatures' cries and who daily told their maids not to speak among themselves in those spotless kitchens of such things as dying sea mammals on the causeway and those terrible visions of hunger and prostration before death. Three hundred dolphins arrived on Monday, by Wednesday there were close to seven hundred, and by the week's end over a thousand; in the midst of their agony they continued to horrify curious witnesses with their grotesque dying smiles as, shrinking further into the suffocating indignity of their last hours, they dreamed still of leaping away on the open seas where, so it had always been known, only one man had ever walked. Why the rass were they so desperately unhappy, everyone wanted to know, and why the backside had they struggled to the land's end of these particular shores? Those questions were never completely answered, Uncle McKenzie told us, but still in horrendous numbers they continued to wash up, continued to die, continued to decompose beneath that trenchant sun with those gruesome grimace-smiles beneath their bottlenoses. Even if they had been edible no one would have dared eat them, for to do so in that region would have been supreme and utter blasphemy of the spirits of those deities who, even after so many years of modern building on their sacred lands, continued to appear nightly in the surrounding waters and in the hills, and who centuries ago had taught the first inhabitants of the region exactly what the sea offered and what it withheld. So that it was finally clear to all, even to the wealthy who stuffed their ears with mango leaves and studied North American TV programs in order to expand the vacancy of their own minds and lose the precious music of their accents, that without doubt the condition of the dolphins was inextricably linked to the nation's condition, which at that time (and, it seemed, forever before and since) was gripped in the stern throes of not-enough, the wretched condition the singer crooned about. A mean little thing, not-enough. But big. Nasty. Which had crept through every tin-roofed shack, pissed its salty waste beneath ragged clotheslines, pecked at the scabby feet of bang-bellied children, cutlassed off a woman's arm for her bracelet on a city bus, buried a woman at age nineteen with deep scars on her wrists and an undetected form in her belly, planted want in sixty hearts in a town of one hundred, burned to death in a rum shop a young man who had in his short life cartwheeled seven times over the taste of Irish moss, raped sixteen virgins in a neighborhood known for fierce allegiances, enticed down the narrow throat of a bewhiskered man the bitter taste of a certain drug (and thereafter his own death), rallied even the soaring black john crows to fight over those slim dung-heap pickings, and frightened away those who, from behind the gilded window bars of their inherited hopes, at the end of those long curving driveways of their aspirations, fled in terror to the warm, palm-filled city of exiles on the northern continent, where not even those palms, though more decorous, were indigenous, and where the only dolphins to be found were those which performed in glass tanks for tourists. It was a terrible time, Uncle McKenzie told us; although the man they called the prime minister was a noble spirit and stouthearted, of a long line of men who had arrived in the world at birth with white hair and blue eyes which, while revealing little of their origins in Africa, yet even at that tender age gleamed with a fierce national pride and love of the people. During the sixth week of the dolphins' visitation, his blue eyes gazing out calmly yet sternly at millions of television viewers one evening, he announced that enough was enough, the dolphins were obviously a sign to everyone that it was time for wide-reaching reforms, *all* of our people have to be fed, we will *not* wind up like our neighboring nations to the north and east, we'll all have to tighten our belts and share the little we've got, I don't want to hear any complaints from those of you with mango leaves stuffed in your ears, if you don't like it we've got five

flights a day to that northerly city of exiles, that noxious sinkhole
of traitorous Swiss-bank quislings and dictators' descendants, make
your choice. Not even twelve hours were allowed to pass until dawn
of the following day, when, in frenzied riotousness, those who
stuffed mango leaves in their ears, along with those who someday
hoped to, launched a national campaign of outrage against the dolphins and the poor who had befriended them. That, Uncle McKenzie
told us, was how he first met Icilda. She was out there on the causeway on the evening of the first antireform protests, a young girl
kneeling by the side of the road in a yellow dress, a pink bandanna
on her head, scorning the clamorous reactionaries who endeavored
to convince her of the wrongful actions of the prime minister, as
she nuzzled against her face a dolphin dying yet struggling to give
birth on that narrow shore. It was the same creature that, the week
before, had with that irrepressible smile shared with her forty-plus
tones of the secret dolphinic language, confirmed in those same secret tones that she and the nation's wisest should never *ever* put
even the smallest amount of their trust in bakra men, confided the
as-yet-unrevealed truth that one distant day in the future the Rastas
would finally be regarded nationally with the proper reverence they
deserved, and with that disarming prescience known to southern sea
mammals assured her that the moon's reflection on night waters
was of course, as always, a matchless ally in the pursuits of youthful
romantic love. Enraptured by that vision of a young woman in a
yellow dress kneeling with the head of that sickly dolphin in her lap
by the side of the road thick with riot noise and human greed and
anger, Uncle McKenzie made his way through the protesters to her
who would shortly become, and remain long after her death decades
later the woman of all his dreams. He begged for her hand which up
until then had known no other man's touch, and, oh, how he'd had
to convince her, he told us, and console her too in her youthful grief
after the dolphin's passing and the appearance of those five stillborn
young; yet he'd managed to assure her that, yes, he too was pro-
reform, progressive, anti-imperialist, and, no, he didn't stuff his ears
with mango leaves, he had no dreams of a large house at the end of
a winding driveway while people suffered in silent hunger on land
and dolphins died on shore, he too despised the transnationals and
the inhuman global straddlers, and no, Icilda, I've never loved anyone up until now, my love, my heart, the spirits of the blue mountains were saving me and all my youth for someone like you, Icilda,
Icy. To hold. To hold this way. Come. They were married one year
later with the white-headed prime minister's blessings and the voice

of the singer behind them. Four years later, guided by the spirits of those dolphins that appeared in their dreams in gratitude and remembered solidarity, they journeyed north to a city of steel, bridges, tunnels, black water, concrete-colored skies, and unsmiling people who raced through their days in order to die sooner, all of which, however unsettling, would grant the two some promise, an agreeable sort of happiness, and years of passage in each other's arms; during their waking hours far only in literal distance from that green island that never left them—"Home," Uncle McKenzie would say then before the grave, watchful eyes of O. K. Griffith and Mr. Winston, "that still my home, you see. And I going home someday to die"— standing very still then, seeing nothing, we thought; seeing again Icilda on that distant shore, the dying sea spirit in her lap; as all of us, moved by that tale of events and places we hadn't yet known and still hoped for, sank back into ourselves, holding within, and in the truest part of our hands, those singular visions which still took the immediate shape of flesh in an old man's eyes. Mr. Winston would touch him on the arm then, lightly, drawing him and all of us back to the present and Sound Hill as the light began to fail with the merest murmur about our shoulders. Then they would depart in silence. Even then it was apparent to us how united in soul and reach they had become, stepping out from within those twilight afterthoughts to descend further, arise ever higher and higher and *higher* into the time-fields, the caresses, the *!!here we are, my love!!* of ghosts.

One. Become one at last. So the words and the news came down to us, over us, quickly and silently taking shape, a whispered intelligence out of that most unending of currents that first slowly and now more quickly was rushing us all on to those final events. The first of which came with a shock: that, all at once, and for some time after, we couldn't tell either of them apart from the other. It was as if, overnight, as we slept, they had traded each completely for the other: it was Mr. Winston, not Uncle McKenzie, whom we watched winter-wrapping Icilda's nine backyard fig trees, muttering all the while about the duppies them that lived pon the hill just so and the damnblasted obeah woman who did live in May Pen, thief from the people them in Mandeville, vex up a whole heap of boogayaggahs in Half Way Tree and then when you hear from the shout did die in Spanish Town with nothing but a blasted rass-goat f' come sniff up her footbottom. It was Uncle McKenzie, speaking with all the life-knowledge so sonorously contained in Mr. Winston's voice —or so we thought, their voices and faces also having somehow become each other's—who laughed out of Miss Ardelia's side-porch step about how he hadn't never in his life trusted no peckerwood and how these folks up north didn't know diddly squat of what they was missin compared to what we had back home—then all at once, in self-conscious laughter, confused NAACP, PNP, and JLP. And then it was quite clear to us from the way that laughter soughed up between them that they had at last discovered between themselves the completely possible yet still unnamed actuality of love; which, while perhaps not yet manifestly real to them except in the current realm of dreams, had, further back in time than any of us could guess, been predetermined by that same constant pair of unseen guiding hands—both through their shared dreams of each other and by way of those spirit-linkages of the past. So that we knew their wives nightly hovered above them in munificent protection as the two of them, furtively at first, and with a hesitation formed by decades of adherence to the most championed and unquestioned conventions, began to reach out and across those dreams to hold first the divined presence of the other, then the actual other; holding each other's dream-specters and then flesh as once they had held their wives; becoming in those still hours wife and husband and lover to each other. The current of that love swiftly filled out every lonely space of the two old men's reawakened hearts, filling them with that presence—mainly their newly discovered love and desire for each other—they had before sensed only on the edge of a further darkness, beyond the edge of the sea, and had never questioned. The current allowed them nothing of fear or shame. For by the time their lips brushed in dreams, then across those luminous and shifting night fields when their shared tongues and skins and even the blood beneath were the same, we knew that they had walked enough with each other along the shores of death and grief so that at last, without any great effort, they were able to read each other's desires in every shade except green, had acquired the difficult skill of summoning one another out of harrowing dreams to the calming kisses and entry of the other, and ultimately possessed no fear whatsoever of wading through each other's night rivers in search of all the untold secrets lying at rest there. It really was as if, aloft in the pursuits of those new vision-gifts, they were finally free, not of care, but of the weighted vain nuisance of hope; for by that time they knew with certainty, rather than hoped with fear, that someday they would be united in complete silence and light with their wives and each other, knowing in that certitude that they could love each other without the abstractions of hope because the gift was already theirs, there remained nothing more to hope for except the gift's expansion into their unity in death.

So watching them, dreaming them, we too learned. Learned that the hunger for those whom we love, knowingly or not, doesn't die. Doesn't die even when the spirit stoking the need fails, or when the watching eye glimpses the ghost-warning of its own impending death. We knew that hunger so keen as Uncle McKenzie's and Mr. Winston's could not at their time of life either die or be destroyed. In our part of that hunger and yearning, as we slept and dreamed of them and moved ourselves back and forth rhythmically across the sheets pressing with our own unappeased desires so urgent and wet against the flesh, we watched them straining along the steep banks of those rivers, burying their faces without rest in all that grew there; their mouths open, then filled, heavy with each other's pulsing flesh; their wrinkled hands moist from those rivers shared, as, amid odors and essences of what only the most private innermost eye reveals, they thought still of resting the head they rested on the other on the bosom of those other two watching ghosts who met one ancient eye with still another, descending—the lover of one, the comrade of another, and friends as they had always been and would be always. There.

—So it was and would be we remembered as our days whitened further into deep winter and the sweep of that new silence all around brought forth the events which began with the memory of the smell of curried goat in a dead woman's kitchen and would finally unite the four of them forever.

That was how it began, we remembered. Yes, right there, slowly, inevitably, the wind currents of that time and the season carrying the predictions of the long endless winter-dark to come and then the attractions of love and recollection beginning in a dead woman's curried goat across the wide and far blue sea and the echoings too of years from that place of blue mountains and trees where so many years ago a young girl in a yellow dress had knelt by the side of a road with the face of a dying sea-creature in her lap: the smells of embraces and memory lifted without end over every horizon of our dreams: then the dreams of the sleeping revolving earth as the singer crooned on about the poor whose bellies could never be full especially with the sad meat of their hearts fed upon by those who lounged at the end of long driveways and stuffed mango leaves in their ears: they at first paying no heed, do you remember, to the miraculous arrival of dolphins upon those shores and later to the memory-scents contained in the smell of curried goat from a dead woman's kitchen carried through that spirit-force to the sleeping nostrils of Uncle McKenzie who beneath spiritual vigilance slept in Mr. Winston's enfolding arms: until he our uncle awakened on that morning which would signal the beginning and end to all things, the first of which was in that moment a walk through the unfolding winter dream that led him down those icy pathways and winter-quiet streets and through the frost-colored late morning out of Sound Hill and up through Baychester and the Valley and then still up and over westward to White Plains Road where the music shops and the food shops and the stores with red black and green in their windows and too with green black and gold lined that avenue so noisy with traffic and the grumblings of that elevated subway above: and now mark that, yes, even in that coldness young men were out feeling their bones and early-morning rage with each other in the streets: mark too how then he Uncle McKenzie with a light step walked past them to that grocery store owned by his country-man who would sell him those two pounds of goat meat he, our uncle, planned to prepare at home for them alone, the two of them who were Mr. Winston and himself, because this was and remains for all time and ever after their story, remember, their story yet be a tale of our remembrance of the past:

—To walk out of there, Uncle McKenzie, white of hair, tall of stance, so lately light of step and always given to that deep music of ageless mountains beating within the blood: walking, yes, still smiling within the welcome hoarfrost of that private dream, except that that day Icilda was not walking with him, she could not come in those looming moments to steer him from danger as had always been her province and willful destiny both before and after her own death, for that day the dolphins of the past were calling her back to them across the channels of memory, beckoning, urging, so that thus called, you understand, so summoned back to that grievous suffering of the past and to that one in particular who with its dead young had returned to her walkways after so much time, she could not refuse: and forthwith journeyed back across the seas and mountains and scorpion-filled deserts to that place and hour of the pro-testers and again to her own youth in a yellow dress and a pink bandanna, holding once again in her lap on that narrow causeway beneath the palms of her youth that desolate bottlenose as she soothed the feverish sorrow plaguing the air so that she couldn't be there, you see, which would be here in this time and place when

*that man she had always loved now walking in a winter dream of
another waiting man held always close in their love and shared
waiting for death, he the aged morning walker of that day suddenly
awakened out of the cycle of snowflakes kissing his face on White
Plains Road to see with horror and shock:—*

They're killing him, Icilda

*—he thought: awakening then yes to see the young men who were
his countrymen two of them or no three no four raining blows down
upon that young boy outside the music shop blaring a song of the
singer, raining blows upon the boy's head, the boy there no more
than fifteen years old holding up his useless hands, screaming, and
now how true it came to be then that oh, revelation, a hungry mob
is an angry mob: Icilda, he thought as they reddened the snow with
their fury and rage and called him Battyman and You goddamned
fucking battyman and Kill him the fucking battyman because:*

*—:oh but they must have heard something about him, you see,
or perhaps they thought he was looking at them in a certain way,
whatever way he was looking at them, if he was looking at all:
which to them would have been that way, the way men do not,
mustn't look at men, that way, they'll kill you for it;—or maybe
who can tell, at one time in the past he might have been clad in
shorts, tight shorts showing too much, too little, the wrong shirt,
the walk too fast, arms too slow, eyes too wide, lips or mouth or
nose or who can tell?—but in any event it was notright notright*

*so now kill the bastard little battybwoy son of a bitch they said
killing him Icilda*

*:—he thought amid the screams, shouts: and in that one instant
he our uncle McKenzie as we watched in our dreams and screamed
for him to leave them alone, not to go near them, we screamed to
him but he not hearing:—he our uncle McKenzie went forward with
cries/shouts/trembling rage of*

Leave him alone

Why you beating him

Leave him alone

*—his greatest mistake we knew as we watched and shouted and
tried to reach him through the dream, pull him back: but couldn't
awaken from it ourselves as we watched the horror dawn on Uncle
McKenzie that his longtime comfort with the world of ghosts who
loved him had scarce prepared him for the world of the living who
did not: nor for the rage-world of the young who loved the old less
than they loved themselves (which they did not) having been taught
by everyone one thing only which was destruction, an outcome for*

which they too (also having known not-enough, the hot piss of it
down their throats, the shame of their bones whitening in the sun
and eternally the unsatisfying blood beyond their hands) were des-
tined;—his greatest mistake, knowing nothing of this rage until

then the noise began filling up the whitening air whoops shrieks
frenzy finding another source for that fear the driving forward of it
seeing only this latest enemy seeing in that hysteria not really him
hearing only the voice forbidding feeling the ancient shame of their
bones whitening in the sun one pushing along the other for O violence we have done/shall do again they thought in that screaming
as their bones whitened in the sun so that in that hour came forth
the screams of the already vanquished yet hopeful the howl deep
within their skins For yet might we live they thought o yes through
the blood they thought live precious precious and the sacrifice blood
and the bones the skin the knife for sacrifice there

then raining blows down upon him upon the thin whiteness of
his head beneath the whitening sky

so there began the red beneath the blows and the sacrifice darkening the skin

darkening the snow and the field of the dream suddenly so dark:
seeing now there in the red Uncle McKenzie on his knees: the goat
meat fallen beneath him: the red over his eyes: the knife glittering
in the red: we couldn't reach you Uncle couldn't hold you through
the dream could only see you there

falling

falling

the red over your eyes now over all our eyes too for we too were
responsible: had been dreaming of safety far too long: believing ourselves safe for a time not only from death but too from that death
we ourselves knew: the self-stalking, the fear: which wasn't to be
feared so much in the night rivers of our dreams but here: right here
always here in our days our violent waking days

So that it was

had always been

Red.

Then darkness.

Leaving him there.

The police were able to identify him because he always carried his
Social Security card. From Sound Hill, they ascertained from his ad-

dress; had living kin who did not reside in either the city or the
state. Who would have to be contacted. Which O. K. Griffith did.
And the victim: would have to be taken to a city hospital, the police
said, since no one was able to say anything about the condition of
his insurance or even if he had any. That city hospital, not far from
the Pelham Bay train station, which was where Mr. Winston and the
rest of us found him: not in a room but on a dirty stained stretcher
in the emergency room because there were no rooms, you see, so
many people were dying, they said, this one and that one: don't you
people know, we've got a fucking huge-ass disease out there that's
killing everyone, and then so many of these sluts coming in with
their faces bashed in, goddamn dope addicts and crackheads and all
these young punks too with their guts or the few brains they have
left shot out, we're living in violent times, it's a violent city, we're
inundated, you'll have to be patient, we'll get an intern to tend to
him as soon as we can, what do you expect, a miracle?—rushing
through the cold white glaringness of so much human misery, holding their breaths as we held ours so as not to inhale those odors,
piss, shit, antiseptics, blood; so as not to believe, please, that Uncle
McKenzie so suddenly was going to die that way in that place he
had avoided for so long while men forty and fifty years younger than
he turned up there without fail and nameless in the redred on nights
of the full moon, bullets deep in their brains, knives plunged up to
the handle in their throats: no, not die there, we said, not on that
low, flat, white, hard, stained, mean metal stretcher jammed between every other and every other going on and on down the hallway
and all holding a dying hand reaching out, a shot-up stomach, a
bleeding head and Lord Lord Jesus we thought what kind of world
was this what kind and what was happening what had been happening to us always? The entire world screaming, except for him: lying
there only; eyes closed; not speaking; not even dreaming for once;
merely waiting as Mr. Winston clutched his hands there; then bent
over him calling *Now you Mac;* putting his own face next to that
face; begging between those dry pleadings, kisses, unheard assur-
ances, *Please Mac. Now Mac. Come on now, Mac, now can you rise
up, Mac, please, or can you hear Mac. It's Win, Mac. Mac.* Then we
looked not at Mr. Winston but into the eyes of those passing who
had looked into his eyes looking into the closed face of his friend
and lover and saw in their eyes beginning the low dark storms of
that incredulous and loathing disgust. The bitterness of knowing yet
knowing nothing, understanding nothing beyond the storm. Then

feeling our own rage. Waiting with Mr. Winston. Seeing nothing more. Waiting.

(Wondering later was it all part of some other dream or real. Knowing that it was real.) Seeing him open his eyes. One time only. Filled with that same redness that never left him. Looking out right then almost steady at the one touching him. Both looking. Deep. Longslow. The fearpain in the redness for a moment leaving him. Then closing his eyes again. Saying something. Quietquiet. Low, from deep down in the red and the night river rising. Saying, *Icilda. Icilda girl, I finish. Finish in this country, Massa God. I finish. . . . Winston. Jesus—:*

*—Don't bother go on with that—*the other touching him saying. Uncle McKenzie's voice coming out of him. Standing over him next to him still touching. Not caring not mattering either who looked or how. But then all at once couldn't find what he was looking for behind those closed eyes. Not anymore. Not anywhere. But wait. Maybe. Maybe . . . but no. Couldn't find it. It was gone. All gone. What he was looking for. What had been there. Inside those eyes. Between the hands. Deep in the chest. The light.

Six hours later Uncle McKenzie stopped breathing. There, amid the noise, in the clutter of all that stench and suffering, he just stopped. There was no time for any of us to say or do. It happened so very fast, was suddenly so quiet. And then, as one of us who had maintained watch throughout the entire time there would later report, it was at that precise moment that a very old woman who yet somehow bore the incandescently transfigured face of a young girl, with dirt on her knees as if she had recently been kneeling by the side of a road, and with a pattern of wetness on the lap of her yellow dress as if an apparition from the sea had only just lain its head there in a struggle between birth and death, walked unseen by all the nurses into that emergency room and over to that particular stretcher, lowering her wet, gleaming face over the face of the man who lay there; saying something to him in that moment which caused him immediately to sit up, lower the stretcher's protective side rods, step to his feet with the renewed vigor and erect stance of a man fifty years younger, beckon with his face also newly transfigured to Mr. Winston watching in disbelief as the woman too beckoned to him, grasped his hand firmly, warmly, and they walked the three of them hand in hand down the dirty passageway under the dim fluorescent lights past the stink and noise and cries, unseen by

the nurses and out the door to where, sheathed in light beneath a
new white straw hat, waited another woman who, with that same
odd yet joyous and almost otherworldly youthful lightness in her
step, joined them—taking hold of Mr. Winston's free hand as he
continued to hold Uncle McKenzie who held also the hand of the
woman in the yellow dress as she smiled back at him and, so walking, led them all on. Farther on. And on. Walking.

The nurse was examining the body of the man on the stretcher.
Then said, quietly, The patient has expired. I'm so sorry. So very
very sorry. Please accept—said something else we couldn't hear. And
made the sign of the cross.

Mr. Winston was found dead in his house in Sound Hill at three
o'clock that afternoon. His eyes were open, gazing out intently at
something which in that wider, more silent distance might have
figured as a distinct and even familiar form taking shape. The gaze
remained intact beneath our ministering hands. It was then that we
noticed his left hand was clenched tight shut, as if around something
both withheld and held. The balled, curled-up fist staunchly resisted
our attempts to open it. It was as if, quite by a last willful effort of
the heart and thereupon inevitable, what remained held so tightly
within had in lasting partnership with the holder sworn that it
would not ever, and could never, be removed—as if the silence out
of which the grasp had been formed exceeded both within and without, on every side and for all time, the imagined silence of death.

The funerals for Uncle McKenzie and Mr. Winston were held two
days later at our church up in the Valley. After the services they
were laid next to their wives and each other.

Yes. We were there.

Watercolour for Negro Expatriates in France

George Elliott Clarke

What are calendars to you?
And, indeed, what are atlases?
   Time is cool jazz in Bretagne,
you, hidden in berets or eccentric scarves,
somewhere over the rainbow,
where you are tin men requiring hearts,
lion men demanding courage,
scarecrow men needing minds all your own
after DuBois made Blackness respectable.
   Geography is brown girls in Paris
in the spring by the restless Seine,
flowing like blood in chic African colonies;
Josephine Baker on your bebop phonographs
in the lonely, brave, old rented rooms;
Gallic wines shocking you out of yourselves,
leaving you as abandoned
as obsolete locomotives whimpering Leadbelly blues
in lonesome Shantytown, USA.

What are borders/frontiers to you?
In actual seven-league sandals,
you ride Monet's shimmering waterlilies—
in your street-artist imaginations—
across the sky darkened,
here and there, by Nazi shadows,

Krupp thunderclouds,
and, in other places, by Americans
who remind you
that you are niggers,
even if you have read Sartre and Hugo.

Night is winged Ethiopia in the distance,
rising on zeta beams of Radio Free Europe,
bringing you in for touchdown at Orléans,
or, it is strange, strychnine streetwalkers

fleecing you for an authentic Negro poem
or rhythm-and-blues salutation.
This is your life—
lounging with Richard Wright in Matisse-green
parks, facing nightmares of contorted
lynchers every night. Every night.

Scatological ragtime reggae haunts the caverns
of le métro. You pick up English-language
newspapers and Time magazine,
learn that this one was arrested,
that one assassinated;
fear waking—like Gregor Samsa—
in the hands of a mob;
lust for a Black Constance Chatterley,
not even knowing that
all Black people not residing in Africa
are kidnap victims.

After all, how can you be an expatriate
of a country that was
never yours?

Pastel paintings on Paris pavement,
wall posters Beardsley-style:
you pause and admire them all;
and France entrances you
with its kaleidoscope cafés,
chain-smoking intelligentsia,
absinthe, and Pernod poets. . . .

Have you ever seen postcards
of Alabama or Auschwitz,
Mississippi or Mussolini?

It is unsafe to wallow in Ulyssean dreams,
genetic theories, vignettes of Gertrude Stein,
Hemingway, other maudlin moderns,

while the godless globe
detonates its war-heart, loosing
goose-stepping geniuses
and dark, secret labs.

Perhaps I suffer aphasia.
I know not how to talk to you.
I send you greetings from *Afrique*
and spirituals of catholic *Négritude.*
Meanwhile, roses burst like red stars,
a flower explodes for a special sister.
You do not accept gravity in France,
where everything floats on the premise
that the earth will rise to meet it
the next day;
where the Eiffel Tower bends over backward
to insult the Statue of Liberty;
and a woman in the flesh of the moment
sprouts rainbow butterfly wings
and kisses a schizoid sculptor
lightly on his full, ruby lips;
and an argument is dropped over cocoa
by manic mulatto musicians
who hear whispers of Eliot—
or Ellington—
in common prayers.

You have heard Ma Rainey, Bessie Smith.
You need no passport.
Your ticket is an all-night room
facing the ivory, voodoo moon,
full of Henri Rousseau lions and natives;
and your senses, inexplicably
homing in on gorgeous Ethiopia,
while Roman rumors of war
fly you home.

Exile (wondering what happened to all the brothers)

Brother Yao

One
my heart splits
with the touch of your fingertips
whip of fantasy
I want you
but you don't want me
that is why
I must go away . . .

this bitter word
gothic with vines
assault of the ancient
mystery, dark old
and alone
it cracks and splinters
it is the shrieking drip of water to stone

I grow old without you

silence strangles;
what is left of lust
has broken into webbed ground
of the desert

this portion of earth so distant
from my own
foreign tongue that whips flesh

they speak to me without respect

gray sky of idolatry
masks of the sun
bricks cracked and filled with soot

prison *"to send a brother away from himself"*

filled with loneliness
until it pushes you out
of your own door
into . . . exile.

beauty another pimped thing
green grass with a whore's glow
Congo Square
to move without shackles in
fenced space
you walk on the grass
and you are escaping

my nightmare has me forget
this confinement
save myself through dreams
and one day I ran out to the grass
without my shoes on
to feel free/not be
but to feel free
and I was shot
in the cool grass on my feet

shackles bitter
but they rub the skin to be
kind
to say
"excuse me, sir,
you cannot go there"

I forget

worse to dance and forget it is a different dance
from any you know
you forget
because there have never been words
for Congo Square
like there are no words
for what things have come to

what has not been taught
the mysteriousness of the destruction
that comes like warm wind
black cloud
you wait for storm after storm
the men cry for exile

bitter death too thirsty
to let my blood and let it
wet my throat
I seek exile

your ballad of the sorrow reigning here
your face
your beauty
in with that vicious band of grass
and distant sun
your sweet smell works for them
to punish me
softly tickle
this man without laughter
tortures me
dances with heels
on my mind

your ballad
your eyes weep for me
forget me not

I will not die in death's arms
instead I will swan dive
and burn in the sky

though I am soot I still burn
though you are mine
I still yearn

that is why I have gone so far away

TWO
where else would a brother go?

THREE
you thought there was no more exodus
you thought we would forget how to bleed
you thought we were trapped in these lives
to either rise or self-destruct

backdoor-exile self-exile

you thought your daddy was crazy
and then you found him hangin' out with
your grandaddy and High John the Conqueror
tellin' ol' lies
without faces
shrinking into the forest
Sambo and Rastus there too
hiding in that dope image

FOUR
in Negroland there are many Black folks
much gold
on treasure island
how did they get there?
how do you get to treasure island?

FIVE
his bitterness turned into opium
there was no magic left to turn things
sweet magic itself became bitter
only magic left
made bitter bland
made sweet bland
made everything taste the same

SIX
the path to the forest has no crossroads
you would not know Legba
and he would tell you
of Negroland and
starving for any land
you would believe him
he laughs

SEVEN
we searched for days
and only found zombies
whose every step
left the footprint of parables
but their clothes stunk of lies
and we who had forgotten spells saw
sunk in their eyes the red storm of tragedy
who opened the backdoor for them
who did these deeds
who gave them tragic, rotten exile

EIGHT
many circles
starving for progress
some Negro
plotted a new course
to nowhere

it appeared that they vanished
from any path known
strange
some dimensional form of travel
he was last seen in his house
acting like a fool
screaming about America
a monkey on his back
picking through his life story for lice
of deception
and then he disappeared
and his son
seeks that path.

The Ballad of the Sad Chanteuse

COLIN CHANNER

CHAPTER ONE

The sun crashed through the window and shattered against the walls. I acknowledged the light, but continued to lie in bed, staring at a spot on the ceiling where water stains had formed a pattern of subtly shifting browns.

A growl in my stomach reminded me that I hadn't eaten in two days.

I went to the bathroom, took a leak, and almost trampled my laptop, which was sitting on a pile of magazines and old Gleaners in front of the toilet. Placed as it was, the computer resembled a bathroom scale; and I found myself pondering what my weight would be if the laws of physics were revised and gravity began to affect psychic burdens. My physical weight was one eighty-five, which at six-four placed me on the meager side of slim. But with my problems factored in, I reasoned, I would've weighed around two twenty, two twenty-five. I felt heavy. I moved slowly. I had been locked in my room for the first three days of my trip to Jamaica.

I took a shower and went out on the balcony to smoke and watch the storm's retreat across the water. It was a little cool after the rain; but the breeze whispered the threat of heat and humidity. Out in the distance at a point where the blue of the sea should have paused to acknowledge the infinity of the sky, a ship floated in the transfiguring mist.

What if there were a stowaway onboard that ship? The question hung in the air for as long as it could have, then fell back to earth, breaking into shards.

The smoke burned my lungs as I inhaled deeply. Cigarettes were a recent habit. I stubbed the butt on the railing and flicked it into the air. What if that ship were carrying drugs? Two tons . . .

I raised my hand to smack the railing in frustration and noticed something that I had scribbled on my palm the day before.

I am tired of struggling. Struggling to develop my writing craft. Struggling against the temptation to give up and go back to the office. Struggling under the weight of financial debt. Struggling with writer's block. Having writer's block is like having nerve damage. It can come on slowly or suddenly. It can last years or just a few days It is devastating. Debilitating. Frustrating. Filled with desperate moments and actions. A writer's mind is like a limb. That's why he needs to nourish it with reading, and strengthen it with experience. In fact, his mind is more critical than his arms. A blocked writer is like a dancer with a stroke. Consider the state of a hobbled Bill Jones, wanting the legs that catapulted him across the stage to merely stir, asking limp toes to assume a less cowardly posture. Try to imagine the fear. The sadness. The anger. The loss. The disappointment.

I got dressed, groomed my beard, and went for breakfast at the Guava Tree, a little café near the hotel. I took a seat at one of the small wooden tables on the sidewalk and watched minibuses and taxis wriggle back and forth like ants on a trail.

Both the café and the hotel were located on the eastern end of Gloucester Avenue, the main tourist strip in Montego Bay. Narrow and winding, with only a single lane in either direction, Gloucester Avenue is chock-full of small hotels, gift shops, nightclubs, and restaurants. The western end, which begins just a little beyond Doctor's Cave Beach, is a little quieter. There the beachfront is interrupted for about a quarter of a mile by a line of low cliffs, at the end of which is Walter Fletcher Beach.

I didn't want to stay on Gloucester Avenue. But I had no choice. I couldn't afford the nicer hotels on the outskirts of town. Neither could I afford to rent a car . . . or the trip itself for that matter. But I had heard that a change of scene was a good intellectual laxative.

I lit a cigarette and fidgeted with my dreads as I trawled the conversations around me for ideas. I needed a character or an incident to begin writing again. I had exhausted all of mine.

After two novels and a collection of short stories, I still didn't feel comfortable introducing myself as a writer. I used to do this. But I had stopped, because I had never met anyone who had heard of my books. So I identified myself as a typesetter, the endeavor that paid my bills.

My waitress edged up to the table. She was a short, fat girl with a face that had the shape and texture of a pineapple. Compounding her cosmetic problems were a pair of crossed eyes and an underbite. She was shy, a real country girl, and she held her head down when she took my order.

"Can I get for you, sah?" she asked timidly.

"What's good?" I asked brightly, attempting to relax her.

She tugged at her sky blue tunic before answering.

"Well we have Jamaican breakfast—ackee and saltfish and eggs with either green banana or hard dough bread and we have American breakfast, sah."

"I'll take the Jamaican," I said.

"You is Jamaican, sah?"

"Yeah. Yardie to de core. Original ruff neck."

She laughed and looked up after I spoke patois with her.

"But you leave here long time," she continued.

"When I was eighteen . . . what's that? . . . fourteen years ago."

"You come back regular?" she asked as she walked away.

I nodded.

She returned about twenty minutes later, by which time the temperature had risen to about eighty-five degrees. Following the cue of a passing street vendor, I removed my shirt.

The eggs were delicious. They were spiced with garlic and scotch bonnet pepper, and I was ravenous. I lowered my mouth to the edge of the plate and shoved my face in my food like a pig, unconcerned with my demeanor until I heard a soft chuckle.

I looked up to see a little boy watching me, which was surprising, because the table was empty when I had begun to eat.

He blushed when our eyes met and clapped his hands over his delicate face. But he continued to watch me through a crack in his fingers. He was with a woman whose face was screened off by a newspaper, so he felt free to play a game of imitation with an indulgent stranger.

I covered my face after he covered his. And when he dropped his hands in his lap, I did the same with mine. Out came his tongue, then came mine, but accompanied by raised eyebrows. He couldn't get his brows up, and as he contorted his soft face, laughter vaulted out of my heart.

The woman's face appeared suddenly above the paper and it became obvious that she and the boy were mother and child.

"Cello! What did I tell you about strangers?" she asked with undiminished alarm.

"Sorry," I said, acknowledging that I understood her fears.

"Don't take it personally," she replied without taking her eyes off the boy. He pulled his chin into his chest and began to pout, then turned to look at me again. His mother cleared her throat. This didn't deter him from waving. He turned his eyes down to direct my vision to his pudgy hand which rested on the table, then he slowly flexed his wrist. I shouldn't have responded, but I didn't want to let him down, so I did the same. His mother caught my movement and turned toward me, glaring.

I looked away as casually as I could and acted on the sudden need to conceal my nakedness.

I heard them rise while my shirt was over my head. When I was through, the mother was facing me from the other side of my table.

She was tall, about five feet nine inches, and had a slenderness that began in her face but was defeated by the resistance of her abdomen. Her skin had a layered brown complexion, like a well-oiled baseball mitt, and she wore a white cotton shirt that was buttoned at the neck in defiance of the humidity. Short hair would have suited her because she had beautiful almond eyes the color of tamarind seeds. But her long hair was not distracting, since she wore it modestly. It was pulled away from her face and coiled in a braid that was held in place with a pin. She appeared to be around thirty-three, and Cello around five or six. Judging from her accent and her clothing, she was educated, professional, and probably Jamaican. She wasn't wearing a wedding ring, which led me to believe that she had not been married to Cello's father, as she struck me as the kind of woman who would have continued to wear her ring to deter the unwanted approaches of men.

"I really didn't appreciate that," she remarked tersely.

She reached into her purse and popped some pills without water —vitamins I presumed—then left with Cello in tow.

I didn't reply. I just sat and watched as she and Cello disappeared around the bend.

I began to think about her as a character in a narrative. I took a sip of coffee and began to give her a history, a context, and a situation. What was her name? Prudence was the first one to come to mind, but it was quickly replaced by Grace. She looked like a Prudence or a Grace, in that the names would have suited her conservative demeanor, albeit in a clichéd way. While debating which of these names was more appropriate, I was overwhelmed by the name Lissanne, which just felt right.

Well what did Lissanne do for a living? I asked.

Businesswoman? No. Musician? . . . classical? . . . piano? . . . acoustic guitar? . . . cello? Businesswoman. Maybe she had a little inn somewhere . . . in Falmouth or Savanna la Mar or one of those little towns. No, she didn't. She was a pharmacist . . . had her own drugstore. But she had some artistic skill . . . the piano. Okay, Lissanne the pharmacist was in Montego Bay on vacation? She was on vacation from Kingston. She was Jamaican, but lived in . . . in . . . Canada for a long time before she returned. . . . Toronto. . . . that's where she met Cello's father . . . Canada but not Toronto. . . . Montreal, and he was French Canadian of Haitian extraction . . . a musician . . . conservatory trained . . . but worked in bars and cabarets because . . . he couldn't get a job in a symphony. She was attracted to him because of his gentle way . . . and because. . . . No. She got involved with him because her parents didn't like Haitians . . . and she was rebelling against them, although she didn't realize it at the time, this rebellion being her first sensation of passion, which, sadly, she mistook for love. But she came back to Jamaica because her former lover had been stalking her. . . . He had become a junkie after she left him. . . . He was a casual user before . . . and . . . she had left him after three years . . . so Cello remembered him. . . . She was on vacation in Montego Bay, and she was renting a villa, she didn't like hotels. . . . She couldn't relax in them . . . but then again villas were kind of expensive. . . . Would she have been able to afford one on a pharmacist's salary? So she owned her own pharmacy. She had brought money back from Canada plus her father was well-to-do and he had left her some property which she had sold. Good, she owned a pharmacy. She worked there fourteen hours a day and she was on vacation with her son, Cello. What if this Lissanne . . . Sedgewick's Haitian junkie pianist ex-lover turned up at her villa, how would she deal with it? If he were no longer a junkie, but had cleaned up? That would be a source of conflict right there . . . because she had never loved him . . . but . . . but . . . Cello wanted him to be in his life, and there was no longer the issue of drug addiction between her and Paul . . . Paul Fouché. And she was a forgiving person . . . and he wasn't a bad guy to begin with. . . .

I was about to begin jotting down an outline when the waitress returned to clear the tables. She went about her duties quietly and didn't seem inclined toward conversation.

I got up to go to the beach to work on the outline. At the same time, a middle-aged English couple took the table where Cello and his mother had been sitting. As I stepped off the curb, I heard a voice calling out to me.

"Hullo, I think you've forgotten something."

I turned around.

"You dropped this," the man said, pushing a book toward me. "It was under your table."

I reached for the book reflexively. The couple turned around and continued their conversation, convinced that I was the rightful owner. It dawned on me that it belonged to Cello's mother, who had probably been too annoyed with me to have heard it fall. I began to flip through it out of curiosity, but stopped when I realized it was a journal. A photograph of Cello's mother was tucked between the pages. She was wearing a strapless evening dress and her hair was down. I held the photograph by the edges because I didn't want to leave fingerprints. I was taken aback. I would have never imagined her dressed like that. I examined the photograph closely, and flipped it over to see if there was an inscription on the back, but there was none. This was a little disappointing, because I was hoping to learn more about her, at least her real name. As I compared my initial impression of her with the one in my hand, I began to find her intriguing. Was she for example a pharmacist or some other medical professional? Did she live abroad at one time? Was she even Jamaican? I knew that at least some of the answers were in her journal, and I was tempted to take a read . . . at least a few pages. But I knew it wasn't right.

Realizing that I was on the verge of violating her privacy, I decided to entrust the journal to the café's manager.

I went inside and inquired, and soon an American woman with tousled auburn hair emerged from an anteroom. She was portly and cheerful, and seemed unduly intrigued by my account.

"What's your name?" she asked, as she placed the journal beneath the counter.

"Colin Robinson," I replied.

"I'm Faith Whistler. Nice to meet you. And where are you staying?"

"The Ocean Front, right down here on Gloucester."

I was about to ask her why she needed this information, when she told me. "I'm gonna write her a little note, so she can thank you in person if she feels like it. I'm from Chicago, and one day I lost my Walkman at a Bulls game and miraculously someone turned it in. And I felt so bad when I wasn't able to thank them, because they didn't leave a name or number or anything. Trust me, she probably will want to thank you."

"It's all right," I replied. "I don't think Lissanne likes me very much."

"Who is that?" she replied with a jerk of her head.

"That's the name I made up for the woman whose book this is," I replied sheepishly.

She looked at me quizzically.

"It's a long story," I said with a finality that didn't convince her to drop the subject.

"That's Anaïs Castro," she said with a flourish, "the singer. She headlines the cabaret at the Shady Grove. Isn't she beautiful? She's Costa Rican. Why don't you think she likes you? Costa Ricans are very loving people. They don't even have an army in their country."

"I think I got off on the wrong foot with her when I played with her son. She didn't really appreciate it," I replied.

"She doesn't have any children. That was probably Cello with her. Cello is her sister's son. I know Anaïs very well. She has breakfast here at least once a week."

A waitress whispered something in Faith's ear and she excused herself to iron out a problem. I was left in a daze. I couldn't believe that I had been so wrong about this woman.

The thought of getting to know her began to intrigue me even more. The urge to read her journal again possessed me. Just a page, I told myself. One page and no more.

I knew I shouldn't have done it. But I did. I looked to see if anyone was watching. Faith was busy scolding two waitresses. The other three were busy. No one would notice. I resisted as long as I could. But my resolve snapped without warning. Before I could stop myself, I had leaned over the counter and snatched it.

I turned to a random page and read quickly.

I imagine that the feeling of a penis in my mouth would be like a guinep . . . round and smooth, hard yet soft. I've been thinking about having a penis in my mouth a lot lately. Maybe it is because I haven't made love to a man in over a year, and so my mind is wandering in perverse directions. I've often wondered if the feeling of a penis in my mouth could ever be as fulfilling as having a man inside my vagina. Having my legs wrapped around my lover's back makes me feel powerful, because I can feel his strength pulsing inside me. Could the feeling of his penis in my mouth give me the same feeling? I need to stop thinking about this. What I need to do is take a lover.

My mouth went dry. I wanted to continue reading, but I felt guilty about invading Anaïs's privacy. I replaced the journal as quickly as I had taken it and headed to the bathroom to wash the perspiration off my face.

I examined myself in the mirror, the sloe eyes, the cleft chin, the high, narrow nose bridge that was built by a European forebear, the wide African mouth that survived to recount that tale.

What kind of men did she like? I asked. What kind of lover was she looking for? Why hadn't she had a lover for so long?

I wanted to know.

I decided to go to the Shady Grove that night. I wanted to see her again.

Intuition told me that the real story of Anaïs Castro was more engaging than anything I could create. She was a foreigner in a strange country. She was beautiful. Artistic. And yearning for love. There was a story there, and I resolved to find it. I thought about the photograph again and remarked to myself that her breasts had seemed smaller in her blouse.

I checked my watch when I left the bathroom. It was noon. The crowd was thinning inside the dining room. Almost half of the purple banquettes were empty. The cooling system was out of service. Fans were going, but they seemed to be whipping the air and making it thicker. Sweat slithered down my back.

The tables were to my right, the L-shaped counter to my left. The passageway ran straight ahead to the front door, which was flung wide open. Through the aluminum louvers, all but one of the sidewalk tables stood empty. Several waitresses were talking by the door. Two were tending tables. I assumed that one of the waitresses in the group at the door was actually overseeing the register and would return to her post behind the counter soon.

One of the waitresses went behind the counter to get an ice cream bowl. She dug deeply, and during her search she placed a number of objects on the countertop. Among the glasses and pitchers was the journal. I swallowed hard when I saw it. The waitress went back to her friends by the door and fanned herself with a menu, leaving the journal unguarded.

I began an internal dialogue.

One more look, I heard myself say. One more look at the picture so you can have her image imprinted on your mind, so you can begin to write about her. One look and nothing else.

No. It wouldn't be right. You've done too much already.

Do it now. What if she returns a minute from now? You'll never get the chance again.

It had been months since I had been able to write anything. It was my first experience of writer's block. I was nervous about its duration. I had a good feeling about this story. So I couldn't afford to lose it.

I looked around and sidled up to the counter.

I grabbed the journal, went to the bathroom, and locked myself in the toilet stall. I tried to find the page I had begun before, but it took too much time. I examined the picture closely, then turned to a random page. I began to read.

Jamaican men are so funny. A man came up to me one day at the gas station by the airport and told me that he loved me. I told him he didn't even know me. And he told me that he didn't need to know me to love me. The guy reminded me of my grandfather. I never met him but I've seen pictures of him when he was young. He came to Nicaragua from Panama where he had gone to build the canal. My father says he came from St. James parish but his father was from Cuba. Maybe that's why I love Mo'bay so much.

When I write my autobiography this journal will be my source. I was born in the Atlantic coast town of Bluefields, which is mainly English speaking, in 1959 to a big family. There are six of us. Father, mother, and four children. A boy then three girls. All spaced exactly two years apart: Eduardo, Emmanuelle, Nora, and me. Eduardo drowned when we were children. Emmanuelle is a part-time hairdresser in New York. Nora is in jail for drugs in Denver.

My father, Zephaniah, is retired. He was a building contractor in Nicaragua; he did a lot of work for the Somozas and the Chamorros, but he couldn't find work in New York so he became a building superintendent. My mother is from Managua, so she speaks mainly Spanish. She has always been a housewife. I miss my mother. I know she doesn't miss me and that is sad.

My family moved to New York in the summer of 1975 because my father was alarmed by the Sandinista uprising. My sisters and I attended boarding school in Managua and finished up at Archbishop Molloy in Queens. We lived in Rego Park in a two-bedroom apartment. Soon after we arrived, Emmanuelle got married to Hugo, a machinist from Haiti, and moved out to Brooklyn. Nora won a scholarship to Amherst College in Massachusetts. It's a pity how her life turned out.

My mother was happy when Manny got married. She wanted Nora and me to get married too. She never had a life because of children, she always use to say. Emmanuelle said Mama hated us because Papa liked having sex with us more than with her. Nora and I made a blasphemous exclamation when we heard this; then we comforted her by not telling her that it had never happened to us.

I began to fear my father after that. I did everything to please him, because I didn't want sex to happen to me. I began to hate my mother even more for letting petty jealousy come before protecting her child. It is Nora's opinion that Mama didn't like us because we weren't her children. According to her, our aunt Martha told her that we were each the child of a different one of our father's mistresses, and he brought us home to the house after we were weaned because Mama couldn't have any more babies after Eduardo and my father wanted to have a big family. I have often wondered if any of this is true. We do not really look like each other, although we share some features like our eyes with our father. None of us look like our mother though. But the idea of her suffering for anyone is too hard to believe. And Aunt Martha is dead.

I think my mother doesn't like us because she is just a horrible person. As simplistic as it may sound, some people are just born that way. My mother can be so verbally abusive and selfish and deceitful. Nothing I do is ever good enough for her.

I admire her for one thing though: that is her voice. It is incredible. It buzzes with tremolo like the wind in the wake of a hummingbird's flight. That is how Somoza himself described it when she sang for him as a teenager, my father says. She has perfect pitch and a five-octave range that begins at mezzosoprano and, according to my father it used to be eight when she sang for the president in the thirties, when she was only sixteen. According to rumor Somoza offered her a scholarship to Madrid to study opera on condition that she sleep with him. I don't know what happened, but she did not go to Madrid. Emmanuelle told me that she slept with him but didn't go because

she was uneducated and thought her accent would sound crude
in Spain. Nora said she slept with him but she was afraid to
cross the Atlantic by boat. I often wonder if I would be a lounge
singer today if she had gone? I wonder if her voice is still pretty?
I haven't heard it in over twelve years.

I turned to another page.

Last night I had a dream about Mr. Markowitz. He was such
a good voice coach. I can't believe that he's dead. Where would
I be today if he was still alive? Maybe I should go back to New
York. But I'm not sure if I'll be able to deal with things. Maybe
it's too soon. Not after what happened to me there.

Another page.

I touched myself four times last night. I kept thinking about
Wesley Snipes. . . . fantasized about being entered from behind,
which surprised me, because I don't like that position. I can't
see a man when he is behind me, and I don't trust men enough
to feel comfortable with my face turned away. I think I fantasized about it because I went to hear Stone Love at Walter
Fletcher Beach and saw a woman leaning backward against her
date and rubbing her buttocks against his groin. Her face was
pure ecstasy. She was wearing a cat suit. I kept watching her all
night. She would lean forward and touch her toes and he would
hold her by the waist and grind into her. It was so sexual. It got
me very excited. But I am not like her. I can't let go. The
thought scares me.

I flipped again.

Sometimes when I am singing I feel that I am the greatest
singer alive. And at others I am so self-critical. Like last night.
I sounded awful. My timing was off, and the band kept altering
its tempo to stay with me.
   I think I was nervous last night because I knew my blind date
was watching from the audience. When I met him I was disappointed. He wasn't my type. He was short and clean-cut, and
when we went out he didn't have any original thoughts on anything. He wasn't like X. It was a pity he turned out to be an

insensitive pig. He was physically very attractive. The color of his skin frightened me. He was so black.

Black skin frightens me because I find it so seductive. I have never analyzed it beyond acknowledging that my father was really black and that might have something to do with it. The only one-night stand I ever had was with a very black man. I was ashamed for months afterward, because I felt I had done something wrong and cheap and low. Men don't respect women who sleep around. And women who sleep around don't respect themselves. Some women who sleep around say they do have self-respect, but they are only fooling themselves. My friends say I am repressed. But if so, then so what? I feel normal. And what is the difference between being repressed and having self-discipline?

What really upset me about that experience is the assumptions he made about me. For example, he took it for granted that I wanted to have sex with him the next morning and began to touch me. And when I refused him he got upset. That spoiled it for me. I did want to have sex with him again, but there was nothing in my manner that said I did. He was just operating on stereotypes of women who sleep around. He began to insist that I was putting up a front in this really mocking self-assured tone, and when I still refused he began to try the soft approach, nibbling my earlobes and the like. Then when this didn't work either, he began to twist my arms so that I would remove my hands from between my legs.

I fought with him, but he was strong and he pinned my arms above my head with one of his hands. I parted my legs to kick him but he used the opportunity to wrench his body up against me. I begged him. I pleaded with him. I didn't realize that I peed my clothes until afterward. The night before he was so tender, but now he was a brute.

I like it. But I can't let him know because I will be proving his point. Scream. I want to scream but I'm afraid it might come out as a scream of pleasure. But my silence seems to urge him on. It is as if he wants to get a reaction from me, and he is doing it harder and I can't hold it in. I want to let it out. Maybe if I move about beneath him it will end quickly and it will never get to the point where I lose control. I don't want him to have this power over me to make me lose control. That's why I like to do it to myself. But if I move against him he might mistake this as a sign of agreement and he won't feel guilty for violating me afterward. I am confused about that incident to this day. It lives with me.

A knot formed in my chest. I shuffled quickly toward the back. I checked my watch. Five minutes had elapsed. I began to panic that Anaïs had already returned and was discussing the whereabouts of her journal with Faith. I was about to close it up and replace it immediately. But something caught my eye. It was a pencil sketch for a business card. And it had her address and phone number. I had no specific plans for the information, but common sense told me to take it down. After this, I closed the book and concerned myself with returning it.

Business was slow and all the employees were distracted. Neither Anaïs nor Faith were anywhere to be seen. I could have walked off with the journal or read it some more.

And it was all up to me.

If negotiations were taking place within my conscience, they were occurring under strict security. I didn't feel any discrete emotions. There was, however, a low-frequency hum that traveled back and forth along my spine to the base of my skull. The book was held firmly between the fingers of my left hand, which was pressed up against the counter.

Elements of my biography wriggled out of the inchoate muck of my mind. Colin Robinson. Born October 7, 1963, at Andrew's Memorial Hospital in St. Andrew, Jamaica, to a pharmacist and a policeman. Christened Anglican. Three siblings. One boy and two girls. Baby of the family. Nine O levels from Ardenne High. Three A levels from Meadowbrook. Member of the choir, soccer team, and track team. Emigrated to New York with family in 1982, leaving distraught girlfriend. Graduated from Hunter College in 1985. Communications degree with Spanish minor. Dropped out of Columbia School of Journalism in 1985 and became an editor at *Interview* magazine. Stayed at *Interview* till 1988, then went to Crabbe Wedderburn Publishers until 1990. From then till present, full-time fiction writer, part-time typesetter. In other words, struggler.

I was halfway across the street before I began to come to terms with my decision.

CHAPTER TWO

I didn't take the journal. Instead I left her a note saying that I was a free-lance writer who had seen her performance and wanted to interview her because I thought she was marvelous. The idea had come to me in flash, and in its aftermath I wasn't sure if it had been the brightest thing. What if she didn't believe me, or simply wasn't interested? That would've left me with only the memory of what I'd read and not much else. I had gambled on the fact that she would be interested, however. She was obviously battling with her personal and artistic worth, so there was the strong possibility that she would call me because she was flattered. But what if she did not call?

I should have just taken the journal, I thought to myself. It would have made things so much simpler. But it wouldn't have been right, I heard myself say. Neither was lying to her, I noted. But in my hierarchy of infractions, theft had always ranked higher than perjury.

I crossed the street to Doctor's Cave Beach, paid the fee at the booth, and passed through the turnstile into the shadowy entrance hall. I took a chair on the esplanade and looked out on the cerulean sparkle of the sea. The sand was littered with sunbathers, and heads bobbed in the water as far as fifty yards from shore. I transcribed the excerpts of the journal from memory, then made a quick plan.

It was simple. I would spend the day getting as much information on her as I could, then approach her at the Shady Grove. I would convince her to do the interview, then spend as much time as possible with her.

After spending the next half hour outlining interview questions, I left to go see her house.

I flagged down a red Lada taxi and jumped in the front seat.

"Weh dis address deh star?" I asked the driver rude-boy style, dispelling all notions that I was a tourist and therefore a sucker. I showed him the information I had written down.

"Dat is out in Ironshore side, outta Coral Gardens," he replied.

"How much fe go deh so?"

"Bout a hundred J," he replied, trying to sound final.

"Sixty me can pay y'know," I replied, more convincingly than he. He looked at me, paused, pondered, then capitulated.

We drove off in a cloud of smoke. The Lada needed a ring job and the muffler was blown. The driver was young, about twenty-two, short and stocky with a deep scar on his right cheek.

The car labored up the steady incline that Montegonians call Bottom Road, past the police station, which used to be a good hotel, and several small guest houses.

"Dread, y'ave any dollars fe change?" the driver asked. "Me can gi yuh a good price y'know."

"You know a place name Shady Grove?" I asked, acknowledging his question obliquely.

"Yeah man," he replied brightly, realizing the relation between his answer and mine. "Right out behind the airport near Sandals and Dragon Lounge and Baba Joe's . . . a new place, on Kent Avenue. Yeah man me know deh so good. Pure money people go deh so. Whitey, y'know. Cause a dem ave de dollars."

"Y'ever go yet?"

"Naw star. Me a-struggle as it is right now because my baby modder a-breed again, dat a-go make it four by she now—she easy fe breed y'know, all me do is take off me shirt and she breed—me cyaan really afford dem place deh. Plus a no really my style still. Dem play pure jazz and dem kinda fuckery deh. Me is a man love dancehall still."

"You know anybody that works over there?"

"Yeah man, me cousin Slacky. Is a waiter. Im live over Flankers near me."

"I'da like meet Slacky."

"We coulda check im now still cause im suppose to deh deh arready, cause im work lunch and dinner."

"At Shady Grove?"

"Yeah man. A jus up yah so y'know, when you pass de rounabout and go roun. You come from Kingston don't?

"Yeah man—"

"Me can tell cause you doan know Bay. Kingston people always know Ochi, but dem doan know Bay. You waan me pass round a Shady Grove?"

"Let's do that when we come back from roun Ironshore."

He nodded in disengaged approval, then there was a hesitation. He asked me in a sheepish voice about the U.S. dollars again. I told him I could change twenty for him.

He smiled and pressed fists with mine, and graced me with his name: Percival Alberga Clarke.

We swung off the main road about two miles outside Montego Bay proper and began the ascent into the sprawling hillside development of luxury villas. The little Lada coughed and wheezed but it brought us to our destination, albeit in reverse, after every other gear had failed on the last curve.

We pulled up outside a two-story pink stucco house with a red tile roof. It was probably the smallest house on the street, but it had an undisturbed view of the coast road and the sea. The fence was rimmed with orange and yellow crotons and the lawn was a bit over-grown. The gate was open but there was no car in the carport. The redwood louvers were all closed as far as I could see.

"You want ah blow?" Percy asked.

"No man, is all right," I replied.

"You want me wait?"

"No man."

"So wha you want me do den?"

"Jus cool."

"Cool cos money y'know dread."

I turned to look at him. His eyebrows were raised expectantly.

"Me wi link you man," I replied reassuringly. His face relaxed

I sketched a picture of the front of the house and placed it in my pocket.

Percy began to chuckle to himself.

"Bloodclaat! Dis dread ya is a artistic dread," he muttered under his breath. I looked at him. Then he spoke up. "Dread, me no really a-laugh still, but it kinda strange fe come all de way up ya so fe draw a ouse y'know. Tink bout it? Suppose police come now? Dem woulda mus tink say we a-plan fe rob de bloodclaat place. Especially like ow you is a dread an me jus come outta jail."

I reached into my pocket and fished out a five.

"Percy, do me a favor. Go up the street and park. I'm going to go inside. If you see a car coming like it coming into this driveway start your engine. It look like I could cut through the bush behind the house up to that road up there." I pointed. "Then if anything, come and meet me up there."

He smiled and took the five.

"If police come me gone dough y'know," he cautioned. "Because Jamaican police doan loaf."

We touched fists to consummate the deal. I was about to get out of the car when I spied someone watching us from the house across the street.

"Percy, cancel that. Somebody watching. Don't look, just drive away," I said calmly, not wanting to alarm him into acting sus-piciously.

He put the car in neutral and let it roll down the hill, and we were gone.

"So you doan want back the five?" he asked rhetorically, when we hit the main road.

I didn't answer. He took it to mean no.

"So what you went to jail for, Percy?" I asked out of professional curiosity. "And how long you stayed?"

We had just passed by the big Texaco station at the little bridge over the creek. Ragged little boys stood there selling fish strung together with twine that looked like strange fruit.

He paused before answering.

"A little rape ting y'know. Set me back about five years."

His answer was casual but thoughtful, as if I had asked him how long he had had his car.

He began to speak before I had a chance.

"So whappen dread . . . you never rape a gyal yet?"

"No," I replied.

"Half you life gone man. When a gyal a-fight you you get de sweetest ride."

"I see," I said distantly, then changed the subject to the heat.

He continued, however: "And some woman like it to . . . fe get hol down. . . . Most gyal wha me hol down . . . from dem see say dat me naah let dem go . . . dem jus start gwaan wid nuff tings. An after de firs time, every day dem jus a-antagonize me fe de work man. Serious ting."

I heard him pause, then through my peripheral vision saw him looking at me with his head turned away from the road. I didn't pay him any attention. I couldn't. All my reserves were channeled into thinking about Anaïs's account of her violation.

We swung onto narrow, deserted Kent Avenue, which used to be the road into Montego Bay before the roundabout and the wide Bottom Road were built.

I looked through the chain-link fence beyond the airport's runway to the bluff above Flankers, where the yawning sore of the gypsum quarry reminded me of the hard truth beneath the greenery of the hills. We passed the big white wall of Sandals on the right and the clapboard facade of the Dragon Lounge and the concrete benches under the poinciana tree by Baba Joe's. The sea hummed as it went about its business of saving the shore from loneliness. Goats and cows grazed between the airport's fence and the taxiway as a jetliner screamed good-bye to the island of contradictions. I peered in all directions, but there was no sign of the Shady Grove. I began to feel uneasy.

I glanced over at Percival. He was lip-synching to a song on the radio. He saw me in the corner of his eye and spoke as though he had read my mind.

"We soon reach dread," he said reassuringly. "Jus hol on."

"I'm not worried," I replied, gripping the door handle.

"See it deh," Percival announced in a faux tour-guide tone. "The Shady Grove."

In the near distance, the top of a white building was partially visible above a stand of poinciana trees.

We pulled up outside the wrought-iron fence and followed the brick walkway to the courtyard in front of the neo-Georgian limestone building. It had a shingled roof, switchback stairs and shuttered windows. In the center of the courtyard was a fountain. And around the fountain were concentric circles of white slatted chairs, and round tables draped in blue linen. The courtyard was shaded by a ring of yellow poinciana trees whose blossoms drifted in the breeze.

I sat at one of the tables and watched the band set up for the lunch crowd and the bus boys decorate the tables with hibiscus posies.

Percival and Slacky returned shortly. Slacky was dressed in his work clothes—a full ensemble of white linen. He was slim, with cheekbones spread like wings. Percy introduced us and we pressed fists.

I gave him my New York writer's line in my New York writer's voice and asked him to tell me about Anaïs.

Percival interrupted and asked if the meter was still running. I dismissed him with a five and told him to go sit in the car. He muttered something about an undercover-artist-spy-journalist-miser-dread and left.

Slacky turned out to be very useful. He was head waiter, well educated and extremely articulate—a Cornwall College man.

He said he had been working at the Shady Grove for five years and knew Anaïs pretty well, although not personally. She was quiet and very focused and always seemed to have something on her mind. Some of the band members thought she had an attitude problem, but he thought this was just their reaction to her criticism and suggestions. She didn't seem to have many friends. And although she was well-known, she was usually out alone.

"What is she like on stage?" I asked.

"Laid-back," he replied. "She is so laid-back that she forces the audience to come to her. Some people say that she sings too slow. But that just adds to her sex appeal."

"Is she considered some kind of a sex symbol?" I asked.

"Oh yes," he replied with a grin. "She wears tight evening dresses with slits up the thigh and high-heel shoes when she performs. But she doesn't seem cheap though, just sexy . . . appealing . . . exquisite

. . . like someone you wouldn't want to make love with. Just someone you want to admire and maybe hold. She is just so dignified . . .
that's the word: dignified. She wears tight clothes, but she doesn't
wiggle. She wears high heels but she doesn't strut. And although her
dresses sometimes have slits, you never see her thighs because she
hardly moves. She sways. Her voice does all the work."

"Is she involved with anyone?"

He shook his head. "Never seen her with a man yet."

"She's divorced I hear," I said, fishing.

"I've never heard that," he replied. "Men are always sharking her
down though. Every night they come with gifts and crowd around
the back by the dressing room. But she don't want none."

"Why is that, you think?" I asked.

"Some women are just like that. Who knows, maybe she has a
man under the quiet."

"Does she have any kids?" I asked, fishing some more.

"Yeah, one, Cello, but he lives in New York with his father. I've
only met the kid once and she never talks about him. Neither does
she talk about the father. That is something that nobody ever asks
about. One time a guy asked her about Cello's father and she had
him fired from the band. She can be vindictive."

"How so?"

"I'd rather not say. . . . She can be vindictive."

I asked him again and he became a little agitated, so I decided to
back off and ask some benign questions, like where she was from.

"Is she Jamaican? I wasn't able to place her accent."

"She is Costa Rican," he replied with a smile that indicated that
he preferred the new line of inquiry.

"Costa Rica?"

I must have sounded overly alarmed because he eased back. I
thought back to my conversation with Faith at the Guava Tree. She
too had said that Anaïs was from Costa Rica. But after reading the
journal I had concluded that Faith didn't have her facts straight.

"Has she actually told you this?" I asked.

"Yes. One day she was looking really down and I asked her if she
was okay. I went into the kitchen and got her her favorite dish,
grilled bluefish. She was sitting out in the back by the water and I
just surprised her and brought it for her. And we began to talk about
something or the other, and she really opened up to me. It was common knowledge that she was from Costa Rica, I mean she often
referred to growing up in Limón. She is a rich girl you know. Her
father was a big real estate developer in Costa Rica, and her mother

was an opera singer in Spain . . . Madrid or Barcelona. As a matter of fact, her mother was Spanish. Man, she loves that woman. She talks about her all the time. How her mother sends her gifts all the time and calls her long distance from Paris just to say hello. Her mother is a big opera teacher in France you know."

"So she's real close to her mother," I said.

"Yeah man. It's nice to see a woman close with her mother."

"Has she ever mentioned anything else about her mother?"

"No."

"Do you know how long Anaïs has been here in Jamaica?"

"I think I heard her mention that she has been here about two years."

"Where did she come from?"

"London; that's where she went to school. That's where she partly grew up. Her parents got divorced when she was five, so she grew up between England, Spain, and Costa Rica. Her father is a professor of architecture in London."

"She's actually told you this?"

"Yes. That same time I brought her the fish."

"Has she ever mentioned siblings?"

"One owns a boutique in a fancy hotel in New York and one is a pharmaceuticals exec in Denver."

"Talented bunch. Did she ever mention why she came to Jamaica?"

"Yeah. She was on a world cruise and she fell in love with Montego Bay when the ship stopped here and she just decided to stay."

"I see."

"Anyway, listen I have to go now, it's running a little bit late."

"So what about the kid's father?"

"I don't want to get into it," he said, rising to his feet quickly. "I don't deal with gossip. Plus the only reason that I am doing this interview is because Percival told me that you would give me six hundred J."

He extended his palm. I reached into my wallet without indicating my surprise and disfavor. Something told me that he was lying about the money, but he had proven to be a good source, and I wasn't about to ruin our relationship over twenty bucks. I placed the twenty in his palm and shook his hand in a single move. I gave him my phone number and told him to call me sometime.

He thanked me. I told him he was welcome.

"So when is the article coming out?" he asked.

"In about a month," I replied. "By the way, who owns this place?"

He told me. I didn't recognize the name.
I watched him walk away. He did not look back.

CHAPTER THREE

A writer's mind is like a revolving lottery drum filled with hundreds
of balls. Each ball represents a specific bit of knowledge or experience, and as the drum turns, the balls collide against one another,
leaving their marks on one another's surface over and over until they
are barely distinguishable, making one experience recall another and
all knowledge related. Sometimes the drum spins too fast for too
long and the balls disintegrate instead of denting and abrading
each other, which is a matter for the shrinks; or sometimes the
drum stops turning for a while and the balls begin to regain their
original shape and settle into neat trays, like eggs in the door of
refrigerator filled with Jell-O, Spam, and Tupperware, and one becomes normal.

Writers fear normalcy, because we are all abnormal, which is why
we all begin our lives as liars. Every single writer that I've known
was a liar in his youth. This is because lying is a child's way of
creating a universe in which he feels okay to be abnormal. It is easier
for a child to create his own abnormal world than to fit into the
normal one, because his abnormality is usually not of his choosing
and is thus beyond his control. Think about it. Who would choose
to be poor, ugly, or unathletic, or to have divorced parents?

When a child feels powerless to change the facts of his world, he
makes up his own, in which abnormalities do not occasion prejudice
and pain. And this disposition toward fiction becomes a permanent
part of his personality because an adult is only a child magnified n
times. Why all lying children do not become writers, I cannot say.
But I can say that those who do are always born with lottery drums
for heads and not refrigerators. They cannot stop their heads from
spinning and the balls from colliding randomly in infinite combi-
nations of knowledge and experience that connect with each other
in infinite numbers of angles an infinite number of times, creating
in that random collision a writer's sixth and seventh senses: the
sense of irony and the sense of metaphor, without which he is
merely a person who writes, a scribe, and not a poet.

As a writer, and therefore an experienced liar, I understood Anaïs
Castro.

She hated her life and had tried to create her own, but had failed.
She failed because she did not believe her own story. Her journal
entries were filled with ambivalence and remorse. A self-deluded

person is always confident in his lie, and it shows even in corre-spondence with himself. He is sure why he doesn't like people and why people don't like him, and being paranoid of discovery, he rarely writes things down in the first place.

Most of Anaïs's lies were easy to understand given my knowledge of her. Her horrible mother had become her good mother. Her un-derachieving sisters had become overachievers. Her social class in America improved her class in Nicaragua. Her fears were under-standable as well. She didn't trust men because her father was an incestuous child molester. She repressed her libido for the same rea-son, the validity of which was driven home by rape. Her mother's talent intimidated her, and she resented her mother because she wasn't affectionate and seemed to have been an accomplice to her child's abuse. Four questions remained unanswered, however. Was Cello her nephew as Faith said, or her son as Slacky said? And if he were the latter, who was his father? Why did she come to Jamaica? And why did she lie about her country of origin?

Anaïs was waiting for me when I got back to the hotel. I had just said good-bye to Percy and asked him to pick me up at seven to go to the Shady Grove when I saw her sitting on a bench beneath one of the royal palms that lined the short walkway from the street to the lobby, legs crossed, fanning herself languidly with a raffia fan whose weave was becoming undone, eyes hard, metallic, and invis-ibly powerful like twin magnets, pulling me in their direction. She was wearing different clothes from when we first met two hours before. She was now dressed in black, which seemed odd in the heat—black roman sandals, long black pleated skirt, black cotton blouse. Her face was blank, which was unsettling, so I did the first thing that came to mind: I smiled, thrust my hand toward her and made a joke.

"How's your dad, Fidel?" I asked.

"Not good since he stopped smoking," she replied coldly.

She didn't take my hand. Neither did she smile.

"We need to speak, Mr. Robinson," she said, looking down at her feet. I followed her gaze and was treated to the beauty of her toes. "I've been waiting for you for about an hour and a half, and I was willing to wait for the rest of the day if I had to. I know that you have read my journal. I know that you have been inquiring about me. I know that you have been to my house. We need to speak, Mr. Robinson. We need to speak."

"Where?" I replied. The words dribbled out of my suddenly dry mouth.

"In private. Let's go to your room."

She got up and led the way through the lobby and up the stairs. I followed her nervously, half expecting her to double back and meet me with a knife around each corner.

"How do you know where my room is?" I asked.

She did not answer.

"How do you know where my room is?" I asked again, more stridently.

"Nervous?" she asked over her shoulder.

"Please," I replied dismissively.

"Okay, so go ahead of me then . . . and let me walk behind you." I didn't answer.

We got to the room and she told me to open the door.

I became intensely uneasy. I dangled the keys halfway between my pocket and the lock, overcome suddenly by a flashback from a spy movie in which two thugs awaited the hero in his room.

"Let's talk downstairs, Anaïs," I said. "My room's a mess, and there is no room service here . . . and we might get thirsty or something."

"That's Miss Castro," she replied. "We are not friends. Can I tell you something?"

"Sure," I replied with a shrug.

"I wrote about you in my journal today."

"What did you write?"

"I'll tell you inside."

I laughed. Her ploy to get me to open the door was so unsophisticated. At this point I was ready to just turn around and leave her standing there and write the whole thing off as a big mistake . . . but then she reached into her bag and took out her journal and began to read.

I am sitting outside the hotel where I have been keeping watch for the last three days, hoping to get a glimpse of the man from the airport. Although I know his name now, Colin Robinson, he is still for me the man from the airport, the man that I saw the day I went to pick up Cello, the tall black man with the dreadlocks that has been on my mind since the first time I saw him because he reminds me of someone. I finally saw him today when he came out from hiding and I followed him to the Guava Tree where I sat at the table next to him and covered my

face with a newspaper because I didn't want him to see my face.
I got into an argument with him over Cello, who was drawing
attention to me when I wanted to remain circumspect. I must
have dropped my diary when I got up to leave. He found it and
I know he read it because he left faint stains from his breakfast
on some pages.

She handed me the journal to dispel any notions that she had been
ad libbing. I handed it back to her and—I am not sure why—opened
the door. She asked me to keep it open.

There were no thugs waiting in the room, only bright light, an
ocean view, and a man and a woman who did not know each other.

Her face registered displeasure at the condition of the room. Books,
paper, cigarette butts, and Coke bottles had settled wherever they
felt most welcome. In a sense the mess was an improvement; it
concealed the blandness of the furniture, which comprised a mir-
rored dresser, a side chair, a bed, and one end table. There was space
for another table; in fact its former presence was marked by a square
of deep yellow that a catalog writer would have called banana or
papaya to distinguish it from the prevailing maize. She cleared some
space on the chair and I did the same thing across from her on
the bed.

"I want to know about you," she said.

"There isn't much to know," I replied.

"Do you have a journal?"

"No," I replied, noting the non sequitur.

"Why not?"

"I have better . . . other things to do with my time."

"Like spying on people?"

She pursed her lips slightly when she said this. I pretended to not
notice her show of emotion, not wanting to make it an issue.

"No, like trying to write," I replied, taking pains to sound unper-
turbed by her presence and mysterious demeanor.

"So you are some kind of writer?" she asked, with a tone that
betrayed disbelief.

"Well kind of. I'm actually a typesetter . . . but I have written
books."

"What about?" she asked, leaning forward and gesticulating
slightly like a job interviewer.

"Different things. Male-female relations . . . war . . . male-female
relations," I replied, casting an eye on the dresser where one of my
titles lay.

"Are you an expert on that?"

"Male-female relations? No . . . not even close."

"Do you have a woman?"

She wet her lips when she asked this—not in an intentionally sexy way. Nervously.

"When I need one," I replied.

"How often is that?"

"Why are you asking me all these questions?" I asked finally, un-comfortable with her intrusion into my life, certain that she had a secret agenda whose revelation would unsettle me.

"Because I want to get to know you," she replied in a voice that could only be described as earnest. "Why did you want to know about me?"

I told her the truth as a reflexive response to her earnestness, re-gretting it soon after when I considered that her earnestness might have been manufactured.

"To write about you," I replied. "I thought you were an interesting character when I saw you and Cello. And then I found your journal by accident and read a little of it and became fascinated."

"What is so fascinating about my life—the fact that it is so hor-rible and that I tell so many lies?"

"I can understand why you say the things you do, though. It's not random. There are things that happened to you, and I can see logical attempts to cover them. But everybody lies sometimes. If you're not hurting anybody, does it really matter? Can I tell you something? I had a very different impression of you compared to what you're ac-tually like. For one I didn't think you were a singer."

"What did you think I was?" she asked, her eyes illuminated.

"A pharmacist."

"I should have been," she replied, shaking her head thoughtfully. "That way I would get my antidepressants for free."

"You take antidepressants? Why?"

"Because I'm always depressed."

"Makes sense," I replied with a chuckle.

She smiled without revealing her teeth. Her lips became relaxed and lost their wrinkles and her forehead resumed its smoothness. I acknowledged our mutual attraction with a smile. There was a ten-sion in the room. I didn't acknowledge it, but it was largely erotic. Left unattended, the tension grew and thickened, miring us in its stickiness as we sat facing each other, transfixed and pretending not to know why. The urge to kiss her began as a warmth that began in my midsection. She wanted to kiss me too, I realized. She articulated her words overprecisely, indicating that she was concentrating on her mouth, which I was commanding telepathically to press itself against mine. Sitting alone with her, engaged in conversation, I discovered her particular brand of sexiness. Her appeal was in her reserve. It kept me uncertain about her feelings, which was disorienting, encouraging me to project onto her my feelings, which she reflected in her eyes along with her incandescent feelings for me.

"Why do you want to know so much about me, Mr. Robinson?" she asked, her voice sliding up to a girlish pitch.

"You can call me Colin."

"Why do you want to know so much about me, Colin?"

"Honestly?"

"Well you have been so dishonest with me that I don't know if saying the word will make a difference."

"I've been having writer's block and I thought if I got to know you I would find a good story to break through it."

I cringed when I realized that I had just wasted the elaborate lie that I had created about being a magazine writer.

"So you kinda need me then?" she replied with another muted smile.

"In a sense, yes."

"I'd like to help you. If I could do anything to help you out of your writer's block, what would that be?"

"Well it's a sorta touchy subject."

"Go ahead."

"Honestly?"

"Here we go with that word again."

"If you let me read your journal."

"I would do that for you," she replied casually, adding a slight emphasis to the last word, personalizing her largesse.

She smiled again.

"Would you?" I asked, leaning forward.

"Yes."

"Why?"

"Because I need something from you too. Maybe we could trade."

I leaned back, subdued by the suggestion of a quid pro quo, the secret agenda whose existence I had suspected.

"What would you need from me?" I asked cautiously.

"For you to make love to me as though it was my last day on earth," she replied, smiling timidly, as though she had said something just marginally outside the norm, like asking me to massage her feet and suck her toes.

I flopped back on the bed and covered my face, laughing quietly. I wasn't laughing at her, or the unexpectedness and melodrama of her statement. I was having an adolescent reaction to the idea of sex. I stopped laughing though when I opened my eyes to see her standing over me, unbuttoning her blouse and removing it, folding it neatly and placing it atop the mess on the chair with a delicacy that elicited a slight quiver from her big, firm breasts. She removed the rest of her clothes in the same deliberate fashion, folding each piece neatly and placing them on top of each other, all the while staring at me as though she were in a trance, her eyes slightly out of focus, as if her attention were possessed by something that lay about two inches beneath my outer body, my soul perhaps. I stared back at her, aroused by the form of her body but unnerved by her mind or rather my lack of familiarity with its shape, dimensions, and orientation. I began to think. Why is she doing this? Do I want to really do this? Should I resist the urge to do this? Do I have any condoms? Should I just kiss her a bit and leave it at that until I get to know her better? What if it is all a plan having something to do with punishing me for reading her journal? Should I get up and close the door? Or would that break the flow and make her change her mind? If so, would breaking the flow be a good idea? Is she usually like this with men? What if she lied to herself in her journal and I had gotten the wrong impression of her and she wasn't prudish or repressed? If she is in fact a prude, do I really want to subject myself to being in bed with her? What if the journal were actually a work of fiction? Are her breasts soft to the touch? Should I take the time to rub down that ridge of fat on her outer thighs right where they meet her hips or should I just slip my hand between her legs? Should I rub down her pubic moss or would it be okay to finger her immediately? But would I really want to place my skin in contact with the bodily fluids of a stranger? Is some thug going to come through the door any minute and beat the shit out of me?

As these thoughts swirled in my mind, Anaïs placed her knees on the bed and straddled me. She unsheathed a smile whose glistening was intimidating and held my face in her hands, startling me by moving toward my face. She bent forward and sliced my neck with her tongue, then kissed me deeply, as though it were truly her last kiss on earth. Her body trembled as her lips approached mine, and she closed her eyes at the moment of contact as though she were shielding herself from the sparks of an explosion.

I wrapped my arms round her slender back, which hummed with the force of the passion that coursed along her spine to her brain. As she ground against me, all reason, and logic, and all questions were turned to powder, and I stopped thinking.

How do you make love to a woman as if it were her last day on earth? Like a horse. You are her horse and she is your rider. You respond to her wishes according to nuances of touch. You let her control your pace and direction, along with something that has no direct equivalent in horsemanship, stroke, although one could posit gait as a crude corollary.

As we made love, neither of us said a word or made a sound. We were quiet, slow, and tender, caught in a momentary peace that we knew could disappear as suddenly as it had manifested itself.

Anaïs fell asleep in my arms. And I joined her moments later. When I woke up, however, she was gone.

The door was closed. The room was set in order. Everything was in a logical place. My clothes were neatly folded and arranged in drawers, underwear and socks together, T-shirts and polo shirts by themselves, shirts hung on individual hangers.

She did not leave a note. Neither did she leave the journal. She did however take the copy of my novel which had been lying on the dresser.

She called about an hour later, her voice calm, her words neatly spaced.

"Thanks for cleaning up. You really didn't have to," I said, after saying hello.

"I couldn't stand the mess," she replied, languidly.

"Why did you leave without telling me?" I asked.

"I don't know. . . . I just didn't feel like being there anymore," she replied apologetically.

I didn't pursue the matter, not wanting her to misinterpret curiosity for territorialism. She went on to explain her absence however.

"I began to read your novel, *Phyllis & Charlie*, and I found it so intriguing that I went out to the bookstore to see if they had it in stock or any of your other books for that matter. The bookstore didn't have any of them, so I went to the parish library. They had two of them, *Phyllis & Charlie* and *The Return of the Don*. I borrowed both of them."

"Another sale lost to the library system," I said jokingly. She laughed.

"I left you something," she said. "Did you find it?"

I told her that I didn't see anything, and she told me to look beneath the pillows. I reached down next to me and felt paper. She had torn pages out of her journal and left them for me. Cute, I thought. Very cute. I was beginning to like her.

"That's what you get for being nice to me," she said. "Three journal entries. Keep being nice to me and you will get the whole thing."

It dawned on me that the whole idea of trading journal pages for sex might not be just a cute way of presenting the idea of sex. This thought however was fleeting, as that sort of thing simply didn't happen in real life. Or so I thought.

"Read them," she said.

"I am," I replied.

"To me, so I can hear my words in your voice. It's all about you. All my thoughts about you since the first time that I saw you at the airport. Read them in chronological order. You will get a better sense that way."

I hesitated.

"You think reading them to me is kinda corny, don't you?" she asked.

"Kinda."

"Okay, then read them to yourself."

"Okay."

There was a little silence.

I didn't know what to say next.

Her silence though was different. She was breathing heavily as if she were holding something in.

"Would you like to spend the day with me?" she asked timidly.

"What would we do?" I asked.

"I guess not, then," she replied. "I know I shouldn't have slept with you like that. I knew that this reaction would come. That's why I . . ."

"You're reading too much into things," I said. "I was simply thinking aloud, you know, trying to plan us a nice time. Let's spend the day together. Where are you?"

"In the lobby."

She laughed. I laughed with her.

"Come on up then."

I left the door open for her, and she didn't close it when she entered the room. We didn't kiss or even hug. It was strange. Two hours before that we had been so intimate. She asked if she could

take a shower, and I waved her into the bathroom. As soon as I heard
the rush of the water, I began to read.

Today I saw a man that made me stop and look hard. I was
at the airport picking up Cello and I saw him as he came out of
customs to the curb to catch a cab. He had long dreadlocks down
past his shoulders and a closely cropped beard that grows high
up on his cheeks. He was deep brown like Belgian truffles,
dressed in a white T-shirt and khaki shorts and he wore some
kind of boots I think. He was wearing sunglasses so I couldn't
see his eyes, but he had a pretty nose and pretty lips. He looks
about thirty or thirty-two, lean and strong. He had a knapsack
on his back and a case in one hand and a duffel bag over one
shoulder. I guess he hardly dressed up. I kept watching him, for
what I didn't know. He was reading a magazine as he waited on
the curb. I guess he was waiting for someone to pick him up
because he wagged his head politely when the taxi drivers ha-
rassed him, cool and absorbed in what he was reading, which
made me curious to see what it was, because it had to be really
engrossing to make him ignore the cab drivers. At one point it
seemed as if we were looking at each other and I smiled but
I guess that I was wrong in that he didn't acknowledge me. I
was watching him and he turned around while I was smiling
and I didn't want to stop smiling abruptly. That would be
rude.

I positioned myself so that I could see what he was reading.
It was a copy of *Transition*, a journal that I've seen before but
never read. I wished for the courage to go up to him and start a
conversation by asking what the magazine was about, but I am
not that kind of a person. I had to leave him when Cello came.
When I came back outside though, he was still there. As I drove
past him in the car, he got into a cab, and on a whim I decided
to follow him to see where he was staying. He sat quietly in the
back of the cab, reading. I began to think about him, put together an idea of who I thought he was. The first thing that came
to mind was musician, guitar—he looked like someone who
could play in a reggae band or something—or rock and roll. I
wasn't sure if he was Jamaican. I don't think so, because he
seemed really uncomfortable in the heat. He could be a painter
too; he has graceful fingers. I think he is an artist, but not a
dancer or an actor. He does not look like a homosexual. I tried

to make up a name for him, but I couldn't find any suitable ones, so I called him Airport Man. As I followed him from the airport I kept sending him telepathic messages to turn around and see me. "Airport Man, turn around now." But he didn't.

I followed him to the Ocean Front Hotel. I expected him to stay somewhere like that. He wasn't the Sandals type and he definitely couldn't afford the Half Moon.

After playing with him I decided to leave it at that.

I smiled to myself, flattered. I began to like her even more after realizing that she had been admiring me, which needs no explanation, because affection is often reflexive. I thought back to my arrival at the airport, and tried to remember if I had seen anyone resembling her in the crowd, or if there was in fact a car following me from the airport. I did not. She liked my complexion. It made sense. She did have an attraction to very dark men. I had read this in her journal. Smiling, I read the next entry.

I woke up this morning in a good mood. I sang beautifully last night and I had a dream about Airport Man. I can't remember the content of the dream except for the last scene before I woke up, where he was standing at the sink in my house pouring himself a beer and we were talking about music. I dreamed about him because I thought about him all day and he was the last thing on my mind before I went to sleep. I kept thinking about him because I kept wondering why I couldn't stop. What is it about him? He is not the most handsome man I have ever seen, and I don't know him to know if he is charming. There is just something about him. . . . I think it may be his skin. I find dark skin like his compelling. But it's not just his skin though, it's that quiet focus in his forehead. I think, but I am not sure, he has the look of someone with something on his mind, a burden. I wonder what it is. I am not sure if I am explaining the reason I am attracted to him or the reason I find him puzzling.

While thinking about him today I got the crazy idea to drive by his hotel to see if I might run into him. I got in the car and drove down to his hotel. Of course I didn't see him, and I drove along Gloucester Avenue down to the roundabout, up into town along Barnett Street looking for him, sure that I would see him along the way. I just had this feeling.

I went to his hotel. I went in the lobby, circled the pool, and went down to the beach, but he was nowhere to be found. I asked the desk clerk for him by description and got her to tell me his name and room number. Colin Robinson, room 5B. I told the clerk that I was an old friend from high school and I hadn't seen him in fifteen years and I wasn't sure if it was in fact him and I wanted to surprise him so she shouldn't tell him that I came by.

I sang like an angel tonight thinking about Airport Man. I can't even use his real name; it doesn't fit him. He looks like he would have a more American name like . . . I don't know . . . Roger Williams. He inspired me tonight. He placed me in such a good mood that I was completely relaxed and in high spirits so there was a fullness of sound and emotion in my voice.

It's a pity that he'll never know how happy he has made me. I was depressed for weeks before I saw him. Maybe it is better that way, because I do not have luck with men, so he might turn out to be horrible like the rest of them. When I went back to his hotel the second time today I was going to leave him an anonymous note to this effect. I changed my mind though. I don't know why. Nerves I guess. The clerk told me Airport Man hadn't left his room since he checked in.

I guess I'm not the only one who is lonely.

The next entry was the one that she had partially read to me when we were standing outside my room. I reread it from the beginning however, wanting to comprehend it thoroughly.

I am sitting outside the hotel where I have been keeping watch for the last three days, hoping to get a glimpse of the man from the airport. Although I know his name now, Colin Robinson, he is still for me the man from the airport, the man that I saw the day I went to pick up Cello, the tall black man with the dreadlocks that has been on my mind since the first time I saw him because he reminds me of someone. I finally saw him today when he came out from hiding and I followed him to the Guava Tree where I sat at the table next to him and covered my face with a newspaper because I didn't want him to see my face. I got into an argument with him over Cello, who was drawing attention to me when I wanted to remain circumspect. I must have dropped my diary when I got up to leave. He found it and I know he read it because he left faint stains from his breakfast on some pages.

Faith kept gushing about him, how nice he was but when I

asked for specifics she wouldn't give me any, she just kept on saying that he just had a nice aura. I was very nervous when she handed me the journal and I kept searching her eyes to see if she had read it. I didn't see any signs. As I inspected it though as I walked away I saw faint stains, egg stains, and I knew that Airport Man had read it. I didn't know how it came into his hands. I just assumed that he picked it up somehow.

I hadn't realized that the journal had been missing until I went home. I went into my handbag to get my antidepressants and couldn't find it. I was very depressed. I didn't know why. I don't need a reason. I think a lot of it has to do with Cello coming. Each day that he grows older he reminds me more of his father, our father, who I'm not sure should be in heaven or hell. Airport Man reminds me of my father too. That just dawned on me. That is why I think Cello was drawn to him at the café. That is why I am drawn to him too and have been all these years when I lied to my sisters about our involvement.

Faith tells me to get off the pills because they can make me suicidal, but I tell her that my first suicide attempt was at the age of sixteen and I wasn't on medication then. I called her and she told me that she had the journal and that Airport Man had turned it in so I went to get it.

I am sitting under a tree now waiting for him outside his hotel, angry with him for raping my privacy. It is a hot day, the hottest day this year I think so far. I went back home after I got the journal from Faith and my neighbor told me that a man fitting Airport Man's description was loitering outside my house. And I phoned the Shady Grove to call in sick tonight and Slacky told me that Airport Man was a magazine writer and was asking questions about me and he had fed him a pack of lies. Everything he told him he said was a lie. I thanked him and he promised to save me the choicest piece of bluefish.

My last meal will be my favorite. I don't know if it really matters that it is my favorite because my appetite might not be very strong. I have tried and tried with life but I'm not good at it, so it is best for me to just go. I think I should take another pill. As I am sitting here waiting for Airport Man I can only think of two things: hating him for violating me and wanting him to be the last man on earth to make love to me. I have chosen him because he reminds me of the one I really love. He stirred something in me that I thought had been dead, the will to live. He stirred it but it did not flourish, but I still love him for that. I don't think we will make love though because we don't know each other, but at least I will be close to him, even if we are angry with each other.

A numbness encased me as soon as I had gone halfway through the journal entry. I wanted to stop reading and check on Anaïs, but the numbness disabled me, preventing me from abandoning the narrow track of sanity that snaked through her written thoughts. As soon as the numbness wore off, I was filled with deep sadness. Cello was her father's child. I read that section over, making sure that I had read the right thing, hoping that some magic would change the facts.

I sat on the bed listening to the sound of the shower, thinking of what to say to her, confused because I did not know her but feeling partly responsible for her grief. I was also afraid, of what I did not know. It was the fear one feels in the dark, a fear grounded in the infinity of fearful possibilities, fear of not knowing exactly what one should be afraid of.

The shower continued, uninterrupted. I made a deal. As soon as the shower stopped I would make a spontaneous decision and go with it irrespective of what it was.

The shower did not stop. I was forced to make a spontaneous decision however.

Anaïs shot herself in the head.

I was sitting on the bed with the pages in my hand, tapping my left foot on the floor in time to a tune I had made up to pass the time. It was a slow tune, I remember. It had a mournful melody and I imagined the lead being played by a plungered trombone. Then there was this crack. A thin, short sound like a limb being fractured or a broom falling on a tile floor. Then there was a moan and a thump, then more moaning.

I do not remember rushing to the bathroom. I just remember being there and seeing her lying neatly on the floor, on her stomach, fully clothed as if she had simply fallen asleep after a hard night's work and had chosen a pool of rich, red blood for a pillow. The Saturday night special had flown out of her hand into the tub, where it lay under the continuous stream of the shower like a sinful soul holding its breath during baptismal immersion, wanting to make sure it was saved and sanctified, nervously aware of all the evil it had done.

Anaïs wasn't dead, but close to it. She was still breathing and moaning softly with decreasing frequency and volume.

I ran to the telephone and alerted the front desk and ran back to her side, kneeling next to her, not really knowing what to do. Intuition told me to stanch the bleeding, so I took off my shirt and tied it around her head, talking to her as I worked.

"Are you okay?" I asked.

She didn't answer.

"You are okay," I told her, staring into her unfocused eyes as the blood from her temple soaked through the cloth.

I kept telling her that she was okay, hoisting her head into my lap and stroking her face, which was serene and eerily beautiful. At one point her body stiffened and I thought she was going to speak, but she threw up green vomit all over her black blouse, then reclined into silence, her face suddenly becoming limp, her mouth falling so that she seemed to be smiling.

In retrospect, I could have done more, like administer CPR. But I did what came to me at the time. I held her and watched over her and waited.

An ambulance did not come. Ambulances are luxuries outside of Europe, North America, and a few countries in Asia. The hotel manager and two lifeguards were the ones to take her to the hospital. I told them that I would prefer to stay behind, and they carted her off, by which time I am sure she was dead, although I did not check her pulse. I did not check it because I did not want to know. Her eyes had rolled up in her head though, and she had stopped breathing.

I didn't notice the journal on the toilet tank until the police came. They asked me if it was mine and I said that it was and they gave it to me after their brief investigation, which was summed up by the statement "Anybody who woulda kill demself shoulda dead fo true."

After they left I went out onto the balcony to smoke a cigarette and think, but my mind could not advance beyond the point of planning to change hotels. So much had happened so quickly that my brain saved itself from overload by becoming temporarily disengaged.

Absently, I flipped the journal to the last page and began to read, ignoring the crowd that had gathered at the door. The last page of the journal was a note to me, which made me feel justified in claiming ownership.

Colin I am sorry that I did this where and when I did this, but I could not go on any more. I will never forget you and I hope you will always remember me. This is for you. I hope you find your story here.

I flipped to the first page and began to read. When I was through I knew a lot more about her. But I did not find out why she came to Jamaica or why she pretended to be from Costa Rica.

Three weeks later, I had a manuscript on my agent's desk. *The Journal of a Sad Chanteuse* was published the following year.

I never heard her sing.

ON AFRICANS AND VIOLENCE

GREGORY A. THOMSON

It's 1989, and I'm in Freetown, the capital of Sierra Leone, West Africa. Sierra Leone is the former British colony where freed slaves and slaves intercepted from "illegal" slave traders were returned, at least as much for "out of sight, out of mind" reasons as for any more benevolent ones. A sprawling city of decaying, mostly wood colonial-era buildings not without charm, Freetown looks something like Kingston, Jamaica, complete with surrounding lush green hills and mountains. As in all of the countries I have visited on this, my first African trip, no place seems completely foreign, and I'm feeling pretty comfortable. The people are cool, even if they aren't as openly friendly as in other West African countries.

But things are not good in Freetown. The economy is falling apart, the government is out of money, and the civil servants and blue-collar government workers have not been paid in over three months. Their average monthly salary of one thousand leones is worth, on the day I arrive, ten U.S. dollars. Yet the day I arrive is a milestone —it happens to be the day the one-hundred leone note is introduced, and it is the largest denomination in the country (the previous largest was a twenty). Required to immediately change one hundred U.S. dollars at the airport, I end up with so many leones I feel like I've robbed a bank. When I tip the baggage handler two crisp hundreds (two bucks!), I give him one-fifth of an average worker's monthly salary (I quickly learn the real deal in Sierra Leone, and get more careful with money). A single loaf of white bread (why is *white* bread always the economic yardstick?) costs five or ten leones, so you know times are very hard for the people. Can you imagine if this shit was happening in America?! The lid on public peace and decorum would have long since blown, and every day would be Rodney Luther King day on the streets. Yet in Sierra Leone, people were making do, scratching and surviving, keeping their dignity and sense of humor to an amazing and inspiring degree.

Yet I counted more Mercedes-Benzes on some downtown streets than you might see on Rodeo Drive. Sierra Leone is not a poor country. It reportedly has more unmined gold and diamonds than South Africa. Sierra Leone was also at that time run by a mild but corrupt governing class which allowed foreign interests to control mining and export and virtually all resulting wealth. Sierra Leone is also incredibly fertile, with coconut and fruit trees of every description growing wild. But the people without Benzes were having a hard time buying even plain white bread.

So I'm in a shared taxi heading to the center of Freetown. It's midday, it's hot, and traffic is getting congested because the blue-collar workers—the ones who haven't been paid in over three months—are angry and demonstrating in the streets. We turn off the main road into a crowded residential district and right into the heart of the demonstration. Traffic is now stopped, and a crowd of demonstrators and onlookers surround the car and the cars directly in front and back of us. No police are in sight. Our driver and others honk their horns insistently, but the crowd doesn't yield and instead grows more dense. A tense and seemingly dangerous situation, but somehow I remain calm.

After a long minute of this, the driver of a pupa green Toyota taxi immediately in front of us gets impatient and tries to drive through the crowd. The crowd is not having it. A tall, lean, muscular young man with an open short-sleeve shirt is especially unhappy about this taxi driver, and he and others encircle the car and shout and slam their fists on his hood. The driver shouts back at them. Though still calm, I wonder if I'm about to witness a homicide or perhaps become the victim of one. But just as quickly the crowd yields a little, and the pupa green taxi and our car are grudgingly allowed through.

If this scene had taken place in America and American workers hadn't been paid in one month, let alone three, and someone tried to drive through such an angry crowd, that person would be dragged from the car and beaten into intensive care if he were lucky. Or, equally likely, police on horseback and in riot gear would charge in and make a bloody mess of things. Either way, violence would win out. Yet in Sierra Leone, where conditions were far worse materially, people did not clobber each other. I was surprised by this, but my Sierra Leonian companion said that "in Sierra Leone, we have not gotten to that point yet."

It wasn't that people were docile, pacified, or dispassionate—there was plenty of passion and justified anger, and people were very concerned about their situation. But could it be that in Sierra Leone, physical violence is much less a way of life than in America? Could Africans be less violent than Americans?

This notion was confirmed repeatedly throughout the five African countries I visited on that trip. I had brought with me several copies of a mixed tape of the latest and best pre-gangsta hip-hop music courtesy of NYC's DJ Red Alert. This was mostly less aggressive, bass line–driven (as opposed to then-more-conventional programmed bass drum-driven) music, and I figured that this type of hip-hop would be most suited to African tastes. My plan was to give these tapes to deejays and other music lovers, hopefully in exchange for local music. But when I reached Africa, this plan derailed, because this hip-hop music—best suited to driving beneath an elevated train line on a Bronx Friday night—was simply too harsh, too aggressively abrasive to make sense in an African environment. I wouldn't even say people didn't get it, but rather this music seemed out of place in a place much calmer and peaceful than the U.S. I was actually almost ashamed to play Boogie Down Productions in Mali, Senegal, Ghana, and wherever else I went.

Violence and environments of violence do not consist merely of obvious, acutely violent acts—beatings, shootings, etc. More important, the *threat* of violence is constant, and daily interaction is filled with a low-level hostility. I believe this starts with a fear among people and a lack of community and social harmony. This contrast became clear to me when I returned from London, a city I had spent much time in. In London, there was a low-level hostility in the very way people moved among one another on the street and in the subway. It was as if people (strangers) didn't like each other and were a little afraid of each other, as if they were expecting to be hit by someone. I had never so clearly noticed this atmosphere. Returning to the States, I found the climate of hostile interaction stark and obvious in New York City. In the South, there was a more subdued, less hurried social climate and an outer layer of civility and gentleness, but I could feel the threat of explosive social violence poised to strike anyone who dared step outside the status quo.

Yet in America, where white people feel an obsessive, almost hysterical fear of Black males, in an era where social policy rapidly moves toward control and suppression of Black males, it is a never-spoken but thoroughly accepted "truth" that Africa and Africans are inherently more violent than Americans and America. Most people, Black and white, reacted with disbelief when I told them I found Africa to be far less violent than America. The concept was completely beyond their grasp.

On one level, how could you blame them? We are continually bombarded with television images of mass violence and death in Africa. You would never know that the majority of Africans get along fairly well, considering their economic and political straits. You would never know that with only a few exceptions, virtually anyone can walk through the poorest sections of Africa's large cities and not be harmed. The often-used Lonely Planet guides to African travel, though mostly written by Eurocentric ex–Peace Corps types, clearly note the relative safety of Africa's big cities.

Not to say that there is not severe, extreme violence in many parts of Africa. Many countries are, after all, experiencing a civil war. Somalia, Ethiopia, Rwanda, Liberia, Angola, Sudan, etc.—the images are familiar. It's as if Africa is covered with Yugoslavia-type situations. But even the often extreme violence that accompanies these situations must be viewed in the proper perspective, and we get no perspective from today's mass media.

There are some fifty-eight countries in Africa. At any given time, several of them may be experiencing severe unrest. Currently, about twelve countries are in this situation. That leaves the other four-fifths of Africa's nations in a relatively calmer state, though even this situation is eroding as conditions for the poor throughout the world continue to deteriorate. Of all the African nations, not a single border was determined by Africans themselves—all of Africa's borders were set by European colonial powers to serve their own interests. Whereas in the nations of Europe, centuries of wars, empires, negotiations, and treaties determined their borders, Africa had no such "natural" process. Everywhere, ethnic groups with long-standing and unresolved hostilities ended up forced to share the same countries. Imagine one country comprising parts of England, France, and Germany and you'll see what I mean. African borders were imposed from without, not settled from within, and they thus created often ungovernable territories. When this is combined with decades of Western intervention in which small elites have conspired with foreigners to the tremendous economic and social detriment of the mass of people in each country, and with an endless supply of arms from superpowers past and present, an explosive and deadly mix is created.

The clearest European exception to naturally evolving borders is Yugoslavia, a country artificially created after WW I out of countries and empire fragments with long-standing hostility toward one another. After communism's fall, Yugoslavia descended into a genocidal civil war. It is no coincidence that this takes place in Europe's most artificially created nation. Rather than wonder why many parts of Africa are so violence-ridden, perhaps we should wonder why every country does not fall apart like Yugoslavia. Africa is in fact a continent full of Yugoslavias.

The painful question that haunts me is this: how can I reconcile the incredibly peaceful Africa I came to know with the horrific violence of Rwanda, Liberia, and other places? People generally tend to be most susceptible to violence when the ties that bind them to each other are damaged or severed, when the emotional scars of suffering and oppression (whether from intrafamily, societal, or international forces) control their conscience, or when they are most desperate. In terms of material deprivation, physical hardship, access to health care, and similar issues, the average African endures exponentially more in his short lifetime than the average American. Yet in Africa, the social fabric and family structure are generally much stronger in the ways that matter most: in providing support for the mental, spiritual, and physical well-being and security of its members. This is not the idealized, sanitized "family values" type of family touted by America's Newt Right, a type of family which often puts too much effort into creating a respectable front for those on the outside, while hiding deep dissatisfaction or dysfunction. It is much more often the real, organic type of family life that keeps people grounded in all but the most desperate times.

Africa has simply endured far more hardship and externally fueled unrest and disintegration than has most of America and Europe. Imagine Manhattan or Houston with every grocery store and restaurant suddenly closed and no hope of a government to come to the rescue. Panic and violence would soon erupt. Imagine Birmingham, Alabama, circa 1963, with every Black and white person armed with their own Soviet-supplied AK-47. In this type of situations, even the family cannot always endure, and once that last levee breaks, there is often nothing else to stop the horror. Africans face this type of situation all the time. It is a wonder things are not worse than they already are, that the lid does not blow more often.

The only way we can effectively combat the "violent Africans" myth is to know in our minds *and* our hearts that it is not true. So the next time you are bombarded with media or everyday conversational images of "tribal violence," "*Africanized* killer bees," or "the enemy" in the "war on drugs," grab a hand-held mirror, reflect that projection right back at the projector, and take a good look. Or, even better, go see Africa and get to know her for yourself. And be sure to tell a friend.

Letter from Foreign

Rohan B Preston

Dear Mum, there are so many things I have
to tell 'bout 'Merica, the place where you said
the streets are gold and there are many people
with good hair (like those in the movies).

'Member when I used to play with the toy helicopter
and fly away a Foreign? Well, Mum, Dearest Grand Mamaa,
I have some news for you. 'Merica is not in the sky
like the planes but is on land, flat land, droopy cornfields
and choking chimneys, with latrines, and doo-doo
and frowsy ragamuffins as good as dead on sidewalks.

Mum, you tell me say God bless America for the people
here good—I have some more news for you.
Sure, some people go to church and chapel
and mosque and synagogue and march and pray
and some smile when they see you on the street
(some don't say "Morning, dog" and sometimes
them cross the street when we pass them—
for one healthy African is a dinosaur
blowing fire at the people with pretty hair
and you know how easy it is for hair to catch fire).

Mum, you tell me that they have scholarships galore.
And, a true. But you never say anything 'bout glass,

'bout aquarium, and how buckra can encase you
in glass so that no matter how loud you scream
no matter how much you bark, the ceiling still there.

I don't want to bring down God on me so I must say
that education here good and that we learn all kinds
of things 'bout Greece and Rome, me speak Italian
now, some French—even Japanese. All these things
that you wanted me to do, Mum, but there is lots of glass
about, you know: lenses, ceilings, bottles, and they're all trained
on me, you know, reflecting, watching, waiting, and laughing,
but I have to follow your lead, almost a century
and still not weary yet, I must never get weary yet.

Look Homeward, Exile

George Elliott Clarke

I can still see that soil crimsoned by butchered
Hog and imbrued with rye, lye, and homely
Spirituals everybody must know,
Still dream of folks who broke or cracked like shale:
Pushkin, who twisted his hands in boxing,
Marrocco, who ran girls like dogs and got stabbed,
Lavinia, her teeth decayed to black stumps,
Her lovemaking still in demand, spitting
Black phlegm—her pension after twenty-towns,
And Toof, suckled on anger that no Baptist
Church could contain, who let wrinkled Eely
Seed her moist womb when she was just thirteen.
   And the tyrant sun that reared from barbed wire
Spewed flame that charred the idiot crops
To Depression, and hurt my granddaddy
To bottle after bottle of sweet death,
His dreams beaten to one tremendous pulp,
Until his heart seized, choked; his love gave out.
   But beauty survived, secreted
In freight trains snorting in their pens, in babes
Whose faces were coal-Black mirrors, in strange
Strummers who stroked Ghanaian banjos, hummed
Blind blues—precise, ornate, rich needlepoint,
In sermons scorched with sulfur and brimstone,
And in my love's dark, orient skin that smelled

Like orange peels and tasted like rum, good God!
   I remember my Creator in the old ways:
I sit in taverns and stare at my fists;
I knead earth into bread, spell water into wine.
Still, nothing warms my wintry exile—neither
Prayers nor fine love, neither votes nor hard drink:
For nothing heals those saints felled in green beds,
Whose loves are smashed by just one word or glance
Or pain—a screw jammed in thick, straining wood.

SOUL REBEL

———

THIS IS WHO I BE

CARLOS MCBRIDE

It's about a comfortable sixty degrees out. Sirens are blaring in the background, piercing the hearing for about two min. No one really pays any attention, it's probably just another bust. In the midst of all this "confusion," as someone might put it, a voice stops me from drifting into one of my daydreams (even though it's about eleven-thirty P.M.). "Aye yo Recles, hurry up kid, pass that damn forty-o, it's getting late, the jam should be jumpin by now!" As I took one last guzzle, I looked around with an unfocused sort of vision, I saw the vandalized buildings, a burned house on the corner, a bunch of girls walking, hooked-up cars parked along the street, and finally all of my boys. In that moment, I passed the forty ounce of Private Stock, and said, "All right fellas I'm ready, let's merc."

That night as we caught a ride to the party, I thought real hard, I said to myself, "This is my home, this is where I live, these are my peoples, and together we are all imprisoned, stuck in the jungle of society's leftovers, struggling, not realizing that we have all accepted this sentence given to us by this so-called righteous society for the mere fact that we are nothing more and nothing less than *minority.* . . .

My name is Carlos Edward McBride. My nationality: Hispanic, African-American. Am I a racist? . . . Racism!? What is the purpose or definition of this word? Do I have a right to be a racist? I didn't start this essay to merely entertain. I do not take great pride in the fact that I'm poor, the fact that in the eyes of "white society" the verdict on my life has been made for me. As a minority, living in the poor section of town, I've had to learn the hard way how to deal with racism. Whether it was in a classroom, in court, or on the streets. I can recall one day I was running to a friend's house, who lived two blocks from me. I wasn't really running, more like jogging, anyway the narcs happened to drive by. They stopped the car right in front of me, threw me on top of the hood, patted me down, and when they didn't find anything proceeded to bombard me with stupid questions. "Where are you going? What's your name? Why are you jogging?" Why am I jogging? What kind of shit is that, I thought. This is only one of several events that I began encountering starting in my youth. No, not all cops are bad, and no, I wasn't a big-time drug dealer, but this is not about cops or drug dealers.

At the age of thirteen, I was kicked out of my home for the first time. At first I thought, "Damn, this is the shit, on my own, no one to answer to, I could do whatever I want!" Little did I know this was the start of what were going to be the most difficult times of my life. Throughout my teenage years I was in and out of my home. Sometimes I was away for as long as two months at a time. Two months is a long time when you don't have a place to go, food to eat, and so forth. I was lucky though, I always managed to find a place to go and somewhere to eat. I wasn't a "problem child." Liquor, which seems to be the remedy to escape this thing called reality, destroyed my family.

My parents were into drugs and liquor. Something I was not proud of. Only later in life did I realize that the lessons that occurred as a result of the drugs and liquor were to be the most crucial and valuable I ever learned. My dad eventually went into rehab for a while, and through a long, painstaking process he beat the beast that tore my family apart. Now he is my mentor. He has become a very successful college professor who has been sober for the past ten years. My mom's continued to drink. In my twentieth year she passed away. I guess I owe all of my life to her. Whenever our paths crossed we got along, we loved each other, and, most important, we learned from each other. No matter how tough things got I was always clean, had nice clothes. Not because of drugs or anything like that. I had a lot of pride for who I was and what I stood for. I was a product of the environment and I made the best out of my situation, *and never, I mean never, did I give the media satisfaction by becoming another statistic!* I have a brother who is seven years younger, and a beautiful sister who is two years younger. We are all doing very well now, thanks to my father who, after going through his own ordeal, has guided us onto the right path to make something of our lives.

I hope people reading this essay understand that the difficulties faced by a poor minority family growing up in "white corporate America" often result in misfortune. For some, a one-way highway to the graveyard or prison becomes a deal almost impossible to refuse. For others, "the savior comes in a variety of bottles and cans, or every two weeks when the government stops in for a visit to pay off the poor and restore dignity in the minority communities." Unfortunately, society has stereotyped the struggles of the poor to the point that the allegations become facts. With the broadcast media focusing on the misfortunes of poor communities and the local section of the newspaper exploiting "the talents" of minorities, what other options do we have in life? "We" do not have the best schools, "we" do not have the "rights" of other middle-class citizens, "we" do not even have decent community centers to develop the raw talent of our youth! "We" only have what society wants us to have. If society feels that "we" have too much, *blam! Gimme dat!*"—it is taken away. So "we" must struggle and struggle until, God willing, "we" reach a level of wisdom and knowledge that not even the devil himself can take. With this, "we" will possess the power and ability to unlock the doors of opportunity and embrace the luxury of *being somebody*. I didn't write this essay for sympathy. I wrote what I felt was necessary for people to know about me and my background. I have sought refuge in education. An alternative school called the Learning Tree has been my savior. I have embraced the opportunity for a second chance in life, to be somebody, somebody great. The guidance from my father, the support from my family, and the spiritual motivation will give me the power to conquer! I will conquer! My name is Carlos Edward McBride, my nationality Hispanic and African-American. Am I a racist? . . . Racism!!??

BROTHER #2

BROTHER YAO

Brothers I know
hold themselves
as children hold butterflies
in their hands
the power to smoosh
or kill
free or help
their wings
dusty
and anxious
a secret
kept
a promise
to be made

WE LIVE

TYEHIMBA JESS

We live.
a million sun-blackened soul-minds
dynamited from
   rocks
   plains
   hills
   savannahs
   middle passages away.

   burned into buffalo heartland
   searching for red, white, and blue consciousness
   We found nothing but echoes coming off the walls,
   silently
   silently
   silently.

We live.
We be your drug taken to forget.
blown into your midnight hour with the cry of nighttime blues
                shifting choruses
                motown whispers
                slowly spitting in your ear.

We live.
not shadows of big lips and tall struts bleedin down your

gone-with-the-wind tiara staircase.
not al jolson charade followed by tv dinner of
the jeffersons
good times
and cosby show kente-clothed niggas.

We live.
AIN'T I A WOMAN she said, and
I AM THE MAN YOU THINK YOU ARE he declared before the
    last bullets rained
on ballroom stage steps.

We live.
and not just the visible ones.
others go unnoticed
    undetected
    unseen
    unheard
    unthought of
until the next prisoner is freed in the middle of the night. (assata!!)
                                                              (assata!!)
                                                              (assata!!)
                                                              (assata!!)

WHO ARE WE?

MICHAEL DATCHER

You have just walked under the overpass (a place where you can get just below the funk) and, down here, we are still trying to find ourselves. We are still rummaging through our tangled souls. Uncovering, turning over, tossing out deficient definitions of our collective self: old hand-me-downs from skewed history books and the Eleven O'Clock News. We are still searching for the truth. Who are we?

Sitting here under the overpass, this question boomerangs through my mind, returning with few answers. The answers I get, I don't want: countless young Black men don't value the lives of the young Black men around them. We articulate our anger about the "white oppressor," but we carry out our rage on each other. Growing up in Crip hood on the east side of Long Beach, I witnessed many consequences of this rage. Two Bloods, undoubtedly trying to build their rep, came to an east side party and pulled out their red rags. Instantly, the whole party converged on them, kicking and stomping on their ribs and heads, stopping only to shoot them both. One bled to death on the dance floor; the other died in the hospital a few days later. All over a red handkerchief. Although I am well versed in the historical and sociological antecedents of this behavior, the bottom line is that young Black men have a penchant for killing other young Black men. Who are we? We are murderers of our own; we eat our young.

This is the answer that I try to evade. In these Afrocentric times, it is so difficult to embrace our ugliness as Black ugliness: as a Black responsibility. We immerse ourselves in kente cloth and syncopated rhythms, while righteously laying claim to the rich Black aesthetic, speaking of it as a manifestation of our soul's beauty. Yet, we are quick to place all the blame on white America for our communal cancerous abscesses. We will luxuriate in our Black beauty, but we will not deal with our Black sores. They are unpleasant to the eyes, tormenting to the heart, and painful as hell when operated upon. We would rather toss our problems in the laps of liberal white men, providing them a vehicle to assuage their guilt. We'd rather wait for their governmental agencies to supply ineffectual opiates that offer short-term relief and produce lifetime addictions (see: prisons and welfare). If Black men are to significantly change our living conditions, we must aggressively seek to reverse this trend. We must accept our cancerous sores as Black cancerous sores and take the responsibility for identifying (and removing) the communal carcinogens. This is what it means to love ourselves.

Who are we? We are struggling. Ironically, this is what encourages me about the young Black male condition today. If we are struggling that means that we are still fighting. Black people know a little somethin' 'bout fightin'. We are the survivors of a Holocaust unworthy of Hollywood's attention, although far more tragic. We are the sons of men and women who waged battles on South Hampton plantations and on East Harlem streets. We are brothers to Panthers who knew where true justice came from: out of the barrel of a gun. Who are we? We are warriors. This is why despite our struggles young Black men will also survive this latest battle. This fight against self-hatred. A self-hatred that results in self-doubt and murder. In this battle, we are our own worst enemy. In this war, we are both victim and assailant.

This unique situation necessitates a slightly different kind of military philosophy. In a conventional war, the oft-quoted key to victory is to "Know thy enemy." In a war against self, the key to victory is to "Know thy self." This means that young Black men must investigate our personal insecurities that lead to injurious behaviors. Insecurities about our masculinity top this list. If we are uncertain of our manhood, we feel a need to prove it to ourselves by proving it to others. This is the type of mentality that moved the two Bloods to come to an east side party and moved the Crips to kill them for doing so. This is why knowing the Black male self also must entail calling into question our historically rigid definitions of Black manhood. The two young Bloods felt they had to define their manhood by how "hard" they were, a hardness established by their willingness to claim their set in the middle of a Crip party. If only they had understood that there are many others types of Black men besides the hard kind. We are short, balding college professors. We are gay football players. We are light-skinned nurses. We are straight ballet dancers. We are lazy secretaries. We are rugged construction work- ers. We are sensitive actors. Yet, we are all Black men. Is anyone of these characterizations more authentically Black than another?

We are at war. A war against self-hatred and bloodletting. Who are we? We are warriors. If we are to win this war against ourselves, by knowing ourselves, we must reach out to understand the many man- ifestations of Black manhood. We must work to know each other, which is to know ourselves. Who are we? We are brothers. We must be our brother's keeper, here, under the overpass.

GALLERY OF CONTRIBUTORS

JABARI ASIM is editor of *Eyeball*, a literary arts journal. His fiction appears in *In the Tradition: An Anthology of Young, Black Writers* and *Brotherman: The Odyssey of Black Men in America*. His poetry has appeared in *Black American Literature Forum*, *Obsidian II*, *Shooting Star Review*, and elsewhere. He has reviewed books for the *St. Louis Post-Dispatch*, *Washington Post Book World*, *Los Angeles Times Book Review*, and *Emerge*. He lives in St. Louis.

CHARLIE R. BRAXTON is a poet, playwright, and journalist from McComb, Mississippi. His works have appeared in numerous publications, including *Black American Literature Forum*, *The Black Nation*, *The Minnesota Review*, and *The San Fernando Poetry Journal*. His poetry also appears in the anthology *In The Tradition: An Anthology of Young Black Writers* (Harlem River Press, 1992). Mr. Braxton is the author of a volume of verse, *Ascension from the Ashes*, and the forthcoming *Reflections on Black Music: From Be-bop to Hip-Hop, and Ya Don't Stop*.

COLIN CHANNER was born in St. Andrew, Jamaica, in 1963 to a pharmacist and a constable. He migrated to the U.S. in 1982 to study media communications. At Hunter College in New York City, he came under the mentorship of Frank Dexter Brown. "The Ballad of the Sad Chanteuse" and "Black Boy, Brown Girl, Brownstone" are part of a forthcoming collection. He lives with his wife, Bridgitte Fouché, and daughter, Addis, in Fort Greene, Brooklyn.

GEORGE ELLIOTT CLARKE is a professor of English and Canadian studies at Duke University. Born in Canada, he has African-American roots; his ancestors arrived in Nova Scotia from Maryland and Virginia in 1815, part of a wave of Black immigrants who entered British America after the War of 1812. Professor Clarke has published three books of poetry, *Saltwater Spirituals* (Pottersfield, 1983), *Whylah Falls* (Polestar, 1990) and *Lush Dreams, Blue Exile* (Pottersfield, 1994) and a collection of Africadian (Black Canadian) literature, *Fire on the Water: An Anthology of Black Nova Scotian Writing, Volumes I & II* (Pottersfield, 1991–2).

MICHAEL DATCHER was born in Chicago and raised on the East Side of Long Beach, California. While a student at the University of California at Berkeley, he edited the Black men's poetry anthology *My Brother's Keeper* with an introduction by Pulitzer Prize–winner Yusef Komunyakaa. After graduating in 1992, he spent two years earning his M.A. in African-American literature at UCLA. During the same period, he began coordinating and hosting the critically acclaimed World Stage Anansi Writers Workshop in Los Angeles's Crenshaw district, which attracts L.A.'s best writers as well as visiting luminaries like Sonia Sanchez and Yusef Komunyakaa. In 1993, he won the Walter White Award for Commentary and in 1994, at twenty-seven, Mr. Datcher was named editor-in-chief of *Image* magazine. He says, "I am a product of America's inner city blues, who has been educated on the verdant campuses of our nation's top universities. There is Black beauty everywhere."

Born in Brooklyn and raised in Queens, GLENN DAVIS was a systems specialist at IBM in Long Beach, California, until recently. He attended St. John's (New York) and California State at Long Beach and graduated from Los Angeles Community College. His writings have appeared in the *Los Angeles Watts Times*, *Upscale*, *Being Single*, and *Celebrity News*. "Eeny Meany Mynie Mo" is an excerpt from his novel-in-progress of the same title. Mr. Davis lives in Atlanta.

MICHAEL ERIC DYSON is director of the Institute of African-American Research and professor of communication studies at the University of North Carolina at Chapel Hill as well as an ordained Baptist minister. He earned his M.A. and Ph.D. from Princeton University. A 1992 winner of the Magazine Award from the National Association of Black Journalists, he has published several books, including *Reflecting Black: African-American Cultural Criticism* (University of

Minnesota Press, 1993) and *Making Malcolm: The Myth and Meaning of Malcolm X* (Oxford University Press, 1995). The letter included in this anthology will serve as the introduction to Professor Dyson's next book.

DANIEL EDWARDS was born and raised in Springfield, Massachusetts, where he attended the High School of Commerce and was a staff artist on the school paper. Neither his artistic nor his writing talents were promoted and encouraged by the school. He joined The Learning Tree, an alternative school for young Black men, where he found direction and in the fall of 1993 he entered Hampshire College as a James Baldwin scholar. His passions include writing and film and the development of his two daughters, Brianah Monet, three, and Kwestchan Topaz, one.

MICHAEL FRANTI is the lead vocalist, composer, and bandleader for conscious hip-hop, funk, reggae, and jazz outfit Spearhead, whose first album, *Home*, was released to rave reviews in 1994. Formerly the lead vocalist for the now disbanded group Disposable Heroes of Hiphoprisy, Mr. Franti is based in Oakland, California.

Thirty-four-year-old poet and attorney **BRIAN GILMORE** was born and raised in Washington, D.C. A staff member at Neighborhood Legal Services, Mr. Gilmore has published work in *Obsidian II*, *Fast Talk*, *Full Volume*, *The Unity Line*, *The Side Bar*, and *Mondo Elvis*. His first collection of poems, *Elvis Presley Is Alive and Well and Living in Harlem*, was published by Third World Press of Chicago and has received great response. His essay "Chico" recently was the runner-up in the Washington, D.C., Larry Neal Writers' Competition.

A 1995 Fellow of the NEA/Travel Grant Fund for Artists, **THOMAS GLAVE** has won artists fellowships from the New York Foundation for the Arts and the Fine Arts Center in Provincetown. His work has appeared in, among other publications, *Callaloo*, *The Massachusetts Review*, *The Kenyon Review*, and *Gay Community News*, and in *The Best Short Stories by Black Writers, Vol. II* (Little, Brown).

LEWIS R. GORDON teaches philosophy and African-American studies at Purdue University. He was a Lehman scholar at Lehman College, the City University of New York, a Danforth-Compton Fellow at Yale University, and he is a fellow of the Society for Values in Higher Education. He is author of *Bad Faith and Antiblack Racism*,

Fanon and the Crisis of European Man, and editor of the forthcoming anthologies *Black Texts and Black Textuality: Constructing and Deconstructing Blackness* and *Existence in Black: An Anthology of African-American Philosophies of Existence.* He recently completed *Her Majesty's Other Children,* a collection of fiction and essays. He lives in West Lafayette, Indiana, with his wife, Lisa Jones Gordon, and their two children, Mathieu and Gennifer.

Founding publishing editor of the Los Angeles magazine *The Drumming Between Us: Black Love & Erotic Poetry* and author of *Hand Me My Griot Clothes: The Autobiography of Junior Baby* (Black Classic Press), **PETER J. HARRIS** won the 1993 PEN/Oakland Josephine Miles Award. His fiction has been anthologized in *Breaking Ice,* his poetry in *In Search of Color Everywhere,* and his essays in *I Hear A Symphony: African Americans Celebrate Love.* Mr. Harris is founding publishing editor of *Genetic Dancers,* a magazine about Black fathers.

CHARLES W. HARVEY is a native Houstonian who in 1987 won the PEN/Discovery Prize for fiction. In 1989, he was a recipient of a Cultural Arts Council of Houston grant for writers and artists. Also in 1989, he was a finalist in poetry and fiction in the McDonald's Literary Achievement Awards. He has published a book of poetry, *Drifting,* and is at work on a novel, *The Road to. Astroworld.* His plays have been staged at the Kuumba House Repertory Theater. His work has appeared in *Blonde on Blonde, The Ontario Review,* and *The Houston Poetry Festival Anthology.*

Detroit-sprung and Chicago-flung, poet and cultural ambassador **TYEHIMBA JESS** won the Sister City/Chicago Poetry Festival "Poem For Accra" Award for his poem "election day u.s. of a.—u. of s.a.". A member of the performance ensemble, drapetomania, he wrote the collection *when niggas love Revolution like they love the bulls: ransom notes from tyehimba jess* and coauthored the play *Blakk Love.* Mr. Jess hosts the African-American Arts Alliance's weekly Monday reading series, "Power of the Word." Self-described as "a work in progress . . . the scribe. resides on the southside vibe. eats baraka, sanchez, wideman for breakfast. lunch is cortez, madhubuti, neal. side of himes. feast morrison and walker for dinner. latenite snack of dumas. member of Malcolm X Grassroots Movement. Writes for liberation of Republic of New Afrika."

IRA JONES was born and resides in St. Louis. A member of the Association of Black Psychologists, he works with the mentally retarded in St. Louis County. He is cofounder of the St. Louis Black Man's Think Tank and First Civilizations. He is a poet and an editor, along with Jabari Asim, of *Eyeball*, a literary journal based in St. Louis. His work has been featured in *Bop, Take Five Magazine, Catalyst, Front Lines*, and other publications, including the anthology *In The Tradition* (Harlem River Press, 1992).

CARLOS MCBRIDE was born and raised in the North End of Springfield, Massachusetts. He dropped out of school and later took and passed his GED. "Reckless" or "Rec," as he is known to those he calls friends, is also a talented deejay and production man whose tapes are renowned in Springfield and Holyoke. In the fall of 1993, he attended the University of Massachusetts in the Continuing Studies department after being rejected by Hampshire College. He did very well, and in the fall of 1994, he was admitted as a James Baldwin scholar at Hampshire College. Together with his significant other, he devotes his life to his daughter Destinee, six, son Nicholas, one, and thirteen-year-old cousin who is HIV positive.

MATTHEW MCGUIRE, twenty-six, is from Washington, D.C., and is currently a graduate student at Harvard.

OMAR MCROBERTS, twenty-three, was born and raised in St. Louis. He earned his B.A. in public policy studies from the University of Chicago in 1994 and is currently a Ph.D. candidate in sociology at Harvard. Mr. McRoberts tempers his social-scientific pursuits with poetic explorations of the complex dynamic interactions of politics, culture, and the sacred. For his selections in this book, Mr. McRoberts thanks the spirit of spontaneous creativity and countless teachers, living and dead, whose "gentle wisdom and peaceofmind" inspire him daily.

TONY MEDINA teaches English at Long Island University's Brooklyn campus. He is the author of *Emerge & See* (Whirlwind Press, 1991), *Arrest the I.R.S.!!!* (Ban Dung Books, 1994), *No Noose is Good Noose* (Harlem River Press) as well as four other books of poetry. His work also appears in the anthologies *In The Tradition* (Harlem River Press, 1992); *Aloud: Voices from the Nuyorican Poet's Cafe* (Henry Holt, 1994); *Long Shot, Eyeball, Negative Capability*, and *Catalyst*. He is also the literature editor of *NOBO: a journal of africanamerican dialogue*.

LENARD MOORE, writer-in-residence for the United Arts Council of Raleigh and Wake County, is the author of *Desert Storm: A Brief History* (Los Hombres Press, 1993), *Forever Home* (St. Andrews College Press, 1992), *Poems for Performance* (Lenard Company, 1989), *The Open Eye* (North Carolina Haiku Society Press, 1985), and *Poems of Love and Understanding* (1982). A native of Jacksonville, North Carolina, Moore was educated at Coastal Carolina Community College, University of Maryland, North Carolina State, and Shaw University, where he is currently coeditor-in-chief of *Shawensis*. He reviews regularly for the *St. Louis Post-Dispatch*, and is a longtime staff reviewer for *Library Journal*.

MARC NESBITT hails from Columbia, Maryland, and attended the University of Wisconsin. The twenty-three year old will attend graduate school at the University of Michigan. "Chimp Shrink" is his first published piece. He describes his writing as "controlled by race and not limited by anything."

KEVIN POWELL, twenty-nine, was born in Jersey City, New Jersey. He is a journalist and senior writer at *VIBE* in New York City. His articles, essays, and reviews have also appeared in *Essence*, *The New York Times*, *Rolling Stone*, *Emerge*, *The Source*, and *L.A. Weekly*. His first book of poetry, *recognize*, was published in 1995 by Harlem River Press. He is the coeditor, with Ras Baraka, of *In The Tradition* (Harlem River Press, 1992). His work also appears in *Brotherman: The Odyssey of Black Men in America* (Random House, 1995). Mr. Powell was featured on MTV's "The Real World," a documentary exploring the lives of seven young people living together in New York.

ROHAN B PRESTON is the author of the collection *Dreams in Soy Sauce* (Tia Chucha/Northwestern University Press) and the forthcoming *Lovesong to My Father* (Tallawa). The Jamaican-born, Brooklyn-reared, and Yale-educated twenty-eight-year-old poet is completing a book on the current Black arts renaissance. Mr. Preston's feature writing has been published in the *Chicago Tribune* and the *New York Times*. He lives in Chicago with his wife, Angela Shannon, a poet and actress.

A doctoral student in ethnic studies at Berkeley, **KERRY RILEY** received his Master's of divinity from Lutheran Theological Seminary in 1990 and his B.A. in humanities from New York University in 1985. His work has appeared in *Image* magazine, among others. An instructor of ethnic studies, including European-American studies, he has won several teaching awards. From September 1988 to August 1989, Reverend Riley was an intern pastor at Bethlehem Lutheran Church in Oakland. His affiliations include the National Council of African-American Men.

JOHN SINGLETON is an internationally acclaimed film director born and raised in Los Angeles. He attended film school at the University of Southern California before writing and directing, at the age of twenty-three, the film *Boyz N the Hood*, for which he received a 1992 Oscar nomination for best director, becoming the youngest ever nominated in that category. His other films include *Poetic Justice* and *Higher Learning*.

Born and raised in Brooklyn, attorney, music aficionado, and world traveler **GREGORY A. THOMSON** currently heads business affairs at Quincy Jones's Qwest Records in Los Angeles. While an undergraduate and law student at Yale, he studied with Anthony Appiah, Vincent Franklin, Henry Louis Gates, Jr., Cornel West, and many other cultural luminaries. He cohosts a weekly classic Black music radio program on Pacifica's KPFK in Los Angeles. Mr. Thomson recently produced and directed a documentary on low-riding.

DANIEL JEROME WIDEMAN, twenty-seven, graduated with honors from Brown in 1991, where he was named outstanding senior in the department of African-American studies. He spent a year at the University of London's School of Oriental and African Studies where he was president of the Africa Society, spearheading a successful campaign to increase Black representation in the faculty and curricula. Mr. Wideman's play *Going to Meet the Light* was produced at the Rites & Reason Theater in Providence in May and June of 1994. He is currently working on a novel, *A Ticket 'Til Morning*, and a book of nonfiction, *The Door of No Return: A Journey Through the Legacy of the African Slave Forts* (Scribner, 1997). Mr. Wideman's work has appeared in *The Langston Hughes Review* and *Uwezo*, and on the PBS documentary "One More Look at You." Born in Philadelphia, the son of novelist John Edgar Wideman and aspiring lawyer Judy

Ann Wideman, he currently lives in Evanston, Illinois, with his wife, Maimuna, a teacher.

JAKE WIDEMAN, twenty-six, grew up in Philadelphia and Laramie, Wyoming, where he excelled in both the academic and athletic arenas. At the age of seventeen he was sentenced to life in prison and is currently serving his sentence. He has earned his GED and is working on a college degree via correspondence courses at Indiana University. In addition to haiku, Mr. Wideman's work includes essays and poetry.

BROTHER YAO (Hoke Glover) lives in the Washington, D.C., metropolitan area. His work has been published in *Fast Talk/Full Volume*, *Catalyst*, and *Nommo II*, as well as in the anthology *Testimony: An Anthology of Young African-American Writers*. He is twenty-four years old, the father of two children, Asha and Dhoruba, and the husband of Karla Wilkerson-Glover.

Jabari Asim's "Days Ahead and Journeys" and "A Photograph of My Mother" first appeared in *Obsidian II: Black Literature and Review*; "Night Vigil" in his collection, *Front Lines*; and "Spitting Image" in *Catalyst*. "Peace, Dog" was produced as a play by The New Theatre, St. Louis as part of a production entitled *St. Louis Stories*.

Charlie Braxton's poems "I Dream of Jesus" and "South Central Olympics" were published in *Eyeball*. "I Dream of Jesus" also appeared in *Drumvoices Review*.

George Elliott Clarke's selections "April 3–4, 1968," "The Martyrdom of el-Hajj Malik el-Shabazz," "Violets for Your Furs," and "Watercolour for Negro Expatriates in France" were originally published in his volume *Lush Dreams, Blue Exile* (Lawrencetown Beach, Nova Scotia: Pottersfield Press, 1994) and "King Bee Blues" and "Look Homeward, Exile" in his *Whylah Falls* (Winlaw, British Columbia: Polestar Press, 1990).

"the fire this Time" by Michael Datcher first appeared in *San Francisco Focus Magazine*, August 1992.

"Their Story" by Thomas Glave was first published in *The Kenyon Review*.

Tyehimba Jess's "Brother less," "Magic," "shadowbox," and "when niggas love Revolution like they love the bulls" were published in the author's chapbook, *when niggas love Revolution like they love the bulls*. "Brother less" and "shadowbox" also appeared in *Freedom Rag*. "trust (the rape of)" earlier appeared as part of the play *Blakk Love*.

"Letter from Foreign" and "Letter to my brother" by Rohan B Preston first appeared in Mr. Preston's collection, *Dreams in Soy Sauce*, Tia Chucha Press/Northwestern University Press, 1992.

FOR THE BEST IN PAPERBACKS, LOOK FOR THE

In every corner of the world, on every subject under the sun, Penguin represents quality and variety—the very best in publishing today.

For complete information about books available from Penguin—including Puffins, Penguin Classics, and Arkana—and how to order them, write to us at the appropriate address below. Please note that for copyright reasons the selection of books varies from country to country.

In the United Kingdom: Please write to *Dept. JC, Penguin Books Ltd, FREEPOST, West Drayton, Middlesex UB7 0BR.*

If you have any difficulty in obtaining a title, please send your order with the correct money, plus ten percent for postage and packaging, to *P.O. Box No. 11, West Drayton, Middlesex UB7 0BR*

In the United States: Please write to *Consumer Sales, Penguin USA, P.O. Box 999, Dept. 17109, Bergenfield, New Jersey 07621-0120.* VISA and MasterCard holders call 1-800-253-6476 to order all Penguin titles

In Canada: Please write to *Penguin Books Canada Ltd, 10 Alcorn Avenue, Suite 300, Toronto, Ontario M4V 3B2*

In Australia: Please write to *Penguin Books Australia Ltd, P.O. Box 257, Ringwood, Victoria 3134*

In New Zealand: Please write to *Penguin Books (NZ) Ltd, Private Bag 102902, North Shore Mail Centre, Auckland 10*

In India: Please write to *Penguin Books India Pvt Ltd, 706 Eros Apartments, 56 Nehru Place, New Delhi 110 019*

In the Netherlands: Please write to *Penguin Books Netherlands bv, Postbus 3507, NL-1001 AH Amsterdam*

In Germany: Please write to *Penguin Books Deutschland GmbH, Metzlerstrasse 26, 60594 Frankfurt am Main*

In Spain: Please write to *Penguin Books S. A., Bravo Murillo 19, 1° B, 28015 Madrid*

In Italy: Please write to *Penguin Italia s.r.l., Via Felice Casati 20, I-20124 Milano*

In France: Please write to *Penguin France S. A., 17 rue Lejeune, F-31000 Toulouse*

In Japan: Please write to *Penguin Books Japan, Ishikiribashi Building, 2-5-4, Suido, Bunkyo-ku, Tokyo 112*

In Greece: Please write to *Penguin Hellas Ltd, Dimocritou 3, GR-106 71 Athens*

In South Africa: Please write to *Longman Penguin Southern Africa (Pty) Ltd, Private Bag X08, Bertsham 2013*